He'll take her to his bed – but
she won't touch his heart!

HIS *Mistress*
HIS RULES

Also available:

HIS WIFE, HIS
Revenge

Three timeless novels from
bestselling authors

D0588509

Ann Major lives in Texas with her husband of many years and is the mother of three grown-up children. She has a master's degree from Texas A&M at Kingsville, Texas, and is a former English teacher. She is a founding board member of the Romance Writers of America and a frequent speaker at writers' groups. Ann loves to write; she considers her ability to do so a gift. Her hobbies include hiking in the mountains, sailing, ocean kayaking, travelling and playing the piano. But most of all she enjoys her family.

Jamie Sobrato's first aspiration as a young child was to join the navy, mostly because she wanted to explore the world by sea and she thought the uniforms were cute. Luckily for national defence, she went on to use her primary talents – daydreaming and procrastinating – to become a writer instead. Jamie lives in Northern California with her two young children and two house rabbits who think they rule the world.

Cathy Gillen Thacker married her high-school sweetheart and hasn't had a dull moment since. Why? you ask. Well, there were three kids, various pets, any number of cars, several moves across the country, his and her careers and sundry other experiences (some of which were exciting and some of which weren't). But mostly there was love and friendship and laughter, and lots of experiences she wouldn't trade for the world. Please visit her website at www.cathygillenthacker.com.

HIS *Mistress*
HIS RULES

Ann Major
Jamie Sobrato
Cathy Gillen Thacker

*M&B™ and M&B™ with the Rose Device
are trademarks of the publisher.
Harlequin Mills & Boon Limited, Eton House,
18-24 Paradise Road, Richmond, Surrey TW9 1SR*

HIS MISTRESS, HIS RULES © by Harlequin Books S.A. 2009

Mistress for a Month © Ann Major 2008
Too Wild © Jamie Sobrato 2004
The Cowboy's Mistress © Cathy Gillen Thacker 1992

ISBN: 978 0 263 86891 3

010-0109

*Printed and bound in Spain
by Litografía Rosés S.A., Barcelona*

Mistress for a Month

Ann Major

To my aunt, Patricia Carson Major, because she's so much fun and she adores all things French. Unfortunately, she never married a French *comte*. At least, not yet.

One

W*ild, zany Aunt Tate dead?*

Amelia flipped her cell phone shut. Then her grip tightened on her steering wheel as she rounded a curve of green mountain, and the tall hotels of Waikiki vanished in her rearview mirror. Why couldn't her mother ever just answer the phone?

Amy punched in her mother's number once more, and again it rang and rang.

After Aunt Tate's horrid French attorney had told her her aunt had died, Amy had stopped listening for a second or two. The next thing she'd caught was, "She left you everything."

Everything should have included only Château Serene and the vineyard in Provence where Amy had once shared sparkling summers with Aunt Tate and her haughty *comte,* but her aunt had not quite finished the process of donating her extremely valuable Matisse to a French museum before her death. She'd left a letter to Amy in her will stating her intentions regarding the painting, but technically the Matisse was hers, as well.

"I'm afraid the property is in a pitiable state of neglect. Luckily for you the young *comte* is ready to make you a generous offer. Naturally he would like to buy the painting back, as well. Surely it belongs on the wall in the home of the family who's owned it for nearly a century."

"The *comte*'s family disliked my aunt. I'm not sure I want to sell to him!"

"But, mademoiselle, the château belonged to his family for nearly eight hundred years."

"Well, *apparently* everything belongs to me now. Goodbye!"

She'd immediately called Nan, her best friend, who'd been in a sulk because she hadn't gotten to go on a retreat on Molokai with her sister Liz and had asked her to cover for her at Vintage, her resale shop, during the sale today. Then she'd tried to call her mother to tell her about Tate and to ask her if she'd work at Vintage so that she could fly to France to check on the château and vineyard.

Imagining her customers lined up outside Vintage, Amy pressed the accelerator, speeding through the mountains and then along the rugged coastline where waves exploded against the rocks. The shop didn't matter. Nothing mattered. Life was short. She wanted Fletcher, her longtime boyfriend. She wanted his arms around her. That was why she was driving as fast as she could to his beach house on the North Shore.

Aunt Tate was gone. On a day like this there should be a rogue wave hurtling toward the Hawaiian Islands or an earthquake about to topple the hotels in Waikiki.

Despite the wind pounding the hood of her Toyota and streaming past her windows, the North Shore of Oahu with its lush, green mountains and wide, white beaches and ocean was beautiful.

Amy felt sad and restless and increasingly nostalgic about Aunt Tate as she kept redialing her mother. If only she could reach her.

I'll never watch Aunt Tate put on one of her crazy get-ups again. I'll never hear her throaty laugh as she bows extravagantly and jokes about being a countess.

The bright blue sky misted. Amy's eyes burned.

No! She wasn't crying!

She was driving too fast, and she never drove too fast. With a shaking hand she dialed her mother again, only this time she mashed her cell phone against her ear.

Sounding out of breath, her mother caught the phone on the eighth ring. "Hello!"

"Mom! *Finally!* The most awful thing has happened! I've been calling you and calling you. For hours." The last was an exaggeration, but her mother deserved it.

"Do you need more money? Me to sign another mortgage paper on Vintage? Where are you, sweetie? You're breaking up. Isn't today your big day? How's the sale going?"

"Mom, I'm not at Vintage. I'm on the North Shore."

"Amelia, I thought *we* agreed you weren't going to chase Fletcher any more!"

Do moms ever step out of the mom role? The last thing she needed was for her mom to start in on how irresponsible and indifferent Fletcher was. Why had she called her mom, of all people?

Because Carol, favorite daughter, *her* sister, had married well—an English lord, no less. Carol lived on an estate an hour out of London, and it was in the middle of the night over there. Because her best girl buddy, Liz, was in Molokai sitting cross-legged at a retreat. Because Fletcher's phone was turned off as usual. Because Mom *was* Tate's sister. Because she was her mom, for heaven's sake. And if she had to go to France, who would take care of Vintage?

Shells crunched under Amy's tires as she braked in front of Fletcher's unpainted house. As always the house and neighborhood looked so shabby they creeped her out.

"*Amelia!* Tell me you didn't drive out to Fletcher's alone!"

Amy gritted her teeth.

"You could do so much better."

"Mother, I'm grown."

"Sometimes I wonder. Carol wouldn't have wasted her precious time—"

"Don't start on Carol, either!"

"This is all your father's fault. He was a loser, but you were his favorite. And you couldn't see through him. You feel comfortable with losers like him."

"You married him."

"Don't remind me."

"Mother!"

"Not that I'm glad he left me or that's he's dead, God rest his soul."

From her car Amy nervously scanned the broken-down cars and trucks in Fletcher's front yard. Then she spotted

Fletcher's yellow longboard in the bed of his old blue pickup and felt a surge of relief.

Her mother sighed.

Amy had never liked the house he'd bought and rented out to surfers or the communal lifestyle that went with it, but real-estate prices were high on Oahu. She was hardly in a position to criticize. Here, people of ordinary means had to compromise. Since the value of her mother's house had appreciated exponentially over the past two decades, Amy had had to move there to save on rent and to help her mom with the property taxes.

"Amelia, are you still there?"

Amy's fingers traced the smooth leather of the steering wheel. "Mom, listen. This lawyer from France with a snotty accent and way too much attitude called me."

"What did he want?"

"Aunt Tate died in her sleep last week."

"I—I can't believe this. I—I just talked to Tate. She said she'd been to all those parties in Paris."

"Mom, they already had a memorial service. She's been cremated and put in a niche or something at Château de Fournier."

"What? And nobody called her only sister? They stuck her in Château de Fournier? She hated that place!"

"Apparently they just found Tate's address book today."

Her mother was silent, in shock, or more likely a sulk. Like a lot of sisters, she and Tate hadn't always been the best of pals. Tate had done what the women in their family were supposed to do. She'd married up, way, way up, landing a French count the third time around. And she'd never let her family forget it. She'd sent newsy Christmas cards every year to brag about parties at châteaux after her glamorous stepson's Formula One races, trips to Monaco and round-the-world cruises on friends' yachts. Her step-children were all celebrities in their own fields. But the main headline grabber had been Remy de Fournier, the handsome, womanizing Grand Prix driver. Not that Tate had boasted much about him lately. Apparently he'd retired from the circuit rather suddenly last year.

After one of Tate's bright cards or calls, her mother would sulk for days, blaming Amy's deceased father for never having amounted to anything.

"You're not going to believe this, Mom, but Aunt Tate left me everything. Château Serene, the vineyard, even the Matisse."

"What? That painting alone is worth a fortune."

"Aunt Tate intended to donate it to a museum."

"You can't afford to be so generous."

"Mother! Your baby's all grown-up. I'm afraid I need to go over there to settle Aunt Tate's affairs, pack her personal belongings and inspect the property. I hate to impose, but could you possibly watch Vintage?"

"I suppose. If it fails, who'll pay the mortgage? I'll need a day, maybe two. After that, I'd be glad to. To tell you the truth, I've been a little bored lately."

Which probably explained why her mother tried to run *her* life all the time.

"Mom, could you help Nan handle the sale today?" This question was met with silence. "Just for an hour or two? Please! Just to make sure Nan's not overwhelmed."

Her mother sighed.

Amy thanked her and hung up. Now all she needed was for Fletcher to hold her and make everything feel all right again.

* * *

When Amy opened her car door, the wind tore it from her grasp and whipped her long, brown hair back from her face. Her sandals sank deeply into the shell road, making each step so difficult she was almost happy to step into the high grass of Fletcher's yard. With less annoyance than usual, she picked her way through scratchy weeds, beer cans, fluttering fast-food wrappers and plastic sacks. Usually she hated the flotsam and jetsam of Fletcher's front lawn.

Lawn. If ever there was a euphemism.

Today she was too anxious to throw herself into his arms, inhale his salty male scent and cling to him forever, to obsess over her issues with his bachelor lifestyle.

He hadn't known Aunt Tate personally, but he'd scribbled Amy a postcard or two when she'd spent those months in France. One-liners, yes, but for Fletcher, that was a lot.

When Amy reached the rickety wooden stairs that climbed the fifteen feet to his deck, she noticed four triangular bits of red cloth flapping from the railing. She picked them up, fingering the damp strings and then the triangles of what appeared to be the tops of two miniscule bikinis. When she heard music, she frowned. Was Fletcher having a party without her?

A singer cried, "Yeah, yeah, yeah." Then the sound of a steel-string guitar accompanied by the heavy thudding of drums.

Her throat tightened, and she flung the bits of fabric savagely into the grass. Avoiding the front door, which stood ajar, Amy put her hands on her hips and marched around to the back of the house by way of the deck. Rounding a corner too fast, she almost stumbled over a bloated male body. His beer gut moved up and down, so he had to be alive. But his shaggy hair was filthy, and his sunburned arms sported several tattoos. She didn't recognize the spider tattoos, so maybe he wasn't one of Fletcher's regular roommates.

No sooner had she scooted around him when she saw six or seven more bodies sprawled on the deck, over the hoods of cars in the backyard and across the lawn furniture. A boom of deep male laughter accompanied by wild squeals in the Jacuzzi made her heart speed up.

Fletcher.

She turned slowly. Sunlight glinted in his tousled curls as he squirmed on the edge of the tub while balancing two topless blondes on his lap.

Amy dug her fingers into the railing so hard a splinter bit into her thumb.

When she cried his name, Fletcher bolted to his feet. He wasn't wearing a suit. To his credit his handsome face turned red. "Aw, baby, you should've called."

The girls toppled into the Jacuzzi with a splash. Squealing, they grabbed at Fletcher's bronzed legs.

Horrified, Amy began to back toward the front of his house.

"Baby!" Fletcher yanked a wet towel off the floor of the deck. Whipping it around his waist, he stomped toward her, leaving big, drippy footprints on the deck.

She ran, leaping over unconscious surfer bodies, plates of half-eaten pie and overturned beer bottles, her feet flying down the steps into the chaos of cars in his front yard. But he was faster. Springing down the stairs with the agility of an orangutan, he grabbed her arm.

"Baby, I know you think you've got a right to be mad, and you do, you do, but I can explain."

His voice was slurred, and he reeked of beer. A smear of lipstick marred one prominent cheekbone.

She jerked free and stomped past the cars to her Toyota.

"Look, I know I should have invited you to the party!" he yelled. "But you hate my parties. You refused to move in with me. You never want to do anything fun anymore. Ever since you got the store, you act as old and boring as those old clothes you buy and sell. And when it comes to sex, forget it! You never want to try anything new."

"Maybe because I'm tired after working all day."

"Which you throw at me constantly."

"Maybe because I want you to grow up."

"Maybe I'm as grown-up as I'll ever be. I have money. I bought this house. I run it. So what if I don't have a real job?"

She looked at him, at the plastic sacks fluttering like ghosts in the over-long grass, at his unpainted house and then down at the beautiful beach. "Is this all you'll ever want?"

"What's wrong with this? My old man worked himself into an early grave. Luckily he left me enough so I can get by. I wake up to paradise every day."

The blondes, wrapped in towels now, were standing on the deck watching Fletcher.

Would Fletcher's girlfriends get younger every year?

Amy fumbled in her purse for her keys. When had everything changed? Grabbing her keys, she punched a button and got her door unlocked. Then she climbed in and slammed it. As she started the engine, she rolled down her window. He ambled over and smiled at her.

Oh, God, his eyes were so startlingly blue, so warm and friendly and sexy even now, but dammit, her mother was right. She couldn't live with him.

But could she live without him?

"You know what, Fletcher? I'm tired of having to feel lucky to be dating the good-looking, popular guy that all the other girls want. I want to be wanted."

"Baby—"

"You're not the only one who needs to grow up." She hit the accelerator so hard her tires slung bits of shell against his bare shins.

"Sorry!" she whispered when he let out a yelp. And she was. She was sorry for so many things. Sorry she'd disappointed her mother. Sorry about her dad.... Sorry about all sorts of dreams that hadn't panned out.

A mile down the road, she began to shake so hard she didn't feel she could drive without endangering innocent strangers, so she pulled over.

She had always loved Fletcher. To her, he was still as gorgeous as he'd been in high school. But this wasn't high school.

She flipped her visor down and stared at herself in its mirror much too critically. Normally when she wasn't comparing herself to naked teenagers with Barbie Doll hair and pole-dancer bodies, she didn't feel *that* old.

Today she'd been too busy because of her sale to bother with her makeup and hair. The wind and humidity hadn't helped. Her brown hair hung in strings. Grief hadn't helped, either. Her hazel eyes were red, and her mascara was running.

Images from the past swept her. She'd gotten a crush on Fletcher in kindergarten. By the sixth grade, maybe because he'd failed a year, he'd been almost as tall and cute and golden as he was now. Back then he'd been reckless and daring and the most popular boy in school, while she, Nan and Liz had been bookworms. Only, one day he'd run up to them at recess and painted a mock tattoo of a heart on Amy's left arm. Then he'd kissed her cheek and stolen her book.

Amy had felt like Cinderella at the ball with her prince. Her cheek was still burning when he'd returned her book three hours later and kissed her again. He'd teased her like that for a few more years. Then they'd become serious in high school. Or, at least, *she* had. She'd told herself she could wait.

She was still waiting.

But not anymore!

London
Three days later

Promise me you won't sleep with her.

When a man is thirty-five and famous—make that infamous, especially with women—he is likely to resent such a command, especially from his mother. Even if she is a countess.

Without warning the slim young woman his mother wanted him to keep in his sights—for business reasons only—sprinted across the street.

Not wanting to alarm her, Remy waited a few seconds before loping after her.

He frowned. His mother had nothing to worry about. The wholesome Miss Weatherbee wasn't his type.

Brown hair, thickly braided. Hazel eyes. Not ugly. But not beautiful. Nondescript really, except for… His gaze drifted to her swaying hips again. Then he remembered all the sexy lingerie he'd watched her buy and wished she weren't forbidden because that made her infinitely more fascinating.

From birth, Remy de Fournier, or rather the *Comte* de

Fournier, had had a taste for the forbidden. His mother and his older, brilliant sisters only had to tell him not to do a thing and he'd do it. As an adult he'd liked his cars fast and his women even faster—until the accident a year ago at the Circuit de Nevers at Magny-Cours had turned his life into a nightmare. Ever since, except for brief trips to Paris, he'd been living in self-imposed exile in London.

Yesterday the highest courts in France had decided not to charge him with manslaughter. As soon as he could make the arrangements he would be going home, which was the reason his mother had given for calling him. She wanted to set up a celebratory lunch in Paris with him and his first serious girlfriend, Céline, whom he hadn't seen in years.

He should have felt relieved that he'd been exonerated, that his mother would even speak to him. Instead, last night he'd dreamed of the crash and of his steering wheel jamming. Again he'd felt that horrible rush of adrenaline as he'd fought the curve and the car and lost, hurtling into that wall at 160 mph before ricocheting into André's car and then into Pierre-Louis's.

With the memory of André's terrified black eyes burning a hole in his soul, Remy had dressed and bolted out of his flat at four in the morning to buy coffee, returning to work on the family's portfolio on his computer. Hours later he'd still been in a cold mood when his mother had called to discuss Céline and her lunch plans and to put him on to Mademoiselle Weatherbee, who was even now sashaying, her cute butt wiggling, glossy red shopping bags swinging against her thighs, toward her sister's flat on Duke Street in St. James.

Why was it that the longer he trailed that ample bottom, the more appealing it became?

Usually he chose leggy blond models or busty socialites and princesses, sophisticated women, who knew how to dress. Céline was his type. Mademoiselle Weatherbee with her wide, trusting doe eyes and thick brown braid was not. Deliver him from naive Americans with no sense of style.

Still, it was growing easier and easier to look at her. The worn faded blue stripes of her vintage cotton sundress made her look innocent even as it showed off her slim shoulders, narrow waist and, okay, hell, emphasized that pert and rather large ass of hers and its moves.

Nice moves. Very nice.

What would she feel like naked under him? Would she writhe? Or just lie there? Damn, if she were his, he'd make her writhe.

His bossy mother's predawn call had annoyed the hell out of him, even more than usual.

"I'm too excited to sleep," she said. "It's all over the Internet. You're a free man. And…Mademoiselle Weatherbee stayed at her sister's flat on Duke Street in St. James last night! And will stay there tonight, as well! Since you live so close, I thought maybe you could…check on her."

"I have back-to-back commitments before I can leave London."

"So far, she's refused all our offers to buy Château Serene, and she seems to want to follow her aunt's wishes about donating the Matisse."

"Isn't she on her way to France?"

"Tomorrow…"

"Well, then, negotiate when she gets there."

"She's in London to do a little shopping for her store. I thought maybe you could meet her and work a little of your magic. But don't take it too far. She probably doesn't follow Grand Prix headlines, and with any luck, she won't check the Internet and the London papers will ignore you."

"I met her once, you know."

"Years ago. If she doesn't recognize you, don't tell her who you are. No telling what Tate told her about us. Or you."

"This town's enormous. If I can't call her or knock on her door and introduce myself, how the hell can I meet her without scaring her away? What would be the point?"

"Improvise. I'm going to fax you a recent photograph of her and her sister's address."

"You want me to stalk her, hit on her and entice her into some pub?"

"But be careful. The last thing we need is more nasty headlines."

When she hung up, Remy crushed his paper coffee cup and pitched it into the trash. No sooner did it hit the can than he heard the fax in his bedroom. Amelia Weatherbee was not someone he'd ever wanted to see again.

Even her photograph brought painful memories. Holding it to the light, he noted the same youthful wistfulness shining in her eyes. Only now, there was a bit of a lost look in them, too, a sadness, a resignation.

He'd met her only that once. What was it—seventeen years ago? He'd been eighteen, she around thirteen. She'd eavesdropped on a private conversation, and he'd vowed to hate her forever for it even though she'd been kind. *Especially* because she'd been kind. Dammit! Who was she to pity him?

Funny how that same vulnerability in her eyes and sweet smile seemed enchanting and made him feel protective now.

He'd forced himself to dress and walk over to her flat, where he'd waited outside, reading the *Times*. When the varnished doors trimmed in polished brass had finally swung open and she'd stepped out into the sunshine, he'd shrunk behind his paper. Bravely armed against the gray sky with her yellow umbrella, she'd looked bright and fresh in her faded cotton dress and scuffed sandals.

He'd been trotting all over the city after Mademoiselle Weatherbee's yellow umbrella and cute butt ever since. He'd watched her shop at Camden Market and Covent Garden, then Harvey Nicks and last of all Harrods Food Hall. But had she eaten? Hell, no! So he hadn't eaten, either. Because of her, he was starving and grumpy as hell.

Americans. What sort of barbarian instinct made her skip lunch, a sacred institution to any man with even a drop of French blood?

During the lunch hour she'd gone into a nail shop, where she'd had a pedicure and had gotten tips put on her ragged nails. A decided improvement. Still, she'd skipped lunch.

At the Camden Market, he'd felt like a damn pervert when she'd fingered dozens of bright, silky bras and panties, holding them up to herself as she tried to decide. In the end, she'd surprised him by choosing his favorites—the skimpiest and sheerest of the batch.

Why couldn't she be the practical-schoolteacher sort who wore sensible cotton panties and bras?

When she'd paid the cashier, she'd suddenly looked up, straight into his eyes. He'd been visualizing her in the red, see-through thong, and her embarrassed glance had set off a frisson of heat inside him. Not good. Fortunately she'd scowled at him and had quickly thrown the tangle of lingerie into a sack and slapped her credit card on top of the mess. After that, he'd kept out of sight.

But she was nearly back to her flat. He had to do something and fast. He'd wasted way too much time already.

She was on Jermyn Street, a mere half block from her building, and he was running out of options when a cab rounded the corner.

Yelling for the taxi, he'd sprinted toward it, deliberately bumping Amelia so hard she stumbled. Her bags tumbled onto the sidewalk, spilling lacy bras and thongs.

All apologies, he dove for the woman, not the silky stuff. He caught her, his long limbs locking around hers at an impossibly intimate angle.

When body parts brushed, she fought a quivery smile and blushed. He felt a heady buzz of his own.

"I'm sorry," he said, letting go of her instantly.

Those soft hazel eyes with spiky black lashes stared straight into his, and she turned as red as she had when he'd caught her buying the transparent underwear. All of a sudden she seemed *almost* beautiful.

"You! I saw you before…"

A shock went through him.

Then she said, "At Camden."

He acted surprised. "Yes, how very strange. Do you live around here, too?"

"No. I'm visiting my sister. She has a flat just…" As if remembering he was a stranger, she stopped and knelt to pick up her bags and the bright bits of sheer lace and silk.

Quickly he knelt and gathered up bras and panties, too, tossing them into her bags but holding on to their handles.

Eyeing his hands on her underwear, she backed away from him a little.

He kept his distance. "If you'd like to have a drink, there's a pub across the street, or there's a tea shop around the corner."

A passerby, a man, gave Remy and the black bra dripping from his right hand a sharp look.

"I'm really awfully tired," she said.

"All right." He dropped the lacy underwear into the appropriate bag and then handed her her things.

Her face again burned an adorable shade of red when she looked up at him from beneath those inky lashes, which were as sexy as her butt.

"In that case, I guess it's goodbye," he said.

"You're French."

"Yes, and alone. Big city. I prefer Paris." Deliberately he allowed his accent to thicken.

"Of course. I love Paris, too. I've been there many times. With my…"

She looked wistful. Was she thinking of Tate? Her quick, sad smile struck a chord inside him. She'd probably loved Tate very much, he thought. His father damn sure had. He himself knew what it was to chase ghosts.

"Are you here on business?"

"Of a sort," he replied.

"I like your accent. It's elegant, but not snotty. You know, sometimes French people are so—"

"I like yours, too," he said before she could insult the French, who were his people, after all, which might cause him to defend them. "You're American?"

She nodded. "I'm on my way to France on rather a sad errand."

The light left her beautiful hazel eyes. "A favorite aunt died. I—I used to spend every summer at her château."

Her château? Like hell. Still, Tate must have been wonderful fun for a young niece, who had no reason to be jealous of her just because the *comte* had adored her instead of his own son. For all her faults, his outrageous, American stepmother had made his father happy. His own pretentious mother had not.

And he damn sure had not.

Remy's teeth clenched, but when Amelia continued to stare at him, a stillness descended on him. Her nondescript face with those spiky lashes and naive gaze wasn't beautiful. It wasn't. But it was growing on him.

Why couldn't he stop looking at her? Why did he feel so…so…

Aroused was the word he was trying to pluck from the ether.

Abruptly he looked away.

She sucked in a breath. "So, you're French and I'm going to France," she said lightly. "How's that for a coincidence?"

"Yes."

"We meet in the market. And now here again. Why?"

No way could he admit he'd stalked the hell out of her. "I can't imagine."

"Maybe it's fate."

Fate. Horrible concept. He could tell her a thing or two about fate. Fate had made him the despised bastard of the father he'd adored. Fate had hurled him into André at 160 miles an hour and then into Pierre-Louis.

She was still rattling on as Remy remembered the long months of Pierre-Louis's hospitalization after the amputation. But at least he'd…

"I mean London is so huge," she was saying. "What is the chance of that?" When her shining eyes locked with his again, she must have sensed his darkening mood. Spiky lashes batted. "Is something wrong?"

Her soft voice and sympathetic gaze caused a powerful current to pass through his body.

He shook his head.

"Good." Amelia smiled at him beguilingly. "Then maybe…maybe…I mean, if your offer's still open, I think I will have that cup of tea, after all, even if we did just meet."

A cup of tea? As he stared into her hazel eyes he found himself imagining her naked on cream satin sheets. Why was that? She wasn't his type. He felt off balance, and that wasn't good.

He should run from this girl and leave the negotiating with her to his agent. He'd had the same cold feeling of premonition right before the crash.

This is it, he'd thought when his steering had jammed and his tires had begun to skid on pavement that had been slicker than glass.

Every time he looked at Amelia pure adrenaline charged through him.

This is it. And there's no way out, screamed that little voice inside his mind.

Run.

Two

If only she could look at him without feeling all nervous and out of breath, but she couldn't. So she fidgeted.

He was sleek and edgy and yet he seemed familiar, which was odd because he wasn't the sort of man a woman with youthful hormones onboard would easily forget.

Curious, intrigued, attracted, Amy couldn't help studying him when he wasn't looking. His thickly lashed eyes were brown and flecked with gold. The brows above them were heavy and intimidating. He had the most enormous shoulders and lots of jet-black hair that he wore long enough so that a lock constantly tumbled across his brow.

He was too amazingly gorgeous to believe, and far too male and huge to be sitting across from her in such a ladylike tea shop. But here he was.

Amy bit her lips just to make sure she wasn't dreaming.

Despite his powerful body, he looked so elegant in his long-sleeved, black silk shirt and beige silk slacks. So grown up and successful compared to Fletcher, who wore old bathing trunks and T-shirts.

"Have you ever been to Hawaii?" she asked, struggling to make the kind of small talk that beautiful, polished Carol would be so good at.

Lame. Did she only imagine that he looked bored?

"No. Why do you ask?" His deep, dark, richly accented voice made her shiver.

"Because I live there. Because lots of tourists come there and I thought…maybe I'd seen you. I mean, you seem so familiar."

"Do I?" Did she only imagine a new hardness in his voice?

He cocked his head and stared at her so intensely she couldn't quite catch her breath.

Continuing to gaze at her in that steady, assessing way, his big, tanned hand lifted his wafer-thin teacup to his sensual mouth. She was too conscious of his stern lips, of his chiseled cheekbones, of those amber sparks flashing in his eyes, of his long, tapered fingers caressing the side of the tiny cup.

A beat passed. His eyes scanned the other women in the tea shop before returning to her. She swallowed.

When he grinned, she blushed.

"I—I'm not usually this nervous," she whispered.

"You don't seem nervous." His low tone was smooth. Everything about him was smooth.

When she touched her teacup to lift it, it rattled, sloshing tea. "Oh, God! See? My hand is shaking."

"Did you skip lunch?"

"How did you…? Why, yes, yes I did! There were so

many things to look at in the markets. Sometimes I forget
to eat when I shop."

"I skipped lunch, as well. Maybe we'll both feel better
if we have a scone. They're very good here."

"Do you come here often?"

"Never. Until now. With you."

"Then how do you know they're good?"

"Reputation. I have a friend who comes here."

Amy imagined a woman as beautiful as Carol. His
friend would be delicate—slim and golden and well-
dressed, the type who wouldn't be caught dead shopping
at the Camden Market. His type.

Ignorant of her thoughts and comparison, her companion was slathering clotted cream and jam on his scone.
When he finished, he handed the dripping morsel to her.
Then he made one for himself. When she gobbled hers
much too greedily, he signaled the waitress and ordered
chilled finger sandwiches and crisps.

Licking jam and cream off the tips of her fingers, she
willed herself to calm down. He was right; she was shaking
because she was starving, not because he was gorgeous
and sexy and maybe dangerous.

She was perfectly safe. They were in a sedate tea shop
with a table and a tablecloth, pink-and-gold china teacups
and saucers between them. They were surrounded by lots
of other customers, too. So, there was absolutely nothing
to be nervous about.

"So, you haven't been to Hawaii," she mused aloud,
staring at his hard, too-handsome face with that lock of
black hair tumbling over his brow. "Are you famous?"

He started.

She bit into a second scone, and the rich concoction

seemed to melt on her tongue. "A movie star?" she pressed, sensing a strange, new tension in him as she licked at a sticky fingertip. "Is that why you look so familiar?"

"I'm an investor." He was watching her lick her finger with such excessive interest, she stopped.

"You don't look like an investor," she said.

"What did you have me pegged for?"

"You have a look, an edge. You certainly don't seem like the kind of man who goes to the office every day."

Did she only imagine that his mouth tightened? He lowered his eyes and dabbed jam on his second scone. "Sorry to disappoint you. I have a very dull office and a very dull secretary in Paris."

"So what do you invest in?"

"Lots of dull things—stocks, mutual funds, real estate. My family has interests all over Europe, in the States... Asia, too. Emerging markets, they call them. Believe me, I stay busy with my, er, dull career. I have to, or I'd go mad." His voice sounded bleak. "And what do you do?"

"I just have a little shop. I sell old clothes that I buy at estate sales and markets."

"And do you enjoy it?"

"Very much. But it would probably seem dull and boring to someone like you."

"The question is—is it dull and boring to you?"

"No! Of course, not! I love what I do. I live to find some darling item at a bargain price, so that I can sell it to a customer with a limited budget. Every woman longs to be beautiful, you know."

"Then I envy you." Again she heard a weariness in his voice. Only this time she sensed the deeper pain that lay beneath it.

"And you don't think I'm boring…because I sell old clothes?"

He laughed. "Don't be absurd."

"No, really, you must tell me." She leaned forward, holding her cup in two hands for fear of spilling. "Since we're strangers, we can speak freely. Was your first impression of me… Did you think I looked boring and old?"

He set his scone down. "Who the hell's been telling you a stupid thing like that?"

"My boyfriend." Why had she admitted that?

"Then dump him."

"I sort of did, but I've always loved him. Or, at least, I thought I did. Maybe he's just been in my life forever."

"So you're the loyal, committed type?"

"Well, anyway, I can't stop thinking about him. All day I thought about him. And the things he said."

His black brows shot together so alarmingly her hands, which still held her teacup, began to shake. "Stick with your decision."

"But I've loved him since I was five, I think," she whispered a bit defensively. "My mother disapproves of him, though."

"No wonder you cling to him."

"No, it's not like that." She smiled. "It's just that I'm not sure I did the right thing to break up with him. I did it so fast, I mean. That's not like me. I spent several years planning before I opened my store."

"Maybe the decision had been coming on for a while."

"But Fletcher—"

"Fletcher?" His handsome features hardened. "Well, you're not boring or old. So, you want to know my first thoughts about you. I thought you were lovely. Fresh.

Nice. Different. Too nice for me probably, but a woman I definitely would want to know better if I were a different sort of man—one capable of commitment. Sexy." He bit off that last rather grumpily. "Sexy in a nice way. You're the kind of woman a nice guy, who has a good job and wants to settle down, marries so he can have a houseful of kids to play soccer with on the weekends."

His dark eyes with those sparking flecks said much more, and she grew hot with embarrassment.

"That's sweet," she said.

When his hand reached across the table for hers, she jumped.

"Responsive, too. That's another first thought."

She yanked her hand free and tucked it beneath her pink napkin.

"This Fletcher doesn't deserve you. But let's talk of something more pleasant. I can tell we'll never agree on this subject, so why argue? Your love life is your choice. Not mine. I barely know you."

He seemed out of sorts suddenly, defensive, almost jealous. But that wasn't possible. A man like him, who was wealthy, refined and movie-star sexy couldn't be jealous of her. Especially not when they'd just met.

"I'm sorry if I upset you."

"So, you have a sister?" He was clearly determined to change the subject. "Here in London?

"Carol. Actually, she lives outside London. On a rather grand estate near Wolverton. She has a large house with a conservatory. And a lovely garden, too. That sounds so English, doesn't it? But she and her husband—he's a lord and a very important person, mind you—keep a flat here in St. James so they can stay in the city whenever they need to, which is usually four or five nights a week. She's a barrister, and he's high up in the government. They both work in the city."

"So how much time do you have with them? What sights are you going to see while you're here?"

"I'm flying to Marseilles tomorrow afternoon. But I hope to ride the Eye and walk across the Millennium Bridge. I'm sure those seem like dull and boring things to you."

"Quit running yourself down. We'll do it, then," he said.

"We'll?"

"If you'll accept my invitation. Are you free for dinner and dancing tonight?"

"But we just met. I bet I'm not the sort of girl you usually ask out."

"What the hell are you talking about now?"

"Just what I said. I'm not the sort of girl you usually hang out with."

"No, you're not. But maybe that's why I like you so much. Why I find you so not boring and old, as you put it, that I want to clear my schedule, which is jam-packed I assure you, and spend as much time as I can with you before you leave."

She was thrilled and yet startled, too. She was in a foreign city, and she didn't know anything about him. Except that he was sexy, and she wasn't sure that was exactly the best recommendation.

"I'll have to check with my sister. She went to Edinburgh on business, but she's going to try to get back tonight in time to have me come for dinner. I came over here in such a rush, and she had a calendar full of engagements and business commitments."

"I understand." He pulled out a little black notebook and tore out a page. Then he scribbled two numbers. "This one's my mobile. The other rings at the flat. Call me if you're free." Then he shrugged in that wonderful Gallic way he had as he handed it to her.

His deep voice was as heated as his gaze, causing her to shiver even before he placed the note in her hand. Instantly she curled her fingers around the scrap of paper. When his fingers lingered warmly over hers for long seconds, her own hand froze.

Soon the heat of his long fingers wrapping hers proved too unnerving. She couldn't think or talk or breathe. Not with her pulse knocking a hundred beats a minute.

"Why do you seem so familiar?" she blurted, pulling her hand away so she could put his note in her purse. She gasped for a breath. "I—I just know I've seen you before."

"I don't think so."

With a scowl, he picked up the bill. Then before she knew what he was about, he lifted her hand and brought it to his lips, turning it over slowly. His mouth against her palm and wrist sent her pulse leaping even faster than before. Then heat swept her body.

"I don't need to call you later. I'll go with you... dancing...everything...tonight," she said in a rush.

"What about Carol?"

"Carol?" Her mind was blank.

"Your sister." He smiled much too knowingly.

"Right." She gasped. "Right. Of course. Carol. I've got to wait until Carol calls. I forgot all about her."

He laughed. "You're wonderful in your own special way. I envy that nice guy with the job who's going to get you. Lucky man."

When he got up, he helped her out of her chair. After he paid the bill, he escorted her out of the shop and said he hoped he'd see her soon. On the sidewalk he lifted her hand to his mouth and said goodbye before walking rapidly toward Piccadilly.

Amelia looked at the little scrap of paper with his phone numbers on it. He hadn't written his name down, nor had he introduced himself properly. He hadn't asked her for her name, either.

Why?

He had impeccable manners.

Was he famous?

Why did he seem so familiar?

France's Highest Court Upholds Dismissal of Manslaughter Charges against Comte Remy de Fournier!

Her mouth agape, riveted by the news headlines, lurid photographs and articles in the newspaper she was holding, Amelia sat perfectly still on Carol's "bloody-expensive" sofa.

Remy de Fournier. No wonder he'd seemed so edgy. No wonder he hadn't told her who he was.

He'd killed his best friend, André Laffite, because he'd driven on bad tires on a wet day to win. Since the wreck, he'd slept with every beautiful woman with a title on the continent, heartlessly jilting them, not caring if he broke their hearts as long as they pleasured him.

So, they hadn't met quite by accident.

She took a deep breath against the hurt that threatened to overwhelm her. He wasn't attracted to *her*. He'd been feeling her out, figuring out a strategy to get the valuable properties he coveted.

Beneath the blaring headline were pictures of the crash that had ended the life of his best friend. Apparently Remy had been determined to win at any cost. More photographs of the wreck were splashed across a back page. There were numerous shots of Remy and the beautiful women he'd dated and jilted. One of the women had even made a suicide attempt after her affair with him. Not that the woman herself blamed Remy. No, she said he'd helped her through a difficult time. There was an awful picture of him smashing his fist into a reporter's jaw.

When she finished reading the articles and looking at the pictures, Amy felt sick. She reexamined them, anyway. When she was done, she shot to her feet and began to pace with the newspaper clutched to her heart. If half the accusations were true, she should despise him. Wadding the paper up, she threw the pages at the wall and then flung herself back down on Carol's sofa.

Bastard. Liar. Jerk.

A memory came back to her. Remy had been eighteen, and she'd been in the garden when the *comte* had hurled brutal, damning insults at him. Never would she forget the torment in Remy's eyes when he'd stormed out of the château and straight into her.

"What the hell were you doing?" he'd thundered. "Spying?"

"But I wasn't."

"Damn little eavesdropper! Get out of my way!"

"No. I—I wasn't. I swear."

"Liar."

"No. I—I'm sorry about what he said. Maybe he didn't mean it."

"Spare me your fake kindness. He meant it, all right. I hope I never have the bad fortune to meet you or your aunt again." He slammed past her and out the gate and she hadn't seen him for seventeen years. Till today.

And now? Outwardly he was much changed from the tall, awkward, angry boy who'd been so rude to her.

Fool. He'd been deliberately charming because he wanted the vineyard and the painting.

Still, he'd gone out of his way to make her like him. Even now when she should be furious because he'd deceived her so he could use her or so his agents could trick her, she wanted to give him the benefit of the doubt.

He is loathsome. So much worse than Fletcher.

But that woman who'd tried to kill herself had defended him.

Why did the bad boys of the world always appeal to her? Why couldn't she fall for some nice, paunchy accountant going bald, someone like Carol's Steve, an upright, type-A achiever? Or even just the normal guy Remy had described: the nice guy with a job who wants to settle down and marry so he can have a houseful of kids to play soccer with on the weekend.

If a hard-partying surfer was the frying pan, Remy, the womanizing, ex–Formula One driver, who'd watched her buy transparent panties and had made her pulse race, was definitely the fire.

She was lying on the couch in a state of utter depression as she tried without success to conjure up a dull ideal mate when the phone rang.

"Hey!" Carol said too brightly, sounding like her overly self-confident self. "I'm at the house. If you took the train from Euston, you'd be here in an hour and I could have dinner ready. The kids and Steve are very keen about seeing you."

The very last person in London she felt like seeing was her perfect, superior, drop-dead gorgeous, big sister.

"I don't feel too well," she heard herself say.

"What's wrong?"

"Something I ate, probably. Or jet lag. I'll have to catch you on my way home."

"I'm so sorry you don't feel well. I worked so hard all day just so we could all be together tonight. Do you need a doctor? Should I come to London?"

Guilt swamped Amy. She felt like dirt. Here she was lying, and Carol sounded so concerned and caring. "I'm sure after a quiet night here, I'll be just fine."

"Well, then, if you're sure…I really am tired after the trip. Maybe I'll just pop by and check on you first thing in the morning on my way to the firm. Maybe bring you a croissant or something."

They talked a little while longer, making tentative plans to see each other in the morning before they hung up.

I can't believe I did that! I've let him ruin my visit with Carol! My mood! Everything!

She stared across the room at the wadded-up newspaper.

All those women, women as beautiful and poised and perfect as Carol. They must've liked him, too.

He'd said he liked her because she was different.

Quit thinking about him!

Usually, Amelia wasn't one for hard liquor, but this was an emergency. She went to the kitchen, telling herself she was after a bottle of sparkling water or a soda, but the bottle of scotch lived in the same cabinet with the sodas, and it spoke to her. She grabbed a glass and poured a shot over some chunklets of ice. Swirling the glass, she returned to the living room, where she settled herself on the couch once more. For a long time, she just sat there, glumly sipping Carol's scotch as she glared at the wadded-up newspaper and the half of Remy's face she could see.

Then she stood. Crossing the room, she picked up the newspaper again. This time a photograph she'd barely noticed caught her attention. His stony face bleached of arrogance and any conceit, Remy was walking through the pits carrying André's helmet under his arm. All she saw in his hard features was shock and grief.

Who was he really? He'd been so nice to her today. He'd been attentive to her needs, and he'd gone out of his way to make her feel special and beautiful. Was he that sensitive, caring person or the man she'd just read about?

He'd had lots and lots of women. He couldn't have had all those women if he wasn't a really good lover. He was French. Frenchmen had a worldwide reputation for being good lovers. She knew it was crazy, but she began to envy those glamorous women whose hearts he'd broken.

Fletcher had accused her of being old and boring. More than anything she wanted to be exciting.

Remy de Fournier had asked her to go dancing tonight. Maybe he was totally awful like the papers made him out to be.

Or maybe he was just the man she needed to show her how to be a more exciting and confident woman. He'd made her feel interesting and beautiful today.

Maybe it was time she learned a new set of life skills. What sort of things could he teach her if she spent an entire night with him?

Her mother was always saying she could be and have so much more if she refused to settle. Maybe it was time to live a little dangerously.

Slowly Amy dug into her pocket and felt for the scrap of paper with Remy's phone numbers on it. For a long moment she studied the flowing black letters. Then with shaking fingers she began dialing his mobile, but after letting it ring once, she hung up, and would have chewed her nails except she couldn't because she had on those new tips.

Damn!

She was still staring at her fake pink fingernails in utter frustration when the phone rang.

Expecting Carol, she picked it up.

"Did someone from this number call me?" Remy's deep, dark voice spoke with such tender concern she almost forgot he was the terrible person she'd read about and not the sweet man she'd met by chance and had liked so much this afternoon.

He sounded *so* nice.

"Me!" she squeaked, forgetting the terrible bit. "That would be me! The girl you bumped—"

He laughed as if he were thrilled, too. "I know who you are." Somehow the way he said that made her feel very special, like she was the only woman in the world who mattered to him. Which was ridiculous. He was a womanizer.

"I was afraid you wouldn't call," he said, again sounding so sincerely worried and humble she could almost feel her heart shatter. He was *that* good.

Or *that* bad.

Either way, this could be a win-win.

Hang up on him.

She plunged in recklessly. "I—I'm free tonight. Carol..." Amy glanced across the room at a silver-framed photograph of her blond sister and Steve and silently crossed herself. "We...we won't be getting together, after all. She...has a headache."

"Nothing too serious, I hope."

"No."

"Excellent. I can be there as soon as you can be ready."

"But I don't have anything to wear."

"I don't really object to that," he teased. "I could bring dinner over, and we could stay in. You could wear... nothing. I wouldn't mind. I swear."

She laughed. "You *are* terrible."

"So I've been told." He laughed. "What do you want, *chérie?*"

If she wanted lessons in love from an expert, she should say, "*You.*" She should say, "Yes! Yes!"

"Fortnam and Masons is only two blocks away. If I could just pop over there..."

"I particularly liked your dress this afternoon."

"I'll call you when I'm ready."

"I can't wait to see you," he said in a dark, eager tone that sent a chill through her.

"Me, too," she responded in a voice that was probably too low for him to hear.

When he hung up, she licked her lips with the tip of her tongue and drew a slow, deep breath. Just talking to him made her feel sexy and daring.

She exhaled a long, shaky breath. And then another. Oh, my God. She was so excited she'd held her breath almost the entire phone call.

Deep down she knew that if she were smart and practical, she would return to Honolulu and regroup. No way should she fly to France to negotiate with his agents or his family about the vineyard or even *think* about the Matisse until she had her head on straight. If she were smart and practical she would tell him she knew who he was and ask him to leave her alone.

But despite everything she'd read about him, or maybe because of it, she wanted to go out with Remy. Which was crazy.

He'd tricked her!

But he'd been charming, devastatingly charming. And he had not pressed his advantage, she told herself.

Not yet, anyway.

Her mind warred with itself, but soon the hunger for adventure with a dangerous, incredibly attractive man won out over good sense and logic.

He was a *comte*. Despite his many faults, that would cut a lot of ice chunklets with her shallow mother and brilliant sister. Definitely, he was a win-win.

Now all she had to do was to find a sexy red dress!

Three

Is nothing more tempting than the bad and the forbidden? Now that Amy knew who Remy was, he fairly oozed danger with every white smile and seductive touch.

Maybe that was why the evening with him was one of the most desperately wonderful evenings of her life. Not that she wasn't bothered by what she'd read about him or by her plan not to let on that she knew.

Her senses were heightened to an extreme state of agitation when she looked out her living-room window as she was putting up her hair in a clip and saw him at the end of the block, striding up Duke Street with a single white rose. When he rang the bell, her throat closed as if a fist circled it. She tore the clip out of her hair and ran to the door.

As he handed her the long-stemmed rose, did she only imagine that his expression was darker and more haunted than it had been earlier? Then their eyes touched, and he smiled. As she sniffed the delicate blossom, he stepped across the threshold.

"I needed this tonight," he murmured as he gazed at her. "You'll never know how much. You're like a breath of fresh air."

He wore the look of a hunted man, and she imagined he must have read the ugly publicity, too. Did he have a conscience, after all?

When she turned around, he gasped. "You look beautiful."

"I don't usually shop in expensive stores," she said, feeling pleased with the flirty red dress and silver strappy sandals that made his intense gaze linger until her skin heated.

Tonight he looked very masculine and elegant in black.

"You don't look like the same playful girl I watched buying silky, see-through knickers in the flea market this afternoon."

Blushing at the memory, she held up her new bag.

"Very nice," he said.

The ensemble had cost a fortune, but as she'd stared at herself in her bedroom mirror, she'd been thrilled with the beautiful girl she barely recognized. For the first time she'd thought she was almost as beautiful as Carol.

"Are those shoes comfortable?"

"Naturellement."

"But can you walk in them?"

She pranced back and forth in front of the sofas as she had in front of her mirror earlier just to prove she could.

"Wow!"

She picked up her hair clip and coiled her hair high on her head. When she secured it, he whispered, "Better down."

She removed the clip again, and he smiled as her hair fell about her shoulders again. "Much better."

She bit her lip and set the clip on a low table.

"What do you say we take a walk first?" he asked.

"First let me find a vase for the rose."

Later in the gloaming twilight when he took her hand and led her across the Millennium Bridge, she enjoyed the warmth of his long fingers entwined with hers and enjoyed the feeling that for the moment, no matter what their differences, she belonged with him.

A young couple was letting their preschool children dash about blowing bubbles. Remy's indulgent grins made her smile. Did he like children as much as she did?

The captain of a small motorboat looked up and waved gaily at the children and their parents. The children stopped blowing bubbles when gulls and a lone pelican swooped low over the gray, churning waters.

The little boy, who had blond curls in need of a trim, pointed. "Bird."

Remy smiled. "What a wonderful age. Life is so carefree. Do you want children?"

Nervousness tightened her throat, but she nodded, anyway, thinking it an odd question from a man like him. "First I have to find a suitable father for them."

"Not Fletcher?"

"Not Fletcher. What about you? Do you want children?"

His eyes darkened beneath his heavy brows. "I'm not sure I would make a very good father."

"Of course you could be a wonderful father—if you committed yourself to it."

"One would hope any man who fathered a child would

do as much. But I'm afraid there's more to it. One must have examples set early in life."

She heard gravity and doubt and profound pain in his voice as he watched the children race ahead of their parents to the other side of the river.

"And you did not?"

He had turned away, and he pretended not to hear.

When Remy took her to the London Eye, the immense Ferris wheel beside the Thames, he hired a private gondola and then treated her to golden champagne and a box of chocolate truffles.

She wondered if he brought the beautiful women whose hearts he'd broken to the London Eye, or if they preferred lavish hotel suites.

He asked her all about Hawaii and about her mother and her sister. At first she was reticent, but soon she found herself talking to him far too easily. Even the difficult years after her father had left and then died, those years when she'd felt like the ugly duckling in a home with her beautiful sister and ambitious mother, Amy described with affection and humor.

"I was too much like my father. He thought there was no point in being rich and famous. I missed him when he was gone. I think Fletcher reminded me a little of him. My mother was always saying neither of them ever wanted to grow up."

"A fatal failing," he said.

"Well, at least I can brag about my sister."

His eyes filled with empathy. "You are not the only one who has disappointed your family, you know."

Pain flashed in his eyes. "I could tell you a story or two. More than a story or two. Maybe someday I will." He pressed the back of her hand to his lips, and his voice was edged with such bleak bitterness she wondered if he was as disreputable as the man she'd read about. What was *his* side of the story?

As their capsule soared high and the city of London was spread beneath them, she stopped talking, hoping he would tell her something of himself. But he didn't. Instead, he pointed out the various parks, the Tower, the Palace of Westminster, Westminster Abbey and St. Paul's Cathedral, to name only a few sights.

"When I come back, I will see them all," she said.

He laughed. "I'd like to show them to you."

Would he really? Wasn't he with her solely because of Château Serene or maybe the painting? Was he between glamorous women and merely bored tonight? Or did he just fling lines like that to any woman he happened to be with?

"It's hard to imagine you sightseeing."

"The simplest things can be fun if you're with an enjoyable companion."

He told her he preferred St. James's Park to all the others because it had the best vistas and was the most royal.

"St. James's Park is the first place I'd take you if I ever had the chance. In summer I often sit beside the lake and work there. If I get bored or stuck on a problem, I watch the pelicans."

"In London?"

"You just saw one when we were on the bridge. The first flock was a gift from the Russian ambassador. These, however, are from Florida. They're quite vicious when you get to know them, sort of like our *paysans* in Provence who will squabble over anything." He smiled.

"And you enjoy that?"

"I understand it. When they fight over scraps, they take my mind off…" A shadow passed over his face, and again she sensed his pain. Did he blame himself for André's death? Was he really as ruthless as the papers made him out to be?

Her own conscience was pricked. Should she confess she knew who he was and suspected what he was up to? No. Even if he was not guilty of the worst, he had deliberately deceived her.

She didn't push him to confide. Finally he drew a deep breath and began speaking of London and Paris. His London that was made up of chauffeurs, private clubs and the best restaurants, shops and hotels was very different from hers. His London had nothing to do with vintage shops or flea markets. He never exhausted himself chasing about the city on the tube.

Not that he didn't listen and ask questions when she described her world—the shop, her bargain-hungry customers, her triumphs at finding something wonderful for them at some insanely cheap price, her life in Hawaii, which was both casual and laid-back, but ridiculously expensive and, therefore, stressful. He seemed particularly interested in hearing about her mother and her sister's sometimes unendurable ambition and conceit regarding Carol's grand marriage to her English lord.

"And do you call her Lady Carol now?"

"Just to tease her. But I must confess, I have a picture of Steve being knighted and a picture of her estate on a bulletin board at Vintage, so I do brag about her when my customers ask about the pictures. Actually, technically, she can't be called Lady Carol. Apparently, titles like that are acquired by birth. She's Lady Burlingsquire, though."

"Sounds very matronly and respectable. Old and boring, if you ask me."

She began to giggle, maybe because she was on her third glass of champagne.

"How about some coffee and a truffle?" he said.

Before she could protest, he'd removed their glasses and set them on a little table, which was too far for her to reach.

If he was bad, shouldn't he be trying to get her drunk so he could seduce her out of her transparent knickers and break her heart? To tell the truth, she felt vaguely disappointed that he was being so good.

"How's the truffle?" he asked, keeping to a safe topic.

She closed her eyes, smiled, sipped her coffee and nibbled on the treat.

"Delicious, I hope," he said. He pressed her hand to his lips when she wasn't looking.

His mouth against her skin produced so much sizzle she hissed in a breath.

"Quite delicious," she agreed.

"You must save the rest of the box for later," he said. "When I'm gone."

He threaded his fingers through hers, which were burning from his kiss, and pulled her trembling body tightly against his chest. More fire shot through her and she grew hopeful that he might be contemplating a swift seduction. Then she looked down and saw trees and the tiled roofs of buildings looming large. They'd run out of time.

As their glass capsule approached the ground, he fell silent, and it was an electric, shared silence that made her want to stay in this magical bubble, Cupid's Capsule, he'd called it, with her fingers burning and her body brushing tightly up against his forever.

She hungered for his gorgeous mouth. Hungered so fiercely her heart began to pound.

Why didn't he lean down and kiss her? And not on her fingertips! She wanted to arch her body recklessly into his, to mash her breasts against his torso, to taste him, to know him, to have his hard arms close around her with wild, savage need.

To be seduced.

She had to be crazy to want a man like him.

But the evil womanizer she'd read about in the paper did nothing the least bit wicked to further debauch his or her reputation, and she was so acutely disappointed she wanted to weep. All too soon, they landed, and he folded those tingling fingers of hers inside his and helped her out of the gondola in the thoroughly gentlemanly fashion that was beginning to frustrate her.

"Thank you, that was fun," she said, but an edge of strain had crept into her light tone.

"Yes," he murmured most agreeably, "it was." When he stared so intently into her eyes she feared he might read her thoughts, she looked down.

"Is everything all right?" he whispered. "Did I say something wrong? Step on your toe or something?"

So, he sensed her edginess. "Everything's too perfect," she replied, her voice clipped.

This time he ignored the edge. "I made reservations at a French restaurant on the South Bank. It's a two-minute walk. But we could take a cab if you're tired…or if those pretty shoes hurt."

"No." She found that she wanted to prolong every experience with him, even walking along a public thoroughfare.

The restaurant was styled as a 1930s brasserie. The earthy odor of truffles mingled with rich sauces, fresh baguettes and buttery croissants. The wait staff seemed to recognize Remy, or maybe they fussed over all their wealthy customers. Remy spoke to the head waiter in rapid French, and they were led to a table in a secluded corner. When their black-coated server brought the menu with a flourish, it was in French, which she thought she knew fairly well, but as is often the case with French menus, there were many long words and dishes that confused her.

"I'm afraid you'll have to translate," she said in dismay. She'd so wanted to seem sophisticated.

He smiled over the dark fold of his menu. "Don't worry, French menus confuse even the French. The chef has rewritten this one since I was last here, and I am unsure about many things myself."

She felt herself relaxing.

"The waiter will love explaining everything. And if you let him guide you, you won't regret it. In France cooking is our highest art form. Our chefs are like gods, you see. Like your rock stars in America."

Charmed, she smiled. "I always eat on the go."

"Ah, you English and Americans. Fast food is one of the worst things about modern life. But I will forgive you that transgression because you did not know better before tonight. You are disadvantaged from birth, you know."

"What do you mean?"

"American and English babies are fed the blandest of foods. Mush—food we would feed the chickens."

"But of course."

"No. Not of course. From birth French babies eat what human beings with taste buds should eat, foods such as sole, tuna, liver, fruits, vegetables, Gruyère, *fromage blanc*."

She laughed even though she knew he wasn't totally joking.

"The palate must be educated, you see. No hamburgers and French fries when they go to school, either. They are served a three-course lunch. Voilà! The child learns to appreciate good food. Even our lower-end restaurants serve excellent food. Not so in your country. You must be wealthy to eat well."

"Surely there are some exceptions.

"They are rare."

After a two-hour meal, which was prolonged by Remy's and the waiter's inordinate care in the selection of every course including the wines, he took her dancing at the Savoy.

Being in his arms for the first time all evening at the landmark hotel made her blood tingle and her body heat. Not that he held her all that close. No. But his hand against her spine burned through the delicate silk of her dress and made her imagine how his touch might feel without the gossamer-thin fabric between them.

It was beginning to bother her that again he played the gentleman, deliberately keeping her at a polite distance. She wanted to snug herself against him, to feel his heat and wildness. His badness.

Every time he stared down into her eyes while their bodies moved together in perfect accord, she wondered what he was thinking. Not once did he mention Château La Serene or the vineyard, but she imagined the painting and the properties must be heavy on his mind even as they danced what was left of the night away.

She closed her eyes and pretended that they were on a real date and that she was glamorous and fascinating enough to intrigue him.

It was two in the morning when he brought her back to Carol's flat. And he at least *pretended* he did so with as much reluctance as she felt. But after holding her hand for a brief moment and pressing it against his cheek like a lover might, he pushed the door of her building open and said an abrupt good-night.

"I—I had a wonderful time," she whispered.

"So did I. I wish you a safe journey." His voice was cool and casual, if a little hard.

Suddenly she felt awkward and shy. "I—I wish you a happy life."

"Good night." He let go of the door.

As the glass door fell shut behind him, he turned and began walking away, his strides long and graceful. Not once had he mentioned the château or vineyard or painting. Why had he gone out with her, then? She stared at his retreating broad shoulders with acute dismay.

Suddenly nothing mattered except that he was leaving. Hardly thinking, she flung the door open. Giving a little cry, she flew out into the night after him.

"Would you like to…er…come up? For a drink maybe?"

He whirled. Looking miserable, he shook his head.

"Oh, please…do come up."

As he stared down at her, his eyes were dark and tortured.

She knew exactly how a Frenchman, especially a man like him, would take such an invitation from a woman at so early an hour in the morning. Still, she stared up at him, her gaze probably too adoring and trancelike, and he stared back as if equally compelled by some dark force.

He must be used to women throwing themselves at him. It had probably happened again and again, especially in the glory days after his races when he'd been a famous champion.

Moving closer, he started to reach for her. Then he scowled and backed away, furiously fisting his hands. Shaking his black head again with more violence than before, she felt as stricken as if he'd slapped her.

Because she felt so vulnerable, his narrowed gaze seemed harsh and unrelenting. "I don't think that would be wise," he said. "You have that plane to catch, remember. Like you said this afternoon, you and I are very different sorts."

When he turned on his heel, she ran after him and seized his hand, pulling him toward her building shamelessly. "I want you to stay. So…much."

"You little fool!" he muttered, gripping her fingers hotly as he reeled to face her again. Anger and some other fierce emotion hardened his features. "Don't you understand anything? I am not the kind of man a girl like you invites home."

"That might be true under normal circumstances."

"I'm not what you think! I don't want you to regret tonight. That's why I can't stay."

She wasn't about to admit she knew who and what he was and that she didn't care.

"I won't regret it. I swear." She flung herself against his chest and was slightly reassured when she felt both his erection and then his heart, which was beating even faster than hers. She ran her hand over his abdomen and then his chest, causing him to shudder.

"You don't know what you're doing," he whispered raggedly.

"I know what I want, and I think maybe you want it, too." She touched his jaw and then his lips.

"I'm a man," he rasped, passion flicking through his words like a whip as he pressed his cheek and mouth against the back of her fingers. "But I don't want to use you…or hurt you like…." He stopped.

This from a man who wanted only a vineyard and a painting?

Her heart beat madly in her throat. "You won't."

"I already have too many regrets," he muttered savagely. "I don't want you on my conscience, as well."

"Then I must make sure that neither of us regrets tonight."

When he glanced down the street as if thinking to escape, her hands flew around his neck and she pressed her trembling body to his. Even though they were fully clothed, she felt his hard muscles and erection against her pelvis.

"In the morning, you can go. I won't try to stop you. I won't be a problem."

He tipped her chin back with a finger and smiled down at her gently. "You're not the problem, *chérie*." Suddenly his arms circled her waist in a death grip. For a long moment he simply held her, and she reveled in the heat of his great, hard body wrapping hers. His heart was still pounding violently when his mouth slanted across hers, unleashing a storm of emotion and other hot, licking sensations inside her.

One kiss and she felt weak and needy and yet powerful, too. And beautiful. So beautiful. Was this how Carol *always* felt?

He kissed her again and again, and each kiss was

more heated than the last, at least until headlights at the end of the street splashed their shadows against the wall of her building.

Then on an undertone of dark laughter and in a low, slurred voice she hadn't heard him use before, he said, "We'd better go inside before I embarrass the hell out of myself and you, as well, by taking you right here against that brick wall."

He tugged her toward her building. Not that she resisted. She smiled when the door closed behind them, locking them inside the glass lobby.

When she punched the button for the lift, he grabbed her again and pushed her against a black marble wall that felt cold to the touch. Here he devoured her lips hungrily until soon they were both shaking so hard she couldn't catch her breath. His hands sifted through her hair and then skimmed over her throat, her nipples, her waist and lower, his wide hand splaying intimately against her pelvis.

She felt a rush of heat as his hand continued to explore her.

"Yes," she whispered. "Yes."

Everywhere his fingers lingered, her skin burned in thrilling awareness. If he'd tried to strip her then and there, she would have let him. When the lift pinged and he pulled free, she ached all over with needs she'd never known she had.

"I haven't ever felt quite like this," she whispered. Leaning forward, she sucked on his lower lip an instant longer.

"Neither the hell have I," he muttered, his tone almost angry. "Dammit. This is the last thing I ever wanted to have happen."

Four

Inside Carol's flat, Remy bolted the door and drew her into his arms again.

"Nice," he drawled as his gaze lazily took in Carol's custom-made coffee table with the family photos in their silver frames and then the sofas covered in beige cotton velvet. Last of all he looked at her. "I didn't really notice how nice it was before. All I saw was you."

He leaned down and picked up the picture of Carol and Steve. Still holding her with one arm, he said, "Is this your sister?"

Amy nodded.

"She's very beautiful. Like a movie star."

Like the women he usually dated.

"You're even lovelier, though."

He was staring at her with the laser focus of a man deeply attracted to a woman. The shadowy room was as quiet as a tomb, and it felt a whole lot smaller with him filling it.

Did he mean what he'd said, or was that just the sort of thing he said to every woman? Seconds ticked by.

Suddenly the tension was too much for her. Feeling embarrassed and out of her depth, she loosened herself from his grip and rushed to the window overlooking the street and opened it.

The night air held a slight chill, and she shivered. Somewhere a siren screamed.

Staring out at the glistening pavement and breathing in the damp, she didn't dare look at him again for fear she'd reconsider what she was about to do.

"I've never done this, you know," she said shyly, still feeling too unsure to face him. Funny, even as she said this, she felt as if the rest of her life had never existed, and as if all that would ever matter was being with him.

He moved behind her stealthily, and she gasped when his warm fingers lifted the black silk shawl from her shoulders and a cool breath of air stole across her naked skin.

"Done what?" he drawled against her ear in that deep voice, which made the last thread of her common sense unravel.

His warm breath against the back of her neck made her shake, or was it his hand moving over her that so affected her?

"Slept with a man the first day I met him."

"Who said we're going to sleep?"

"You know what I mean."

"I'm not the sort of man who has a right to care if you've slept with a dozen other men."

"You prefer an experienced woman?"

"Did I say that?" he whispered.

"You probably do this all the time."

For an instant that haunted look she hated came into his eyes. "Not lately. But, yes, in the past. I'm not proud of it. But I didn't want it to be like that with you."

"Why not?"

"I don't know. Maybe I don't want to be the person I've been most of my life. Or maybe I just think you deserve someone better than me."

She felt a flicker of conscience. What would he think of her if he discovered that his badness was the reason she'd invited him up? Would that ruin his good opinion of her?

"So, you think a person can change?" she said to divert him.

"You're not asking a man who knows much about such things."

"Then what do you know about?"

"Hell. Did you invite me up here just to talk?"

Before she could answer, his mouth touched the back of her neck and began to nibble with a practiced expertise that made exquisite little shudders ripple through her. Even as new longings flooded her, his callused finger feathered across the softness of her throat and moved lower to caress her breasts.

"Incredible," he said as her nipple peaked beneath a fingertip.

When he began untying the delicate silk straps that held her halter top up and more intense pleasurable sensations pulsed through her, she sucked in a breath.

She felt weak, blindsided by her own needs. Losing her nerve, she gave a little cry and grabbed the straps. Holding them up, she danced away from him and hit the light switch with the heel of her hand. Everything went black and she sank against the wall.

"I don't want to make love to you in the dark," he said huskily. "But I will, if that's what you want." He strode to a cabinet, punched some buttons, and almost instantly soft, seductive music filled the room.

"Why did you invite me up here?" he asked.

She was too aware of his tall, dangerous body, of his smoldering eyes searing her from the dark. She sensed the strength of his will and the formidable ruthlessness that had made him a champion race-car driver and a predator in the bedrooms of all those beautiful, glamorous women who'd hungered for his touch. Horribly, his badness excited her even as it frightened her.

When he said nothing more, the awful wildness began to rise in her again until she was so hot for him she wanted to tear off her clothes and turn on the light and spread her arms and legs wide open and lean back against the wall.

Why not surrender to that untamed part of her nature? Just this once? He of all men should understand and revel in such primal female wildness.

She began to undulate slowly to the music. At first her frozen limbs could barely move. Only gradually did her body come alive and heat to his male presence in the dark. Very slowly, she let the silk straps fall and drift down her breasts to her waist.

Too aware of him, she caught her breath and held it. Cool air caressed her breasts as she unzipped the back of her red dress.

Maybe he heard the rustle of silk or the purr of her zipper as it slid down or her silk gown slithering down her hips, because he hissed in a sharp breath. Or maybe he could see her in the dark.

When he didn't move, the charged, pulsating seconds ticked by slowly. Then he punched a button, and the next song was faster, wilder, its beat flooding through her like a jungle drum.

Leaning down, she loosened the silver straps of her high-heeled sandals. Kicking them toward him, she watched as they sparked like falling stars before landing softly right in front of him. With a fingertip she caught her transparent, red thong panties, which she'd bought because of a crazy dream she'd had about Fletcher, and stepped out of them. The darkness made her feel safe, but this wasn't about safety. It was about sex and sensuality and reckless-ness, about learning that she was a beautiful sexy woman who was not afraid of that part of herself, which until tonight she'd never fully explored.

She slammed her fist against the light switch, and the chandelier blazed to life. She threw her red thong at him. Then, bathed in light, she arched her golden body against the wall. She was wet and hot and trembling.

Dry-mouthed and mindless with fear, she froze.

His dark eyes devoured her.

"Voilà," he whispered. Her thong dangled from his tanned hand.

Her palms grew damp. "I—I can't do this." She stabbed wildly at the light switch again, but couldn't find it. "I thought I could."

He dropped the thong on the carpet and moved lightly, swiftly toward her. She was sobbing when he reached her. Instantly his hand hit the light switch and the room melted into darkness. Then he began stroking her hair and her damp cheeks, his voice crooning hushed words of comfort.

"Don't cry. *Chérie,* you are a magnificent woman. Very brave. You were made for all this…and more." His awed tone held her in thrall. "You are very beautiful. Perfect. Exquisite. Flawless. And I like very much that you're shy. Tonight I'm the luckiest man on earth."

Still terrified by what she'd done and the desires she'd revealed, she remained stiff and unyielding even when he began kissing her tenderly.

"There are many things to cry about, but not wanting to make love to a man who wants you as much as I do is not one of them." His mouth moved over her throat and breasts. "We can stop any time you want to. I'll go."

Amy's confusion and alarm seemed to dissolve under his gentle words and kisses.

"No! Don't go!"

"So beautiful," he murmured, kissing her damp eyelids and cheeks. "All night I fought this. Dancing without really touching you drove me crazy. I wanted you so much."

"You did?"

"I wanted you even in that damned tea shop."

Boldly she pushed herself away from the wall and pressed her length against his body. "Then I want you naked, too."

"Ah. Finally."

His strong arm encircled her. All too quickly, his kisses and his words made her feel so hot and desirable she forgot who and what he was and all the reasons sex with him was probably a really bad idea. Magically her tears vanished.

Wanting to touch him, she slid her hands inside his shirt. He felt sleek and solid and as warm as a baguette straight from the oven. She was desperate to have all of him. Soon her shaking hands were unbuttoning his shirt, loosening his belt and unfastening his slacks. In a frenzy she ripped his shirt loose and his belt out of the loops.

He was magnificent naked. Much larger, darker and more powerfully built than Fletcher. He had long, muscular legs and large feet, which she quite liked. She stared at his broad, square toes for a while because she was too shy to look at the rest of him. Finally her eyes traveled up his legs. He was huge and erect, and she was pleased with that part of him, too.

It was nice, this being naked together. Things were somehow simpler, more equal. No longer did he seem the *comte* and she the naive ugly duckling from America.

When he took her hands and made her touch him *there,* she took a deep, steadying breath. He began to stroke her, too, and she liked the things he did. She liked them so much that her hands began to move over his body with natural wonder and delight. Soon she was quivering from his slightest touch even as she felt his flesh respond beneath her lightest caress.

His low growls of pleasure made her ache for more, and her breathing quickened. He began to breathe fast and hard, too.

"Where's the bedroom?"

When she pointed, he lifted her into his arms and carried down the hall. Ripping off the bedcovers, he laid her down on Carol's fine, embroidered, laundry-scented sheets. When he straddled her, she ran her fingers over his wide shoulders, his furred, muscular chest and waist, her fingertips lingering over the warm, sinewy muscles of his arms and abdomen. He was stroking and kissing her, too, with an easy familiarity that made her feel she had always belonged to him and always would.

"I want you so much," she said, her tone low and urgent.

His hand drifted between her damp, open thighs. "I know."

"Then why don't—"

"You Americans are always in a hurry. Some things like food and sex are better if you take the time to savor them."

He pressed his mouth gently to her lips so she couldn't talk. Then he began caressing her again until her entire being felt radiantly aglow, until the slightest flick of his fingertip anywhere against her bare skin made her jump. She was now so hot for him that his lightest touch became the most exquisite torture, but, of course, it wasn't torture at all.

Without giving her any warning, he eased himself down her body and lodged his head between her thighs. Before she could cry out, his hot, open mouth began to caress secret silky places, his tongue dipping, circling, tasting until one flick made something burst inside her like liquid lightning. Exploding, her whole body pulsed. Screaming, writhing, she dug her hands into his powerful shoulders and hugged him closer.

Afterward he moved up and pulled her into his arms so that her head lay on his muscular chest. Then he patted her hair and stroked her cheeks as she shuddered and clung. Finally, when she was calm again, he brushed her hair out of her eyes and said, "*Chérie,* you are the sexiest woman I've ever known."

"I…I…I'm not really…I mean not usually—"

"I don't want to hear about other men."

He got up and left the room. When he returned he was

wearing a condom. He kissed her brow and lips before easing himself on top of her. Then as if it were the most natural thing in the world, he parted her legs, stared straight into her eyes so that she felt their souls were connected and plunged into her.

He stroked deeply, powerfully, his body and hers growing burning hot. Incredibly, desire rose in her again like an out-of-control fever, only this time she blazed even hotter. When he exploded inside her, she cried out. Then she began trembling and clinging to him as before. Only this time she wept, as well, tears cascading down her cheeks, which caused him to hold her closer.

Where was the ruthless heartbreaker she'd read about? The man who held her was as tender and compassionate as he was wild.

He was right. They didn't sleep much.

He made love to her again and again, teaching her exactly how to pleasure him. He was patient and gentle and yet strong, too.

She barely knew him as a person, and yet she learned his body that night. Never had she imagined that making love could be so glorious. And yet even in the midst of rapture, she felt a piercing sadness at the thought of parting, because she knew such feelings, however wonderful, would never have the opportunity to deepen into something more than this one magical night.

When she grew sleepy, he wrapped her tightly in his hard, warm arms, snuggling her bottom against his groin. As she lay curled against him, she tried not to think beyond the bliss of his body enveloping hers beneath the sheets.

She had this one shining moment. That was all she could ever have of him, all she must ever want.

He was bad. Not the sort for her in the long run.

But he'd proved to her beyond a shadow of a doubt that she could be sexy.

The next morning she awoke to city sounds, to the obnoxious roar of a garbage truck lifting cans and garbage spilling against metal sides, to cans crashing back down on the pavement, to the shrieking of sirens and horns two blocks away.

She sat up, rubbing her eyes and squinting in the brilliant golden light. Muscles and feminine tissues she'd never known she had felt raw and burned.

With a shy smile she turned to face the lover responsible for these changes in her body and nearly wept when she found no one there.

She hugged herself tightly, fighting tears. He'd left without even a goodbye.

Feeling bereft, she hugged herself. Had he been real? Only those tender, well-used tissues and the dent in the pillow where his head had been told her she hadn't dreamed him.

Chérie, *you are the sexiest woman I've ever known.*

She lay back, thoughtfully stroking the pillow that still carried his scent. Remembering how he'd sucked her naked breasts so lovingly, she threw off the covers so that the warm sunlight could stream across her and heat her skin as his mouth and tongue had. She ran her palm over her belly, and as she thought of his lips on her flesh, her stomach quivered and perspiration beaded her brow.

Oh, God! She was pathetic. She wanted him more than ever.

She sat up. With a feral scream, she threw his pillow at the wall and then shot out of bed. Thinking she would go mad if she didn't get out of the apartment, she raced toward the bathroom just as the phone rang.

Thinking it was Remy, she lunged for it. *Pathetic!* Maybe she should confess she'd known all along who he was. No! Then he'd *really* know she was pathetic.

"Hello there," she murmured.

"You don't sound at all well," Carol said, her tone anxious and much too big sisterly.

An acute shudder of disappointment moved through Amy, but she forced herself to get a grip. Putting her hand over the receiver, she closed her eyes and drew a long, steadying breath.

"Amy!"

"I—I'm just a little tired, that's all," she whispered.

"You're all better, then?"

"Much better, thank you," she murmured. Stretching heedlessly, she gave a twist to her spine and made all those soft tissues burn.

"Ouch!"

"Amy!?" Big sister's voice was shrill.

"Sorry. I'm fine. Really. I am. In some ways I've never been better."

"You sound...depressed."

"Aunt Tate, I—I suppose." She stopped, horrified at how easily she lied.

"She did adore you. I mean the *Matisse...*"

"I'm going to give it away."

"Only if you're an idiotic, idealistic little fool, which knowing you, you will be!"

"Carol!"

"Sorry! It's horrifying how much I sound like Mother sometimes."

As Carol talked, Amy barely listened.

She was thinking about Remy and aching on a soul-deep level to see him again.

Would he be at Château Serene when she got there?

Or would he play it smart and avoid the hell out of her—unless she thought of some way to lure him back to her bed.

Because she wanted him again.

Five

Remy said hello to Marie-Elise, his secretary. Then he directed her to hold his calls and to make no appointments until the next day. Before she could say much, he strode past her into his own starkly modern office and shut the door.

When he flipped on the lights, his gaze went to the only decoration in the room—a framed photograph that lay facedown on his chrome-and-glass bookshelf.

He forced himself to walk over to the shelf. Carefully he picked up the snapshot of himself and André Lafitte when they'd been boys. In the picture they were grinning from ear to ear as they stood in front of their racing karts. They'd been fourteen. André's doting father, Maurice, who despised Remy now, had been full of pride and joy in both boys when he'd taken the picture.

Remy's hands were shaking by the time he set the picture upright on its glass shelf. He stood there, staring at the tarnished frame and faded picture in silence for as long as he could bear. The picture had lain facedown for a year.

After a few minutes alone in his office, he began to feel so alienated and full of self-loathing he almost flew back out to Marie-Elise's office. Instead, he swallowed and turned toward the window.

Outside, the morning was gray and bleak, but no bleaker than the darkness of his own guilty heart.

Slowly he turned away from the window and sat down at his desk, which was piled high with envelopes, flyers, brochures and telephone messages. Determined to accomplish something his first morning back, he emptied the contents of the first envelope. It was a letter from his estate agent, complaining that Amelia was balking. Several telephone messages and faxes from the agent were attached to the envelope, one with yesterday's date. The agent called her obstinate and difficult.

Amelia was the last person Remy wanted to deal with. He should never have agreed to meet her. Or kept his identity a secret. Or bedded her. Hell.

No use in thinking about her now. But despite his efforts to put her out of his mind, he constantly imagined her on the bridge laughing about the bubbles or dancing in his arms or writhing underneath him, and an ache in his soul would rise up to torment him. Determined to banish her, he wadded up the agent's messages and threw them in the trash. Then he slashed into envelopes, tossing garbage onto the floor beside the can with a vengeance. When he couldn't stop thinking about her, he decided to return his phone calls. Not that that worked any better.

Somehow he passed the morning slogging through the piles on his desk and returning his calls. When it was almost noon, and his desk still had numerous piles, he regretted his promise to lunch with his mother, whose preferences dictated long, formal meals. The hour was nearly upon him, and he was getting up to go meet her when Marie-Elise slipped into his office and quickly shut the door. She was a thin, efficient girl with a pale complexion. She always wore dark, loosely fitting clothes, large glasses and shoes with thick rubber soles so that she could move about like a shadow and not attract attention, especially male attention. He suspected she was much prettier than she appeared.

Once she'd implied she'd been in a bad marriage. She hadn't gone into the particulars, and he hadn't asked.

"Maybe you should go out the back way, monsieur. A man is here to see you."

"I said no appointments."

"I told him, but he laughed and ordered me to give you this. *Ordered* me! He assured me that he needed no appointment." Blushing, she handed him a business card. "If I may say so, he's a very pleasant young gentleman, monsieur."

Marie-Elise had never complimented a man before, at least not to him.

With a lift of his eyebrows, Remy took the card. In the next instant he was smiling, too. Then he was laughing. "Didn't take him long to charm you."

She blushed—Marie-Elise, who never blushed or took the least notice of *any* man.

Remy stared at her for a long moment. "His wife left him a year ago. You could do worse."

Again her cheeks reddened becomingly, making him think she really could be pretty if she tried.

"Sorry," he said. Feeling like an idiot, he rushed from his office into hers.

"Remy!" A short, painfully slim man gripped the sides of his chair and pushed himself to his feet. Gripping his cane, he steadied himself. Then he grinned from ear to ear.

He was hospital pale, and he looked years older than thirty. Years older than last year.

Dammit, he was alive. And his blue eyes were sparkling, instead of glazed with pain. *He was alive. Standing. Walking slowly toward him.*

"Pierre-Louis!"

"It's good to be back in the real world."

They hugged fiercely for much longer than was necessary.

"It's so good to see you," Remy said in a voice choked with raw emotion.

"No appointments?" Pierre-Louis teased. "No exceptions, your fierce little secretary said."

"I'm late to meet my mother and an old friend for lunch, or I'd suggest we go out. But you're always welcome—here or at the château. But then, you know that."

He studied the dark circles under Pierre-Louis's eyes. Maybe they weren't quite as dark as they'd been three months ago when he'd last seen him at the rehab hospital. He was standing, walking apparently. Remy tried not to think about the amputated leg that the doctors had worked so hard to save.

"You look good," Remy whispered.

"Thanks to titanium we'll probably be jogging together in six months. Hey, but what about you? I wasn't the only one who hit a rough patch. I'm glad you're back. At last. Wonderful news in the papers last week!"

"The newspapers want me charged. Hell, did you see the editorial two days ago where the writer said men like me make him want to bring back the guillotine?"

"They'll forget. But more importantly, *you* should forget."

Remy stared out his window at the brick facade of the office building across the street, which blocked the sun and made him feel trapped in its long shadow. "Maybe I should have stayed in London."

"No. Don't look back. Just concentrate on the future. I've recently taken a job with Taylor's team."

"Driving?" Remy asked, hoping his alarm didn't show.

Pierre-Louis shook his head. "Administration. That's why I'm here. Taylor asked me to look you up. Have you given any thought to what you're going to do now that you have these obnoxious legalities behind you?"

"Work for my family."

"You became a driver because that wasn't enough for you. And not just a driver—the best damn driver there ever was."

"A lot has changed."

"But have *you* changed?"

"Too much." Remy paused. "So what do you want?"

"*You*. Taylor wants you on our team."

"I told you before that I retired a year ago. For good."

"We don't want you in a car. Taylor wants your brains, your administrative and organizational skills. He's not getting any younger, but he's got the ambitions of a young man. He says we need men with your kind of dedication, brilliance and energy at the highest level if we're going to keep Formula One a global television spectacular. As the technology improves, you can help us make the sport safer and better. You can save lives, Remy."

"Taylor's a bastard to send you. You're the one person I hate saying no to."

"Good. Then maybe soon I'll convince you to say yes. If ever there was a born mogul of the pit lane and paddock, it's you, Remy."

"Thanks," Remy said, but his voice was cold.

"But no thanks?"

"Formula One is a murderous sport. Like I told you before, I don't want to have a hand in killing anybody else."

"It wasn't your fault that the steering jammed."

"Look, I've rerun that race a thousand times in my head. I could have taken that curve more slowly. I should have. I was reckless, out of control."

"We were all pushing the edge that day. That's what drivers get paid to do."

"I can't go back. Not ever."

"Just think about it."

Remy shook his head.

"You know, you're the last man I'd ever peg for a quitter."

"Hey, thanks. I know what you're trying to do." Remy hesitated. "I've got to go now. But it was good to see you. I'll call you."

"You haven't heard the last of me. You were there for me during the worst time. I won't forget that. On a different subject—how long has your cute secretary worked for you?"

"Marie-Elise? Cute?"

"Is she married? Children?"

"Divorced. One little girl. And she doesn't date."

"Maybe the right man hasn't asked her."

"Marie-Elise is sensible and sensitive. She's been hurt—badly."

"Marie-Elise. Pretty name. Very pretty." His eyes were warm. His smile was as big as his heart.

They shook hands and embraced again, even more fervently than before. Remy felt good that Pierre-Louis looked so much like his old self.

Remy showed him out and then raced down the hall to the elevator that went down to the underground parking garage. When the doors opened in the basement, he loped to his red, vintage Alfa Romeo Spider.

He started the engine and backed out, but when he hit the remote door opener and the garage doors rose, reporters who were bunched just outside on the sidewalk started shouting at him.

A tall man held up a grainy photograph from a front page of a notorious Paris tabloid.

Amelia—laughing as Remy led her from the Savoy.

Bastards.

Even though the shot was grainy, and her face was partially turned away from the camera, Remy's stomach knotted.

"Who's your new girl?" A cameraman shoved his camera against the sports car's window. A flash burst in Remy's face. More flashes and sordid questions demanding to know the details of the relationship followed.

Seething, Remy tapped the accelerator and inched forward. What he really felt like doing was hitting the brakes, leaping out of the car and throttling the bastards. But he'd slammed a fist into one reporter's jaw last year, and they'd gotten all sorts of shots of that. Then they'd sued him and garnered more nasty headlines, all in an effort to exploit him to better their own bottom line.

He grabbed his wraparound sunglasses off the passenger seat and slammed them onto his face. Without waiting for a break in the traffic, he jammed his hand on the horn and tore into the traffic. Tires squealed. Brake lights flared as he shot ahead of them. Other drivers made lewd hand signals. He roared ahead of them, anyway.

As he sped off, a dozen motorcycles stuck to his tail while others swarmed like maddened bees on all sides of him.

He drove faster than the flow of traffic, and the paparazzi snapped pictures from their bikes the whole time. Long before he reached the grand old Hotel de Crillon on the Place de la Concorde, he was furious. Jumping out of his car, he flipped his keys and a thick wad of Euros into a doorman's palm.

"Take good care of my biker buddies," he muttered.

The doorman blew his whistle and reinforcements ran to help. Leaving the shouts behind him, Remy jogged briskly into the sanctuary of the Hotel de Crillon's marble lobby. Not that he paid much attention to the opulent eighteenth-century Louis XV architecture and décor, which included sparkling mirrors and chandeliers.

The paparazzi were tenacious. He hated that they'd gotten a picture of her. Even though it was blurry and she wasn't named and he didn't plan to see her again, she might still be at risk. The last thing he wanted was that sweet girl to be hounded by the paparazzi because of him.

His mother's cheeks were even brighter than the peachy marble walls of Les Ambassadeurs, which meant she was well into her second glass of Pinot grigio or maybe her third by the time he arrived at her table.

While six waiters watched them in deferential silence, Remy leaned down to kiss his mother's rosy cheek.

"Sorry I'm late," he said as he sat down opposite her. "A friend dropped by the office at the last moment."

She folded her menu. "Anybody I know?"

"Pierre-Louis."

Her lips thinned. "Ah, yes. But I thought you said you were through with all that."

Anything that had to do with Formula One had always been extremely distasteful to her. No wonder. Her lover, his biological father, had been killed racing Formula One. Their affair had destroyed her marriage. Remy had gone into Formula One as much to even the score with her as to get revenge on the *comte* for detesting him. After that dreadful afternoon when Remy had discovered that he was the bastard offspring of her illicit affair with Sando Montoya, the champion Grand Prix driver, Remy had hated her. But time and maturity had lessened those initial hot feelings. After all, she was his mother, and in her chilly way she adored him—if you could call her obsession with running his life adoration.

Well, those mistakes were in the past now, and like many people with regrets, they could do nothing but move on.

Her remarks on the subject of Pierre-Louis's health were cool and dutifully polite. She was clearly impatient to move forward with her own agenda.

"I've invited Céline as I promised," she said, her dark eyes sparkling.

He smiled, wishing he could postpone seeing Céline.

It was strange. Before Amelia, he'd been curious about Céline. Today he would have preferred to dine with his mother alone. For some reason he needed time to get past that night with Amelia in London. She'd left him shaken. And not because he'd probably made negotiating with her more difficult.

"How did it go in London...with *her?*" the *comtesse* asked.

An image of Amelia's soft body coiled in a tangle of sheets that smelled of sex in a bedroom filled with moonbeams and shadow slammed into his mind so vividly his heart jumped into his throat and beat madly.

He'd felt an overwhelming desire to sink back into that bed and bury his face in her perfumed hair and hold her warm body tightly. And never let her go. Instead, he'd run. Even now when he saw his actions as reckless and selfish, he still longed for her warmth and kindness. He knew that peace could only be an illusion for a man like him, but he'd felt something awfully like it when he'd lain in her arms.

"Meeting her was a mistake. Nothing was accomplished." Deliberately he kept his tone flat and low to indicate he had zero interest in the subject. "I would prefer to forget about it."

"What happened?"

"I never found the right opening to bring up the vineyard. She didn't seem to want to talk about it. Since I didn't introduce myself, nothing happened."

Watching him closely, she lifted her wineglass to her lips. Instead of drinking, she swirled the wine so that it flashed like liquid gold.

"*Some*thing happened." Her laserlike gaze seared him. He snapped his menu open and sank lower behind it.

"I wish you were right. So...have you had time to look at the menu? Have they told you the specials?" He signaled for one of the hovering waiters.

"We can't possibly order yet." His mother closed her menu when the waiter came. "We're waiting for a third party. Perhaps my son would like a glass of wine to calm his nerves."

Seething, Remy spent far more time than necessary in his selection of wine. When the waiter vanished, Remy launched into a new topic. "I've been on the phone all morning with the engineer overseeing the foundation repairs for our villa in Cannes. I need to go down there, so I won't be able to return to the château until Mademoiselle Weatherbee is gone."

His mother's eyebrows rose ever so slightly as she continued to study him in silence.

"This *is* serious," she said at last.

"What?"

"You. You're deliberately avoiding her." His mother leaned down and pulled the same French tabloid from her purse that the reporter had shoved in his face.

A single glance at Amelia's grainy profile made Remy stiffen.

"You slept with her."

Since he was not going to discuss that relationship with his mother, he gripped his menu and studied it, even though the words were a blur and he no longer gave a damn what he ate. Fortunately, before she could continue to pry, a tall, slim blonde dressed in a black suit and pearls caught his eye and that of every other man as she glided into the dining room.

"Céline!"

Smiling, he jumped up and hurried toward her.

She was thinner since her husband's death, and there was a new sadness in her blue eyes that made her seem both fierce and fragile. On the whole, though, she was much more hauntingly beautiful than she'd been as a girl when he'd dated her in Paris. He brushed his lips across her hand, which was warm and satin soft. She'd been a sweet young thing in Paris. He'd always remembered her fondly.

She smiled as if she were very glad to see him. Suddenly he was genuinely pleased his mother had invited her. At least now, with his mother distracted by her match-making project, he would be safe from more questions about Amelia.

His mother's eyes were triumphant when he pulled out Céline's chair. No doubt she saw in the lovely, tragic Céline everything she most desired in a daughter-in-law—beauty, breeding, brains, style and old money.

An image of Amelia with her childish braid and faded cotton sundress arose in his mind's eye. Could his mother be so pleased if such an unpretentious girl were his choice?

Lunch was long and pleasant. How could it be other-wise in Les Ambassadeurs with the musky perfume of white Italian truffles, butter, garlic and fresh herbs drifting in the air? And with two such charming companions ready to shower him with their undivided attention?

Still, at least for Remy, something was missing. Despite Céline's efforts at flirtation, he was constantly distracted by visions and memories of Amelia's sweet face and of her intimate caresses. Why couldn't he forget how hot and silky she'd felt when she'd been naked underneath his body? Or how sweet and responsive she'd been? Or how utterly trusting? She'd been gentle and kind and sexy as hell.

Suddenly he wanted to forget about Cannes and rush down to Château Serene. What was she doing down there all by herself? Did she miss her aunt terribly? He wanted to put his arms around her and console her. He wanted to hold her naked and make love to her again.

Had she thought about him at all? Did she miss him, at least a little? Or had some newspaper article or old photograph of him she'd found in one of her aunt's albums made her hate him? How stupid he'd been to seek her out in London.

"Remy, what are you thinking about?" Céline's sweet voice chided when she asked him a question and caught him staring past her.

Muttering a swift curse under his breath, he forced his attention back to the lovely Céline. "Sorry," he said.

"It must be difficult…coming home, facing everybody…even me." She laid an affectionate hand on top of his. "It's too soon, isn't it?"

He froze, unable to answer until she lifted her hand.

She continued to flirt under his mother's pleased, watchful gaze, and he played along.

Thus they made it through their long, elegant lunch.

Did the *comtesse* hate her or what? Or did she simply despise having to deal with someone she considered so much her inferior?

Amy held the phone against her ear with growing impatience as the *comtesse* told her how disappointed she was that they could not come to an agreement, *disappointed* being a euphemism for *very pissed off*.

If only Remy would call, instead of his mother or his

agent, who were always so unfriendly and snobby. But no, he, apparently, was avoiding Provence. And *her*.

Well, if she couldn't have Remy, she'd much prefer to enjoy her breakfast in the garden in peace.

"Bless you, Aunt Tate," Amy whispered to the ghost, who she believed was still very much in residence, "for having stood the *comte*'s first wife as a close neighbor for so long."

"My agent informs me that you are going to give the Matisse away and that you still refuse to sell us Château Serene," the *comtesse* was saying.

Did she know Remy had contacted her in London? She would probably have apoplexy if she knew the whole story.

Bees droned in the purple lavender. A fat tabby licked its fur on a terra-cotta wall beneath the deep shade of a cherry tree. A plump black dog lay in a lazy coil under the rosemary hedge with a plump paw over his eyes.

Amy hadn't had her coffee yet, and the heat was making her feel as lazy as the animals.

"My agent informs me that you refuse to sell Château Serene," the *comtesse* repeated.

Amy pushed the phone closer to her ear, but the *comtesse*'s tone was so strident she pitied Remy and was soon concentrating on the purple shadows and sparkling sunshine, instead. What would Matisse have captured from this scene?

"I'm having breakfast in the garden alone. Do you mind if I put you on the speaker phone?" Sipping her strong, steaming-hot espresso, Amy punched the appropriate button.

"Are you alone?" the voice barked from the center of the table.

Much better.

"Quite alone!"

"Why do you refuse to sell?"

Amy stared at the pool and chaise longues surrounding it. Not that she really saw them. No, instead, she imagined Remy's darkly chiseled face and glowing dark eyes as he'd held her in his arms after making love to her.

Last night she dreamed that he'd come here and seduced her on one of those chaise longues in the moonlight.

"I had forgotten how divine the early-morning light is here," she said. "It's a gold haze, really. And I love the smell of warm pine needles, wild thyme, baked earth and lavender."

Happily the château with its crumbling biscuit-colored walls, its rambling garden and vineyard were in much better shape than she'd been led to believe. From the terrace Amy had a view not only of the pool, but of the lavender fields that stretched to the woods on one side and to the vineyard and village and purple mountains on the other.

"I asked you a question." Clearly Amy's enthusiasm for the place did not delight the *comtesse*.

"Oh, yes." Amy bit off the tip of her fluffy brioche swirled with chocolate and suddenly found herself dreaming of lying in Remy's arms again. "Some things are hard to let go of."

"That is how we felt when my ex-husband gave the Matisse to your aunt on their wedding day and willed the château and vineyard to her upon his death." The *comtesse*'s soft tone bit like a viper's hiss.

"I cannot sell you the Matisse. It is priceless, and my aunt's last wishes were for it to be given to the French people. As for the château, I like the way it has been modernized since my last visit, especially the bathrooms. Have you seen the skylights and the deep stone tubs and the showers? Well, they're really quite lovely. Last night after Etienne gave me a tour, I took a long, hot bath staring up at the stars."

She did not say that she'd fallen asleep wondering where Remy was and if he would come, or that she'd dreamed they'd made love out here by the pool.

"I never realized before that Château Serene was set on an area of Roman ruins," Amy continued.

"Who told you that?"

"Etienne showed me."

"Are you saying you want more money?"

Amy's gaze drifted to Etienne's stooped figure in camouflage trousers and a beige sweater. He was working among the vines where plump, purple grapes exploded in dark bunches. "The vineyards seem to be under capable management, too."

"Only a fool would trust that foul-tempered old devil. The vineyards are certainly not as we would like them to be."

"You seem extremely anxious to buy them."

Keeping her gaze on Etienne, Amy brought her cup of espresso to her lips again.

"Name your price," the *comtesse* said coldly.

"I need more time."

"I don't understand. You live in Hawaii. You have a shop. You need money. What could a girl like you possibly want with a château in France or a vineyard?"

Amy frowned. Annoyed, she said, "Do you always snoop so deeply into everybody's affairs?"

"Why won't you do the intelligent thing, the logical thing, and sell?"

"Maybe you should ask your son!" She remembered Remy in her bed and then her empty bed the next morning and the desolation that gnawed at her ever since.

There was an audible gasp. "What?" For the first time the *comtesse* seemed to be at a loss for words.

"Oh, did he forget to tell you? We met in London, I thought by chance. Until I saw the newspapers and figured out who he was. I don't like being tricked or lied to. If you and he want to buy the vineyard as passionately as you say you do, then send him. If I decide to sell, I'll discuss my terms with him. *Only with him.* Until then, goodbye."

Maybe her voice had been calm, but she was shaking. It was a long time before she could relax enough to find delight in the stone walls and shutters that glowed in the warm, golden sunshine again.

Remy. Just thinking that he might come increased her trembling.

This was the exact spot where she'd first seen Remy after she'd overheard his father yell something on the order of "You want to know why I've always hated you? All right, I'll tell you! Because you're the bastard spawn of Sandro Montoya, that damn womanizing Grand Prix driver, whom God in his infinite mercy annihilated in Monaco six months before you were born! I should have divorced the *comtesse* then! If you want a father, dig up his corpse!"

Remy. Bastard. Bad boy Grand Prix driver. Heartbreaker. Womanizer. And the present *comte*. Not to mention her tender lover in London.

Who was he really?

Did he want Château Serene badly enough to come?

If so, would he agree to her terms?

Six

Twenty-four hours had passed without so much as a word from the *comtesse* or her agent. Or Remy.

Where was Remy?

The late-afternoon sun with its dry heat was so intense the dogs and cats shared the same pools of shade beneath trees shrill with the songs of cicadas. Even with the shutters closed, the main living room felt oppressively hot to Amy. As she knelt over an album entitled *My Life—It Was Fun While It Lasted* and flipped through a carefully edited group of pictures that depicted the highlights of Aunt Tate's glamorous life, perspiration beaded Amy's nose and brow and glued her blouse to her rib cage.

The house was oppressive in other ways. Was that because emotions lingered in houses after a person died? Or were her own memories of happier days all that haunted her?

With a sad smile Amy turned the last page of the album.

Every picture either flattered Aunt Tate, showed her decked out in some outrageous costume or standing beside a celebrity or the Matisse. Funny that her last husband, the *comte*, was the only husband she'd included in this pictorial record of her life.

Mountains of boxes, stuffed with all that was left of Aunt Tate, surrounded Amy. Some were taped shut and labeled; some gaped open. Amy felt guilty about having to tear up Aunt Tate's house and sort through her personal things. Every time she put something in a box, she glanced over her shoulder, praying that Aunt Tate's ghost wasn't watching.

Life was short. With a start Amy realized she was thirty, which was half Aunt Tate's age at her death. Aunt Tate had already divorced two husbands by the time she was thirty.

Amy stood and went to the shadowy wall where a sensational copy of Aunt Tate's colorful Matisse hung. She flipped on the light that illuminated it, and the vivid colors came to life. The painting was of a small reclining nude. The *comte* had told Tate he'd fallen in love with her at first sight because she reminded him of his favorite possession. Tate, who'd been sunbathing topless on a secluded beach near Nice, had begged to know what he'd been talking about. He'd promised to tell her someday, and on their wedding day he'd presented the Matisse to her, saying she was the painting come to life, and that he was the luckiest man in the world. To thank him Tate hadn't worn any clothes for a month.

Amy was reaching for a red, blown-glass bud vase that she'd bought Aunt Tate in Venice when a loud knock boomed at the thick front door. Next, Remy's compelling baritone echoed through the house. Her heart began to race. Without even bothering to wrap the bud vase, she flung it into a box. Then she ran barefoot through the dark house.

The front door stood slightly ajar—he'd arrogantly pushed it open. Not that he was anywhere to be seen.

"Hello?" When she peered out the door, a shrill burst from the cicadas greeted her.

Had she only imagined his voice? Hating that she looked such a mess, she ran her hands through her hair and smoothed her blouse as she tiptoed outside onto sunbaked stone.

"So, you refuse to sell—until you talk to me?"

She jumped.

"I would have thought you'd never want to see me again," he said.

"I'm not too smart—especially where men are concerned," she said dryly.

He laughed. He was leaning against the wall wearing aviator sunglasses with impenetrable reflective lenses. His tall, dark figure was drenched in brilliant, lemony light that caused his elongated shadow to slash across the warm flagstones.

With difficulty she squared her shoulders. He shifted his weight from one leg to the other as if he, too, felt on edge. Then he fell back into his slouch against the stone wall.

"If this isn't a good time, I'll go."

His low, guarded tone caused her heart to race all over again. Obviously he was eager to run.

"No…it's a great time."

She squinted against the warm glare. He wore stone-washed jeans and a long-sleeved, white shirt rolled to his elbows. He looked good, too good. Taking a breath, she wet her dry lips with her tongue.

He whipped off his glasses with a defiant smile. "I should have told you who I was in London."

His hard stranger's voice made her chest knot. She swallowed, hoping that the fist in her chest would ease. Maybe she should confess that she'd known who he was almost from the first. Instead, she stared at him in sullen silence.

"I won't blame you for hating me," he said.

"But I don't…" She shook her head. "Not that I think what you did was right."

"You're too generous," he continued. "I'm not the most admirable person."

Guilt gnawed at her.

"But I expect you know that by now. I did warn you that you'd regret—"

She held up a hand. "Don't overestimate my virtue. And please stop with the apologies. I don't know what I feel, okay? I read a few newspapers, a few unflattering stories about you."

"I was charged and found guilty of murder by the media."

"Your steering mechanism failed."

"I killed my best friend. I have former friends and even family members who won't speak to me. André's father was my father's mechanic. As a kid I loved hanging out with him in the garage. He taught me about cars, about girls, about everything because my own father never took the time." His brilliant eyes pierced her. "And you and I…know why. Maurice Lafitte despises me now."

"It was an accident," she said softly, feeling a strange need to soothe him. "The track was wet."

"I was stupid, reckless, arrogant. I pushed myself and

the car to the max. Beyond the max. I was out of control on and off the track."

"Who taught you to drive like that? André's father?"

Remy moved toward her. "And for what? Surely not to kill his son!"

"To win."

"Yes! I had to win! It was the most important thing in the world to me then, because I had to prove..." He stopped. "I had to prove to a man who wasn't even my father, a man who was dead, that I mattered."

As she had in the garden seventeen years ago, she felt the heaviness of his pain and fought the need to throw her arms around him. "It was your career. You were paid to win races."

"Tell that to André and his father!"

He came so close that she caught her breath. When he raised his hand, she thought he might touch her.

But he lowered it, instead, and swallowed tightly. "I'm sorry. I have no right to want anything from you. If you're smart, you'll forget you ever met me. I have nothing to offer you. Not even friendship. I regret how I treated you."

"So you want to be as harsh and condemning of yourself as the newspapers?"

"My old life is over now," he said bitterly. "Fame. Easy fortune. *Women.* Funny, some part of me thought those glory days would last forever. They never do, though. Now I have to find a new path. I've made a lot of mistakes in the past year."

"Anybody would have under that kind of pressure. You were hounded."

"I've hurt some people I could have avoided hurting, only I was too locked in my own misery to think of them.

I went to bed with women to distract myself, never thinking of them."

"You're thinking about them now."

"When it's too late." His dark eyes locked on hers. "Look, I don't expect your forgiveness for deceiving you in London when I can't begin to forgive myself for it. But I'm sorry. I didn't want to hurt you."

His heartfelt apology only made her feel more despicable for remaining silent about her own deception.

"So why did you seek me out in London?"

"You know why."

Her heart sank. "The vineyard? Château Serene? The Matisse?"

"My mother called and told me where you were."

Some part of her wished he'd said he found her so beautiful and irresistible he'd had to deceive her.

"Because she wants them back?"

"I think it's a point of honor. Tate took her husband and Château Serene. Now she wants what he gave her back."

"And you work for her?"

"For the family. Since last year. I've caused them immense pain. It's time I repaid them for their trouble. And I am, even if ironically, the present *comte*."

"Yet you've stayed out of the negotiations all this week. Why?"

"To spare you."

"Don't lie to me ever again!"

She turned quickly, so he wouldn't see how stricken to the core she suddenly felt. Why did he evoke such wild emotion so quickly? So easily?

Placing her hand against the warm stone wall, she splayed her fingers and fought not to succumb to tears or more foolish passion. "You were afraid you'd jeopardize the negotiations." She hissed in a hot breath. "You don't give a damn about me—or about sparing me."

"*Chérie...*"

She whirled on him, no longer caring if her eyes were red. "Don't call me that. Not in the same voice you used to seduce me."

"You invited me to come up, remember?"

"Don't remind me of my stupidity!"

He held up his hands and fell back a step. "All right. The last thing I want is to make things more difficult for you. But you did ask me here." He paused. "Look, I've said what I came to say, so I'd better go."

With a shrug he turned to leave.

"Wait! The painting, which is in a bank vault in Paris, is not for sale. Aunt Tate used to tell me that an important piece like that shouldn't be privately owned. Before she died she was negotiating with several museums. She left me a letter entrusting me to complete the transaction for her, and that's what I want to do."

His jaw tensed. "That's very generous of you, considering..."

"Considering what?"

"That you're not a wealthy woman."

"Money isn't the only thing that makes a person wealthy."

"And I thought you were intimidated by your sister." His gentle smile made her throat tighten.

"Not always. And if you still want to buy Château Serene, you'd better listen to my terms."

"You'll sell?" His eyes narrowed with new interest.

"I live in Hawaii. What could I possibly want with a vineyard in Provence?"

"How much?" he said.

"Come to dinner...a little later...and maybe for a swim. It's too hot and I'm too tired to discuss business matters now."

"You cook?" His tone softened. "Not hamburger, I hope."

"Eight o'clock sharp."

"You speak enough French to know there's no way to translate eight o'clock sharp in Provence."

"You speak enough English to understand the term. Eight o'clock sharp. Bring the contract. And your bathing suit."

"Do we really need bathing suits...in the dark?"

His gaze slid over her with more than enough male interest to make her skin grow warm and her neck to perspire under her limp collar.

Which was good. The bargain she had in mind would never have occurred to her if he wasn't sexier than hell and hotter than the Provençal sun.

The sky was thickening with dark, rolling clouds as Amy bathed and moisturized and perfumed herself in the most intimate places as she stood in the largest of Aunt Tate's modernized stone bathrooms. Carefully she selected a translucent white thong. Next she chose a gauzy white dress, pearls and white, high-heeled white sandals.

When she finished blow-drying her hair, she barely recognized the vibrant young brunette who smiled back at her from her mirror.

Gone was her casual vintage look that made her look too much like an unfashionable hippie. Before her stood a sophisticated woman who could appreciate the best things in life, including a very sensual Frenchman.

Still wearing the same stone-washed jeans, now with a black jacket, Remy arrived fifteen minutes after the hour.

"Eight o'clock sharp?" she teasingly reminded him as she took the chain off the door.

"I did try to warn you." His grin was sheepish as she stepped back to allow him to enter.

He handed her a bottle of Pinot grigio. "I intended to return to Château de Fournier, change and grab my bathing suit, but when I stopped in the village to buy the wine, of course, Faustin, the wine seller, invited me to share a *pastis*. And when one led to another, he started in on politics, as he always does, and I ran out of time. Every time I come home, Faustin and I must have this same frustrating conversation, which he, at least, enjoys so much."

"And you don't?"

"What is the point of arguing? You can't change someone's mind."

The damp air smelled of rain and lavender and pine and *him*. She smiled, savoring his scent as she had when he'd lain beside her in London. "I suppose you're right," she said.

"You look beautiful." He grinned as he stood inside the foyer. "I drove through some heavy rain on the way over," he said, attempting polite conversation. "But that's normal for August."

She stared past him at the black sky and swaying tops of the pines and cypresses, but said nothing. He pulled the contract out of his briefcase and handed it to her. Silently she thumbed through the pages and then tossed it on a low table near the door. "Later. How about a glass of wine?"

When he nodded, she carried the bottle of Pinot grigio into the kitchen, where she tried to open it. But her hands shook with such excitement that all she accomplished was drilling out bits of cork. Her ineptness made him laugh.

"Allow me." When he swept the corkscrew and wine bottle from her, his hands grazed hers. Then he deftly yanked the cork out. "It just takes practice. Obviously you need to drink a lot more wine." Quickly he poured two glasses.

"Feel like watching the storm?" she asked, not wanting to be confined inside with him. Without waiting for his answer, she picked up a platter of cheese and crackers and glided past the stacked boxes out onto the terrace under the eaves.

He was slow to catch up because he stopped to admire the copy of the Matisse. A burst of wind sent leaves flying across the terrace when he came out of the house.

"I can see you've been busy packing," he said.

She led him to a small green table near several potted tangerine trees and sat in one of the chairs.

"I've made some progress, but there's a lot more to do. I can't stay here forever. I talked to my mother today. Luckily she's okay with watching my store for the rest of the month."

He leaned closer. "You'll be here a whole month?"

"Hopefully no longer. So I'm anxious to come to an agreement that is mutually satisfying—to both of us—within that time frame."

"And the Matisse?"

"Like I told you. It belongs to the world."

"An idealist." His dark eyes glinted.

"I don't know anything about art or museums, so it might take me a while to figure out the right thing to do."

"Maybe I can help you."

Their gazes met, and immediately she felt as if he lit her being.

"And the château and vineyard?" he continued.

"I'm willing to part with them."

The wind howled, causing the *cigales* to stop chirping in the cedars. She lifted her wineglass, and the Pinot grigio slipped down her throat like cool silk.

"Then I see no reason we can't wrap up this negotiation tonight," he said.

"I don't think so," she replied.

"Look," he said. "We want this property. Very much. The price has always been negotiable. You say you'll sell. So what will it take to make you a happy seller?"

When he gave her a quick, uninterested glance as he sipped his wine, she lowered her eyes and hesitated for an awkward moment.

"You," she said, staring at the flagstones like a shy schoolgirl, instead of a wanton seductress. *"For a month."*

She looked up, hot-faced and terrified.

Equally startled, he raised his eyebrows and gazed at her so long the air between them grew charged. "Me? I don't understand."

Her mouth felt dry, and she ran her tongue over her lips. Taking another quick gulp of wine, she said, "Remember when I told you that my boyfriend accused me of being boring and old?"

"Fletcher," he growled.

She felt rather than saw his gaze on her wet mouth when he whispered, "Damn him."

"Let me finish, please…before I lose my nerve completely."

Draining his glass, he swiftly poured himself more wine. He was as flushed with high color as she probably was. He sat up taller and shrugged out of his black jacket even though the night air was cool and damp.

"I—I told you that my life is dull back in America, that I own a second-hand store and that my boyfriend says—"

"To hell with him. He's wrong. I should know."

She felt her skin grow even hotter. "Maybe not with you. Not that once. Which brings me to the point I'm trying to make…"

In an agony of embarrassment, she stared down at her sandal-clad feet, which were cocked in a childish, pigeon-toed angle. Quickly she straightened them.

He smiled. "Go on."

"I need more practice…with an expert. According to all those newspapers, you're a very experienced lover. So, I—I want you to teach me to be sexy."

"Don't you know that those damn papers make up lies and use sex just to sell more newspapers?"

"But what if London was a fluke? What if I'm a dud the next time?"

He took a deep breath. Leaning back, his bleak, dark eyes stripped her. Then he frowned. "You aren't listening!"

"I know you usually date all those beautiful, wealthy women—"

"You don't know a damn thing!" He sat up abruptly. Seizing her hands, he stared deeply into her eyes. "You are a dazzling woman. Would you stop selling yourself short? *Believe* in yourself!"

"If you'd do this one little thing for me, maybe I could."

"This one little thing, as you call it, would compound the mistake I made in London—which was to deceive and sleep with a sweet, innocent girl!"

"If you'll make me your mistress for a month, I'll sign your contract for the price your agents have offered and not a penny more."

Shaking, she pulled her trembling hands from his and brought a fingernail to her mouth, but since she was wearing tips, there was no way she could chew on it.

Gently he pulled her hand from her lips.

"Don't! I hate that habit," he said, kissing the offending fingertip before letting her hand go. Then he shot to his feet. "No! Hell no!"

She stood, too. "Because I'm not sexy enough? Because I'm too dull?"

"Dammit, don't put another man's words into my mouth!"

The valley was thick with swirling mist and the sky was nearly black, holding the promise of rain. She stomped through wild thyme and made her way toward the grove of wet pines behind the pool, anyway. The damp wind moaned, tearing through her hair. Not that she cared.

Embarrassment and hurt at his rejection made her bend at the waist and hug herself as if in unbearable physical pain.

"Amy…" His voice and footsteps were cautious as he approached through the crackly thyme.

"Amy!"

In the next instant she felt the heat of his hand against her spine. She tried to jump away, but very gently he pulled her back.

"London was wonderful for me, too. I was afraid I'd hurt you. That's why I came over this afternoon. I've thought about you all week. I didn't want to obsess. But I couldn't stop myself."

"Don't say things you don't mean."

"Okay. Let me repeat myself—the best thing for you is to stay as far away from me as possible. Name your price, sell the vineyard and go home!"

Her hands curled, fake tips digging into her palms. "I named my price—you for a month. You're the perfect person to teach me what I need to know. All my life my mother and sister and Aunt Tate saw themselves as beautiful adventuresses who deserved grand lives. My mother failed, and I opted out of their game because growing up with such a beautiful, elegant sister made me too insecure to try to compete. So I never became the woman I could be, the woman you showed me I *might* be—if I ever dared to let myself…dare. I want to be good at sex, the way I was with you."

"Good with other men, you mean?"

"Yes!"

His fingers wrapped around her upper arm. "You little fool! Sex isn't a skill like playing the piano. When a woman gives herself to a man, she gives more than her body. You don't just hire a teacher because you read he's slept with a lot of beautiful women."

"I don't see why not. Especially since I know from experience just how good you are."

His grip tightened, and he turned her so that she faced him. "Amy, Amy. I like you just the way you are. I don't want to be the one to change or corrupt you."

"This is *my* idea, not yours. I was a bookworm in school. I believe in lessons and study, and now I want to study…sex!"

"Don't be ridiculous!"

As the wind whipped her hair, he slowly brought his

long, tapered fingers to her cheek. "Go back inside before you're blown into this pool, and I'll forget we ever had this idiotic conversation."

"Why shouldn't we?" She circled his waist with his arm and pulled him to her. "You want Château Serene, and I want you. Or rather, what you can teach me."

When she stood on tiptoe and leaned toward him, he took a quick breath. With a shaking hand she stroked his cheek and then his lips. He stiffened. For a moment longer he stood motionless. Then as if drawn by an irresistible force, he slowly bent his head and kissed her, sending wild shards of sensation to every nerve ending in her body.

"You're good," she whispered breathlessly, pressing herself against him. "The best. That's why I'm choosing you."

"It's called chemistry. It's because I like you and you like me. But you're the last woman I'd ever choose as my mistress."

"Ouch!"

"I meant that as a compliment. Trust me. It would be more dangerous for you than you think. You've read about the women I've hurt. Women always want more than I can give. I always walk. I'm not capable of the kind of love and commitment people like you need. I was abandoned young, so I can be cruel."

"I don't care. All I'm asking for is a few more lessons in bed."

"Dammit, you'll get hurt."

"How, if I have no illusions about how bad you are? How, if I could never love someone as low-down as you? Besides, a sexy bad guy has to sleep with someone. Why not me? Especially since you'll get Château Serene for your trouble. If you're cruel, why do you care?"

A bolt of lightning crashed near the pool, the stark, white blaze lighting the grounds and his scowling face.

"Do we have a deal or not?" she asked softly.

"Who else will you make this offer to if I don't accept? I should call your mother," he said in a low, seething tone. "And tell her you need somebody to watch over you while you're here."

"Why can't that be you?"

His dark eyes stared straight into hers. Then he went still, and she saw something of his real desire.

"Go! Run!" he growled.

"No!"

"All right. Have it your way."

He scooped her into his arms, and his mouth came down hard on her lips, her throat, her breasts, causing her blood to heat and her heart to pulse like a drum. Then he hauled her into the house.

Once they were in the kitchen, he wrapped her in his arms. Glancing up at her aunt's calendar on the wall, she said, "In one month, at this hour, I'll sign your contract." Pushing loose from his tight embrace, she grabbed a red pencil and circled the date.

"As if I give a damn right now," he said. "The important thing is that after one month with me you'll be so sure you're sexy, you'll never question yourself again."

"You swear? On a hundred Bibles?"

"This isn't a child's game." Leaning down, he caught her bottom lip with his teeth and tugged gently. Then his tongue invaded her mouth.

A long time later he said, "Who's making up our first lesson plan?"

"You! You're the teacher, *mon amour*."

He pulled his mobile phone out of his pocket and turned it off. Then he kissed her very slowly until his heart was thudding and his breath was rough.

"Strip," he said, his voice hoarse and low as he let her go.

"While you just stand there and watch me…like I'm some woman you're appraising in a brothel?" Startled, she backed away from him an inch or two.

"You're my mistress. I want to see you naked. It's your job to satisfy my wishes."

"You think I'll be too scared and shy to do it, don't you? You think I'll just sell the vineyard without…you having to live up to our bargain?"

"If you have a grain of sense, dammit, yes!"

"Then I guess it's up to me to show you once and for all that I'm dead serious about being a satisfactory mistress."

Her hands went to her ears and she plucked her pearl earrings off, one by one. Next she removed her pearl necklace. Then she began to unbutton her gauzy white dress, touching herself and sighing as she did so.

When the soft fabric slid down her erect nipples and thighs and pooled at her feet, she felt feverishly warm, even though she wore nothing but the transparent white thong panties he'd watched her blushingly buy at Camden.

She moved toward him and boldly traced her fingers over his shoulders, down his broad back. She cupped his hips, his thighs and, last of all, his erection. His entire body was hot. He was fully aroused.

"Am I beautiful?" she whispered. "I do so want to be beautiful for you."

With a groan, his arms wrapped her close. His mouth sought hers in a long, demanding kiss that made her body tighten and quiver.

"Yes, dammit, you're beautiful."

Lifting her gently, he carried her through the house to her bedroom.

Seven

A callused fingertip ran the length of her body in the velvet dark. Only dimly did she hear the rain beating against the stone walls and roof tiles and racing off the roof into the gutters. Blasts of lightning shot the night with fire. Not that she could see much blindfolded. And only vaguely was she aware of the bursts of thunder.

"They say that the blind are more sensitive to touch," he'd whispered when he'd locked her in her bedroom.

Amy's eyes were still covered by a strip of black silk. She was naked, and her arms were stretched above her head and tied loosely with a long, white, silken scarf. Why had she let him tie her up?

Why not? He was the teacher. This was his lesson plan.

"If you're going to be sexy, we must break down your inhibitions. You must be wild and free and willing to try things you've never tried," he'd told her.

"Like making love in the rain out by the pool."

"If the lightning stops," he promised.

Her ankles were wide apart and tied by scarves at each corner of the bed. His head was lodged between her open thighs, his tongue tracing silky, satin circles and delving deeply inside her, tasting her essence.

For an hour she'd lain helplessly beneath him as his mouth and tongue had roamed her body, licking the soles of her feet and between her toes, licking her in the most intimate places until she'd become a wanton, quivering mass of flaming female sensation. When she cried out, feeling hot, on the edge, ready to explode beneath his next kiss or flick of his tongue, he slowed his exquisite torture.

"Don't stop. Please," she begged.

"Anticipation," he murmured, kissing her secret femininity, "is everything. Sex is mainly in the mind, you know."

"You're killing me."

He eased himself higher along her body. "No, I'm loving you. I want you to know how totally, how completely sexy you are." He kissed her temple and she quivered. Then he gently kissed her lips. "You are the most responsive woman I've ever known."

"But I'm afraid."

"I won't hurt you. Though sometimes a little fear enhances the thrill."

"Kiss me. Hold me," she pleaded.

His mouth found hers. Their lips and tongues joined, tasted. In utter bliss at the taste of him, she sighed. He settled down on top of her, his hips aligning themselves over hers before he slowly entered her.

His skin was even wetter and hotter than her own as

he hovered above her, barely moving, each stroke expert. Suddenly he plunged harder, and she was screaming and weeping. When she began to writhe, he exploded. With a cry, she tore the scarves loose, and her hands clutched his shoulders.

"Yes," she whispered, wrapping her legs around his waist and arching herself upward. "Yes."

He buried himself even more deeply when she shuddered and dug her nails into his back.

Afterward, as he lay on top of her, his shaft still buried inside her, she reveled in the utter completeness she felt to be thus joined to him and held by him.

She'd missed him so much. How was that possible?

He kissed her brow, her cheeks, her eyelids and lashes, even the tip of her nose, muttering low, sweet words in French that she only partially understood.

"You could be insulting me and I'd never know."

"You'd know. And I'm not insulting you."

"I didn't think you were."

His stomach grumbled.

"Hungry?" she whispered.

"You did say dinner at eight o'clock sharp? And even for a Provençal, we're long past that hour."

"Oh, yes, dinner." She got up slowly. "And I was thinking about making love in the rain."

"With a mind like that you damn sure don't need me to teach you to be sexy."

"Oh, but I do."

They dressed, and he followed her into the kitchen where he surprised her by proving that he could be as useful behind the stove as in her bed.

Together they chopped fresh vegetables and made pizza—or rather, three pizzas, mushroom, cheese and anchovy. He tossed a salad while she put the finishing touches on a steaming casserole of roasted chicken and mushrooms that she'd prepared earlier.

After lingering over dinner and sharing a crème caramel, she thought he would surely leave. Instead, he stayed to help her wash and put away the dishes. She turned out the lights and locked up. When they reached the front door, instead of stepping outside so she could lock it, he took her hand and led her outside into the mist.

"You said you wanted to make love in the rain," he reminded her.

She shook her head. "Not now."

"How about a quickie?"

"I don't think I could."

"A sexy girl's got to have a quickie lesson." He pushed her against a cool stone wall, stripped off her jeans, unzipped his and penetrated her. His dark eyes glowed with intense black heat as he thrust into her again and again.

Slam. Bam. Instantly she was aflame. Why hadn't she thought she wanted this? She held on to him, begging, clinging, wanting all of him.

"Condom," she whispered several strokes later.

"Damn."

"Damn," she agreed as he withdrew.

Panting hard, he stood before her.

"Wait here," he finally managed between hoarse breaths.

Gasping too, pushing her hair out of her eyes, she nodded. "As if I could go anywhere."

When he returned, he kissed her tenderly on the brow and eyelids and lips before shoving himself inside her again. As before, his movements were hard and fast. For long, glorious moments her body strained with his. She screamed at the exact moment he clutched her shoulders and drove into her with a final shudder.

When her knees buckled, he pulled her close. "Wrap those legs around my waist."

When she did as he asked, he walked with her inside the house and slammed the door.

"You're a quick study. I don't think you need a month of lessons, *chérie.*"

"That's not our deal," she whispered.

She thought he would say goodbye and go. Instead, he carried her back to her bedroom where they slept wrapped in each other's arms just as they had in London.

Only, the next morning when she awoke to brilliant sunshine and that delicious soreness between her thighs, his black head was on the pillow beside hers. Snuggling closer to his warm body, she smiled. How nice he felt. How right. How pleasant it would be to have him always.

Her eyes snapped wide open. As she stared at his furred chest, her heart pounded.

His long lashes fluttered lazily open.

"One month?" he murmured. "You look like you're having second thoughts. You sure you really want so much of me?"

"One month," she insisted. No way could she confess the depth of the terrifying tenderness she felt for him.

"Usually my affairs never last that long."

She swallowed. His comment hurt, more than it should have.

"So, this will be a growth experience for you, too," she said, attempting a lightness she didn't feel.

He frowned as if something was bothering him, too. Was he already tired of her?

"So far I have no complaints," he said. "It's been fun."

"For me, too," she agreed even though she suddenly felt miserable.

When she got up, he lay on his back with his arms crossed under his head and his dark, brilliant eyes watching everything she did. Taking her time, she put on a soft, pink cotton dress that had faded from red. Slowly, self-consciously, she braided her hair.

What was he thinking as she used a pencil to darken her eyebrows and a tube of lipstick to make her mouth redder? Was he bored? Did he think she was using him? Did he feel resentful? She would give anything to know. But she did not have a right to his thoughts.

She had rights only to his body. And only for one month.

When she was dressed, she asked him what he wanted for breakfast.

"I know a café in the village."

"Won't everyone know about us then? Even your family?"

"Probably. The villagers are terrible gossips. Especially about the de Fourniers. But they know I want to buy your vineyard. If we bring the contract, perhaps we can fool them into thinking we're conducting business."

"With your reputation?"

"You're leaving. Do you really mind if they suspect you're my mistress?"

When she shook her head, a slow, possessive grin spread

across his face. If she hadn't known better she might have believed he wanted everyone to know she was his.

"But what about you, your sisters and your mother? Your mother could barely stand talking to me the other day. You know how much she disliked my aunt."

"Don't worry about my family," he muttered, pulling her close and kissing her. "I'll deal with them."

With the top of his Alfa Romeo down, he sped down the slick, narrow roads that climbed through the fields of lavender to the red-roofed, medieval village perched on a cliff.

He drove so fast her thick braid whipped her face, and tires screamed around the curves. She should have expected speed from him and recklessness. Not that rubber ever veered once off the asphalt. Nor did he come too close to the cyclists on the edge of the road.

The car was nimble, his concentration complete, his expertise profound. He knew the road, the car and his abilities, and soon, instead of fear, she felt exhilaration.

She'd never been in a car with butter-soft leather seats like this, in a car with a driver who could make her feel like she was flying in bed and out of it.

"So what kind of car is this?"

"A '67 Duetto Spider."

"It's cute."

"Cute." He snorted. "It was the best damn sports car made that year. Not that it ever caught on—even after starring in a major film. Did you ever see *The Graduate*?"

She shook her head.

"Someday soon we'll have to watch it together."

He slowed when they reached the village, which was

crowded because it was market day. He cruised the narrow, winding lanes overflowing with haphazardly positioned stalls that sold all kinds of wares. Young gypsy women in tight bustiers and shiny skirts ran up to the Alfa Romeo, shaking long plaits of garlic and lemons in Amy's face.

When she reached for them, he said, "No shopping," and kept driving until he found a parking space near a fountain two blocks from his favorite café. "I'm starving."

As they got out, the clock tower chimed. He took her hand, and they walked up the hill past galleries and benches that would have been perfect for people-watching. Everywhere there were stalls selling everything from olives and fresh bread to terrines and Disney toys.

He tugged on her hand when she edged toward a yellow-and-white canopy. "No shopping," he reminded her.

"But he's selling fresh croissants."

"We're nearly at the café."

Two minutes later they were seated on a rooftop terrace under an arbor dripping bougainvillea. He laid the contract on their table, and then they ignored it and chatted until their omelets laced with pungent truffles arrived. The food was so delicious they ate in silence. No sooner had he finished his and was sipping café au lait when his mobile rang.

He fished the phone out of his pocket only to frown when he saw who it was.

"Sorry. It's my mother. I had my phone turned off until a few minutes ago. I guess I'd better talk to her."

Amy nodded.

"Bonjour." After this brief greeting, he was soon scowling. "You shouldn't have done that," he said in sharp, staccato French. His gaze on Amy, he listened with in-

creasing irritation. "You're right," he snapped. "I'll be there as soon as I can."

He flipped the phone shut and jammed it back in his pocket.

"Let me guess. She knows we're together and she's not pleased?"

"Gossip travels fast. She didn't fall for the contract on the table, and she's not happy I didn't return to the château last night. Apparently she'd made plans—"

"I knew we shouldn't have eaten in such a public establishment so early in the morning."

"My personal life is none of her business."

"She's your mother."

"I'm thirty-five. The trouble is she's always been able to dictate to my sisters. She failed miserably with my father, and her schemes frequently annoy the hell out of me."

He stared up at the impressive Château de Fournier, which topped the highest hill above the village, and then fell into a gloomy silence.

Amy knew his family had lived there for hundreds of years. Once she'd told her aunt it must be wonderful to belong to a family with such ancient roots and traditions like the de Fourniers.

"They're ridiculously conservative," Aunt Tate had replied. "His first wife was so out of touch with the modern world, she drove him into my arms."

Amy looked at Remy. "Surely if you tell your mother you're merely seeing me because you're negotiating the sale of the vineyard, she'll be more understanding," she began.

"The last thing I intend to do is discuss our relationship. Not with her. Or anyone else."

"I know you were trying to improve your relations with your family, and I don't want to be a problem."

Remy's hand closed over hers. "No problem. At least it won't be after today." Squeezing her fingers, he lifted them to his lips.

Seeing the tender gesture, the proprietor winked at Amy and made a pleased little bow before darting back inside.

A short while later the man reappeared, beaming. Remy held up his hand for the check. Grinning widely, the owner zoomed over and slapped it on top the contract.

As if still preoccupied by the phone call, Remy did not attempt to make conversation with the man or with her. As soon as he paid, he led her out onto the street to find his car.

Rocks crunching beneath their shoes, they walked in silence. Despite Remy's mood, Amy was enjoying the brightness of the sun, the vivid red geraniums and the sweetness of the lavender as they topped the hill in search of the Alfa Romeo.

Just as they reached it, she heard a roar, and a green Renault careened straight at them. Swerving almost into Remy the driver hit the brakes at the last minute. Jumping out of the way, Remy grabbed Amy and circled her with his arms protectively.

Yelling Remy's name, the driver charged out of the Renault like a bull.

The solid fellow looked tough enough to do real damage even though he barely came up to Remy's shoulder. He wore rough, faded work clothes, and his blue eyes burned so hotly Amy wondered if he'd already been drinking.

"Murderer! You think you're smart because they let

you off? You think your money can buy anything, even justice for my son's death!"

"I'm as sorry about André as you are, Maurice."

"You! You don't know anything!"

Maurice held up a fist. Then he took a step backward and slammed it down on the hood of the Alfa Romeo with so much force he dented it. He began to hurl further abuse at Remy, making violent hand gestures as he did so. His vernacular French was not entirely comprehensible to Amy, but Remy turned so pale she began to tremble.

White-lipped, Remy grabbed Amy's arm. Leading her around to the passenger side of the car, he yanked her door open and said, "Get in."

When he raced back around to the driver's side, Maurice hurled himself at Amy's window.

He spat heavily on the ground. "Stupid girl! You should have nothing to do with this man. He killed my son! He's dangerous! He hurts everybody he touches—especially women! He drives like a maniac!"

Remy strode back around the car. "Maurice, you'd better leave her alone."

"Or what? You'll call the police? You think you're safe because you own this town, don't you."

"If you want to talk to me, make an appointment with my secretary." Remy held out a business card. "I'll be happy to see you anytime."

Maurice grabbed it and shredded it, then hurled the bits at Remy. He spat on the ground again. "I'll see you in hell. That's where I'll see you."

"Fine." Remy got into his car, slammed the door and jammed his key in the ignition. The engine roared to life.

Careful of Maurice, whose bulk was blocking half the

lane, Remy shifted and drove up on the curb to avoid the man and get away. Only when they were outside the village did he speed up, but his face remained grim. He gripped the wheel so hard, his knuckles punched the skin like bleached bones.

Even when the village was several miles behind them, his fury, grief and self-loathing remained such a presence in the car that Amy grew close to tears. What must he have suffered this past year?

"Are you cold?" he asked her. "Do you want the top up?"

She pushed her braid back. "No, I'm fine."

"Right." Jamming his foot down on the accelerator, he sped toward Château Serene as if chased by demons.

She thought he wanted to be rid of her so he could be alone. But when he pulled up in the curving stone drive of Château Serene and stopped, he reached across her to open her door.

"I wish I could have spared you that little scene," he said.

"I'm okay."

He drew a deep, resigned breath. For the next few minutes he was silent. "Look, if you've changed your mind…about seeing me for a month, I'll understand."

She buried her face in her hands and shook her head.

"I can't see you until tomorrow. Apparently I have a previous engagement today."

"Oh." Looking up, she fought to hide her disappointment. Not that she asked questions. He had a life.

His jaw was set. His expression was so dark and cold, her eyes began to burn. Determined to escape before she broke down completely, she quickly scooted toward her open door. But when she would have gotten out, his arm snaked across the back of the seat and pulled her to him.

"You're not crying, are you?"

"No!" When she felt dampness oozing down her cheeks, she sniffed. "Sinuses. I'm allergic to the cypresses."

"Liar." He crushed her to him, stroking her face and hair. "I'm sorry. I had a great time until my mother called and Maurice showed up. I'll miss you today." He kissed each cheek, tasting her hot, salty tears. "What will you do with all your free time?"

"Pack."

"You're sweet. I don't deserve you," he whispered. Then he let her go.

She got out slowly and walked hurriedly up the drive. Before she reached her door, he was roaring away.

She would have waved if he'd ever once looked back. Since he didn't, she watched the Alfa Romeo until it disappeared over the first hill.

Where was he going? Who would he spend the rest of the day with?

She opened her door and walked into her dark, empty house that without him, seemed colder and gloomier than a tomb. She'd been his mistress for only one night and already he felt like a dangerous obsession.

If she were smart, she'd call his agent and agree to sell immediately.

Eight

Remembering it was market day, Remy parked the car in a shady alley beneath the château. He opened the car door and then closed it again. For a long time he sat hunched over the steering wheel, staring at the ancient stone wall.

Mistress for a month? What the hell was he doing? Hadn't he sworn to quit focusing on what he wanted without thinking of the consequences for others?

An affair with him was not in Amelia's best interests. With women like her, sex was a messy business. She might say no strings in the beginning, but she wouldn't even remember the bargain once her emotions started complicating matters.

But what if she was right, and he succeeded in making her believe she was a sexy femme fatale? Just the thought of her doing the things that she was doing with him now with her Hawaiian beach bum, made his gut clench.

Fisting his hand, he shoved his door open and angrily flung himself up the lane toward the château. Fifteen minutes of climbing had him standing beneath the famous lion carved above the lintel. Glancing up, he saw his mother and Céline in a high window. Céline's back was to him, but his mother's gaze, cold and fixed, was on him. She'd been watching him for some time.

On the phone she'd said she'd invited Céline down for a few days. The problem was she hadn't seen the need to inform him. Dreading straightening out the mess she'd created, he bolted up the wide stone stairs that angled twice before climbing even higher.

The last thing he wanted to do was offend Céline. But he'd committed to Amelia's bargain, so the next thirty days were hers.

He would have preferred to confront his mother first, but long before he reached the portal and the ornate doors with their bronze knocker, he heard high heels clicking much too rapidly on stone for the person who approached to be his sedate mother.

When he rounded a curve, Céline ran toward him. Her face alight, she looked gorgeous in a simple white dress and white sandals with laces around her slim ankles. Her golden hair, tied back by a white satin ribbon, bounced about her shoulders.

"Remy!"

Blue eyes locked on his face. How flushed and perfect she was in the lemony light. If only he wasn't involved with Amelia, he might have been happy to see her.

"I feel so terrible," she began, gushing concern. "I just realized that maybe your mother hadn't told you I was coming. You have other plans for the weekend, don't you?"

"I'm negotiating the purchase of Château Serene."

"I see."

"I'll call you in…say, a month or so."

"I've waited this long. I guess I can wait a little longer."

"You always were more patient than I."

"A month from now. I'll write it on my calendar," she said gaily, reminding him of Amelia circling the same date with her red pencil on her calendar.

"Since we're such old friends, I'll be blunter than I probably should be…Your mother has hinted that…she has certain fond hopes."

"She's always liked you, so I can well imagine her hopes. I was not opposed to them until…like I said, this…er… other business obligation developed."

"Château Serene? For exactly a month?" she murmured. Her eyes were filled with questions before he looked away.

Remy's interview with his mother the next morning in the grand salon was difficult, especially after he mentioned his need to go to Cannes to oversee the renovation of the family villa and his desire to invite Amelia to go with him.

Wearing black silk and diamonds, Alexis de Fournier looked like a countess from another era as she stood under the gigantic crystal-and-gold chandelier, studying her son with cold, calculating eyes.

"You can't possibly be serious about taking that conniving little witch of a niece to our home in Cannes."

"I will take her, if she'll accept my invitation," Remy stated bluntly.

"How can you be so stupid? Not to mention blind? She's Tate all over again. Simply everybody is in Cannes right now. People will see you with her."

"So?"

"She's trying to catch you in a weak moment."

"How well you seem to know her. Have you even met her?"

"All your sisters agree with me."

"Why do you always have to involve them?"

"They are brilliant women. And they want the best for you."

"Spare me their concern. I never interfere in their lives. Did you ask for my help with Château Serène or not?"

"Yes, but I didn't mean for you to—"

"Be happy, then. In this I am giving you your way. I promise you that in one month Miss Weatherbee will be gone, and you'll have your precious Château Serène all to yourself. When and *if* I feel like it, I will call Céline and invite her down for a long weekend, and we'll see how it goes. No promises, though. Until then, I belong to Miss Weatherbee."

"This is absurd. Why should you have to spend so much time with her? Is this just because she doesn't know anybody else?"

"I enjoy her."

"What could you possibly have in common with a...a shop girl? Why do you always have to be so difficult?"

"Maybe because I'm your son."

"You attack me just like your father used to."

"Which father—Montoya or the *comte?*"

A flush swept her neck and cheek, but she refused to be distracted. "Remy, I'm sure she has designs on you just like Tate had on your father."

"That's untrue."

"How do you know?"

"For one thing she read and believed the terrible tabloid

stories about me. For another she is nothing like Tate. She is naive, shy…"

His mother's eyes narrowed. "Shy? Naive? *Remy!* Listen to yourself. I haven't heard you talk about a woman like this…maybe ever. This woman arouses tender, protective feelings in you. I don't believe she could if she thought you were vicious and treated you accordingly. Quite the contrary. I am more convinced than ever she's after you."

"I won't hear any more."

"I want to know exactly what is going on between the two of you. Young, ambitious women can be very manipulative when they want a man. Very charming. Oh, Remy, I thought the worst thing you'd ever do was drive those horrible cars that reminded me of…"

"Montoya?"

Her face went the deep, dead purple of an overripe grape. "Do you have to say his name? I—I regret him. He ruined my life."

"And me? Do you regret me?"

"Of course not! You'll never know what I went through during each race you drove," she continued when she'd regained a small bit of her composure. "But this is worse. I will never speak to you again if you allow a serious attachment to develop between yourself and Tate's niece. *Never.* Do I make myself understood?"

"Perfectly. You can be stubborn. So can I. I refuse to discuss my relationship with Miss Weatherbee with you again. Do I make *myself* understood?"

When she didn't reply, he said, "I need to check the train schedules to make sure Céline's train to Paris is on time."

"What? She won't be staying? You two won't be—"

"You heard me." He turned on his heel.

"Remy!"

Without looking back, he kept walking down the great hall.

"Remy!"

Amelia was happily enjoying the glorious morning with its bright blue sky. She walked briskly along the road edged on both sides by perfumed clumps of lavender. Lebanese cedars cast long shadows over the road. The air smelled of cedar and pine and lavender and freshly mown grasses. She was thinking that even though she hadn't heard from Remy in nearly twenty-four hours, he'd promised to see her today. So when she saw his red sports car zooming toward her, her heart leaped with pure joy.

Remy! She ran out into the middle of the road waving wildly to flag him down.

He'd hit the brakes long before she saw the beautiful blonde beside him. The woman, with her creamy skin and glamorous silk beige jacket, was even more beautiful than Carol.

Immediately Amy felt like her ugly-duckling self. Why had she worn her oldest and baggiest pair of jeans with the holes in the knees and a faded shirt that wasn't even all that clean? Why hadn't she at least put on lipstick?

When he pulled alongside her, he said, "Hi there, neighbor," as if she were no more than a casual acquaintance.

Sucking in a sharp little breath, Amelia tried to appear casual and uninterested.

"I saw you waving. Did you have a breakdown? Do you need a ride somewhere?" he asked.

The blonde's icy blue eyes narrowed as they raked Amelia. Her shapely, glossy-pink mouth thinned before she looked away.

Judged and found lacking.

Amelia felt stricken. If she'd been in her ugly-duckling mode when the gorgeous pair had driven up, she was definitely in an acute stress molt now.

"Oh, I was just taking a walk before it got too hot," she said, feeling desperate to escape them.

"I want you to meet an old friend. I'm driving her to the station. Céline, this is Amelia Weatherbee."

Céline barely glanced at her. She was clearly anxious to be on her way with Remy.

He nodded to Amy. "Well, if I can't give you a lift, enjoy your walk."

"The day is so lovely, how could I do otherwise?" she muttered, her voice so soft it was almost inaudible.

"See you later, then." He tossed her a careless smile before hitting the gas.

Hugging herself tightly, she watched the Alfa Romeo until it was no more than a blurry red dot against the horizon. Then she bit her lips, squared her shoulders and cut directly across the vineyard toward the château. An hour later she was inside the house alone packing furiously when she heard the Alfa Romeo roar up her drive.

Remy killed the engine and knocked. When she didn't answer he banged more loudly and began shouting her name.

Squeezing her eyes shut and pressing her throbbing

temples, she held her breath. How could he think she'd want to see him this morning? When his banging grew even louder, she hugged herself and began rocking back and forth.

When the front door slammed open, she jumped. Calling her name, he stomped through the rooms looking for her.

"Go home, why don't you!" she yelled. "I'm busy!"

"So, *here* you are!" He grinned at her from the doorway. "I knew you'd be angry. That's why I came as soon as I could."

She yanked a pink ballerina figurine off the shelf and pretended she couldn't decide whether to pack it in the box for the antique dealer or the one for her mother.

"Well?" he said when she just stood with her hands frozen around the slim porcelain legs. "Whatever you do, don't throw it. Not at me, anyway!"

"As if I'd waste a valuable porcelain on the likes of you! You are so not worth it!"

He laughed. "Don't be mad."

"You think I'm jealous, don't you? Well, I'm not!"

"Did I say the j-word?"

She set the ballerina down on a low table for fear that she might throw it at him. "I'm not!"

"Of course you're not." His voice was mild. Was he teasing her? "I'm just the scoundrel you chose to be your sex teacher. You couldn't possibly have feelings for me."

"Right. And you certainly don't have to account to me for every second you spend with someone else! I don't care who you're with! Or where you go! And I won't ever!"

"Excellent. You are the perfect mistress for a man like me. We have a rational arrangement, and you made the rules."

He stepped forward and picked up the ballerina and turned it thoughtfully in his hands. "So as a rational person, aren't you even the slightest bit curious to know more about her?"

"No!"

"Well, just in case you're a little bit curious, she's an old friend."

"Define friend. No! I said I don't care, and I don't."

He smiled. "We dated years ago. Before I was the kind of man who stars in tabloid newspapers. She's a Parisian fashion designer and the widow of a German prince."

He couldn't possibly know that she'd once dreamed of designing clothes. And what was she doing, instead? Recycling used clothes.

"My mother and sisters adore her." He set the ballerina back down and knelt beside Amy. "They all agree she's perfect for me."

"I don't care who she is or what she is or what she is or was to you!"

"Right. Well, since you're not the least bit jealous or curious, I commend you. But the fact remains that she came to Provence to see me. But because of you, I sent her away. I made her and my mother unhappy. And now I'm sort of at loose ends."

"Not my problem."

"Who demanded to be my mistress for a month?" he queried in a goaded undertone. Standing up, he took her hands and pulled her up beside him. "I am in need of a woman. Are you up to the job or not?"

Before she knew what was happening, he'd wrapped his arms around her and was holding her close against the muscular length of his body. Much to her utter amazement, he was fully aroused.

When she placed her hands against his chest to push him away, she felt his violently thudding heart. Had the beautiful Céline turned him on?

"Let me go!" She twisted, using her hands to beat at his shoulders. "I have to pack. I won't be manhandled."

"As my mistress, you do have certain duties," he whispered, gripping her tightly. "Unless you want to resign?"

"No!"

"Good!" Before she could say more, his mouth closed over hers, his tongue hot and seeking.

Foolish person that she was, her heart began to pound and soon she was melting against him.

"Sometimes I hate myself," she murmured.

"For what?" His mouth was nibbling her lips as he tore off his shirt and ripped open his jeans.

"For being so easy. For liking this so much. For wanting you so much."

"For being sexy? Isn't that the whole point of our affair?"

"You talk too much," she said.

"So the hell do you."

She could not wriggle out of her clothes quickly enough.

"Do you want me? Or her?"

He encircled her wrists with his hands and drew her close. "Dammit, who the hell am I with?" he growled. "I told you, my mother invited her. As soon as I saw Céline, I explained that I had other plans and suggested that she take the first train back to Paris. She agreed."

His black head dipped toward hers, reclaiming her mouth.

Was he telling the truth? Amelia didn't know.

She only knew that when he laid her down on the oriental carpet and slid inside her, she'd never wanted anything more than him filling her, completing her, loving her. She was so touched by his return and his ardor and his concern that she might be hurt and jealous, tears leaked out of her eyes as he brushed his mouth down her throat, over her breasts.

Maybe he cared about her feelings, but he did not love her.

And he never would. His coming back meant nothing. They had a business arrangement. That was all.

Not that the true nature of their relationship was easy to remember as his kisses deepened and her senses swirled. And when he made love to her, he swept her away to a new dreamlike reality.

When they could breathe again, he carried her to the bed and began sucking her bottom lip as if he had all the time in the world to make love to her a second time.

"You're not mad at me any longer?" he whispered.

She drew back. "I never was. We will not arouse deep emotions in each other. You will teach, and I will learn."

"And we will both enjoy."

"If only temporarily."

When he caught her closer, her body urged him to take new liberties, even as her heart told her to be cautious.

She was only his mistress for a month. Céline, or someone like her, would win in the end.

"But I have him now," she whispered to herself after her third climax. "I have him now."

"What did you say, *chérie?*" he murmured, his hot breath tickling her ear.

"Nothing important. Nothing the least bit important."

"I believe you have the makings of a perfect mistress. You just get better and better."

Smiling, she lay back. Never had she felt more beautiful.

Nine

Cool, soft moonlight glimmered across the surface of the pool. The night smelled of pine and lavender and starlight.

Remy's manhood was still deeply embedded inside her as she lay beneath him, her naked bottom on the scratchy chaise longue. She sighed, feeling warm and sated from their lovemaking.

With a fingertip he slicked a tendril of her hair back from her hot face. "You work much too hard to be a satisfactory mistress. All those boxes…"

During the past week, she'd packed and organized Aunt Tate's clothes all day, and then every night he'd come and they'd made love, swum and had dinner. She hadn't thought of the beautiful Céline waiting in the wings too often, but when she had, she'd told herself she was just being realistic, that this month with Remy meant nothing beyond her original intention. She was learning to be sexy, and that was all.

"If I'm to leave in a month, I must get certain things done," Amy said, trying to keep her tone casual.

"You said you wanted to be my mistress. I have business in Cannes—a villa in need of some rather extensive repairs. I need to go inspect the job and talk to the engineer. Because of you I've delayed going too long. A real mistress would accompany me."

"Who will pack Aunt Tate's things?"

Caressing her hair with his hands, he kissed her throat, causing her pulse to beat madly.

"Cannes is much too crowded this time of year. Too many English. Too many tourists looking for bargains. Certain friends of mine have told me they'll be there, and that they want to see me. A dutiful mistress would accompany her lover." He lowered his voice. "I swear—the trip would be unbearable without your delightful company."

"That's sweet of you to say."

"What if it's the truth?"

His eyes devoured her features with a fierce hunger she wasn't ready to believe was anything more than sexual interest. After all, they were still hot and naked and wrapped in each other's arms.

"The view is lovely from the villa," he continued. "You need a break. Besides, I'm sick of my mother's silences and dark looks. I'm not used to spending so much time with her. She doesn't ask about you, but you're constantly on her mind."

The cool night wind shivered in the pines before dancing across her hot skin.

"I'm sorry."

"She doesn't like being thwarted. In Cannes, even though it's crowded, we might have some real privacy. Everybody here is her spy."

"Do you really want me all to yourself?"

"Why don't you come and find out?"

She nodded absently as she realized how lonely she'd be without him. Besides, she loved beach towns. But what if some former lover as beautiful as Céline were there to tempt him? Or Céline herself? Amy was startled by how much the thought chilled her.

This wasn't a real romance. It was unwise to feel so possessive, but she couldn't seem to stop herself.

"Good," he said. "Tomorrow, then! Ten o'clock in the morning."

He sounded so thrilled her heart began to pound.

"All right." She grinned, happy that he'd been so determined to take her with him.

He kissed the tip of her nose and slid halfway off her. "Why me?" he murmured so tenderly against her ear that a lump formed in her throat. "Why did you pick me?"

His intense gaze made her heart skip.

Feeling too raw and unsure about revealing her true feelings, she had no choice but to tease him. "Timing I suppose. You just popped into my life when I needed somebody with your skills. All those awful things about you in the newspapers definitely tipped the scales in your favor."

He cursed low in French before adding in a strained tone, "You chose me because you think I'm bad?"

She nodded.

"Well, since I'm training you, I advise that when you're with your next lover, you not be so brutally honest."

"Oh, I won't, I assure you."

She laughed. He didn't.

"Réellement, chérie."

"You aren't like my future lovers or the husband who will father all my soccer players. We both know you're a heartless womanizer—a man without a heart, who's so focused on what he wants, he can't be hurt."

"Right! You've read the papers, so you know me well." Tensing, he eased even farther away from her. Even though his face was in shadow, she could tell his jaw was clenched. Every muscle in his body felt coiled and hard.

"You are becoming like me, even in the short time we've known each other," he said in a controlled tone. "More than you know."

"I don't understand."

"If you weren't like me, you couldn't make love so enthusiastically with a man you can't really care about."

"We both agreed I would be stupid to let myself care about you. This month is about empowerment, not love. You can't possibly understand what it's been like for me. My sister is super-gorgeous. She was always the winner, while I... I just decided not to try—until I met you."

"You think this is a game? Okay, I won't argue. You have your opinion and I have mine."

"Then why are you suddenly so angry?"

"Dammit, who's angry?"

Abruptly he jumped off the chaise longue, strode to the pool and dived into the deep end. As he swam rapid laps, the moonlight glittered across the bunched, muscular curves of his tanned arms.

She sat up. Somewhere in the forest, a lone nightingale broke into song. Feeling chilled, Amy wrapped herself in a towel. The longer she watched him, the more awkward and rejected she felt.

Why was he so angry? Had she hurt him? Surely not.

Why did she care so much that she might have hurt him? Or that he thought she was as bad as *he* was?

He was wrong. She wasn't like him. No matter what, she would stick to her plan.

It was becoming more and more difficult for Amy to pretend that she could be with Remy and not come to care about him.

Constantly she reminded herself that he wanted only one thing from her, Château Serene, just as she wanted only one thing from him—sexual confidence. She'd made the rules for their relationship. Now all she had to do was live by them.

So knowing all this, she shouldn't be so excited about going to Cannes that she spent half the night packing for the trip. She'd choose an outfit, lay the pieces out on the bed and eye them critically before trying them on. Then she'd work endlessly with her shoes, jewelry and purses, only to discard her selections in a heap and run to the closet and yank more things out. Nothing seemed right. She grabbed some sleep and then resumed packing in the morning. She was still at it when she heard his Alfa Romeo in her drive.

When he saw all the fancy clothes strewn about her aunt's bedroom, he laughed.

"You're overthinking this. It's hot. The sun is bright and burning. Braid your hair. Wear sunglasses. Pack a bathing suit and sunscreen and shorts."

"But won't we go out at night?"

"Throw in a dress."

"You're a man. Which means you think you know everything even when you're clueless."

She ordered him to wait in the garden while she finished, and he did. Only, he drove her mad by yelling, "Are you ready yet?" about every ten minutes.

And she drove *him* mad by yelling back, "You're not helping."

Finally they were in his car jammed in between all the other cars and trucks clogging the highway that went south to the Riviera.

"Looks like everybody and his dog is going to Cannes," Remy said.

Despite the traffic the drive down was fun. They talked and laughed and sang along with the radio.

"I usually hate the drive," he said. "But with a proper mistress to amuse me, it's not half bad."

She didn't admit that she'd never had half so much fun in a car with anyone. Before she knew it, the gates of his magnificent, rustic, limestone, hilltop villa swung open, and a guard in a brown uniform waved them inside.

They drove past a swimming pool and sunbathing terraces. Then Remy braked in front of the villa, and a servant came running out to help them unpack. No sooner had their luggage been placed on racks in the grandest suite of the villa than Remy led her from room to room as eagerly as a boy, showing her dazzling, panoramic views of a city that reminded her a little of Waikiki.

Holding her hand, he named the glittering hotels and beaches. Then he pointed out the palm trees, crystal-blue water and distant islands. He was so attentive and the surroundings so beautiful she felt like pinching herself to make sure it was real.

But it wasn't real. They were playing a game. Why was it becoming so hard to remember that he didn't really care about her? And that she couldn't let herself be foolish enough to care, either?

"The villa is yours?" she asked, pulling her hand free of his.

"The family's. We share it."

"Have you brought other women here?" she asked, and then steeled herself for his answer.

"You mean other mistresses? *Real* mistresses?" His dark eyes flashed. "Jealous?"

"Sorry for the questions. None of my business."

"Would it be so terrible if we treated each other like real human beings?"

When she couldn't answer, he watched her for a long moment. "Right. You could never care about a man like me who's done all the terrible things I've done."

"Which is good," she said with false gaiety, "because my heart is safe with such a man."

She tried to move away toward a window, but he seized her hand and pulled her closer. "Is it?"

In vain she struggled to twist free of him.

"Is that all that matters to you—being safe?" He took her hand and lifted it to his lips. "Why did you ask me to make you your mistress if you didn't want a little danger?"

At his dark look or maybe because his kisses against her wrist made her heart leap, she began to tremble. When he stopped kissing her and watched her face as if hanging on her next words, she wondered what he was hoping for—that she'd prove herself to be a little idiot and beg him to love her?

She stiffened and said nothing.

"All right, I'll stop," he said.

A gloom fell over him and he was silent for a while. Not that he let his bad mood linger for long. As if determined to make her happy, he took her hand and showed her the rest of the house, and when they returned to the bedroom, he pulled her into his arms again.

"Those other women...you should forget them. I have. They don't matter to me anymore. In fact, that life matters less and less to me. *You* matter. More than I bargained for."

"I—I can't let myself believe that."

"Why the hell not?"

"You're a *comte*. Those other women, they were so beautiful. Céline is even more beautiful."

"*Chérie,* haven't I taught you anything? You are a darling, precious woman. Sexier than hell, too. You don't fake anything. You're just you. Your hair doesn't come out of a bottle. When you laugh or kiss or hold me, you mean it."

"My nails are fake."

"*You're* real." He pulled her closer and held her fiercely, his dark eyes blazing, his heart thudding, and soon her own heart beat with equal violence.

In spite of her jealousy of those beautiful women both in his past and in his future, she began to burn for him with a consuming need that was all too real.

She stroked his cheek, kissed him greedily, and then let her tongue slide between his lips. One taste of him had her breathless and aching for more.

He cupped her chin. Breathing as hard and fast as she was, he tightened his arms around her body.

More than anything she wanted to make him forget all the others, at least while she was with him. Her kisses and exploring fingertips became white-hot. She poured her soul into every caress, into every feather-light kiss. He was equally ferocious and needy. His kisses were so ardent and scorchingly intimate, he swept her away, and she wondered what he might need to prove.

They made love violently on the enormous bed and then tenderly in the gold-trimmed marble shower. Afterward she clung to him, breathing hard, while his hands and lips continued to caress her with such reverence and hunger she felt totally adored. Which made no sense. Still, she turned her wet head, snuggling closer against his hot, tanned shoulder, her pulse beating faster than it should have.

"You're a good teacher," she whispered, trying to lighten the mood.

"Is that all you think that was?" His voice and eyes were dark and hard. "Sex lessons well learned from an experienced teacher? Dammit!" He jerked free of her.

"Remy!"

He slammed out of the shower and snapped a towel off the rack.

Cold air rushed into the shower, chilling her.

Whipping the towel around his waist, he charged out of the bathroom.

"Remy!"

He didn't answer or return.

She laid her head against the cold, wet marble as steam seeped out of the shower.

She felt desperately unhappy, and she couldn't bear to think why.

Ten

Too furious to call his engineer or even to dress, Remy stormed to the bar. Floor-to-ceiling glass windows revealed an expansive view of Cannes. Dark clouds were sweeping across the Mediterranean. Not that Remy gave much thought to the view or the weather.

He grabbed a crystal glass and splashed scotch into it so recklessly the liquor sloshed all over his hands.

Hard liquor on an empty stomach. Before dinner. He was drinking like an American.

He bolted the shot, grimaced against its fire and his fierce need for more of the same. He picked the bottle up and then put it down. Shoving his glass away, he turned from the bar.

Damn her! He remembered rolling with her on the big bed, their legs and arms entwined, his mouth sucking and licking all her secret satiny places until she quivered and moaned. He shuddered as he recalled how good she'd felt when he'd thrust inside her that final time. No woman had ever felt half so good, so hot or moist, so tight or wildly responsive. God, she was sweet.

She's playing a silly game, and you're her toy, you fool. The trouble is you're not playing. Not anymore.

She'd made it very clear she was using him. He had to get a grip. He knew too well what it was like for life to take a dark turn, and for mistakes to become irreparable.

He wouldn't make another one.

He wasn't falling in love with her.

He wasn't that stupid.

This was about sex. That was all she wanted, so it couldn't be about anything else.

Amy was leaning toward the brilliantly lit mirror with an eyebrow pencil cocked above the curve of her eyebrow, when Remy knocked.

She started. "Come in."

The door opened. Instantly her hand began to shake so badly she had to put the pencil down. Only, her hand moved too jerkily, and the pencil spun onto the floor and rolled across the polished marble straight at him.

Leaning down, he picked it up. He stood up slowly, tension radiating from him as he slowly set it on the counter.

"You look nice," she said, noting his dark jacket and slacks.

When he said nothing she picked up the pencil and rushed to fill the awkward silence with words.

"Did you make your calls?" she asked.

"No. I had a stiff drink. Then I went for a short run. Nothing like the miracle of booze and endorphins to improve one's mood."

She smiled. His attempt to do the same was fleeting and tense.

"You were fast, too," she whispered. "Much faster than me."

"Take all the time you need. I still have to call my engineer and the architect. When you're ready, I'll take you out. Oh, and dress up. We'll eat somewhere fancy, and maybe later we'll dance. Or if you prefer to gamble, there are two casinos where we might run into friends, and I can show you off."

She would have preferred to stay in the villa with him, but perhaps being alone with him wasn't the best idea. She felt too vulnerable and needy, too much her real self. And despite his run, he seemed edgy.

After he left, she went into the bedroom and opened her suitcase, rummaging through it until she found the flirty red dress and silver shoes she'd worn in London. She spread them on the rumpled sheets where they'd recently made such sweet love.

When she was dressed, she walked through the house until she found him on the phone in the grand salon. His eyes lit up as they had the first time he'd seen her in the dress.

She twirled, and he nodded his approval. Then he turned away to finish his conversation.

She felt vaguely disappointed that he had not complimented her as passionately as she would have liked. Oh, what was wrong with her? Why did she feel so needy and anxious and confused when she'd had so much fun with him?

He hung up the phone. Taking her hand, he kissed it, before leading her out to the car. "I'm sorry I got angry earlier," he said when they were in the dark garage. "You've been very honest about what you want out of this relationship. I thought I was being honest, too. Apparently I didn't know what the hell I was doing."

She swallowed uneasily.

"Don't worry! No further discussion on that subject is necessary." His tone was so clipped and dismissive she felt rejected and hurt.

Later after they'd driven down a narrow, twisty road under darkening skies and through several miles of construction in tortured silence, Remy's mood seemed to improve a bit. By the time he'd parked the car, he was talking to her again. On the famous Promenade de la Croisette, he held her hand as they walked and occasionally kissed her cheek or brought her fingers to his lips as if they were an ordinary couple.

"La Croisette takes its name from a small cross that used to stand east of the bay," he said, pointing in that direction. As they walked, he pointed out other sites.

She began to relax and enjoy the promenade with its views of the Mediterranean, the Lerins Islands, and the Esterel Mountains on one side and the palms and *belle époque* hotels on the other. "If only the sun were shining, it would be perfect," she said.

"It's incredible during the film festival." He smiled. "Someday we'll come..."

Imagining it, she smiled, and then she remembered that would never happen. Still, she was glad they were past their quarrel.

A few minutes later they ran into a glamorous couple he knew. He introduced her. Not that either the man or the woman paid much attention to her. They were too busy taking turns insisting that they wanted to see more of Remy now that he'd come home for good.

The wind began to blow too briskly off the Mediterranean, so the man said a quick goodbye and would have gone, but his wife lingered. Pressing Remy's arm in a familiar fashion, she said, "Why don't we meet for drinks later?"

She didn't let go of Remy. She was beautiful in her fine linen dress and gold jewelry, and Amelia began to feel plain in comparison and wished he'd decline. Instead, he said he'd missed seeing her and suggested an hour for them to meet at Jimmy'z in the Palais de Festivals.

"And if you see any of our old crowd, invite them, as well. The more the better," he said. "I've been lonely for all of you, and I want our old crowd to meet Amelia."

Why? Did he want to be with them or just avoid being alone with her? When the dark cloud passed over them uneventfully and the sun came out, he took her shopping in several trendy boutiques. He bought Chanel for her at Bouteille's and Provençal olives for her at Cannolive. In both stores, the shop girls rushed to help him and stared at her as if fascinated.

"Did those girls know you?" she whispered when they were safely out of the second shop.

"Yes. They know my entire family."

"Why did you take me there, then?"

"A man buys expensive presents for his mistress, *n'est pas*? Maybe I'm playing your little game."

Too well, she thought, but just the same she would treasure his gifts when she was back in Oahu.

They came upon a flea market, and he laughed at her sudden enthusiasm and helped her bargain. Afterward, when she'd filled several shopping bags, he took her to the Palme d'Or on the first floor of the luxurious Hotel Martinez.

The haughty maître d' made such a fuss over Amy that he soon had her blushing. The man even lavished kisses on her hand, which seemed to please Remy immensely. Then he showed them to a wonderful corner table with a magnificent view of the promenade.

Every dish was served with a flourish. Amy ate slowly, savoring each bite. She was amazed by how many people Remy knew. Glittering couples waved at him or stopped by his table and demanded to be introduced to Amy.

Remy was charming to all, but seeing how popular he was with such a glamorous set made Amy feel his elevated place in the world. He was a *comte* and a Grand Prix champion, a celebrity in his own right. She sold old clothes and barely made enough to cover her mortgage payments.

When his friends left them alone, they sat quietly for a while, she feeling a bit strained because he felt at ease here in a dining room like this with dazzling people. Carol would fit in to this lifestyle, but Amy was much more at home in the garden of Château Serene with Etienne.

"It was a mistake to come here," he said.

Thinking he was disappointed with her, she poked at a roasted potato and rolled it around her plate.

"I'm beginning to see I don't belong with the people I've lived with all my life," he said at length. "It's as if I've lived on the surface with all of them. They know where I live, who my family is. They know I became a celebrity driving for Formula One. But they know nothing of me. You know me better than any of them."

"Me? How is that possible?"

"Think back to that day in the garden seventeen years

ago. Are you aware that no one besides me knows the truth about my birth but you and my mother? Not even my sisters."

Startled, she met his intense gaze. "I'm sorry I had to be there. I had no right to invade your privacy like that."

"It wasn't your fault. I hated you that day because I felt so humiliated. But I never should have gotten so angry with you. Now that I know you better, I'm glad you know. Maybe it's why you've become special. You know the worst. With you I have nothing to hide."

"But I felt terrible about that day for years."

His hand reached across the table and closed over hers. "I was horrible—hurt, furious, and I took it out on you." He pressed her fingers. "Our family has a great deal of false pride."

"Your family has a long history to be proud of."

"Along with dark secrets, which we keep, even from each other, so that we can remain proud and feel superior to people like you, who are more open and honest and, therefore, more fun to be with. You're so real."

"But your life and your friends are so much more exciting."

"Do you ever listen to a damn thing I say?"

"I can't imagine what your life must be like."

"I was trying to show you a little of my world this weekend. Maybe I wanted to impress you, I don't know. Maybe I wanted you to know me, the real me or the person I thought was the real me. Maybe I just wanted to show you off. I don't know why, but suddenly I'm as confused as hell."

"Show me off? That's ridiculous. I'm nobody."

"You're somebody to me."

"I run a used-clothing shop! I still live with my mother—in my own room—because housing is so expensive on Oahu, I can't afford anything better!"

"Listen to me! How is that so different from how my family lives? We've had certain properties in the family for hundreds of years. And we all stay in them as need be."

"Trust me on this," she said. "It's different. Your villa is like something out of a fairy tale. *We* park our cars on the grass in our front yard."

"Don't run yourself down to me. I'd rather be with you than any of them." He paused. "But back to that awful day we first met."

She swallowed. "I wish you'd let that go."

"When you found out who my real father was and that the *comte* hated me, I wasn't ready to face the truth and even less eager to share it. I'd worked all my life to get him to love me. You saw my pain. You understood, but when I stared into your compassionate eyes, I didn't want to accept those truths. Your sympathy forced me to face the reality, and I got angrier because all I wanted to do was run away and hide. You were very understanding. Now, you're even more so. And me, I was a jerk then and an even bigger jerk to deceive you in London. I took you to bed when you were feeling vulnerable because of your aunt's death and the breakup with your boyfriend. You were alone in a big city. And what did I do? I all but stalked you! Again, you were quick to forgive."

"Please. You're much too hard on yourself."

"Maybe. Or maybe I've been so damn anxious to prove I was more than Sando's unwanted bastard that I couldn't tolerate mistakes, especially my own. I raced, solely to prove I was something. I killed a man, a lifelong friend, and to prove what? What does any of it matter?"

"Everything matters. Or nothing matters. Take your pick. Just quit torturing yourself."

"You're so honest about who you are. Maybe it's time I started being equally honest. So what if I was born a bastard and ended up a *comte*? I loved and admired André. I didn't mean to kill him."

"It was raining. The steering jammed."

"Yes. But back then I was arrogant enough to think I could control everything—life and death. Maybe I still would be if you hadn't come to Château Serene and made your crazy bargain with me. You're making me see things in a whole new way. I've relaxed. This time with you has been special. Even here in Cannes, I've been happier than I've ever been." He lifted her hand and turned it in his. "Why is that, do you think?"

"I can't imagine. I'm sure you've been here with much more famous people and more glamorous people."

"Yes, and I was taught those were the only people who counted. I was taught to be closed-off and materialistic, to keep secrets. You have made me rethink the values of a lifetime. When I was a boy I wanted my father, or the man I believed to be my father, to notice me."

"As any little boy would."

"But he never did. When I learned Sandro Montoya was my real father I read everything I could about him. I went to all the houses where he'd lived, to the wall in Monaco where he smashed himself to pieces, searching for what? I felt nothing. It was just a wall. I went into Formula One to impress both my fathers, neither of whom had given a damn about me. During that time, I made no real friends. I was so blindly focused on winning, on proving myself to a ghost and a man who wasn't my father that I failed to connect with the people who might have cared about me."

"Stop blaming yourself."

"Famous people are just people. Being with you has taught me that what's in a person's heart matters much more than fame or status." His dark gaze was intense.

"You may think that now, but if we were serious about each other, you'd see I'm too different to fit into your world."

"Maybe it's not my world anymore. Maybe I want to be me, go to work, come home on the weekends and play soccer with my kids. All I know is that I've never enjoyed being with anyone as much as you."

"Don't," she whispered. "Don't make this more complicated than it already is. For both our sakes, you have to stay that heartless rogue I read about in the newspapers."

"Is that really who you want—the killer-womanizer in the newspapers?"

"In a week I'll be home without even a glass slipper to remember you by."

"I was beginning to hope...that you and I...that maybe you could stay a while longer. People buy old clothes even in Paris."

Terrified, she sat up stiff and straight. "Don't! Please!"

"I want to know you and for you to know me. And you want what—a few sex lessons and then to be rid of me? Is that all you want?"

She looked away. Long seconds passed. Finally, he released her hand and signaled for the bill.

She expected him to drive her home. Instead, he took her gambling at the glittering Casino Croisette where he played high-stakes games and lost enough money to make her feel tense and guilty because she was the reason for his reck-lessness. Then his luck turned, and he won most of it back.

"Do you always gamble so wildly?" she asked.

"Isn't that what your newspaper lover would do?"

Stung by his hard tone and words, she looked away.

He took her for drinks at Jane's Club, where they danced mechanically or sat at their little table in silence.

"I want to go home," she said.

"We're meeting people."

It was late by the time they walked into Jimmy'z. A large group of his friends sat at a large table near one of the dance floors. Céline was with them. A few minutes later, Willy Hunt, a Grand Prix driver, came over to say hi to Remy and asked if he could join them.

The music was loud and lively, and so was the conversa-tion, which was in rapid French. It was difficult for Amy to catch much of what was said. For a while Remy was com-pletely absorbed with his friends. But finally he turned to her, and seeing that she was watching the dancers more than she was talking, Remy pressed her fingers and asked her to dance.

Even though they were on the dance floor away from Céline, Amy couldn't relax. He moved stiffly as if he were equally tense.

"I'm sorry," she said. "Earlier you were trying to be honest, and I was the way you were that day when your father disowned you—trying to hide from my true feelings because they scare me so much. I—I know you're not the man I read about. I knew who you really were even that first night in London—because I'd read a tabloid. I think I went out with you because unconsciously I knew the papers had it all wrong. André's death hurt you just like the *comte* hurt you. I responded to that hurt, furious boy.

Only, you aren't a boy. You're a man. A very sexy man.
And I'm afraid of feeling anything real for you."

"Why?"

"I think you know."

"Tell me."

"You've lived such an exciting life. You'll soon tire of
someone as dull as me, so I tried to make a game of it. Sex
lessons. I thought I could be like an actress playing a part.
I promised you I wouldn't let myself care."

"To hell with our stupid promises!"

"Remy, I swear, the last thing I wanted to do was fall
in love with you!"

"Oh, Amy, Amy. You're the best thing that has ever
happened to me." He bent his head and kissed her with a
wild hunger, and as she kissed him back, her heart seemed
to explode with all the turbulent emotions she felt—
passion, fear, desire and all sorts of insecurities. She felt
more than saw the crowd at their table watching.

"Let's get the hell out of here," Remy said hoarsely. "I
have to be alone with you."

"That's all I've wanted all night."

Cameras held high, two men who'd just entered the
club raced toward them.

"It's him!" they yelled. *"Remy de Fournier!"*

When she turned, flashes burst in her face.

"Leave her alone, you bastards!" Furious, Remy lunged
through the tables toward the two cameramen, but before
he could reach them, several waiters seized the pair and
hustled them back to the entrance.

"Chérie, we've got to get the hell out of here! The last
thing I want is your name dragged into the mud because
of me!"

Taking hold of her hand, he led her toward the front door, but when they stepped outside, rain was coming down in sheets. The engines of the dozen or so motorcycles that were lined up beside the building began revving. Paparazzi. Several men jumped off their bikes and swarmed Remy, shouting his name and hurling obscenities at Amy in the hope he'd look their way or try to punch them and they could then snap a valuable picture.

"Ignore them," Remy muttered, pulling her close and shielding her from the rain and cameras.

When the Alfa Romeo was being brought over, Remy's dark eyes blazed, maybe with the memory of that wet afternoon at the Circuit de Nevers at Magny-Cours. Almost defiantly, he grabbed the car keys from the bellhop.

When she and Remy were in the car, he expertly maneuvered onto the wet street. His windshield wipers slashing violently, he called the villa and warned the guard at the gate that they might be followed.

Snapping his phone shut, he concentrated on the heavy traffic and the motorcycles buzzing on all sides of them. From time to time a bike got too close and sloshed water all over their windows.

Despite his pale, tense face, she liked watching him drive. He exuded power and willful determination. His car was nimble, even on the slick, dark road, and he maneuvered it skillfully, changing lanes constantly to get ahead of his pursuers. Before long they were climbing toward the villa. When they reached a part of the road that was under construction, the rain started to come down even harder than before. Then the road narrowed to a single, bumpy lane walled in by concrete. Despite the narrow lane and the sheets of falling water, the motorcycles maintained their aggressive speeds. Several were ahead, two behind, and two on either side of them.

"Suicidal nuts," Remy said in clipped tones, easing off the gas pedal when brake lights flashed up ahead.

Suddenly one of the motorcyclists on the right gunned his engine and skidded just as the lane narrowed even more. To avoid being hit, Remy swerved to the left, which sent the Spider into a controlled skid straight at the concrete barricade and one of the other motorcycles.

"Damn!" Remy jerked the wheel to the right. Then slamming on the brakes because the bike on his right was too close, he veered back to the left. The Spider hit deep water and skidded wildly, whirling on two wheels before it rammed into the barricade on Remy's side. Amelia screamed as she flew forward. Then her seat belt grabbed, and everything went black.

When she regained consciousness, the windshield wipers were still on and the wind-driven rain was beating down even harder than before. She heard water hissing as if from a broken hose, and the stench of hot oil burned her nostrils.

Icy fingers pressed against her throat.

"Amelia?"

In cold horror she realized Remy was searching for her pulse. At the same time members of the paparazzi were shouting his name and jockeying to get better pictures of the famous crash victims.

A flash went off, and she blinked.

"Damn." Remy's face was inches from hers. His mouth was thin and set. Every time another flash went off, terror flicked across his white, strained face.

"Amelia!" His voice was barely more than a thread now.

"What happened?" she whispered shakily. "Did we have an accident?"

"We should be in a modern car with airbags, not this antique. Are you okay?"

"I'm fine," she said even though she'd never felt more helpless or inadequate.

"The damn fool on my right swerved straight into us. I had to cut to the left."

Funny how he remembered every detail, and she couldn't remember a thing. Still she murmured, "It wasn't your fault."

Her legs hurt. The front part of his car seemed to be crumpled in on top of them.

"Can you get me out?"

He leaned out of the car and yelled to the paparazzi to help him. When they just stood there, staring and yelling at each other, he pleaded with them, saying gasoline was everywhere and that they had to get her out just in case. Only then did they look ashamed and spring forward to assist him.

Just as Remy and two of the men lifted her from the car, she heard the first of the sirens.

The police had arrived. Remy knelt on the wet tarmac cradling her against his sodden body and shielding her blood-streaked face with his hands from the rain and the paparazzi who'd begun shooting again. Someone brought a tarp and covered them with it, but the flashes never stopped.

"Don't those damn bastards ever get enough pictures?" he muttered.

As it turned out they had way more than enough to destroy him.

Eleven

Gone was the lover who'd kissed her so passionately on the dance floor. Remy's face was as white as a death mask behind the wheel of the nondescript car he'd rented for their return to the vineyard the day following the accident. He'd barely spoken since the police chief had released him. He was free to leave Cannes, but would have to return immediately for more interviews. The police planned a thorough investigation into the accident.

"Surely they don't think you were to blame," she'd said.

Remy had cut her short. "He's just doing his job."

Despite a fierce headache and crowded, bumpy roads, Amy had devoured the morning's horrible headlines and stories about the accident. Maybe it wasn't surprising that the pounding in her head was worse than ever.

Former Grand Prix Driver Nearly Kills Mistress on Rain-Slick Road!

Police Investigation Pending!

There were pictures of Remy kissing her at Jimmy'z, and the grainy picture of Amelia that had been taken in London now had her name. Lengthy articles speculated about the exact nature of their relationship that first night in London. A waiter at the Savoy claimed they hadn't been able to keep their hands off each other. Every time Amelia reread the man's awful words, she cringed.

Worst of all the journalists compared the recent accident to the one a year ago and wondered if Remy, who'd behaved high-handedly and negligently last year, should even be allowed to have a driver's license. "Witnesses told investigators that the Alfa Romeo had been weaving in and out of traffic on the seaside promenade of Cannes earlier," she read.

Amy looked up from the newspaper to the lavender fields flying by. Was he driving too fast now? Or was she just so jittery from the accident and the terrible stories that it seemed so?

"Scared?" he muttered, easing up on the gas pedal. "Of me?"

"No. Of course not. You know the roads. You're an expert driver."

"Am I? Or am I a crazed, arrogant devil with no regard for anyone's life but my own?"

"You're just anxious to get home. And so am I."

"To be rid of me?"

"I didn't say that."

"I wouldn't blame you. I come with too much baggage—enough to sink an ocean liner."

The doctor Remy had summoned to the villa last night had ordered her to rest, but her headache and nerves had prevented her from doing more than shut her eyes.

She was shaking now, maybe partly because Remy was so upset. How she dreaded Remy's reading all the accusatory stories and seeing the awful pictures. The shots of them kissing at Jimmy'z were particularly invasive, and she hated the especially unflattering picture of Remy being held by two men as he shook his fist at a photographer last night when the man had refused to help get her out of the car.

Not that the articles about André's death weren't equally terrible. They included recent quotes from Maurice Lafitte saying Remy had always been jealous of André and had been gunning for him deliberately that day. Maurice even went so far as to accuse Remy and his mistress of trying to run him over in the village.

There were stories about Aunt Tate and the *comte* and the Matisse he'd given her. Anonymous village sources recounted in lurid detail Aunt Tate's love affair and marriage with the late *comte*. They said that the young *comte*'s affair with Tate's niece didn't surprise them, that the niece was an American gold-digger just like her aunt, that the niece was refusing to sell the world-famous Matisse back to the French family to whom it had rightfully belonged for a century, that she planned to leave the country with it.

Without looking at Remy again, Amy folded the last newspaper and laid it in her lap on top of the others.

Remy came to a crossroads, touched a blinker and then turned onto a back road, which was fringed on both sides with lavender. She knew from her walks that the rural lane cut a swath through the vineyards that led straight to Château Serene.

"If you don't go back to Hawaii quickly, there'll be even

worse stories," he said. "Now that they've tasted fresh blood, yours, they won't let up. In all probability they'll be waiting to pounce on you at Château Serene."

"Surely not."

"Whatever you do, don't grant an interview. They'll twist your words to prove their viewpoint."

When they rounded the last curve, she gasped when she saw a television truck, three motorcycles and two men with binoculars and cameras standing at the ready by the gate.

"Oh, no," she murmured as the men rushed toward their car, cameras held high.

"So now you know what it is like to be Remy de Fournier's mistress. You will be hounded like this until you leave France. Not a fate I would wish on anyone. If we continue to see each other, they will want pictures of our every assignation. We may even find a photographer under your aunt's bed."

"That's disgusting."

"You heard the police chief. I have to be back in Cannes tomorrow."

"I'll go with you if that would help."

"No! You should cut your losses."

"But—"

"Don't you understand we've lost our chance?"

"Is there no standing up to them? Are you going to let them ruin your life forever?"

"Look, I learned a long time ago that I'm not in control of what is written about me. I'm trying to protect you. You have to go home as soon as possible."

"But I love you!"

"If you decide to sign the sales contract early, I'll do

everything in my power to expedite the purchase so you can leave without any extra hassles. But I must warn you—buying and selling real estate is not as simple in France as it is in the U.S. We have many bureaucrats in need of salaries. There will be many documents and much red tape. And finding a home for the Matisse won't be easy, but I do know a reputable art dealer who could help you."

"Bottom line—you want me gone."

"It's for the best."

"So, it's over."

He didn't deny it.

Her chest felt strange and tight. Her eyes burned, but she could think of nothing to say. He wanted her gone. It didn't matter that she'd told him she loved him.

Fifty yards later, he turned into the drive that led up to the château.

Without a word, he braked, got out and carried her bags to the door. She let herself out of the car more slowly and walked gingerly toward the house. When she reached him, he didn't smile. He didn't touch her or kiss her or even offer to carry her bags inside as he would have in the past. All seemed so frozen and changed between them. It was as if the past few hours had killed every tender feeling he'd ever had for her.

"Do you want to come in?" she asked.

He shook his head. "Don't you get it? Photographers with high-powered lenses could be hiding anywhere to take our pictures," he muttered.

"No more making love out by your pool, either." He opened the door and slid her bags inside. "No telling what technologies these guys have. They're like spies. They can probably take pictures in the dark."

"Is this goodbye, then?" she whispered.

"Like I said—tomorrow I have to talk to the police chief. I don't know what will be involved or how long I'll be gone. Or if I can satisfy him."

"You should let me come."

"If we don't see each other, the reporters will leave in a few days, and you'll have your privacy back."

"What about you?"

"You forget, I'm an old hand at being lynched by the press. I'll survive." He stared unseeingly in front of him.

Would he? Was he already a haunted man on the run from his demons again?

"Be sure to call me. At least tell me how the investigation goes."

He shook his head. "I don't think that's smart. There are lots of techies out there who know how to listen in on cell-phone conversations."

"Then this is really goodbye?"

"It's for your own good," he muttered. "I knew better than to let you become involved with me."

She bit her lip and looked anywhere but at him. Then her head began to pound even more viciously.

"Remy, please…please don't be like this."

"Goodbye," he said in a soft, tender voice. "I won't ever forget you. And I will call…in a few weeks, when you're safely home and the bastards are chasing new prey. Hopefully I'll be able to tell you that all this has blown over."

"But on the dance floor at Jimmy'z, we said… I—I thought that you and I—"

"Dammit, I drove you into that wall! I was driving an old car! The seat belt didn't work. I nearly killed you! Now these jackals are writing awful stories about you! Who the hell knows what the police will accuse me of next? What does it take to show you it has to be over?"

When her telephone began to ring, he began backing away. "You'd better answer that. It's probably your mother or one of your friends wanting to grill you, chastise you for having anything to do with a man like me."

"Remy, no! Don't leave me like this!"

"I have to do what's right, for a change. We always knew this had to end. I'm sorry I let things go so far."

She stared at his face and felt nothing. He was leaving her forever, and she felt nothing. How was that possible? Shock?

He took a deep breath and stared at her for a long moment. Then he turned and walked back down the drive to his car. He got in, slammed the door and drove away, as always without looking back.

The phone had stopped ringing by the time she went inside, but within five minutes it began again.

Thinking it was her mother and she might as well get the interrogation over with, she picked it up.

"Baby! It's Fletcher! Hey, you sound like you're just next door."

Fletcher, who never called, wanted to know how she was and what she was up to. Last of all, he said he was sorry about the girls and for how he'd acted, that he'd been awful, and that he wanted her back.

"I got a real job—selling insurance—to prove to you that I'm ready to grow up, baby."

"Don't do anything rash on my account, Fletcher."

"Is this cold attitude because of that count? There's no way a rich guy like him would be interested in you for anything except that painting or the vineyard."

"You don't know anything about him."

"You're too—"

Much to his surprise, she hung up on him.

Her headache, if possible, was worse, and her eyes burned. Feeling lost, she walked through the house, her footsteps echoing hollowly. She stared at the stacks of boxes and at her aunt's things that still needed to be packed. She felt overwhelmed as she wondered how many more hours it would take before she had everything packed.

The job seemed endless, and someday she would have to figure out what to do about the Matisse, too.

Instead of unpacking her suitcases or lying down, she fixed herself a cup of tea, went outside and stared at the blue chaise longues by the pool until a slight movement from the trees warned her that someone was probably spying on her and taking pictures.

Running back inside, she slammed and locked the door. Then she shut all the windows and drew the curtains.

Alone in the house, the long, lonely day stretched ahead of her. Would her head ever stop pounding?

She was almost grateful that she had no mind, no heart, no senses. Still, she knew that when they came back she'd be in hell.

What would she do without Remy?

Why was it so wrong to love him?

On the second day after Remy had dropped her off, when she'd heard nothing from him, she was beside herself with grief and worry. She wished Remy would call and tell her how the investigation was going. Was he in even more trouble? She grew frantic from missing him.

Thus far, her only source was the media. All the newspapers ran editorials demanding that the police take a firm stand with him. The talking heads on television wanted the same thing. To buy newspapers, she had to drive into the village or send Etienne, and this meant dealing with the reporters camped at her gates. They followed her, yelling at her and demanding interviews.

Why couldn't she forget how much she'd enjoyed Remy in bed and out of it? Constantly she told herself Remy was right not to want to see her. What future could they possibly have? She might as well suffer the pains of withdrawal now.

To stay busy she'd contacted his estate agent and told him she was ready to sell the vineyard. He brought the documents over, and they discussed them. In between packing more boxes, she even signed a few.

She was tired by the time the sun began to go down, lingering forever on the horizon. Never had a day seemed longer or more unbearable. She was thinking maybe a shower would make her feel better when the phone rang.

Remy? She dived for it, answering in eager, breathless French.

"Et ma fille, Mademoiselle Amelia Weatherbee, *avec château?"* said an all-too-familiar voice with a terrible American accent.

"Mother, this is me!" Wisely Amy refrained from correcting her mother's French.

"Why haven't you called?"

"I was going to!"

"Are you his mistress or aren't you?"

"Puh-leeze! That's such an out-of-date term, Mom!" Not that she hadn't used it herself, but that was different.

"From what the papers say and from what Tate used to tell me, your race-car driver is a fast sort and much worse than Fletcher. Enough said. And by the way, Fletcher's actually called. You may be hearing from him."

"I can't believe you discussed this with Fletcher."

"I didn't have to discuss anything. One of his more literate friends saw the stories on the Internet."

"Well, he called. He wants me back."

"You broke up with him?"

"Before I came here."

"Well, I hope you said hell no."

"My decision. Not yours."

"Which gives me chills! So how can you fall for a man even worse than Fletcher?"

"I'm a grown woman, Mother, so stop with all the questions and assumptions!"

"Then act like one. The de Fourniers despised your aunt Tate, and she never got her name dragged through the mud. I can't imagine what they must think of you. Carol certainly never embarrassed me or herself like this."

Amy took a deep breath and counted to ten—twice.

"When are you coming home?"

"Soon. I do have a few papers to sign and a little more packing."

"Carol is most concerned. She'd really like you to stop by in London. If you don't, who knows when you girls will see each other again? Besides, you could use some sound advice from a rational individual like your brilliant sister. At least she's made something of her life. She's a barrister, and she's married to—"

"Must you always throw Carol at me?"

"Just trying to be helpful, dear."

"Well, then, if that's the truth, it would be really, really helpful if you could watch the shop a bit longer."

"Of course, dear. I've been having the time of my life running your shop. Not that I don't have a legal pad full of helpful suggestions for you. The way you order…"

"Okay. Okay. Then if you'll really watch the shop, I would love to stop in London, although I'm not really in the mood for advice from my brilliant sister."

"You never are, dear."

Amy hung up, furious, but at least her anger toward her mother distracted her from worrying so much about Remy.

"I can't believe it! 'Probably something I ate, or jet lag,' you said. My, what a cool liar you were! And I bought it! Me! Brilliant, little ol' me, big-shot lady barrister who can see through liars like they're made of glass. And now you say you have a headache. Ha!"

"Did Mother put you up to this?"

"As if I needed to be told to call my *notorious* sister when all my friends are just dying to know what's going on." Carol giggled. "They're all simply wild to meet you, too. If you come, Steve and I'll throw a big party to show you off. You're a celebrity!"

"No party! And I don't need this! Not right now!"

"None of us blame you one bit. Your *comte* sounds positively dishy. Rich, too! And a celebrity! If he's half as good in bed as he looks, I may fight you for him!"

"Carol!"

"Just kidding. But I do want details."

"Carol, I'm sorry I lied to you, but I really *do* have a headache tonight."

"Right."

"For your information I've had one ever since the accident. So I'm going to hang up, stare at the ceiling and sulk if you don't stop with the teasing. This is not a funny situation."

"Oh, my God, you're not in love with him, are you? Amy? You're *not*, are you? Because he's a *comte*…and he's had all those women! He couldn't possibly care about—"

"Carol, please, I'm begging you—back down."

"Okay, okay. I'll save it until you get here. But I want to hear all about him then. If you've been sleeping with him, you've got to tell me *everything* because, and I hate to say this, a good marriage can become so dull, so routine after a few years. Not that the sex isn't kinda nice."

A phone call from her mother and another one from her sister in one night! Amy was shaking when Carol finally hung up.

She walked into the kitchen and poured herself a tall glass of chablis. As she sipped it, the wine both soothed and made her more vulnerable to her feelings.

She missed Remy. For weeks she'd seen him every day. What if he was in serious trouble with the police? What if there was something she could say to them that would help him? She had to talk to him.

Since he'd warned her against using cell phones, she called the Château de Fournier instead. But as the phone rang, Amy felt panic rising within her. When a woman answered, she almost slammed the phone down.

"Is…is Remy there?"

"Just a moment please."

She bit her lip. Then another woman came on the line. "This is Céline."

"I—I want Remy."

"I'm sorry. He went to Cannes yesterday."

"I know. This is Amy Weatherbee. Do you have any idea how the investigation is going?"

"I know who you are, Mademoiselle Weatherbee. We thought he'd be back today. But he hasn't even called."

"Well, if you hear from him, would you tell him to call me, please?"

"Of course, mademoiselle. Excuse me…"

When Amy heard muffled voices, she had the feeling that Céline had covered the phone to speak to someone else.

Céline returned almost at once. "I'm sorry about the interruption. The *comtesse* would like to speak to you."

The *comtesse*'s voice was cold. "Madamemoiselle Weatherbee, I'm delighted about the sale. Does this mean you will be leaving soon?"

"As soon as possible."

"I don't wonder, all these awful reporters snooping about. Céline can't even wander down to the village without having one of the beasts pop out and take her picture."

"I'm sorry about all that," Amy said even as she wondered what Céline was doing in the village if Remy wasn't coming back.

"I did warn Remy. He should have protected you," his mother said.

Amy saw no reason to tell her he'd tried. "If he calls, would you please tell him I'd like to see him before I go."

"I don't think that will be possible. His secretary and a good friend of his are getting married in Paris. He's going to be best man. It's rather sudden. As soon as Remy's finished in Cannes, he has a direct flight to Paris."

"So, he...he has no plans to return to Château de Fournier?"

"Not as far as I know." The *comtesse*'s quiet voice held icy triumph.

Amy's eyes felt hot as she hung up, but she didn't cry.

Like Cinderella after the ball, her world was reduced to cinders.

It was over. In a few days she'd be home.

Twelve

The cicadas were roaring as Amy sat dully beside the pool and sipped black, double-strength coffee that was so hot it burned her tongue. Between sips, she bit into her buttery breakfast croissant. Make that her second croissant, both of which had been slathered thickly with orange marmalade.

She was full, but still eating. She shouldn't take another bite, but she'd been on something of an eating binge since she'd talked to the *comtesse* two days ago. Not that she wanted to think about how tight her jeans were. She simply wanted to eat and forget.

Funny how everything about Château Serene made her miss Remy. The sweet scent of lavender made her remember making love to him out here under the stars. The glimmering water made her think of the times they'd skinny-dipped. Under those pine trees, he'd held her and they'd made their bargain.

Such thoughts were an indulgence. She had to quit torturing herself. With a supreme effort of will, she looked past the pool to the lavender that rolled toward the distant mountains. The château and vineyard were a picture postcard come to life. Her heart ached at the thought of leaving it all forever.

She loved him. She knew that no matter how long she lived or who else she loved or what children she might have, she would never forget this poignantly lovely place, and it would always remind her of him.

How strange. Remy had taught her to be sexy, but it didn't matter because she wanted no one but him. He hadn't just imparted skills. He'd given himself. He was the magic that made her come alive in bed.

Suddenly, above the humming of the cicadas, she heard a car sweep up the drive. Her stomach tightened in both anticipation and dread.

Even though she knew Remy was supposed to be in Paris, she got up and ran around to the front of the château, anyway. And oh, how painfully her stomach knotted at the sight of the tall, slim blonde in pristine, white slacks, her hair an elegant coil at the nape of her slender neck.

Céline, too lovely for words as usual, was knocking on the front door. Amelia felt like running away and hiding. Instead, she called, "Hi, there."

Tension flowing out of every invisible pore of her creamy face, Céline jerked around. Her eyes were as huge and desolate as Amy's heart. "Oh, there you are," she said without the least bit of enthusiasm.

Why wasn't Céline in Paris? Amy wondered. She said, "I—I was just having breakfast in the garden."

"I thought maybe you'd already left for America. I promise I won't keep you long."

"Would you like some coffee?"

Céline shook her head and then changed her mind when she saw Amy's cup. After Amy prepared the coffee to Céline's liking and they'd talked about all the boxes in every room and the dates the movers would come for them and which was the best moving company in the area, Amelia led her out to the garden.

"I could tell you were probably expecting Remy when you heard the car," Céline said softly. "You looked unhappy to see me."

"But he's in Paris."

"Yes. I do dislike disappointing you, but I *had* to see you." As if at a loss for words, she stared at Amy. "I—I have only one question." A desperate look chased across her pretty face. "Do you love him?"

Amy jerked her chin higher.

Céline's blue eyes were luminous, and she was twisting her hands. "I *have* to know because…because you see, I love him. I love him very much. I've loved him all my life."

Each word felt like a blade cutting Amy's heart. How stylish and beautiful Céline was with her flawless skin and doll-like features. She was much lovelier than Carol. Remy and she would make a beautiful couple. What darling children they would have—dark-headed boys and blond girls. Little weekend soccer players. Amy winced.

"If you don't love him, Mademoiselle Weatherbee, let him go. Because like I said, I do love him. So very much."

"Shouldn't you be telling these things to him? After all, I'm going home—alone. If he's in Paris and you live there, why are you here?"

"I don't believe he's ready to love anyone right now. He isn't over what happened last year. But in time, he will be."

"And you'll be there?"

"If he wants me to be."

"And does he?"

"We dated when we were young. But something happened to him. I never knew what, and he grew so remote. A year or so later, he went into Formula One. He drove himself with a vengeance, and I never knew why. None of us did. He was so different, so competitive and so ruthlessly ambitious on and off the track. He was not the same sweet, gentle boy I'd loved. But even during those years I would see him from time to time because his sisters were such dear friends of mine."

"His sisters?"

"They encouraged me not to give up on him. Racing careers are often brutal and short. We thought that if he survived, he might become his old self again and we would marry. So, I waited. But he won more and more races. He grew famous. Women threw themselves at him, and I saw him so little that I gave up and married another man. And I was happy. But not like I'd been happy with Remy. Still, my husband, Ivan, was good to me, and I was content. Then Ivan's plane crashed in the Alps the same month Remy had his awful accident."

"I'm so sorry."

"Yes. It was terrible. I was numb for months. But something terrible like that teaches you, too. I can understand what Remy is going through. I knew André when he was a boy, you see. I understand suffering and what it is to be damaged, to blame yourself. I had encouraged my husband to fly that day. I believe that I can love Remy and understand him and help him get over André as no one else can. His family adores me. Especially his mother. Family approval is so important when it comes to marriage, don't you agree? And you would never have that, would you?"

Amy was cold and shivering in the heat long before Céline finished. Whatever hope she'd had of Remy changing his mind in a few months and coming to find her vanished like smoke blown away by the wind. Céline would not let that happen.

Amy must have said goodbye as she walked Céline around to her car, but later she had no memory of even leaving the garden.

As she stared at the lavender and pines, she knew that everything Céline had said made perfect sense. Céline would make Remy a perfect wife. Once Amy was gone, he would forget their brief time and turn to Céline.

The only role Amy would ever play was the one she had chosen—to be his mistress for a month.

Their month was over.

Thirteen

Standing beside Pierre-Louis at the city hall in the Fourth Arrondisement, Remy ground the wedding rings into his palm even as he forced himself to relax.

He was here. He'd actually made it on time to the wedding. He'd been exonerated—again. More than exonerated. The chief had blamed the paparazzi.

The Cannes police chief had grilled him relentlessly for hours before finally releasing him a mere forty-five minutes before his plane for Paris had been due to depart.

Much relieved, Remy knew the police chief's decision would anger the bloodthirsty media. No doubt, every journalist in France would be howling for his head.

He wanted to call Amy and tell her he was a free man, but she was the one person he could never share his thoughts or feelings with again. With much effort he concentrated on the enraptured faces of Marie-Elise and

Pierre-Louis. Only slowly did their happiness make his own tension and dark mood lighten.

The wedding ceremony was as romantic as the city hall was dull and official-looking, with its blue-and-white-trimmed walls, French flag and severe portrait of the French president. But if ever there was proof of the power of love to transform two people, the couple's shining eyes as they looked at each other were the living evidence of it. Gone was Remy's plain, efficient secretary hiding fearfully behind her thick glasses and her ill-fitting clothes. Today she was a blushing vision of utter femininity in her ivory-lace gown and clouds of tulle. The froth became the bride. Pierre-Louis was tanned, muscular and robust, even fitter than he'd been before the accident and his tragic divorce.

One minute Remy was staring at Marie-Elise's glowing face, and the next he was losing himself in the memory of a pair of fine, hazel eyes that had been equally radiant when they'd devoured his on the dance floor at Jimmy'z. Her lips had been so soft when he'd kissed her after she'd told him she loved him. She'd put her heart and soul in that kiss and offered herself to him forever.

Love. It had the power to give fresh hope, new meaning and immense happiness to anyone who dared to risk his or her soul again.

Why the hell was he letting her go?

For her own good, you fool. You don't deserve her.

But if she loves you…

As he focused on the bride and groom, he couldn't help visualizing Amy in a white dress and veil.

Slowly the dull, hopeless self-loathing that had afflicted him ever since André's death lifted. He had to call Amy.

No sooner had he made this decision than he began to

chafe for the ceremony to be over and for the wedding documents to be signed, because now, at last, he knew what he had to do.

He had to find Amy and see if she would still have him.

But when the ceremony was over, Pierre-Louis reminded him he'd promised to stay for the reception. As the best man he could not refuse.

Then at the reception, Taylor and several members of his Formula One team showed up, including his two top drivers, and, wouldn't you know it, they all joined forces with Pierre-Louis.

"You planned this, didn't you, Pierre-Louis?" Remy accused when he was surrounded.

"You did say if I ever wanted anything, you'd be there. I want you to listen to what Taylor has to say."

Cornering him, the men pressed him to reconsider joining their team.

Taylor, a tall forceful man with a shock of thick, gray hair, said, "We want you because you weren't just a brilliant driver, you were intuitive. You found speed that was beyond your intellectual limit and then you notched it even higher, so much higher than anyone else's. You were incredible. You know the business on a profound level, as well. A man with your talents could do so much for Formula One."

As Remy stood shaking his head beside Pierre-Louis and the other men while they showered him with praise and told him about their new car and invited him to help with its testing, as they described in detail what he could do for them, he began to feel a flicker of the old excitement and heady self-confidence that had driven him for so long and had made him one hell of a competitive Formula One driver. His head stopped shaking. Formula One had been his life for a lot of years. Maybe this was his second chance to make things right.

Did grief have a life of its own and a death, as well? Suddenly more than anything he wanted Amy. If he felt alive enough to listen to Taylor again, it was solely because of her.

The mistral tore over the mountains and ripped through the pines as Remy stood in the garden staring at the pool and blue chaise longue where they'd made love. A shutter banged. The house was empty of Tate's things. All the boxes had been moved.

Amy was gone.

What had he expected? He had told her it was over, and he'd sent her away.

With slumped shoulders, he walked around the crumbling stone house where Céline waited in the car. He didn't feel like being with her, but she'd insisted on coming.

Even though Amy's leaving without even writing him a note or saying goodbye was his fault, he felt as small and lost as he had the day he'd learned the *comte* hated him because he was Sando Montoya's bastard.

Remy got in the car and jammed his key in the ignition. But instead of starting the car, he just sat there.

"Why don't you start the car?" Céline whispered.

"We've got to end this thing."

"What are you talking about?"

"This. Us. Whatever the hell you're doing. Your surprise visits. Your sudden coziness with my mother."

"But I thought—"

"I thought I made myself clear."

"But you said in a month…"

"It hasn't been a month. Not that that matters."

"But she's gone."

"I'm sorry, Céline."

"I thought that when she left, maybe you and I…"

"I'm sorry."

"But if she's not coming back…"

"Don't say that. Don't even think it. I've got to find her and make her understand that I was wrong, so wrong about everything."

"You love her?"

"I've never been in love before, so I've behaved rather stupidly. But, yes, I guess I am in love."

"Oh, Remy, then I've done something truly terrible, so terrible I don't know if you can ever forgive me."

He looked at her. "I've done terrible things and have needed forgiveness and compassion myself. Why don't you try me?"

"It's about Amy…."

Geography. Songs. Scents. These are the things that transport you in time and bring old memories so acutely into focus that they hurt again. Thus, London, with its black cabs and double-decker red buses and cool, humid air made Amy long too keenly for Remy as she walked toward Carol's flat after a long day of shopping.

The straps of her heavy shopping bags cut into her arms. Her feet ached, but she stopped at the exact spot where Remy had bumped into her and knocked her bags to the ground.

For a long moment she held her breath. Everything was the same, but nothing was. Loss filled her. How long would it take before she wasn't haunted every minute of every hour by his absence? If only she could make a wish and turn the clock back and have him here.

She bit her lips. Visiting Carol had seemed like such a good idea, just the thing to help her get over Remy, just as shopping today at Camden Market had seemed like a good idea after her mother had faxed a list of things for her to shop for. But she'd thought of Remy all day, and there had been no fun in any of her purchases.

Carol was coming into the city to take her to dinner, and she needed to get ready. But she dreaded Carol's questioning and advice. Glancing at her watch, Amy realized she'd better hurry. Perfect Carol was always on time.

Just as she was about to resume walking, a tall, dark man with lithe, long-legged strides dashed across the street straight toward her.

When she turned, he slowed his pace. Even before she really looked at him, her skin began to prickle with excitement. Her breathing became very fast and shallow, and her legs suddenly felt like spaghetti.

A lock of black hair fell over his brow and he pushed it back, and the gesture was so familiar her breath caught.

"Have you been out buying see-through knickers again?"

"Remy? *Remy!*"

Then her bags were falling from her hands, their contents spilling everywhere. But she was running and yelling his name over and over again, too happy to care.

"I love you," he said as he folded her into his arms. "I love you. I hope I'm not too late."

"All that matters is that you're here now."

"And I'll be here forever if you'll have me. I need a wife, not a mistress. Will you marry me?"

All the love in her heart flew to him. She wanted to say yes, yes, yes, but she was so filled with emotion, the words caught in her throat, so she kissed him, instead, long and steadily. Forever.

She was going to be his *comtesse*. That would take some getting used to for a lot of people, like his mother and his sisters. And maybe her own mother, too.

Or maybe it wouldn't.

"My mother always told me that fairy tales were real. She used to promise me that someday I'd grow up and be a princess."

"I'm afraid you'll only be a *comtesse*."

"Being your *comtesse* is way better than being an ordinary princess," she said. "Will we live in your château?"

"Not unless you want to live with my mother. I have an apartment in Paris. My office is there."

"Definitely Paris."

"When you give birth to our first soccer player, we'll have to look for a bigger place."

"Oh, Remy, I'm so happy."

"Me, too."

He kissed her again, and he didn't stop for a very long time.

* * * * *

Too Wild

Jamie Sobrato

To the Wild Writers, who've been there for me from the start. I'm blessed to have the friendship and support of such a wild, wonderful group of women.

1

WHAT JENNA CALVERT NEEDED was a large, tattooed man with a look of death in his eyes. Perhaps someone with a prison record and an intimate knowledge of firearms. Some guy named Spike or Duff.

But even Bodyguards for Less was out of her price range. Jenna listened a second time to the phone recording that described the business's services. No way could she swing the eighty dollars per hour the burly voice on the recording stated was the base price without additional services—and what additional services could a bodyguard provide, anyway?

She hung up and exhaled a ragged breath.

Without a bodyguard, the only protection she had was Guard-Dog-In-A-Box. For twenty-nine dollars and ninety-nine cents, she'd purchased as much peace of mind as she could afford—a sorry amount indeed. Thirty bucks had bought her a motion-sensing device that simulated the sounds of killer dogs barking at any unsuspecting intruders.

Unfortunately, it also barked at neighbors passing in the hallway, at pizza delivery men and at Mrs.

Lupinski's many elderly lovers traipsing in and out of the building at all hours of the day and night.

Jenna hadn't had a good night's sleep in a week, and everyone else in the building was getting tired of her canned guard dogs, too. Even Mrs. Lupinski, who was normally otherwise engaged, had yelled obscenities out her door at Jenna last night when she had heard her in the stairwell.

Guard-Dog-In-A-Box had looked so promising there on the shelf at the store, but now that she'd lived with her faux protection for a week, she saw just how desperate she'd become to even buy it.

She was cooked meat.

She never should have started researching the underbelly of the beauty-pageant industry. Ever since she'd begun the research a month ago, her life had been turned upside down by someone who didn't want her writing the story. Jenna had racked her brain trying to figure out who among the people she'd interviewed or spoken with might wish her harm, but no one jumped out as a likely culprit. She hadn't even uncovered any information that seemed worthy of death threats. But the voice-altered phone calls and the threatening mail had included comments like "back off the story" and "you're risking your life if you write it."

Jenna surveyed her apartment, wishing now that she had a roommate, or at least a parakeet. Someone to comfort her and tell her that it wasn't such a bad thing to get three death threats in the past month. Someone who could also remind her that it was really quite normal to nearly get run down by a car in San Francisco. Two days in a row.

Yes, a roommate would be nice right about now. A roommate, a bodyguard and a really big weapon. But all Jenna had was Guard-Dog-In-A-Box. She resisted the urge to hurl the waste of money across the room and eyed the double locks on the apartment door. If anyone really wanted to get in, they wouldn't have much trouble. The wood of the door frame was rotting away in places, and the locks looked as if they'd been installed before Jenna was born.

Sure, the front door of her apartment building was supposed to remain locked to nonresidents, but Mrs. Lupinski liked to prop it open for her lovers and the ever anticipated sweepstakes-prize delivery people. Getting buzzed in on the rare occasions it was locked was as easy as claiming to be a pizza delivery guy.

Jenna leaned against the decrepit door and closed her eyes. She let her mind drift to happier days, when home security was the least of her concerns. Only two months ago she'd been a relatively carefree journalist who'd made a decent career of writing for women's magazines, and she was embarking on the story she was sure would finally turn her career from decent to well paying. No more squeaking by on a paltry freelance income that barely paid the high rent in the city. The beauty-pageant exposé was supposed to be her ticket to success.

When the buzzer on the door sounded, she jumped so hard that Guard-Dog-In-A-Box clattered to the floor and began barking. It sounded about as menacing as tin-can recorded dog barks could sound—that is, not menacing at all.

Her hand shook as she pressed the intercom button and said, "Who is it?"

"Ms. Calvert? My name is Travis Roth. I need to talk to you about your sister, Kathryn. May I come up?"

Kathryn? Jenna stared at the intercom, dumbfounded. She hadn't heard from or spoken to her twin sister in years. Could this be a ploy someone was using to get inside the building?

"What about her? Just tell me now."

"I really need to speak with you face-to-face. It's a sensitive matter."

A sensitive matter? Did bloodthirsty criminals talk like that?

"Haven't you ever heard of the telephone?"

"I've been trying to call you for days with no answer."

Oh. Right. She'd unplugged the answering machine after the strange calls started coming in, and finally she'd just stopped answering the phone.

"Look, if you're here about the pageant story, I don't have any idea what your problem is with it!"

She turned off the intercom and pushed her sofa against the door, then climbed on top of it and pulled her legs to her chest. She was beginning to think journalism had been the wrong career choice. What she needed was a nice, safe job. Maybe in forestry, or library science.

No, that was just fear talking. She loved her work. She'd always dreamed of being a freelance writer, and now she was one. Was she really such a coward she'd let someone bully her out of writing the truth? Scared as she might be, in her gut, Jenna knew she wasn't about to stop working on the article.

Fifteen minutes later, she was still sitting in the same spot staring at her chipped toenail polish when she heard Mrs. Lupinski hollering about the whereabouts of her free pizza, a sure sign that the guy with the sensitive matter to discuss had gotten into the building.

Someone knocked at the door, and in spite of herself Jenna jumped again.

"Ms. Calvert, this is urgent. It's about your sister's wedding."

Kathryn was getting married? No surprise there, if he was telling the truth. Her sister had been dreaming of a rich Prince Charming ever since they'd been old enough to date.

"She needs your help."

"Right, now I know you're lying. And why isn't she here asking for my help herself if she needs it?" Kathryn would no sooner ask for Jenna's help than she would wear a designer knockoff dress.

"I'll explain, if you'll just give me a chance."

"Go away before I call the police!"

She peered through the peephole at him to see his reaction. Yow! What a cutie. Smoky green eyes, sand-colored hair streaked with blond and cut meticulously short, the kind of stern, masculine mouth that begged to be kissed into submission. Not exactly the face of a thug, but what did she know? Maybe criminals were going for the *GQ* look this year.

"I understand you and Kathryn haven't spoken in some time, and you didn't part on friendly terms."

Okay, somehow he'd found some personal information to make his cover seem authentic. Jenna sank back down on the couch and chewed her lip.

"Jenna, this is really urgent. Open the door."

She eyed the fire escape. Today was not a good day to die. For one thing, her roots were starting to show, and she had a zit on her chin. She'd look like hell in a casket. Maybe this guy was legit, but she couldn't afford to find out. It would only be a short drop from the bottom of the fire escape to the ground.

She hopped off the couch, grabbed her backpack purse, slid her feet into the nearest pair of sandals and hurried to the fire-escape window.

The gorgeous maybe-assassin started pounding on the door, and Jenna pushed her window open and squeezed through it. Her breath came out ragged, and she imagined herself in an action movie as she climbed down the fire escape and dangled herself over the bottom edge for the drop. Five feet, no problem. She let go and landed with a thud in the scraggly mess of weeds that made up her building's backyard vegetation.

Now what? She hadn't exactly formulated an escape plan. Jenna eyed the tall chain-link fence that surrounded the backyard and tried to envision herself scaling it. No way—she wasn't risking it unless there were no other options.

If she hurried, she might be able to go out the alleyway to the street and slip away before he realized she wasn't in her apartment anymore. Jenna hurried to the rusty gate and eased it open, then ran down the alley to the sidewalk.

She'd only made it past the neighbor's house when she heard a man's voice call after her, "Jenna, wait!"

Him again. What, did he have X-ray vision? Jenna ran, and the sound of footsteps quickened. He caught up with her as she rounded the corner of the next street.

"Kathryn said you'd resist helping, but she didn't tell me you were crazy," he said over her shoulder, and something about the perplexed tone of his voice made Jenna stop and look at him.

He was even more gorgeous in person without his features distorted by the peephole. Up close, he was half a foot taller than her, and he stood with the kind of assurance that suggested he was accustomed to being in charge. Jenna's fear was suddenly overcome with a pang of desire. Wow, did she ever need to pay more attention to her love life, if her would-be assassin was suddenly turning her on.

His clothes—a navy wool sport coat, an open-collared white oxford and a pair of beige summer wool slacks—were tailored, expensive. The way they fit, the way he looked so carefully put together, gave Jenna the urge to muss him up.

He was studying her, probably trying to make sense of the differences between herself and her high-society identical twin. "You *are* Jenna Calvert, right?"

Jenna kept her hair long and dyed various shades of red—this month it was Auburn Fire—while Kathryn had always been fond of short debutante haircuts in their natural blond color. And Jenna had always asserted her independence and uniqueness from her twin through her wild wardrobe, while Kathryn's taste tended toward the classic and exorbitantly priced.

"Yes," she said, secretly thrilled that she'd managed to distinguish herself from her identical twin so well.

"I'm Travis Roth. It's good to finally meet you." He withdrew a business card from his pocket and offered it to her. Jenna took it and read the raised black lettering on a tasteful white linen card. Travis Roth, CEO, Roth Investments.

Whoopee. Any bozo could get business cards made up and call himself a CEO.

Jenna stuck it in her pocket.

"What color are Kathryn's bridesmaid dresses going to be?"

"Excuse me?"

"The colors in the wedding—dresses, flowers, everything. If you know that, I'll talk to you."

He appeared to be giving the matter some thought. "I'm afraid I don't know."

Jenna wished she'd remembered to grab a kitchen knife on the way out the window. "If you know Kathryn, you'd know what colors are in her wedding."

A look of understanding softened his features. "Some kind of purple? Lavender, right?"

Lavender was Kathryn's signature color. Ever since they were kids, she'd worn lavender, while Jenna'd had to wear identical outfits in pink. But that was one of their many differences—Kathryn had embraced being dressed up as a sideshow act by their mother, while Jenna had hated every moment of it. She still couldn't look at the color pink without feeling slightly nauseated.

Kathryn could never understand why Jenna had felt the need to differentiate herself from her twin with wild clothes and different hair colors, while Jenna couldn't understand her twin's obsession with being one of an identical pair.

"Okay, so what's your connection to my sister and her wedding?"

"I'm her fiancé's brother, and I'll explain everything if you'll just give me a half hour of your time."

Her curiosity was piqued now that she had some assurance this Travis guy wasn't a hardened criminal. What sort of urgent matter could bring Kathryn to turn to Jenna for help? And why had she sent her fiancé's brother to talk to her?

She looked Travis up and down. Okay, considering his sex appeal, he was a pretty good messenger. She could stand to spend a half hour with him, though she could think of much more interesting things to do with him than talk about Kathryn and her prenuptial problems.

"I'll listen, if you'll buy lunch," she said, her stomach rumbling because she'd skipped breakfast. "There's a diner around the corner."

TRAVIS DID HIS VERY BEST to focus on the business at hand, but Jenna Calvert had thrown him completely off track. She wasn't at all what he'd expected. Yes, Kathryn had described her as a rebellious type, as someone who liked to shock others and be contrary just for the sake of conflict, but she hadn't mentioned how damn sexy Jenna would be.

A waitress with three nose rings and threads of purple in her braided hair arrived to take their order, and Travis tried to take his mind off Jenna long enough to choose a lunch. His gaze landed on meat loaf, and he wasn't sure if he'd ever even tasted it, but he'd seen it on TV and decided that's what he was having.

"I'll have the meat loaf, and…" Certainly wine wasn't the appropriate beverage. "Iced tea."

"You want green tea or black?" This was San Francisco, after all.

"Green will be fine."

He caught himself staring at Jenna's lush pink lips as she placed her own order for a cheeseburger, chili fries and a chocolate shake, and when the waitress disappeared, he forced his gaze back to Jenna's eyes.

The gorgeous redhead had managed in the space of ten minutes to muddle his thoughts and set his senses on high alert. It took a monumental effort to keep from letting his gaze fall even lower than her sensuous mouth to the front of her tight black tank top—to keep from thinking about the fact that she apparently wasn't wearing a bra.

And curse the guy who invented bras if all women could look like that without them.

She wasn't even remotely his type. Her look wasn't classic Coco Chanel, as he'd always preferred, but rather rebel-without-a-Nordstrom-card. With her dyed burgundy hair; her short, unpolished fingernails and her tight, faded jeans, she was about as opposite to Kathryn Calvert as she could get and still be the woman's twin sister.

When he looked into her ice-blue eyes, he saw sparks of fire that weren't present in her sister's. Perhaps Jenna had spirit, something he suspected lacking in Kathryn. Travis was undeniably intrigued by this wilder twin, and he was curious to know her in spite of his suspicion that she probably had a tattoo hiding somewhere on her body.

Where and what that tattoo might be—the possibilities were endless. A little red rose on the satin skin of her inner thigh, or a tiny heart hiding beneath her panties… Whoa, mama.

What on earth was going on here? He didn't like tattoos, and he didn't even know if Jenna had one. But she certainly had his imagination in the gutter all of a sudden.

There was no sense in fantasizing about Kathryn's bad-girl twin anyway, because if she agreed to his offer—and he knew she would—then she would be transformed in the next few days into an exact replica of her sister. It was his unwelcome job to make that happen.

Jenna sat across from him with her elbows propped on the table, her slender arms sporting two chunky bracelets in various stones and faux gems, displaying an utter lack of grace that Travis found oddly charming. As he explained his acquaintance with Kathryn Calvert and her engagement to his younger brother, Blake, she listened closely, never taking her gaze away from his eyes.

But next came the sensitive part, the reason he'd driven all the way from Carmel in the hope of bringing Jenna back with him.

"The wedding plans were moving along just fine until last week, when Kathryn flew to Los Angeles for what she claims was supposed to be a week-long spa treatment. She decided to get some minor plastic surgery while she was there, and—"

"What kind of plastic surgery?" Jenna's eyes had grown perfectly round.

Their conversation was interrupted by the waitress delivering their meals and drinks. Jenna continued to watch him as she dug into her burger.

When the waitress left, Travis continued. "Some kind of procedure where the doctor takes fat from one part of your body and injects it into the cheeks and lips. Kathryn is outraged with the results, and she refuses to come home until the problem has been corrected."

Jenna laughed out loud. "What, her face is too fat now?"

Travis smiled. "Something like that. She says she looks lumpy." He couldn't begin to understand why anyone would endure such a procedure, especially not for beauty's sake, but of all the people he knew, Kathryn was the easiest to imagine having fat injected into her face.

"Now I've heard it all."

"The problem is, we can't postpone the wedding or any of the prenuptial events. For one thing, Kathryn doesn't want my family to know she was off having facial enhancements done. My mother hasn't exactly welcomed her into the family."

"I can imagine how important it is for Kathryn to impress her future mother-in-law."

"She has a long list of people to impress, I'm afraid. Kathryn initiated a project with Blake to establish a women and children's shelter through the Roth charity foundation, and she is supposed to meet with a couple interested in donating land for the project later this week."

"So reschedule."

"They're already hesitant about the project thanks to Blake's reputation for flakiness. Kathryn doesn't want to give them any reason to back out, because such a prime piece of land so central to the Bay Area is nearly impossible to come by."

Jenna frowned. "Sounds like she's got herself in a real bind."

"Not just herself, but my business, too. Our family's investment firm has suffered recently as a result of Blake's inability to handle responsibility, and this wedding is our chance to give some of our clients a better impression of him, to leave them feeling warm and fuzzy about Roth Investments. We need everything to come off without a hitch."

Jenna's expression turned wary as she bit into a French fry. "Why can't you just tell everyone that the bride has come down with pneumonia or something and is too sick to go through with the wedding?"

Travis took his first bite of meat loaf and decided he'd been missing out all these years. He made a mental note to ask the family chef to prepare the dish regularly.

"Any postponement will look like flakiness on the family's part, no matter what the excuse, and that's an image we have to avoid at all costs. Several of our biggest clients have threatened to leave because of Blake's unreliability. This marriage will show them that he's settling down and becoming a family man."

"Why doesn't someone just fire your brother?"

If it were only so easy. "My father has forbidden it. Blake is Dad's favorite."

"This all sounds a little crazy, and I don't understand how you think I can help."

"The doctors have assured Kathryn that her face will look normal before the wedding, but she still refuses to come home until the damage has been undone."

"So you just have to hope she'll come back in time for it."

"And that's exactly what I'm doing, except that still leaves us without a bride for the prewedding events my parents have planned, along with the land donation meeting."

"Does your brother know about Kathryn's little problem?"

"No, and he cannot find out. He's awful at keeping anything secret. He's expecting Kathryn back from her trip on Monday, but she obviously won't be back."

"Isn't he going to notice when his bride doesn't show up for the rehearsal?"

Travis took a deep breath. "That's where you come in. We need you to impersonate Kathryn until she returns."

Jenna dropped her cheeseburger onto its plate and stared at him as if he'd just sprouted antennae.

"You're out of your mind," she said matter-of-factly, her cheek full of half-chewed cheeseburger.

"You haven't even heard my offer yet."

"Sorry to disappoint you, but I'm not going to help Kathryn or the dimwit who agreed to marry her."

Kathryn had never explained why she and Jenna were estranged from each other. Apparently the rift was a deep one, judging by Jenna's reaction, but Kathryn had mentioned how she and her twin had switched places many times as children—how it had in fact been one of their favorite games.

"You'll be quite well compensated." He noted a gleam of interest in her eye that she quickly subdued.

"I'm earning a good living already. I don't need anyone's charity."

From the looks of Jenna's neighborhood, Travis was willing to bet she was barely scraping by on her meager freelance earnings, and that she could definitely use the money he had to offer.

"Not charity. Payment for a job completed."

"Yeah, whatever. I still won't do it."

"You don't even know what the compensation will be."

"Not enough." She turned her attention to her milk shake.

He could tell by the tenseness in her narrow

shoulders that he had to pull his final punch. "Twenty-five thousand dollars."

Chocolate milk shake spurted from her mouth across the table and onto the lapel of his favorite jacket. She stared at him wild-eyed.

He dipped his napkin into a glass of ice water and dabbed at the spot until it disappeared, and when he looked back up, she was scooting out of the booth.

"Where are you going?"

"Away from you and whatever crooked scheme you've cooked up." She stood and shrugged on her small leather backpack.

Travis stared after her as she headed for the door.

He hadn't anticipated her walking away once he'd started to talk money. Nor had he imagined he'd be so mesmerized by the sway of her hips in those faded Levi's that he'd be frozen in place, speechless and unable to form complete thoughts. No, things weren't going the way he'd planned at all.

2

JENNA CLIMBED THE STAIRS to her apartment, her mind playing over and over Travis's proposal. Had she made too rash a decision? Twenty-five grand was a lot of money to walk away from, yet the thought of not only helping Kathryn, but actually taking over her life, was just too much to contemplate all at once.

Jenna had spent every moment since she'd left home ten years ago trying to forget that she was not unique in the world, that she had an identical twin out there and that she wasn't even the best liked of the two. Kathryn had always been their parents' favorite, their teachers' favorite and the one who had more friends and more boyfriends. Kathryn knew the art of getting along to get along, while Jenna had been born with a rebellious streak that angered authority figures and scared away the faint of heart.

An image of Travis Roth popped into her head. A perverse little part of her wondered if he was faint of heart, or if he'd be the kind of guy who could hang on when life with Jenna got unpredictable. Crazy thoughts, considering a guy like Travis and a girl like Jenna would never get together, not in a thousand years—unless, of course, some sort of paid services were involved.

Like being hired to impersonate her sister.

The thought gave Jenna a shudder. Impersonating Kathryn would be like taking a giant leap backward in time. She'd be admitting that all her rebellion in the past ten years had been for nothing—that with a bottle of dye, some scissors, a change of clothes and a bit of makeup, she was just a duplicate of her ever-so-proper sister.

The wild hairstyles, the sexy clothes, the wild men, the wild nights out...

All for nothing.

The choices she'd made to prove herself an individual could be wiped away in one fell swoop.

Jenna reached her floor of the apartment building, and the first thing she saw was her door standing ajar. She froze, and her stomach contracted into a rock.

Could Travis have gotten it open before he came outside and found her trying to escape? Possible, but how could he have so quickly gotten around the couch she'd jammed up against it earlier? That, along with getting past the locks, would have taken more time than he'd had to come back outside and catch her sneaking away.

She took a step closer and saw that the locks hadn't been broken, and an image of the open fire-escape window flashed in her mind. In this neighborhood, no one left fire-escape windows open unless they wanted to find all their valuables and not-so-valuables for sale at a swap meet the next weekend.

Her heart raced. Should she go in or just leave and call the police from a neighbor's place? Common sense told her to leave, but curiosity had her aching to peek inside, if only for a moment.

Her computer—she had to know that it was safe.

Jenna held her breath and stepped into the doorway, thinking of how she was going to pitch Guard-Dog-In-A-Box out the window at Travis Roth's head if she saw him outside her building again. Slowly, she eased her head around the half-open door, until she could see the interior of the apartment.

It took her a moment to make sense of the changes since she'd last been there an hour ago. Couch overturned, cushions ripped open, papers and books strewn everywhere, bookshelves emptied and her laptop missing from her desk.

Jenna's heart pounded in her ears as she realized the months—the *years*—of work saved on her hard drive that now might be missing, and she didn't see her box of floppy disks anywhere among the mess.

She gripped the door frame and resisted the urge to rush in and search for her laptop and files before she knew for sure that the intruder was gone. She needed to think, make a plan…. First she'd go to Mrs. Lupinski's and ask to use the phone.

She backed away from the door and crept up the stairs.

Damn it.

Was Travis Roth a diversion for someone to break into her apartment? No, that didn't make sense. He hadn't come expecting that she'd flee out the window, that they'd end up having lunch at a diner down the street… But he could have had some other plan to get her out of the apartment. Could that whole story about her sister have been an elaborate charade?

Her mind raced from thought to thought, and her hands began to shake as the reality of what she'd likely just lost sank in.

Jenna raised her fist to knock on Mrs. Lupinski's door, but the door swung open at that moment and her neighbor, in mint-green curlers and a red satin robe, peered out.

"Shouldn't have left your window open, huh! Saw some guy climbing up the fire escape, and twenty minutes later he walked right out the front carrying a black bag full of stuff."

"Did you call the police?"

"How was I supposed to know if he was up to no-good? Could have been a friend of yours for all I knew." Mrs. Lupinski's robe slid open in the front to reveal a black lace nightgown. The sounds of a daytime soap opera could be heard in the background.

Jenna shuddered. She knew better than to argue with her cantankerous neighbor. "I need to use your phone. My apartment has been robbed and ransacked." *While you were up here minding your own business.*

Damn it, damn it, damn it.

She wanted to throw up or kick something. Or both. Tears burned her eyes, but she blinked them away, determined not to let her neighbor see how upset she really was.

The elderly woman eyed her suspiciously but stepped aside and motioned her in. Jenna had never actually been inside the apartment before, and she half expected to see a heart-shaped bed in the living room, mirrors on the ceiling, maybe a few pieces of emergency resuscitation equipment in case any of her lovers went into cardiac arrest at an inopportune moment.

What she saw instead was a two-room flat almost identical to her own, except for the matter of décor. Mrs. Lupinski had stopped decorating sometime in the late sixties, when she'd apparently been enamored with orange-and-green flower prints.

She pointed to a telephone next to the couch, and Jenna was surprised to note that it actually had a rotary dial. The feel of catching her shaky fingers in the small holes as she dialed 911 took her back to childhood for a fleeting moment, until an operator came on the line and she found herself recounting the relevant details of the break-in.

The operator warned her not to enter her apartment again until the police had secured it, so Jenna was stuck waiting for them to arrive in the company of Mrs. Lupinski. Luckily, her neighbor didn't see any need for small talk. Without saying a word, she simply planted herself in front of the TV and watched with undivided attention the plight of Rafe and Savannah, a couple who seemed to be very upset over the resurrection of someone named Lucius.

Jenna, left to her own thoughts, didn't want to consider what might be missing from her meager belongings. Nor did she want to contemplate whether the break-in was connected to her research of the pageant industry. If it was, and if her files were missing—

A sense of violation rose up in her chest. *How could they?* How could someone have taken her things, violated her privacy, stolen her work—the thing that mattered most to her?

It was bad enough that she'd taken to cowering behind her apartment door, afraid to venture out in public like a normal person. Now her home had been invaded, and she had nowhere to cower.

No, she had to stop thinking this way. This was exactly the kind of fear they wanted her to succumb to.

She shook herself mentally and her thoughts landed instead on Travis Roth. Where did he fit into this puzzle? Her gut told her he was telling the truth, and her libido told her he was an undeniable babe. But what if he were a hit man, hired to lure her away and kill her, then dump her body in a shallow grave? There was one way to find out, even if it meant calling her mother, Irene Calvert-Hathaway.

She picked up the phone again, dialed directory assistance, and went through the motions of placing a collect call to Palm Springs. Moments later, she heard her mother's voice on the line. It should have been a comforting sound, in light of the circumstances.

"Mom, it's Jenna."

"What's the matter, dear? Are you dead? Did you get thrown in jail?"

"No, Mom. If I were dead, I'd have trouble dialing the phone. My apartment was just broken into and I can't go back in yet, but that's not why I'm calling."

She heard her mother's put-upon sigh. "I told you not to move to that crazy city. Probably drug addicts—I've read how they steal things to support their habits."

"I'm calling about Kathryn, actually. I hear she's getting married."

"To an absolutely magnificent man!" Her mother's voice had changed from nagging to dreamy in an instant. "The wedding is in two weeks. I told Kathryn to send you an invitation, but the way you two fight…"

Yeah, yeah, whatever. No need to invite the black sheep of the family to the social event of the season. Kathryn probably couldn't imagine her lowlife sister rubbing elbows with her country-club friends. Not that Jenna considered herself a lowlife, but she knew her lack of a six-figure income and her less than glamorous lifestyle were a major embarrassment to her family.

While Kathryn had stepped right into their mother's social climbing footsteps, Jenna had never been much impressed by status symbols and excessive wealth. Her rejection of the material life was a constant source of discord between herself and her family, and Jenna imagined Kathryn and their mother shaking their heads and tut-tutting every time the subject of Jenna's rattletrap car or seedy apartment came up.

"It doesn't matter. Do you know anything about Travis Roth, the brother of Kathryn's fiancé?"

She could almost see her mother's surgically youthful eyes narrow. "Why do you ask, dear?"

"He, or someone claiming to be him, contacted me today."

"About what?"

"First, tell me what you know about him," Jenna said, already feeling relieved that at least there *was* a Travis Roth.

"I've only met him a few times, but he seemed like quite the gentleman. Handsome, too. He has a stellar reputation, from what I hear. Runs the investment branch of the Roth family empire, isn't married, lives in Carmel near his brother and their parents."

"What does he look like, exactly?"

"Tall, sandy blond hair, green eyes, nice physique, in his mid-thirties."

"Do you happen to know if their family is connected to any beauty pageants?"

"No, and why on earth do you ask?"

"Never mind." Jenna relaxed back onto the sofa, releasing a mental sigh of relief. It sounded as if her lunch companion wasn't a fraud and knew nothing about the break-in.

"What are all these questions about?"

"I can't say, but don't worry. I'm not going to ruin Kathryn's wedding or anything."

Soon after Jenna ended the call with her mother, the police arrived, checked out her apartment, took statements from Jenna and Mrs. Lupinski and dusted for fingerprints. The biggest clue the police found was a note scrawled on the bathroom mirror in red lipstick that read, "Don't write the story, bitch."

The only story Jenna was working on was the beauty-pageant exposé, so she'd given the police all the information she could remember about whom she had contacted during her research and promised to let them know if she remembered anything else. They'd advised her to take some time off and leave town, maybe stay with family or friends, but to give them an address and phone number for wherever she went.

An hour after they'd left, Jenna sat alone in her ransacked apartment, nervous and depressed. Her laptop and all her files had indeed been stolen.

She didn't allow herself to think about the years of work that were now gone. Instead, she focused on the mess. She wandered around and around the small space surveying her once orderly surroundings.

And strangely, her thoughts kept going back to Travis Roth. His offer wasn't sounding so outrageous, now that her normal life had suddenly turned into a bad dream she wanted to wake from. As if she hadn't been scared enough before, now she knew for absolute sure that someone didn't want her writing the beauty-pageant exposé.

Jenna twirled a strand of hair between her fingers in a nervous habit she'd engaged in since childhood. Any minute now, she figured her eye would start twitching, and then some outrageous behavior wouldn't be far behind.

Her entire life, she'd always relieved tension by doing something wild. In elementary school, there'd been that incident with Mrs. Joliet's desk chair right before the big Little Miss Twin America finals. In junior high, there had been the liberation of the science-class rats after her mother had filed for divorce from her father. In high school, there'd been the time she'd cut class and gone cruising with the biggest badass hunk in school, right before refusing to ever do another beauty pageant.

Later, she'd discovered a little fun in bed had the same effect. Preferably, outrageous fun in bed. And here she was with the greatest need for a tension reliever she'd ever had, and no boyfriend or even the prospect of one in sight.

Jenna sank onto her bed, fighting back the big melodramatic sob that threatened to escape her throat.

Not now, not when she had to think.

Two weeks and twenty-five thousand dollars. She'd get to leave town, forget about her own mess of a life for a little while. Maybe that would give the police enough time to catch the scumbag who'd just trashed her apartment. Or maybe not.

But she'd get to leave town. Even if it meant impersonating her sister, perpetrating a fraud, it was an offer she couldn't turn down now.

And maybe the offer had advantages she hadn't even considered yet. She envisioned Travis Roth in all his tall, blond, broad-shouldered, suntanned glory. Maybe a few weeks in close proximity to him was just what she needed…and maybe a little negotiating was called for.

She smiled, and an outrageous impulse came bubbling up from her subconscious.

Negotiations, yes.

Something to take her mind off her worries. Something to remind her that she was still Jenna, still in control of her own destiny.

Something wild.

Yes.

A calm settled over her for the first time since she'd laid eyes on her ransacked apartment, and an idea formed in her head. An outrageous idea, guaranteed to make her forget her problems, sure to dwarf all the other outrageous stunts she'd pulled over the years.

She withdrew Travis's business card from her pocket and stared at it. After a few moments and a silent prayer, Jenna dialed his number.

TRAVIS HAD DECIDED to drop in on an old college friend at his office downtown before leaving the city. He was just starting the car, wondering what his next step with regard to Jenna should be, when his cell phone rang.

"Travis Roth," he answered.

"It's Jenna Calvert. I've been thinking about your offer, and I may have changed my mind."

"So you're willing to help?"

"Maybe. I have a condition of my own I'd like to discuss, in person."

"Of course. I'm open to negotiating."

"I'd like you to come here to my apartment and pick me up, if you don't mind." She sounded almost…scared. And far less sure of herself than she had a few hours earlier.

"Is something wrong? You sound upset."

She expelled a strained laugh. "You'll see when you get here."

"I'm just leaving downtown, so I'll be there in about fifteen minutes if traffic is light."

Travis pressed the end call button on his phone with no small sense of satisfaction. Mission accomplished. Now there was some hope of saving the wedding from ruin, once they'd overcome the next big obstacle—transforming Jenna into an exact copy of her polished, elegant sister.

No matter how daunting the task, it had to be done, and quickly—without any more getting distracted by sexual attraction. Travis drove back to Jenna's apartment reviewing the necessary steps in his head and trying damn hard not to be thrilled at the thought of a weekend alone with the redheaded vixen.

Before they returned to Carmel, he'd be taking her to a house among the vineyards of Napa Valley, where he'd have the privacy to school Jenna on Kathryn's life without raising any eyebrows. But for the life of him, he couldn't stop the images of other things they might do alone at the country estate from invading his thoughts.

There was the matter of the condition Jenna mentioned placing on helping him, but whatever it was, he couldn't imagine it being much of a problem. More money? He'd pay it. A new car? Consider it done. A nicer apartment? She clearly had the need for one.

The central San Francisco neighborhood where Jenna lived was an urban jungle of decrepit Victorians, tenement apartment buildings and seedy business fronts. The people who walked the streets weren't the sort who hung out at wine-tasting parties or attended charity art auctions. Rather, many looked as though their favorite forms of entertainment might get them arrested.

Travis questioned his own sanity when he found a spot on the street for the second time that day and maneuvered his Mercedes into it. His car had gathered plenty of looks as he'd driven along, and now he'd be lucky if it were still here when he returned. He activated the security system and hoped there weren't any smart car thieves around.

The door of Jenna's building was propped open with a brick, so he went inside and climbed the stairs to her apartment. After knocking on the door, he took time to note the peeling paint on the door frame, the worn hardwood floors, the dingy walls. Jenna's landlord needed to do some building maintenance, that was for sure.

After several minutes, there was still no answer, and Travis fought the sneaking feeling of panic in his gut that Jenna had changed her mind. He knocked again and waited some more. No one came.

He tried knocking harder, then heard a door open on the floor above.

"You trying to get in to see that red-haired girl?" A woman's voice called down.

Travis looked up the stairs toward the source of that voice, but all he could see was the landing, lit by what must have been a twenty-five-watt bulb.

"Um, yes," he said.

Then came the sound of footsteps, and the sight of fuzzy pink house slippers descending the stairs. Next came a red satin robe, and finally he had a full view of a small elderly woman with green curlers in her hair.

"She told me to let you in," she said, eyeing him with interest. "I'm supposed to ask what your name is."

"Travis Roth."

"Yep, you fit the description."

"Did she have somewhere to go?"

"Don't ask me what that crazy girl's up to." She put a key in the door, unlocked it, then presented the key to him.

"I'm supposed to give this to you so's you can return it to her."

Travis took the key, then stared at it in his palm, dumbfounded.

"You get finished with her," the woman said, "and I'm available right upstairs." She waggled her eyebrows at him and flashed what must have been her version of a seductive smile.

"Thanks," he said, forcing a neutral expression. "I appreciate your help." He pushed the door open and stepped inside Jenna's apartment before their encounter could get any more bizarre.

"The thing about us older women you can't get with a young one like that," she said, nodding in the direction of Jenna's apartment, "is that we know more."

"I'm sure you do."

"Honey, I could play your body like an accordion."

Travis shuddered at the image.

"Have a good night," he said as he closed and locked the door.

Turning away from it, he looked around the small room. Jenna was nowhere in sight, much as he'd expected, but the sound of running water came from behind a nearby door. Light was visible in the space between the door and the floor, so he figured Jenna had decided to take a shower.

He took in the mess that surrounded him. Either Jenna Calvert was a lousy housekeeper and a woman with violent feelings toward her sofa, or someone had trashed her place. But, if there had been a break-in, maybe even a struggle, it could have only just happened. Maybe Jenna wasn't even alive and well in the shower. An image of her murdered body being soaked in a bloody shower flashed in his mind, and he panicked.

"Jenna!" He raced to the bathroom door and flung it open.

There, behind the transparent shower curtain, was the unmistakable silhouette of Jenna's body, standing up, seemingly alive and well. He couldn't help admiring the perfect proportions, the tantalizing curve where her waist met her hips. Steam from the shower dampened his face, and he caught the scent of her shampoo, something feminine and fruity.

"Jenna? It's me, Travis."

She peeked out from the edge of the curtain and smiled. "Oh, hi. You got here faster than I thought you would."

Even the sight of her bare shoulder and her crimson hair, slicked back away from her face, aroused Travis. He'd definitely been working too hard lately, neglecting his social life, because instantly, he had a hard-on.

Cardiac arrest was the only appropriate reaction to what she did next. As Travis struggled to keep his jaw from sagging, she slid the curtain open and smiled a wicked half smile.

"Care to join me?" she asked, her tone playful, but her gaze leveled at him with a look of absolute daring.

There was simply no way not to look. He admired the full, round perfection of her damp breasts, the small pink nipples forming tight peaks; the narrow expanse of her waist; the incongruous but tantalizing triangle of blond curls at the peak of her thighs; the delicious shape of her long legs. Not a tattoo in sight. Rivulets of water formed all over her skin, and the only coherent thought Travis could form was that he wanted to lick them off.

Finally, he recovered the ability to speak. "It's a tempting offer…."

She sighed. "But you don't think it would be appropriate."

"Um…" Surely he could say something more profound than "um," but nothing came to mind.

Instead, he could only think of pinning her to the shower wall and burying himself deep inside her. To hell with propriety, to hell with everyone's expectations—he could do something wild and improper for once in his life, couldn't he?

Couldn't he?

Apparently not.

"I've shocked you speechless, I can see." She slid the shower curtain closed again. "I'll be finished in a minute, if you want to wait in the living room."

Travis closed the bathroom door, then leaned against it, barely resisting the urge to bang his head on the wall. His inability to seize the moment was so typical, so thoroughly Travis Roth, it made him want to yell.

Everything he'd accomplished in life had been through careful study and hard work. Never risk taking. His lack of daring had slowly brought the family investment firm out of a slump and into steady profitability, but as his little brother frequently pointed out, the risk takers were the ones who dominated the business world. Calculated risk, their father had always preached, was the hallmark of success. Since he'd been the man who'd built the family fortune, he had the right to preach.

And here was Travis, presented with the erotic invitation of a lifetime, and he couldn't take it. But so what? Business and personal matters weren't the same, and risk taking had entirely different kinds of repercussions for each. He wasn't going to beat himself up for not hopping into a shower with a woman he'd only just met. Getting involved sexually with Jenna would be a huge mistake anyway.

He glanced around again at the mess of her apartment, finally remembering why he'd rushed into the bathroom in the first place. At least he knew now that she was unharmed, but that didn't explain the chaos in her apartment.

Was she just the world's lousiest housekeeper? Was she mentally unstable? That could explain the shower incident, too.... Yet he had the feeling this was definitely a mess someone else had made.

On the other side of the door, the water cut off, and he heard the shower curtain slide open. Travis pushed aside thoughts of Jenna's naked, wet body and walked across the room to look at the books strewn around the bookcase. He bent and picked up some of them, placing each one on a shelf after reading the title. Classics, mysteries, biographies, romance novels, memoirs, philosophy—Jenna seemed to read it all.

He supposed he shouldn't have found that surprising, since she was a freelance journalist. That career suggested a certain intelligence and curiosity, both traits Travis had to admit he considered incongruous with her wild image.

He'd just bent to pick up a copy of the *Atlantic Monthly*—definitely not typical vixen reading material—when Jenna emerged from the bathroom dressed in a pair of faded jeans and a white sleeveless top that laced up the sides. Her damp hair had been pulled back into a sleek ponytail, and her face was scrubbed clean of makeup except for a hint of red on her lips.

Her gaze lingered on him, and rather than looking embarrassed by the shower incident, as Travis imagined he did, Jenna seemed amused.

"I guess Mrs. Lupinski let you in, no problem?"

"She offered to play me like an accordion, but yes, she let me in." He winced at the image and held out the key that was still in his hand. "Here's your key back."

"Thanks. Don't worry, my place doesn't normally look like this."

"What happened?" He was almost afraid to ask.

"While we were having lunch today, someone came in the open window and ransacked it. They stole my laptop and all my backed-up files."

A sense of outrage rose up in his chest on behalf of Jenna. "I'm sorry."

"Not as sorry as I am."

"But why would someone take all your files? Do you have other copies anywhere?"

"It's a long story, and yes, I do have some hard copies and disks of some of my work, but a lot of the newer stuff is lost. I'd hidden emergency back-ups in my closet, but I wasn't very methodical about backing up regularly."

"We've got a long drive ahead, so you can tell me on the way why someone would want to steal your files."

"A long drive where?"

"To Napa. My family has a country home there, a private place where we can get you up to speed on impersonating Kathryn."

"We haven't even discussed my condition for helping you yet."

Up until a few minutes ago, he'd been pretty sure whatever she wanted wouldn't be a problem, but now he knew firsthand that Jenna could be...unpredictable. Outrageous. Wild.

"Okay, let's hear it."

She stepped over a mangled couch cushion and sat on the arm of the sofa next to him. He could smell the fruity shampoo scent from her hair, and that, combined with her proximity, was intoxicating.

"First, I want to apologize for my behavior in the bathroom."

She certainly could have done worse. "Apology accepted."

"I have these sort of urges when I get stressed out."

"Urges?" He couldn't wait to hear her explanation.

"Yeah, urges." She paused, giving him a once-over. "Whenever life gets stressful, I tend to react by following my impulses, which can lead to rather outrageous behavior, as you saw in the bathroom."

Travis shrugged. "No harm done." Other than the image of her lush body burned in his memory for eternity.

"I'm getting this vibe about you."

"What sort of vibe?"

Her eyes sparked mischief. "An uptight one."

"Thanks, that's just the impression I was going for."

"You strike me as one of those guys who's going to die at an early age from a heart attack or a stroke, before you ever get to relax and enjoy life."

Travis ignored the protests of his ego and bypassed her insult. "I'm still waiting for your condition on the deal."

"That's what I'm talking about. You and I, we have a mutual need. I'm stressed out by crazy people stalking me, and you're stressed out by your job or my sister's wedding or whatever. We both need to let off some steam."

He thought of the way he'd snapped at his brother that very morning before coming to meet Jenna. Blake had simply been acting like his usual irresponsible self, turning in a report late, and even though Travis always set artificial deadlines for his brother to make sure the work really got to him when he needed it, he'd exploded right there in the office, in front of his secretary—which meant the entire office building knew about it by now.

Yeah, he definitely needed to let off some steam.

"So what does that have to do with the deal?"

"I'll impersonate Kathryn starting next week. But until then, I'm Jenna. You can coach me on acting like Kathryn, but after hours, I'm still me. All weekend long, we work on unwinding."

Travis didn't quite see where she was going, but he played along. "Okay, I've always found the wine country to be relaxing. Slower pace, quiet—"

"That's not what I mean. The most effective place I know to relieve stress—to *really* relieve it—is in bed, and I don't mean sleeping."

Travis blinked. He couldn't argue with her there. Nothing like sex to put the spring back into his step. But he hadn't even had a serious date lately, let alone—

She continued. "You're single, I'm single, we're attracted to each other, I think. No one will have to know."

"Let me get this straight. You want to make a sexual relationship part of our business agreement?"

"Not when you put it like *that*. I'm just saying I need a little companionship this weekend, and I think you do, too."

Travis frowned. A weekend alone, letting off steam, as Jenna put it, with one impossibly sexy woman. It was either the best idea he'd heard in a long time, or it was absolutely nuts.

3

JENNA SURVEYED THE apartment she'd called home for the past year, feeling yet another burst of anger at the person who'd invaded her privacy and stolen her most valued possessions. It took all her willpower not to kick something—more proof that she needed to unwind. She glanced down at the duffel bag and backpack that held everything she planned to take with her, then up at Travis Roth, who apparently was stunned silent by her proposition.

"I'm not saying I wouldn't like to...unwind," he finally said, "but don't you think it might be awkward?"

"If it is, we won't do it. Just give it a chance tonight, and if it feels wrong, we'll pretend we never had this conversation. Deal?"

If he turned her down, Jenna really was going to kick something. Namely, him. In the ass. Right out her door.

"Okay." He smiled, and the sexy gaze he pinned her with warmed her body in all the right places. "You have a deal. I'd be crazy to turn you down, after all."

She did a mental happy dance. *Look out Travis Roth, you're in for the weekend of a lifetime.*

Jenna switched off all the lights except the one near the door, then started to pick up her bags, but Travis grabbed them first. After he took them out the door, she switched off the last light and locked up her tiny apartment, with the odd feeling that when she returned, her life was going to be very, very different.

While Travis loaded her bags into the trunk of his pristine silver Mercedes, Jenna settled back into the plush gray leather of the passenger seat and tried not to think too hard about what she'd just gotten herself into. She'd focus on the fun part for tonight—do a little flirting, find out what had put all that tension into her companion's shoulders, and do her best to work it out.

It seemed her desire to focus on the positive was not to be fulfilled though. They'd barely been on the road for five minutes when Travis brought up the one subject she most wanted to forget for the weekend.

"Care to tell me why you think someone broke into your apartment and ransacked it?"

"I guess you won't leave the subject alone until I do."

"Probably not."

"I'm researching a story that someone doesn't want written. This was supposed to be the piece that established my reputation as a serious journalist."

"What's the subject?"

"An exposé on the beauty-pageant industry—on the exploitation and behind-the-scenes stuff most people don't know."

Travis nodded. "Sounds interesting. How can you be sure that's why your apartment was broken into?"

"Pretty quickly after I began researching the story, I started receiving threatening phone calls, then other strange things started happening."

"Like what?"

"I was nearly run down by a car earlier this week. It actually drove up onto the sidewalk where I was walking, and it didn't have license plates on the front or back."

His eyebrows shot up. "You don't think it was an accident?"

"An almost identical accident happened with a different car the day before."

"Who knew you were writing the article?"

Jenna pressed her fingers to her temples. Her left eye was starting to twitch, a sure sign that she was overstressed. "More than a few people. Let's talk about this another time, okay? Right now, I just want to pretend I have a normal life."

"So tell me why you and Kathryn don't speak to each other."

Yet another pleasant subject. Jenna stared out the window at the city lights passing by on the East Bay. The eye twitch was getting worse.

"I think I have a right to know what I'm deal-

ing with here. Kathryn said she had no idea why
you hated her so much, but I'm betting she wasn't
telling the whole story."

"You'd win that bet."

"She has a tendency to only remember stories
that make her look favorable, doesn't she?"

"Yep, that's my sis."

"So tell me your side."

"My mother used to enter my sister and I in
these horrible beauty pageants all the time—Little Miss Twin California, Little Miss Twin U.S.A.,
Little Miss Twin America—we did the whole circuit." She scoffed. "I hated it, and Kathryn adored
it. That basically sums up our differences."

"You didn't ever want to be Little Miss Twin
America?"

"I hated dressing up, wearing makeup, being
gawked at by crowds, the whole bit. By the time
we were eight, we knew how to apply mascara
flawlessly."

"Makeup on an eight-year-old?"

"You think that's young? I have photos of myself wearing lipstick at the age of three."

"So that explains your interest in the beauty-
pageant story."

"I've wanted to do this story as long as I've
been a journalist."

Travis nodded. "I had no idea your mother was
such a..."

"Wacko? That's why I'm not exactly close to
her, either."

"Wacko is not quite the word I was looking for, but if you had the kind of mother who dressed you up in matching twin outfits, why not matching names, too, like Kelly and Nelly?"

"It's almost as bad, Jenna Kathleen and Kathryn Jennifer."

"Oh." He fought a smile. "But these pageants were when you were kids, right? Why all the bad feelings after so many years?"

"That was just the beginning. Kathryn always resented me for dropping out of the pageant circuit during our freshman year in high school, thereby ruining her chances of being Miss Twin Anything. It was her big dream to win a pageant, and she never did."

"And that made your mother angry, too?"

"She never said so in so many words, but I knew she was disappointed. She always identified more with Kathryn, and by the time we were teenagers, my sister and I had an all-out rivalry going. She stole my boyfriends, my favorite sweaters and my study notes."

"So you rebelled?"

"In a big way. Where Kathryn was always Miss Perfect—at least to the outside world—I turned into the wild one. I started dating the bad boys she wouldn't dream of being caught with, wearing clothes way too sexy for her taste and I dyed my hair whatever color suited my mood."

"I have to admit, that sounds like an effective way of solving your problems with her."

Jenna smiled nostalgically. "She never once stole one of my black lace see-through tops."

"How long has it been since you've spoken to Kathryn?"

Jenna frowned, unable to immediately recall. "Maybe at a family Christmas get-together a few years ago. And even then, I doubt we said more than 'pass the turkey.'"

"That's too bad. I know Kathryn isn't the deepest person in the world, but she seems to have matured in the time she's been dating my brother. Maybe this wedding will give you a chance to reconcile with her."

Reconciling with her sister sounded about as appealing as diving into a pit of snakes, but she kept silent as she mulled over the possibility. Maybe it was time to let go of her resentment, forgive Kathryn and move on. Or maybe it was just time to get a good laugh at her sister with her new jumbo lips and chipmunk cheeks. Part of Jenna did secretly hope they remained permanently inflated.

"What about you and your brother?" she asked, not ready to discuss something as heavy as forgiveness. "Your relationship with him can't exactly be normal if you're going through all this trouble to hold his wedding together, and I remember you saying he's your father's favorite."

"Blake has never grown up. He's still a little boy playing office at our family business, and our clients can tell."

"So you have to cover for him?"

"In his business life only, up until now."

"You don't have to go around covering for my sister's mistakes, too, you know."

"If I want this wedding to go smoothly, I do." His grip seemed to tighten on the steering wheel.

Jenna stared at his profile as he drove, trying to fathom exactly how much loosening up Travis needed. Definitely more than she'd first suspected.

"What about the rest of your family—do they know what a screwup your brother is?"

"Everyone else finds his boyishness charming. Father wants him at the forefront of the company because he says Blake has the personality to win clients and keep them. He thinks I'm too stiff and serious."

"Hmm. Do you agree with him?"

"I've brought in most of our newer clients myself. When people look for someone to invest their money, they want to know they're leaving their savings in stable hands."

Stability. Why did that quality suddenly sound so sexy, when applied to Travis? Okay, so he could probably make doing a crossword puzzle look sexy, and maybe recent events were causing her to crave stability in her life, but still…

"Have you ever let things slide? Just relaxed and not worried about other people's mistakes?"

"Not when it comes to business—no."

Jenna studied his profile again. He seemed to be in deep thought, and she imagined him fantasizing about suddenly not being so responsible.

Maybe she was helping him loosen up already.
She settled back into her seat and stared out the
window, content with the silence after such a har-
rowing afternoon.

They'd been driving for almost a half hour
when Jenna came out of her trance and glanced
over at Travis again. His gaze dropped to the dash
as they passed a sign for a town in another mile.

"We'd better stop to find some dinner and a
gas station. Are you hungry?"

"Starved. I know a place at the next exit that has
great ribs." She'd stopped there once with a friend
on their way back to the city after a weekend hiking in the mountains.

She decided not to mention that it was a bit of
a biker bar. Or that she fully intended to get Travis
drunk and make him forget all about his worries
for the night.

TRAVIS FOLLOWED Jenna's directions to a gravel
parking lot populated with more than a few Har-
ley-Davidson motorcycles and an even larger
number of pickup trucks. The restaurant with the
great ribs turned out to be a seedy-looking joint
named Lola's Place, and Travis had the distinct
feeling that it wasn't a restaurant so much as it
was a biker bar. The flashing Budweiser sign in
the front window was further support for his
suspicion.

But he gave no protest, since she was probably
expecting him to refuse to go in. He felt strangely

compelled to defy her expectations, whatever that might entail.

He thought to remove his sportcoat and leave it in the car, but before they entered the bar, Jenna gave him a once-over and shook her head. Without so much as asking, she began unbuttoning his shirt cuffs and loosely rolling up his sleeves. After she'd done that, she reached up and mussed his hair a bit, then nodded her approval.

"Wouldn't want you to stand out too much," she said with a little smile.

Then she took his hand and led him inside. Travis was amazed at the way she took charge. He couldn't remember the last time a woman had dared to assert her will on him. His dates were always so careful, so appropriate, so obviously trying to impress him with their polish and impeccable manners. They were even polite in bed.

He'd pretty much given up on dating in the past year. It seemed a futile effort, since he attracted nothing but gold diggers. And one thing he wanted to be sure of before he ever got serious about a woman was that she wasn't marrying him for his money. Short of disguising himself as a janitor, he wasn't sure how to find a woman who really wanted him and not his family fortune.

Inside the dimly lit bar, they found a booth near the dance floor and sat down, gathering quite a few stares along the way. Travis surveyed the crowd and decided that even with his sportcoat abandoned and his sleeves rolled up, he stood out.

The menu consisted of ribs, chili, nachos and French fries, so they both ordered the ribs when a waitress showed up at their table. Just as Travis was about to ask about the selection of imported beers, Jenna ordered a Sam Adams for each of them.

"Was I about to embarrass myself?" he asked.

She smiled. "We'll never know now."

"Is this bar part of your effort to loosen me up?"

"Maybe."

"Am I going to get any direct answers to my questions tonight?"

She laughed. "If you ask me to dance, I'll say yes."

Travis glanced out at the empty dance floor. "Right now?"

"Sure. Or later, if you'd prefer."

"I'm not much of a dancer."

"Then later, after you've had a few more drinks." Her eyes crinkled with amusement.

"That beer is going to be my first and last drink. Remember, I'm driving."

Jenna shrugged. "I can drive, and I don't need alcohol to loosen up."

"What makes you think I do?"

"Just a guess."

And a correct one. Not that Travis usually drank more than a glass of wine with dinner or a scotch on the rocks with friends, but the few times he'd ever really forgotten his inhibitions, alcohol had been involved. Still, he didn't plan on admitting to Jenna that she was right.

Nor did he plan on getting drunk and acting like a fool in the middle of a biker bar.

"If I were drunk enough to get on that dance floor, what makes you think I'd be able to give you directions to our destination?"

"Hmm, you've got me there. Guess you'll just have to dance with me without the aid of alcohol."

The waitress arrived with their drinks, relieving Travis of the burden of continuing a no-win conversation. He took a long drink of his beer and decided he'd do his best to relax and have fun. After all, how often did he have the chance to spend an evening out with a woman as gorgeous and interesting and carefree as Jenna Calvert?

"Tell me more about your journalism career," he said, genuinely interested.

Jenna picked at the label on her beer bottle. "What did Kathryn tell you?"

"Just that you write for women's magazines."

"Ah, the cleaned-up version. Actually, so far I've specialized in sexual issues for women's magazines. I write those articles with titles like 'Sex Secrets of a Dating Diva' and 'Everything He Wishes You Knew about His Body.'"

"You must be fun in bed," Travis blurted and immediately regretted it. Still, he couldn't help wondering….

With a slight smile, she studied him. "I've had some good reviews."

"For your writing or your skill in bed?" What could he say—she brought out the devil in him.

"Both."

And, to think he actually had the opportunity to find out. Amazing. He had a hunch Jenna would be anything but polite between the sheets.

He forced his mind back to the present. "So are you giving up the sex articles for hard-hitting journalism?"

"Maybe. The beauty-pageant piece is supposed to be my chance to get some real recognition. I like the sex pieces, but I'm running out of angles. There are only so many aspects of it to write about."

"Do you already have a publisher for the story?"

She nodded. "*Chloe* magazine paid me an advance for it, but if I can't recover my research and get the article written, I'll have to pay it back."

"Do you still want to write it?"

"I'd like to sound brave, but lately I've been thinking maybe it's not worth getting run over by a car for."

He felt a protective impulse surge in his chest. He generally didn't have urges to fight, but if he could get hold of the person or people who'd tried to harm Jenna, he'd like to give them a thorough pounding.

Instead, he lamely offered, "Surely the police can track down whoever is responsible for harassing you."

Jenna took a long drink of her beer. When she plunked it back down on the table, Travis caught a mischievous glint in her eyes. "How about you take me out on the dance floor now and help me forget all about my career problems?"

"I think our dinner will be here soon. Maybe after—"

She stood and grabbed his hand, then pulled him up from the booth. Before he could offer a protest, she had him on the dance floor, which was now populated with a few couples. The jukebox was playing a bluesy rock song he didn't recognize.

Then Jenna started to dance, and he was mesmerized. He had some vague recollection of moving his body to the music as he watched her hips sway and her torso twist, her long, heavy ponytail draped over one breast.

When her arms snaked around him and urged his hips to move in time with hers, his body came alive in a way that he was pretty sure it hadn't since high school.

He'd just started to appreciate dancing in a whole new way when he felt a tap on his shoulder. Travis turned to find a large bald guy with a tattoo of a snake twisting around his bulging left bicep glaring at him.

"My turn to dance with the lady," Tattoo Guy said.

Why was this bad movie scene happening to him?

"Sorry, she's with me," Travis said, making an effort to keep his voice assertive but neutral.

He turned back to Jenna, whose expression had grown wary.

A large hand grasped his shoulder and tugged him backward. "I *said* I want to dance with the lady."

Tattoo Guy inserted himself between Travis and Jenna, though Travis only needed to take a glance at Jenna's expression to guess that she wasn't going for the new dance arrangement.

When the guy tried to slip his hands around her waist, she took a step back. "Back off! I don't want to dance with you."

Travis stepped between them again. "The lady has made her wishes clear. Now if you'll please—"

He didn't have time to finish his sentence before a fist came barreling into his stomach, and the next sound he heard himself utter was an "umph" as the air left his lungs and pain pierced his gut.

Bringing to mind every lesson he'd learned from watching boxing, Travis ducked to avoid the next punch, then did his best Muhammad Ali impression on Tattoo Guy.

He heard Jenna screech for help from somewhere nearby, and a moment later he and his opponent were scrambling on the ground. Then someone was pulling him up and a burly guy in a leather jacket was picking his opponent up off the ground and dragging him toward the door.

Jenna pushed through the sudden crowd on the dance floor to his side. "Are you okay?"

"I'm fine," he said, though his insides were feeling a bit off-kilter.

A large-hipped platinum blonde wearing a Lola's Place T-shirt approached them. "Sorry about that," she said. "Reuben's a troublemaker I should have banned from here a long time ago."

"It's okay, no harm done."

She extended her hand to him. "I'm Lola, and your dinner and drinks will be on the house tonight, to make up for your trouble."

Travis looked at Jenna to gauge whether she actually wanted to stay. She shrugged and thanked Lola, then took Travis's hand and led him back to the table. Again he had the distinct sensation of every eye in the place following them.

They sat back down at the table where their ribs and fries were already waiting.

"You probably don't have much of an appetite," Jenna said.

Considering that several of his internal organs had just been pounded, Travis probably shouldn't have felt like wolfing down the rack of ribs on his plate, but suddenly he was ravenous. He had the urge to go out and hunt for something, haul it back to the fire over his shoulder and eat the charred meat right off the bone.

"Travis, are you okay?"

Jenna slid her hand across the table and grasped his.

"I'm fine."

"You just look a little wild-eyed."

"I guess it's the adrenaline."

"Thank you for defending me. It's been a long

time since a guy has put himself in danger to protect my honor."

And after he ate the meat he'd bagged himself,
he wanted to take his woman back to the cave and—

Whoa. Where was all this caveman stuff coming from?

"You're welcome, but it was nothing."

He turned his attention to the ribs and dug in.
Neither of their appetites seemed to have been
harmed by Reuben the Tattoo Guy, and by the time
they finished their dinner, Travis had nearly forgotten he was sitting in a biker bar. He'd also managed to relax and almost forget that his association
with Jenna was a bizarre arrangement necessitated
by her sister's botched face enhancements. Their
conversation faded into an easy silence marked by
occasional small talk of the sort he usually only engaged in with longtime friends.

When they left the bar and walked out into the
cool night air, it seemed perfectly natural to slip
his arm around Jenna's waist and guide her to the
car. She stopped at the passenger door and turned
to face him, putting their bodies in close contact.

He recognized the wicked gleam in her eyes.

"Now that we've danced and had dinner,
there's only one logical next step," she said as her
hand wrapped around his neck and into his hair.

He absolutely could not resist the urge to lean
his weight into her, pressing her against the car.
Their bodies fit together too perfectly for it to be
a coincidence.

"What's that?" he whispered, but he already knew.

"Kiss me," she said, and he was there as soon as the words left her mouth.

4

JENNA KISSED LIKE a woman on a mission. Her tongue caressed Travis's lips, then slipped inside his mouth, and a moment later he felt her hands gripping his buttocks, pressing him into her as she snaked one leg around his. Her enthusiasm was just as intoxicating as the rest of her.

Travis's pulse raced, and he returned her hunger with his own, deepening the kiss as one hand held the back of her head and the other slid up her rib cage. When she began to suck on his tongue, he found his thoughts moving into X-rated territory, wondering what other parts of him she might toy with so provocatively.

His hand inched upward and cupped her breast, which was just as full and lush in his palm as he'd imagined. With his erection straining against her, his entire body on fire, he wondered how the hell he'd manage to drive the rest of the way to Napa without pulling off to the side of the road and taking her in the passenger seat.

When they came up for air, Jenna's lips were swollen and her eyes half-lidded as she smiled up at him.

"Are you feeling relaxed yet?" she asked.

"Far from it."

"Guess I'll have to try a little harder then."

"If you try any harder, the last thing I'll be is relaxed."

She bit her lower lip, then slowly released it and sighed. "We'd better be going, hmm?"

Going where? Oh, right, to the country house. Travis tore his gaze away from Jenna and surveyed the parking lot, idly wondering where the nearest hotel was. A couple climbing aboard a black motorcycle eyed them with interest. He spotted the gas station lit up across the street and remembered that they needed to fill up.

"Yeah, we'd better. I think we're still a half hour away." But if they happened to pass a hotel along the way, he wasn't sure he'd be able to keep himself from screeching into the lot and dragging Jenna to the nearest available room.

An image of making love to her on a cheap bedspread in a sleazy motel room flashed in his mind, and he banished it. How had he so quickly gone from respectable businessman to crazed guy who got into bar fights and fantasized about frenzied motel sex?

He looked back at Jenna, and he knew in an instant. Reluctantly, he peeled himself off of her, and they got into the car.

They drove to the gas station, and Jenna said something about buying some weekend reading material before disappearing into the twenty-four-hour convenience store. Travis watched her moving through the fluorescent-lit store, unable to tear his gaze from her as he pumped gas and then used his credit card to pay at the pump.

When she came back out, Jenna flashed a wicked smile at him before she got back into the car. As he was pulling out of the lot, she produced an issue of *Cosmopolitan* from the bag.

"This caught my eye," she said as she read the cover. "'The All-Sex Issue. Ten fun erotic quizzes to share with your guy.'"

Travis felt his mouth go dry. Erotic quizzes? He was in even bigger trouble than he'd thought.

"Mind if I use the reading light while you're driving?"

"Go ahead. You're not going to quiz me while I'm driving, are you?"

"Don't worry, these are no-brainer questions— all in good fun. They might even help you relax."

"That's doubtful."

He heard pages being flipped through as he got back on the highway headed toward Napa Valley. When he glanced over at Jenna and spotted the curve of her breast in the skimpy white shirt, her nipples slightly erect, his groin stirred all over again.

The last thing he needed was an erotic quiz. No, he needed a cold shower and a stiff drink. Not that he was a prude—he just wasn't altogether sure he was cut out for a casual, no-strings-attached sexual fling with a woman he barely knew. Even worse, she was the sister of his soon-to-be sister-in-law, which meant they'd be bound together by family in a matter of weeks.

Travis liked his sex hot, but he kept it restricted to uncomplicated relationships, even if they had been few and far between recently.

Jenna, though… Her effect on him was impossible to ignore, maybe even impossible to resist. Just this once, he was willing to let propriety fall by the wayside and see what happened. Hell, maybe he would even find himself refreshed and relaxed as she said, ready to face the world again with renewed energy after this weekend was through.

"Ooh, here's a good one. 'Intimate Questions for Intimate Fun,'" Jenna said. "Make sure you answer these as honestly as possible. No editing your responses to suit what you think is the right thing to say."

Okay, so what did he have to lose? Besides his self-respect?

"You'll be answering them, too, right?"

"You answer the first quiz, and I'll do the next."

"That hardly seems fair."

"You choose the quiz I have to do, okay?"

"I'm driving."

"I'll read them aloud to you."

"I'm not going to win this argument, am I?"

"Not likely. Question one," she said, declaring herself the victor. "'What's your wildest sexual fantasy?'"

She was sitting right next to him, but Travis decided it would be better not to admit that. "Do I have to answer this?"

"No, but what's it going to hurt? Have you ever had sex with a woman who knew your most intimate fantasies?"

"I don't think so."

"Sex is hotter when your inhibitions are gone. If you tell all from the start, what inhibitions could you have left?"

"Okay, wildest sexual fantasy..." He had a feeling he was about to reveal himself as a meat-and-potatoes kind of guy when it came to sex. "I guess I've always had this fantasy about having sex with a stranger on a cross-country train."

"Oh, the old train scenario."

"You mean it's a common fantasy?"

"Right up there with airplane sex."

She stretched out her long legs, and Travis recalled the feel of her leg snaked around his, which led to an image of both her legs, naked and wrapped around his hips. He gripped the steering wheel tighter and glared straight ahead at the road.

"So if I have a common fantasy, does that mean I'm a boring lover?"

"No, it just means you have a conventional fantasy life. I'll bet you're anything but boring."

"Based on what?"

"The way you kissed me in the parking lot."

Oh, that. Just the mention of it set his blood

boiling again, and he caught himself scanning the horizon for motel signs.

Something had to give.

"I've never had any complaints," he felt compelled to add, then felt foolish for trying to boost his own image.

"Question two. 'What's the most scandalous place you've ever made love?'"

Travis flipped through sexual encounters in his memory—bed, bed, bed, bed... Okay, so his love life was a bit predictable. "The back seat of my father's Jaguar after the prom?"

Silence.

Travis glanced over to see Jenna's expression. She was staring at him with a look of...pity? Great, he was worse off than he thought.

"What?" he demanded, glaring at the road again.

"We'll fix that."

"I wasn't aware that I needed fixing."

"Not you, just your sense of adventure."

"So what's the wildest place *you've* ever done it?"

"I'm asking the questions here," Jenna said.

"Afraid to tell me?"

"No, I just don't want to ruin my air of mystery."

"I've ruined mine."

"I'm not telling."

"Then I'm not answering any more of these ridiculous quiz questions."

"If you think these are ridiculous, then you'd better not read my recent article, 'What Your Favorite Sexual Position Says about You.'"

Travis bit his lip to keep from smiling. "How, exactly, did you go about researching that?"

"Sadly, the research wasn't as hands-on as you might imagine. I mainly interviewed sex and relationship experts. But I learned a lot, and I bet I can guess your favorite position."

Travis tried to imagine himself having this conversation with any of his previous girlfriends. They'd all been comfortable discussing stock options, European vacations, who among their mutual acquaintances had most recently acquired the most impressive car or house…. But favorite sexual positions?

Never.

"I admit, I'm intrigued. What's my favorite position?"

"Girl on top, of course."

Travis pretended to be intently focused on the highway ahead. "What makes you say that?"

"Guys like you, who are always in charge, always responsible for things outside the bedroom, often like to give up control between the sheets."

"You seem awfully confident that you've got me sized up."

"I'm a pretty good judge of these things," she said, sounding supremely satisfied with herself.

Travis had to admire her confidence. Even if she didn't know him from Adam, she put up a good front. "I'll let you believe what you want."

"Okay then, next question—"

"No more quiz questions right now. I'm having trouble driving and talking about sex at the same time."

"That's okay. I can understand your not wanting to reveal your insecurities to me so quickly." He could hear the playful taunting in her voice, and he found it inexplicably sexy.

"What do these sex questions have to do with my hypothetical insecurities?"

"They're never more apparent than when sex is the topic of discussion."

"Ah, I see. You've been reading too many of these fluffy women's magazines."

"Hey, I write for these fluffy women's magazines."

"Oh, that's right. Do you have any articles in that issue?" he asked, knowing he was going to feel like a real ass if she said yes.

"As a matter of fact, I do. 'Ten Ways to Keep Him Begging for More.'"

He doubted she even had to do any research for that one. Jenna seemed to be a woman who knew her own sexual power. One kiss and she nearly had him begging for more.

He shifted in his seat and adjusted his grip on the steering wheel. "Do I dare ask about the content of that one?"

"*Do* you dare? I'm thinking a weekend-long hands-on demonstration is called for."

Demonstrate away, baby. "If you insist," he said, a slow smile spreading across his face. "I'm looking forward to it."

Understatement of the decade. If he didn't get a grip, he was going to completely lose sight of why he'd hired Jenna in the first place. He had to remember: business first, pleasure second. And that shouldn't have been difficult, since it was basically the philosophy by which he'd lived his entire life up until now.

Up until now.

Damn if he wasn't itching for a change.

JENNA SURVEYED the grounds of the Roth family's "country house" and expelled a sigh of appreciation. Even in the darkness, she could see that the property had a prime location among the vineyards. The well-manicured lawn led up to an imposing estate that seemed a bit extravagant for a so-called vacation home, and the hint of hills she could see spreading out into the distance suggested beautiful views in the daylight.

Then she turned to see Travis removing her bags from the trunk, and she experienced an entirely different kind of appreciation. He was a stunning male specimen. Ever since their kiss in the biker bar parking lot, her body had been on fire, her senses hyper-alert. She couldn't remember the last time she'd wanted a man so badly.

And teasing him in the car with the magazine quiz had gotten her far more hot and bothered than she'd expected. Something inside her was driven to push his limits. It was that mussing-up impulse again, only now more than a few hours ago, she had an idea of just how much mussing he needed.

But this estate—whoa.

It served as a reminder of the wide gulf that separated them. Guys like Travis and girls like Jenna didn't get together. Not in real life, not unless girls like Jenna were career social climbers, which she wasn't. And she didn't want to be mistaken for one, either. It occurred to her for the first time that maybe her little erotic stress plan could be seen by Travis as an attempt to get her hooks into his wallet via whatever means necessary.

That couldn't have been further from the truth, but she had no idea how to broach the subject. When he locked the car and carried the bags to where she stood on the sidewalk, she decided straightforward was the best approach.

He nodded at the house. "So what do you think?"

"It's beautiful, but there's one matter we should address before we engage in any, um, stress relief."

"Sure." His gaze searched her, and then he said, "Why don't we get you settled in your room first, then talk?"

Jenna followed him into the house, along the way admiring the grand entryway with its Spanish tile work and high ceilings. The house was dark, so Travis switched on lights along the way, pointing out rooms as they went.

"Over there is the formal living room and the library. In the back you'll find the kitchen, and up here," he said, as they began to climb the stairs, "are all the bedrooms."

He led her down a hallway with walnut floors, the walls lined with photos of distinctly similar-looking people who, Jenna assumed, were various members of the Roth family, and then he stopped at a door on the left at the end of the hall. She resisted the urge to stare at the pictures and hurried to catch up.

"I thought you might like this room," he said as he opened the door and switched on the light. "It's the one female guests tend to use."

Jenna stepped inside and took in the antique black-walnut furniture, the inviting decor of red-and-pink stripes and prints, the double doors leading to the second-floor balcony.

"Wow, this is beautiful," she said as she went to the door and looked out at the sprinkling of lights in the distance.

"The bathroom is over there," he said, nodding toward a closed door. "I'm going to make myself a drink. Would you like something?"

Jenna raised an eyebrow at him. "I thought you didn't need alcohol to loosen up."

"Trust me, a glass of wine won't do much more than make me drowsy."

"I'd love a glass, actually."

"If you follow the downstairs hallway to the rear of the house, you'll find the back door to the pool area. I'll meet you out there once you've had a chance to settle in."

She watched him leave the room and couldn't help thinking the drinks were an excuse to get as far away from Jenna's bed as possible. She could tell he was more attracted to her than he wanted to be. The heat they'd generated with their kiss earlier had been scorching. Jenna would have bet he wasn't accustomed to such chemistry.

On the other hand, *she* wasn't accustomed to lusting after high-society hotties.

Jenna turned and eyed her grungy old bags, looking forlorn against their elegant backdrop. She dug out her toiletries and cosmetics, then took them to the bathroom. It turned out to be four times the size of her little bathroom at home, complete with jetted bathtub, a separate stand-up shower and a gigantic vanity with a dainty padded stool for leisurely beauty routines.

She placed her drugstore cosmetics on the marble countertop and gave herself a once-over in the mirror. Her hair was still damp from the shower earlier, but it was so thick it might stay damp for days if she didn't release it from the ponytail to let it air-dry. After pulling out the hair band, she ran her fingers through the tangles and surveyed the results.

Her hair was naturally wavy, and it tumbled over her shoulders and down over her breasts in a riot of burgundy waves. Perfect for seduction. Her lipstick was gone now, but she knew that most men liked the fresh-from-the-shower look just as much as they liked a woman with a perfect makeup job, so she opted to leave herself bare.

She wandered back downstairs and through the house until she found a large living room with doors that led out to a veranda, where she could see lights on and Travis sitting at a wrought-iron patio table, sipping a glass of red wine.

When he heard her open the door, he looked over and smiled. "I thought you might like a medium red. It's from the family vineyard."

Jenna sat down across from him and looked out at the pool, a brilliant azure blue lit up in the night. "Thanks." She took a sip and let the vaguely fruity, spicy flavor settle on her tongue. "It's nice."

"What do you want to talk about?"

"This house—it just reminds me that you and I, we aren't exactly a likely pair for falling into bed together."

His smooth, strong forehead creased. "I'm not following you."

"I want you to understand that I have no interest in you for your money. Whatever happens between us this weekend—it's purely sexual. You've got needs, I've got needs, and I picked up a box of condoms at the gas station. This is all about sex, okay?"

"I didn't think you were gold digging, if that's what you're afraid of."

"Good. Because I'm not. When this weekend is over, we'll go our separate ways—at least as well as we can until Kathryn shows up again. Deal?"

He hesitated. "Deal."

"Good." Jenna downed the rest of her wine, then smiled at him as she placed the empty glass back on the table. "Have you ever gone skinny-dipping?"

"Does a hot tub count?"

"Yes, if it's outdoors."

"Hmm. I guess I'd still have to say no, then."

"Is there a hot tub here?"

He nodded toward the west side of the house. "In that gazebo over there. I took the cover off and turned it on in case you want to use it later."

Interesting. Very interesting.

The night air wasn't cold, but it wasn't quite warm enough to justify a dip in the pool. A hot tub sounded like the perfect skinny-dipping solution.

"Later? How about now?"

A smile played on Travis's lips. "I'm not finished with my wine."

"Bring it with you." Jenna grabbed the bottle from the table, along with her empty glass.

She started toward the gazebo without looking back. If he didn't have the sense to follow her, she had other ways of enticing him. When she reached the gazebo, she could hear the bubbling water. The inside of the hot tub was lit up, providing just enough light to illuminate the benches and walkway that encircled it.

Jenna found a small table beside the hot tub and placed the wine and glass on it, then withdrew the condoms she'd stuck in her pocket before leaving her bedroom and put those on the table, too.

She hadn't heard any footsteps yet, so she pulled her shirt over her head and tossed it aside onto a bench. Next came her sandals, then her jeans, tugged down over her hips as seductively as she could manage. She kept her back to Travis, but she knew without a doubt that he was enjoying a view of her rear end in white thong panties.

She reached behind her back and unsnapped her matching white lace bra, then tossed it on top of the growing pile of clothes. Last came her panties, which she took her time sliding down over her hips, down her thighs, taking care to bend over enough to give Travis a glimpse of pleasures to come.

As she stepped into the water, she looked over at him. He was standing up from the table, his glass of wine forgotten. She sank into the water, and he came toward her. She kept her gaze locked on him, suggesting with a little smile that she was enjoying the game as much as he was.

His own expression could be described as nothing short of hungry. He wanted her, and she'd offered him a dish he couldn't refuse. She settled back against the side of the tub, her breasts just under the water, her entire body below the surface enveloped in the water's delicious, bubbling heat.

Her nipples went rock hard when he began to unbutton his shirt, and her insides heated up to the boiling point. How she'd gotten herself into this situation with a gorgeous man she'd just met had to be a testament to the current level of stress in her life. Surely, after a weekend of sexual abandon, she'd come to her senses again.

"You've got a way with convincing people, don't you?"

"I've been called resourceful," she answered, intending to sound flip, but instead her voice was strained and a little uncertain.

He shrugged off his shirt and tossed it beside her own pile of clothes. When he removed his T-shirt to reveal a chest and abdomen so perfectly proportioned, so well sculpted Michelangelo could have taken credit for the work, Jenna's mouth went dry. She suddenly needed a drink of wine like she needed air to breathe. As he undid his belt buckle, she poured herself a glass.

When she looked back up, she saw that his navy-blue boxers did nothing to conceal an impressive erection, and as he rid himself of the rest of his clothing, she couldn't tear her gaze away again. In a matter of moments, he was gloriously naked, climbing into the hot, bubbling water.

Jenna's heart raced as she watched him. With his lean, muscular athlete's body and his penetrating eyes, Travis was far more than she'd bargained for. She felt as if it was her first time, and all her former bravado seemed to have drained away. She sat frozen, gripping the stem of her wineglass.

He settled in beside her and took the glass from her hands. "Is something wrong?"

Jenna forced a smile. "I wasn't expecting to be so attracted to you."

"Same here. You're a hell of a lot sexier than your sister."

He watched her as he took a sip of the wine, and his gaze had a warming effect. Jenna found her confidence again. Here she was, in a hot tub on a beautiful night, in a gorgeous setting, with the hottest guy she'd met in a long time. She would not waste this opportunity.

Instead, she got up onto her knees and straddled him, the damp skin of her torso growing cool in the night air. He started to set the glass aside, but she took it.

"There's more than one way to enjoy a good glass of wine," she whispered as she arched her back and poured the wine over her naked breasts.

He must have agreed with her, because he made no comment. Instead, he slid his hands around her waist and pulled her against him, taking her left breast into his mouth. She gasped as he sucked the sensitive flesh of one breast, then the other. He licked the wine from her chest, then her belly, and his hands moved down to cup her bottom.

The sensation of his fingertips, so close to ground zero, was almost more than she could take. She lifted his face from her belly and dipped her head down to give him a long, hungry kiss as a breeze picked up, but she couldn't be sure if the gooseflesh that appeared on her skin was from the night air or his touch.

When he tugged her hips down onto his lap, letting his erection strain against the sensitive flesh between her legs, Jenna couldn't resist grinding against him, rocking her hips to simulate what they really wanted. But he was oh-so-close to slipping inside her; it was too dangerous a game with a man she barely knew. She backed off and slid her hand down between them to grasp his erection.

He closed his eyes and let his head fall back as she massaged him in a slow, steady rhythm. All the while, his hands explored her, filling her with a building sense of urgency.

When she was sure she couldn't take another moment of waiting, he reached down and stilled her hand. "No fast finishes tonight," he said with a little half smile.

"Would you like some more wine?"

"There are other things I'd like more," he said as he trailed his fingertips lightly up her rib cage, along the underside of her breasts. "But wine would be nice, too."

Jenna reached for the bottle and offered him her breast as she began to pour. The wine trickled down over her flesh as he caught her nipple in his mouth along with the crimson liquid. When she'd emptied the bottle, she set it aside again and plunged her fingers into Travis's hair as he tasted every inch of flesh that had been touched by the wine.

He tugged her down against his erection again and said, "You're not trying to get me drunk and have your way with me, are you?"

"I thought it was pretty obvious."

"Getting me drunk is unnecessary," he said as he brushed a strand of hair out of her face.

"Does that mean I can have my way with you now?"

The rich, fermented scent of the wine rose up from her skin and from the hot tub. Jenna never would have considered the smell of wine one of her favorite scents until that moment.

"Only if I get to have my way with you, too."

She reached for a condom and tore open the package, then slipped the condom on Travis. When she positioned herself over him, with his head straining against her, she knew they were at the point of no return.

Consequences be damned, she was about to have sex with a man she should have been keeping a safe, wide distance from, and she was about to add yet one more item to the list of crazy stunts she'd pulled when the going got tough. But given the fact that she could already barely remember what had gotten her so stressed out in the first place, Jenna decided her strategy was a sound one.

She needed this, and so did Travis.

She shifted her hips, and he slid inside of her with one long, delicious thrust.

5

TRAVIS WATCHED the transformation on Jenna's face as he began to move inside her. Her eyes half-lidded, her lips parted as she emitted soft gasping sounds, she grew more lost in the motions of their bodies with each thrust. Gripping her hips, he let go of all his reservations and gave himself up to desire.

Sweet heaven, she felt too good to be real. She was his every adolescent and adult fantasy, all rolled into one irresistible package, here for his taking tonight and all weekend. Travis slid his hands up her torso, over her rib cage to her breasts, savoring the lush weight of them as he built momentum with each slow, deliberate thrust.

Unbelievable.

He wanted to take his time, to commit every sensation to memory, to be sure that when he went back to his boringly cautious life, he'd have this one wild weekend to recall, to remind himself that he was indeed alive.

The hot-tub water bubbled up around them, slapping against their skin as they rocked in unison, and Travis tweaked Jenna's erect nipples into even-tighter peaks until she leaned forward and offered one up to him. He took her into his mouth greedily, like a starving man, tasting and sucking each breast in turn until the lovemaking sounds she made nearly caused him to come too soon.

He pulled back and willed himself to regain control of his body. Then Jenna dipped her mouth to his and their moans mingled together as they made love with their tongues. After a few moments, she broke the kiss and whispered into his ear.

"You *do* like girls on top, don't you?"

"I like you on top, yeah."

"So I was right," she said, and he drove himself deeper inside her, hoping a little distraction would end the conversation.

"Hardly. I have lots of other favorite positions."

"Lots?"

Travis stilled himself. "Yeah, lots."

"Like what?"

"I could demonstrate."

"Absolutely," she said, sounding breathless. "We've got all weekend for demonstrations."

Reluctantly, he pulled out and grasped Jenna's hips, then lifted her onto the edge of the hot tub. "Is the air too cool?"

"Not as long as we keep heating it up, no."

"This is another one of my favorites," he said as he braced his knees on the steps of the hot tub and positioned himself between her legs.

A moment later, he was buried inside her again. She shifted her hips to better accommodate him and wrapped her legs around him. Leaning back on her hands, her breasts thrust up toward him, her head lolling back as she closed her eyes, she was a visual feast. Travis took in the sight of her and knew that he wouldn't last much longer, knew that he needed to have this fast and frenzied encounter, that he could then make the next one last long enough to be truly savored.

The spiral of tension coiling inside him, he pumped himself into her faster and faster. Caveman sounds erupted from his throat, sounds he could hardly recognize as his own. He'd turned from a respectable businessman into a sex-crazed animal, and he was driven by the single-minded goal of spilling himself into Jenna.

She was his sexual conquest, the catalyst for his transformation into a more primitive kind of man. He slid his hand down between them and caressed her clit with his thumb, until her quakes and gasps alerted him that she was as close as he was to release.

And then, when he could last no longer, he sent her over the edge. She clutched her legs tight around him and cried out as the orgasm coursed through her. The feel of her climax around him sent him over the edge, too. He grasped her hips tightly and succumbed to the final few thrusts as he spilled himself, giving over his very male essence to Jenna's power.

He heard himself cry out in one last caveman groan, and then they were kissing desperately, as if they'd only just found one another.

Jenna slid her hands around his neck and whispered, "That's one of my favorite positions, too."

"So you don't have one favorite, either?"

"That's for me to know and you to find out."

"Is that a challenge?"

"It's a promise."

"I'm beginning to like your promises."

Travis pulled her back into the water and onto his lap. The water bubbled up to their chests, and Jenna's still-erect nipples beckoned in a way that made conversation somewhat difficult. But with his heart still pounding from climax, his body still recovering, he needed a few minutes to rest.

"I think the wind is picking up. Maybe we should take this indoors," she said.

"I don't think I could get any more blown away than I already am."

"I'm mainly concerned about catching a cold."

"Good point. We can try out the heated pool tomorrow night, if you want."

"And tonight?"

"I've got another favorite I'd like to demonstrate."

"Oh yeah?" She smiled a wicked little smile.

"We just need to find a nice flat surface…."

"Like a bed?"

"Bed, table, floor, anything will do."

"Now you're talking like a man who knows how to relax."

He pulled her closer and placed a soft kiss on the side of her neck.

Some unnamed emotion swelled inside of him. Gratitude, he decided. That's what it had to be. He was thankful that Jenna had recognized a need in him, that she'd walked into his life at a time when he needed her most, that for one unforgettable weekend, she was his for the taking.

He couldn't even recognize himself tonight as Travis Roth. He was someone altogether different. A wild man. A man ruled by his appetites and able to toss aside propriety in favor of hot, frenzied sex.

Whatever he'd turned into, even if only for the weekend, it sure as hell felt good.

JENNA OPENED HER EYES and blinked at the bright sunlight pouring through the double doors. Odd that she was in a room that looked nothing like her own. She sat up and stretched, feeling more relaxed than she had in weeks.

The fog lifted from her brain, and she smiled at the erotic details that emerged from the night before. Travis, the wine, the hot tub, the staircase, the bed. She couldn't quite remember how they'd made it up here to the bedroom, but she had distinctly pleasant memories of what had happened once they'd gotten here.

She arose from the bed and found the bathroom, where she took a quick shower and tugged on a pair of old jeans and a stretchy little black tee, all the while wondering where Travis had disappeared without saying good morning.

Jenna wandered downstairs, led by the scent of coffee and something else—burned eggs, maybe. She found her way to the kitchen and was surprised to see Travis, dressed in a pair of well-worn khakis and a faded polo shirt, along with a crisp white cooking apron. He was frowning at a cookbook, with a plateful of unidentifiable squares sitting on the counter.

"I made breakfast, but something went wrong," he said, turning his frown from the book to the burned food.

"Is that…French toast?"

"Maybe I should have tried something simpler."

"Do you cook often?"

"Never."

Jenna repressed a smile, trying not to take the gesture for more than it was. She had to admire him for trying, anyway. "So they're a little crispy. That's okay." She went to the counter and picked up the plate of French toast, then carried it to the table, which had already been set.

"You really don't have to eat those. I had the maid stock the refrigerator before we arrived."

"You have a maid for your vacation house?"

"She only comes by once a week when no one's here, more often during our vacations."

Jenna tried to imagine how much work needed to be done weekly to a house that no one lived in, then decided it was too early in the morning to be thinking about it.

Travis retrieved butter and syrup from the kitchen and brought both to the breakfast table, then sat down and surveyed his work. He gave Jenna an apologetic shrug. "Maybe this will help disguise the burned flavor."

Not likely, but Jenna couldn't remember any man ever having made French toast for her before, so she wasn't about to complain. She simply flashed him a huge smile.

"What?"

"What did I do to deserve a homemade breakfast from a guy who never cooks?"

He poured himself a cup of coffee from the pot on the table. "Last night calls for something more than scorched French toast. I'll have to make it up to you with lunch."

Last night. Memories flooded her mind, and Jenna felt herself growing warm in the cool, air-conditioned kitchen. Yes, last night had been unforgettable.

"You're going to cook again?"

"Maybe not *cook*. But I'm sure I could assemble a nice picnic lunch. There's a gorgeous path through the vineyards. I thought you might want to take a hike."

Jenna forked two slices of toast onto her plate, slathered each one with butter and drenched them in syrup, then took a bite. Not bad, except for the overpowering taste. "See, these taste fine."

"I appreciate the flattery, but it's not necessary." She watched as Travis took a tentative bite of his breakfast, grimaced and swallowed it with some effort. "You really don't have to eat this."

Jenna took another bite, ignoring the charred flavor. Living on a tight budget in such an expensive city, she'd learned to pretend that even crappy food was a treat, and she never let a meal go to waste.

"So why don't you start catching me up on the details of my sister's life?"

"Oh, right. I'd almost forgotten that's why we're here."

Jenna, too, had almost forgotten why she'd run away from San Francisco. The thought of her ransacked apartment, her stolen computer and files, the threatening note scrawled on her bathroom mirror—it was all too much. She didn't want her weekend ruined by harsh reality.

"What's wrong?" Travis asked when he saw the change in her expression.

"I was just thinking about real life. Stuff I'd rather forget right now."

"The person trying to keep you from writing that story?"

Jenna made an overzealous cut into a piece of French toast. "Let's talk about Kathryn. Fill me in."

"Okay, but you can't avoid this topic forever. I want to make sure you're not in any immediate danger."

Having someone suddenly looking out for her

safety felt good—amazingly good. It took all her willpower not to gaze at him like an adoring puppy.

Travis picked up a file folder she hadn't noticed before, lying on the other side of the table. "I took the liberty of making notes for you to study, based on what Kathryn said you'd need to know."

"Oh. Um, great." Her sister must have gotten quite a laugh out of Jenna having to study for this task as if it were an important school exam.

"We'll go over some of the highlights orally, though. For instance, you'll need to know that Kathryn quit her job at a local art gallery a few weeks ago. She wanted to leave in time for final wedding preparations."

"Couldn't she have just taken a vacation?"

"She'll be devoting her time to the women and children's shelter after the wedding."

Of course. Jenna should have guessed—abused women had always been Kathryn's pet cause, and while Jenna used to suspect it was just a pageant gimmick, she now saw that her sister's interest was quite possibly genuine. If so, it was one of her few redeeming qualities. "Is that what you'll want your wife to do, too? Devote her time to charity work?"

His eyes sparked with amusement, and he produced a charming half smile the likes of which she'd never seen before. This was a glimpse of Travis when he wasn't being a type-A personality. "I don't have even the remote prospect of a wife. Why do you ask?"

"Curiosity."

"I've never given it much thought. I wouldn't expect my wife to do anything she didn't want to do."

"Good answer."

"Kathryn is also working with a personal trainer right now. I mention this because she's been pretty obsessed with it recently, working out for two hours a day to get ready for the wedding."

"Does she plan to sprint down the aisle and wrestle your brother at the altar?"

He smiled fully then, and it was a warm, brilliant expression that lit up the room. Jenna found herself staring at his mouth, aching for a replay of last night.

"I hope not. I believe she wants to look good in her wedding dress—and on the honeymoon."

Kathryn had never had a problem staying thin, but Jenna could certainly see her sister freaking out about a five-pound weight gain and going to extreme measures to correct it.

"So does that mean I'll have to do these grueling two-hour workouts? Won't her trainer notice my sudden lack of muscle tone?"

"I'm sure you can get out of the workouts, for the most part. But I have to warn you, I've heard her personal trainer is a bit of a fanatic."

"Where does Kathryn live now?"

"She had been renting an apartment in town, but last month she moved into the house she and Blake just bought."

"What? Won't your brother have his own key and be stopping by whenever he wants?"

Travis grimaced. "It's not an ideal situation, but if you've made it clear you don't want any physical contact right before the wedding, that will deter him, I hope."

"There's no way we can pull this off."

"We can, and we will. Kathryn said you switched places all the time as kids."

"Playing fool-the-teacher isn't quite the same as impersonating someone's fiancée."

"True."

"Your brother's going to know something's up."

"He might think Kathryn is behaving strangely, but you can explain it away as prewedding jitters. And I'll help you avoid him as much as possible."

Jenna took a deep breath and reminded herself of the money. She *could* do this, right?

Right.

"What about the rest of the family? You really think they'll buy the act?"

"Absolutely. They don't even know Kathryn has a twin," he offered, seeming to realize a moment too late that Jenna might not be impressed by that fact.

"Don't worry, I'd be shocked if she went around voluntarily telling people about her low-class twin sister."

Travis opened his mouth to protest, but Jenna stopped him.

"I don't have any illusions about my relationship with Kathryn, and frankly, I don't care."

"It seems like a shame to have a twin and not have a relationship with her."

Jenna shrugged. Maybe she had missed out a little, but she'd also saved herself plenty of headaches by not pursuing a relationship with her sister. "You must have a pretty close-knit family."

He smiled. "I've never really thought about it, but yeah, we stick together. How about the rest of your family? Kathryn doesn't talk about them much."

"We're bourgeois middle class—that's why she stays quiet. But no, there aren't any strong ties between us."

"I've met your parents at least once. They seemed like nice people."

"You met my mother and her latest husband. Our father skipped out when we were ten and hasn't been heard from since, and Mom's on her third husband now," she said, then took a drink of orange juice that tasted as if it had been fresh squeezed.

Glancing over at the kitchen counter, she spotted the pile of discarded orange halves. He'd *squeezed orange juice* for her? She repressed a satisfied smile.

"Do you like your stepfather?"

"We get along fine, but he's always been kind of oblivious to me. He makes my mom happy, though, so I don't have anything against him. It's my mother who drives me crazy. She doesn't approve of my lifestyle."

Travis's gaze darkened. "What lifestyle?"

"Don't worry. I'm not a lesbian dominatrix or anything. She just thinks my living alone in San Francisco and working as a freelance writer is a recipe for disaster."

It didn't escape her attention that her mother had been at least partly right. Her life *had* recently turned into a disaster, after all.

"Is this what you want most to do with your life?"

"Yes. I love writing, and I love being a journalist without the constraints of only writing for one publication."

"Then she should be happy for you. Not many people ever follow their dreams." He poked at his French toast with a fork, but didn't take a bite.

"How about you? Are you following your dreams?"

He shrugged. "I've always known I'd become a part of the family business."

"Spoken like a man with thwarted dreams."

"To be honest, I never gave much thought to whether or not it was what I wanted to do. I just did it because it was expected."

"Don't you think you should? Give it some thought, I mean?"

He let his gaze roam down to her chest and back up again, a slow grin forming on his lips. "We're supposed to be going over the details of Kathryn's life."

"How about I look over the file today, and you quiz me later?"

"Sounds fair. I'm having trouble keeping my mind on Kathryn anyway."

"Oh? Where exactly is your mind wandering?" Jenna flashed him her most scandalous look. She knew he'd enjoyed himself last night. It was the best sex she'd ever had, and she'd have been willing to bet he would say the same.

But still, great sex didn't mean much in the long run. It didn't equal mutual respect, love, commitment or any of the other things relationships were built on. There was no reason to think of her weekend with Travis as more than an extremely odd business arrangement.

Travis was looking at her as if he could read her mind. "Last night was amazing."

She smiled. "I told you sex was the great stress reliever."

"It wasn't just that. There's a strong chemistry between us."

Was there ever. "Animal lust. It's what drives the natural world."

"I wouldn't say that."

"Let's don't overanalyze it, okay?"

He shrugged. "You've got a way with a wine bottle."

"And you've got a way with your hands." And his mouth, and his hips, and his...

Jenna stood up from the table, too, eyeing the swimming pool outside. What she needed right now was a cold swim, a cold shower—anything to cool off the warming sensation that started in her belly and grew to a throbbing heat between her legs. No way would she be able to memorize all the details of Kathryn's life if all she could think about was making love to Travis Roth.

6

TRAVIS PEERED OUT the window at Jenna. She was standing at the edge of the pool, dipping one toe in to test the water temperature. And she appeared to be about to take a swim in her bra and panties. He'd forgotten to mention to her that she might need a swimsuit on the trip.

He gripped the window frame, all too aware of how badly he wanted to race outside at that moment and make love to her right there beside the pool. And why couldn't he? What was stopping him? She'd be game for a little more stress relief, as she liked to call it.

But something just didn't feel right about the way she wrote off their attraction as mere animal lust. He didn't want to think of it that way. However, if that's what it took for her to justify a weekend fling to herself, then so be it. He could understand the need to keep an emotional distance, and if he weren't such a fool, he'd do the same.

Travis found an old pair of his swim trunks in the chest of drawers and undressed, then put them on. By the time he made it out to the pool, Jenna was swimming laps in the water, her long red hair slicked back as it had been last night in the shower.

She stopped swimming when she saw him. Holding herself up on the concrete edge, she smiled at him. "Come on in. The water's arctic cold."

"I forgot to tell the maid to turn on the water heater. I just switched it on, but it'll take a while for the pool to heat up."

"That's okay. I needed a cold dip." She pushed herself up and sat on the tile edge of the pool with her legs dangling in.

Travis couldn't help but stare at the way the skimpy fabric of her bra and panties revealed the treasures beneath. They were both black, but he could see the outline of her erect nipples, and other equally tantalizing details. Her skin had a natural warm peach tone that seemed to glow in the sunlight, and as he watched rivulets of water trail down her belly, he felt his groin stir.

"I didn't bring a swimsuit."

"Do you hear me complaining?" He smiled, then dived into the pool and swam a quick lap back and forth before coming up for air.

The brisk water took care of his budding erection but did nothing for the desire coursing through his veins. When he stopped swimming and looked at Jenna, it was like finding Lorelei perched at the edge of the pool, singing her siren song and luring him toward a deadly crash into the rocks of the Rhine River. He swam over to her and pushed himself up to sit beside her.

"I have to admit, seeing you like that is putting ideas in my head."

"What sort of ideas?"

"Bad, bad ideas."

She licked her lower lip and looked at his mouth. "My favorite kind."

"But we agreed that our stress-relief activities would be limited to after hours."

The rise and fall of her chest as she breathed was almost enough enticement to make him reach out and cup her breast in his hand. Instead, he balled his fingers into a fist.

She was still staring at his mouth. "Seems like a silly rule to me."

"So I wouldn't be making a breach of ethics by kissing you right now?"

"I'll make it easy for you," she murmured as she leaned forward and tilted her head, placing a long, soft kiss on his lips.

Travis grasped her by the torso and tugged her onto his lap, then slid his hands down to the cool, damp flesh of her bottom as she pressed herself against his erection. So much for restraint.

He was just thinking of ridding Jenna of her wet bra when a strange voice interrupted their kiss.

"Yoo-hoo! Mr. Roth, are you here?" called the voice from inside the house.

It took an agonizing moment for him to recognize that it was Ramona, the maid. Before he could remove Jenna from his lap, he heard a gasp from the veranda.

"Mr. Roth? I'm sorry, I—I didn't realize—" She was backing herself into the house again when she seemed to recognize Jenna. "Miss...*Calvert?* You changed your hair—"

There was an awkward silence as Ramona looked back and forth from Travis to Jenna. A wiry middle-aged woman who bore an odd resemblance to the Chihuahua she often brought along with her and left tied to the front of the house while she worked, the maid let her jaw sag as her expression grew more and more distressed. "Oh my! I'm very sorry to interrupt!"

Travis looked at Jenna, realizing a moment too late that Ramona thought she'd just interrupted an affair between himself and his brother's fiancée. With her eyes wide, Jenna scrambled up from his lap, and Travis went after Ramona, who'd disappeared into the house.

"Ramona? Ramona! Please wait." He found her in the foyer, about to leave. "I'd like to explain what you just saw."

"Really, Mr. Roth, there's no need. You have my word I'll never speak of this again."

He stopped himself. What would be worse? Having word leak out that he and Kathryn were having an affair, or having any news leak out that might compromise his plan to keep Blake's wedding afloat? Ramona had no reason to tell anyone about the "affair" and risk losing her job, so as much as he hated to have her think of him as a scumbag—even temporarily—he decided that was the safest option.

"I appreciate your being discreet," he forced himself to say. "Was there some reason you stopped by?"

"I just wanted to see if you needed anything— I was in a bit of a hurry when I was here yesterday."

"You did a great job, and thank you for stopping by again. We'll be fine."

She nodded, avoiding his gaze as she left. Travis stared down the hallway at the damp footprints he'd left on the way in, and as his swim trunks dripped, he ran one hand through his wet hair.

That encounter had only been a taste of awkward—and potentially disastrous—moments to come if he and Jenna continued their fooling around. As much as he hated the thought of not touching her, of not making love to her again, he had to consider that maybe that was the safest option. The most sensible one.

Travis found a couple of towels in the kitchen and used them to clean up the water from the floor, then tossed them in the laundry room before going back out to the pool.

He found Jenna stretched out in a chaise lounge, sunning herself. When she heard his footsteps, she lifted one arm to shade her eyes from the sun and looked at him. "She thought I was my sister?"

"And that we're having a torrid affair."

"But you set her straight, right?"

Travis sat down on the chaise lounge next to hers, making an effort not to let his gaze roam over her lush body. "No, I let her believe we're having an affair. I didn't see any point in explaining why I have you here."

Jenna pushed herself up in her chair and glared at him. "How could you?"

"It seemed like the safest option."

She stared at him for a few moments, then leaned back in her chair again and sighed. "This is so weird."

"It's only going to get weirder. I think we need to reconsider our deal."

"You want to back out?"

"Hell no, but will we really be able to pull off this charade if we can't keep our hands to ourselves?"

A breeze picked up from the west, and Jenna hugged herself. "I hadn't thought about it that way."

"Neither had I until Ramona caught us. I think we'll have to be careful how we behave toward each other, or else someone's going to notice our attraction."

"I guess you're right. So what do we do?"

He tried to force the words from his mouth, but they didn't want to come. *Stop having sex* was what he intended to say. Was what he should have said.

But he made the fatal mistake of letting his gaze drift down to Jenna's cleavage, accentuated by her crossed arms, and memories of licking red wine from those lush breasts came to him then.

What had happened to his newfound sense of daring? Where had the risk-taking Travis gone? He'd run for cover just as soon as things got dicey.

That was going to change.

All the problems waiting for him in Carmel—his brother's missing fiancée, his rocky investment firm, his constant family obligations—they could continue to wait until Monday. He *needed* this weekend alone with the sexiest woman he'd ever met, and he wasn't going to waste the entire time drilling Jenna on her sister's favorite foods or best friends' names.

No, he was going to accept the risk, because the immediate payoff was damn well worth it.

He smiled then, willing the tension to drain from his shoulders. "How about we just cross that bridge when we come to it? I'm sure we can handle ourselves like mature adults."

Jenna looked at him curiously. "Why the sudden change of heart?"

"I won't deny that you lying there wet in your underwear has a little to do with it."

She let her gaze travel over him, lingering at his waist, then at his thighs. When she met his eyes again, she said, "I think we've still got some tension to work out of you, anyway."

Did they ever.

"Do you feel up to that hike through the vineyards now?"

"I didn't bring any shoes that would be good for much more than a brisk walk."

"That's okay. It's not a hard trail, and if you get tired, I'll carry you."

She smiled. "Well, if you're offering to carry me... Before we go, I was wondering if you have a computer with an Internet connection here at the house."

"Can't stand to spend a full day disconnected from the world?"

"Actually, I just want to e-mail my editor to let her know what's happened with the story and why I'm taking a break from it."

"There's a DSL connection upstairs in the study, and you're welcome to use it. You still intend to write the story?"

"Yes, I do. I've decided I can't let anyone scare me away from it."

"Good. The police will catch the person who broke into your apartment, I'm sure."

"Whether they do or not, I'm writing the story. There must be even more than I've discovered if someone is trying to stop me."

A wave of protectiveness rose up in Travis's chest. He admired Jenna's determination to uncover the truth, but the possible danger to her had him worried.

"I hope you'll be careful."

"You sound like my mother."

Great. He'd managed to convey just the wrong image again. Travis watched her in silence, pondering his avoidance of risk taking. He had a thing or two to learn from this wild vixen who didn't seem to know the meaning of the word *risk*. Not for the first time, he wondered if it would really be possible for Jenna to masquerade as her much tamer sister for two entire weeks.

"Why don't you go get dressed and send your e-mail while I throw some lunch in a backpack for the hike?" He stood and offered a hand to Jenna.

She let him pull her up from the chair, and the contact of her hand in his was enough for his pulse to race. He willed his gaze away from her body as she walked into the house, and only when he was sure she'd reached the staircase did he make his way to the kitchen.

Explosive was the only way to describe the chemistry between them. He hadn't imagined what he'd be getting himself into when he agreed to Jenna's side of their deal. And for the next two nights, he refused to let caution get in the way, even if it meant getting burned.

JENNA STARED at the message on her e-mail account. The subject line read, "Want Your Files Back?" and the sender had used an address she didn't recognize. Her heart raced as she debated whether or not to open the message and possibly ruin what little bit of relaxation she'd been able to achieve since last night. Curiosity won out finally, and she double clicked on the message.

Don't think you can hide. The only way out is to drop the beauty-pageant story. I'll do whatever it takes to stop you. Oh, and you want your files back? Too damn bad.

Jenna reread the words, her stomach clenched

into a ball. Had this person been watching her when she'd left with Travis? Was it possible that they'd been followed all the way here to Napa County?

No, she was just being paranoid. But why was the beauty-pageant story dangerous enough to elicit death threats?

She closed the message and sat back in the plush leather office chair, her heart racing nearly as fast as her thoughts. Until now, her career hazards had included an occasional paper cut, possible carpal tunnel syndrome and bad eyesight from staring at a computer screen. Now she faced the possibility of death if she wrote a story she truly believed needed to be told.

Anger rose up in her chest and won out over fear. To hell with whoever had sent that message. She would not let cowardly threats stop her. She might be lying low for a couple of weeks, but that didn't mean she couldn't start reconstructing her research when she had the time, and it didn't mean she wouldn't dive back into the story head-first as soon as her obligation to Travis ended.

She opened a blank message and began typing a note to her editor, explaining why she'd been forced to leave town for a few weeks. With assurances that she had every intention of recovering her research and continuing to pursue the story, she finished the e-mail and hit the send button. That left her staring at the threatening message again.

She went to her bedroom and opened her backpack, dug around in it until she found the business card of the detective who was on her case and went back to the office to call him.

After a few rings, a familiar voice answered. "Detective McNeely."

"This is Jenna Calvert from the apartment break-in yesterday. I just got an e-mail message from my stalker."

"Did it give any new information?" His voice had perked up.

"Just confirmed that the beauty-pageant story is the one he doesn't want me to write."

"You've got my e-mail address on my card, right?"

"Yes."

"Forward the message to me. I'll see if we can track down a source. Probably not, with all the ways there are to set up an anonymous account, but it's worth a try. We might get lucky and find out we're dealing with a dumb criminal. We did find some unidentified prints in your apartment, but no matches in our database yet."

"Okay, great. I'm staying in Napa with a friend for the weekend, and then I'll be going with him to Carmel for two weeks."

"What's the best way to get in touch with you if anything turns up?"

"I've got my cell phone with me, but I keep it turned off. You can leave a message on my voice mail."

After she'd hung up with the detective, Jenna

swung around in the desk chair to find Travis standing in the doorway.

"Sorry, didn't mean to eavesdrop. I was just coming to tell you we can take off whenever you're ready."

"That was the police detective who's investigating my case."

"Did something come up?"

"Sort of. Take a look at this." She nodded at the computer and reopened the message for Travis to read.

He came into the office and leaned over her chair to see the monitor. When he'd finished reading, his expression grew dark, and he looked at Jenna.

"It sounds like this guy was watching you."

Jenna clicked the forward button and typed in the detective's e-mail address. When she'd sent the message to him, she turned back to Travis. "Maybe, or maybe the 'you can't hide' comment is just a coincidence. I'm not going to attach too much significance to it. This scumbag could be watching my apartment this weekend, noticing that I'm not coming or going from it, but that doesn't mean he knows where I am."

"We're talking about your safety. I think that's significant."

"Let's just forget about this for now, okay? I don't want it to ruin the weekend."

"We can't be certain you're safe here. If this person was watching you, that means he could have followed us here."

The sick knot in her stomach grew. This was supposed to be her temporary sanctuary, her escape from all the crap that had happened in the city—and now she had to contemplate the possibility that someone could have followed her here?

"Jenna?"

She shook herself out of a daze and blinked at Travis. "So now what?"

"I'll have a private investigator come check things out, maybe keep an eye on the place and let us know if he spots anything odd."

Jenna would be willing to bet he didn't have anyone of the Bodyguards For Less caliber in mind.

"That's a little drastic, don't you think?"

"It's nothing, and I'll feel much better knowing someone has an eye on things."

"So make the call, and then let's put this out of our heads."

Travis frowned. "I'm not going to be able to relax until I know you're safe. Maybe we shouldn't plan to leave the house until someone has come to check out the property."

She could think of worse things than being stuck inside a palatial Napa Valley estate with a gorgeous male, but she wasn't going to let irrational fear change the course of her weekend. This was her stress-relief time, and she'd done enough cowering behind locked doors already thanks to the jerk who was stalking her.

"I'm not going to sit around feeling vulnerable. I've done enough of that."

He sighed. "Is this another challenge?"

"Yeah." She smiled. "Minimum risk, maximum reward. How can you say no?"

"When you put it that way…" He flashed a smile that could melt panties. "Why don't I give my private investigator friend a call and then we can take off?"

"Now you're talking."

Jenna's thoughts immediately turned to the night before. She'd expected Travis to be a little cautious as a lover, maybe need some coaxing, but he'd caught her off guard with his enthusiasm. She felt as if she'd unleashed his inner wild man, and she couldn't wait to see what further risky business they'd find together.

She leaned back in the office chair, erotic images crowding her head, the last vestige of her stress melting away.

TRAVIS DROPPED the backpack in the shade of the tree and turned to look out over the vineyards below. They'd chosen the perfect spot to stop for lunch. Jenna stood nearby, admiring the view, as well. For the beginning of July, the weather was pleasantly mild, and they'd managed to hike several miles barely breaking a sweat. Along the way, Travis had quizzed Jenna about Kathryn's life, since she'd had a chance to look through the file on her sister before they left the house.

Now he wanted to get a taste of how well Jenna could play Kathryn.

"Okay, so now you're Kathryn and someone you don't recognize starts talking to you like you're the best of friends. What do you do?"

"Play along?"

"But how?"

"I know how to act. Sort of."

She wasn't exactly inspiring his confidence with her shaky tone of voice.

"Let's do a little mock scenario. I'll play the acquaintance, and you convince me that you're Kathryn."

"Is this really necessary?"

"You've got to do something to earn your pay this weekend." He produced a mischievous smile, and Jenna tossed him an annoyed look.

"Okay, so… I'm Kathryn. Now what?"

"Now, you act." He did his best impression of one of Kathryn's well-bred and utterly boring friends. "Kathryn, darling, you look fabulous this evening."

He watched Jenna fight off laughter at his bad female voice. Then, with a little tilt of her head, a modest half smile and a well-timed flush to her cheeks—a sort of coyness he'd never seen Jenna display—she transformed herself into her sister. "Why, thank you. You look absolutely stunning yourself," she said in Kathryn's trademark carefully enunciated tone.

"Did you see Lily Carlyle's new diamond? I heard it's a full two carats."

He watched as Jenna tried not to roll her eyes.

And then she was right back into character. "How lovely for her."

Good, noncommittal reply, and it sounded exactly like what Kathryn might say.

"And where's *your* diamond, Kathryn, dear? Too big to lug around on your finger?"

Jenna produced another coy smile. "I'm afraid I've overdone the working out a bit. My engagement ring got too big, so I'm having it resized."

Travis couldn't help being impressed. "Wow, that was good."

"She *is* my twin sister. For better or worse, I know how Kathryn thinks."

"This really is going to work," he said, feeling more hopeful than he had all weekend.

"You think so?"

"I've had my doubts, but as long as we can get you up to date on Kathryn's life, we'll pull it off."

Jenna stared out at the perfectly spaced rows of the vineyards, a slow smile spreading across her lush lips. "And if it doesn't work, do I still get paid?"

"Of course," he said, feeling a ridiculous stab of annoyance that she was most concerned about the money.

He was the one who'd offered the payment, so why should he be surprised that she wanted it? Clearly, he'd lost sight of what their arrangement was about, and it wasn't going to do him any good to lose sight again. Theirs was a business arrangement—unethical as it might be—and nothing more.

After having a lunch of wine and French bread

slathered with Brie under the shade tree, they continued their hike, managing to wander away from the trail Travis knew, until they came to a rock wall that Jenna insisted scaling, certain it would provide a shortcut back toward the house.

Foolishly, Travis had agreed, in spite of the fact that he had no idea how to rock climb, and he now had the bumps, bruises and sore muscles to show for it. He'd been so intent on proving to Jenna that he could take a risk, he'd lost his last shred of common sense somewhere about halfway up the cliff.

Back in the comfort of his bedroom, Travis closed his eyes and buried his face in the pillow, savoring the feel of Jenna's hands working the muscles of his back. "This isn't necessary, you know."

"Want me to stop?" she said.

"Hell no."

"I guess you weren't kidding when you said you didn't do a lot of rock climbing."

Travis winced when she hit a tight muscle. "I've *never* rock climbed before."

She began giggling uncontrollably and collapsed on his back.

"What's so funny?"

"That makes two of us," she said between bursts of laughter.

"You lied to me," he said in a tone of mock horror. After all, he couldn't very well be angry about a little deception when he'd let her believe he was familiar with the sport.

"I never actually said I'd done it before. I just

said I knew *how* to do it. As in, I've watched it on TV a few times."

Travis succumbed to a fit of laughter, too, then, as he pictured himself following Jenna's "expert" instructions on the side of the cliff and nearly getting himself killed. "Next time you decide to fake expertise at something, could you pick a subject that doesn't involve risking life and limb?"

"Hey, you had fun, didn't you?"

He would have had fun sitting and watching the clouds pass by with Jenna, but yeah, he'd had more fun today outside of bed than he could remember having in a long, long time.

"I had a pretty good time," he said, careful not to show too much of how he felt.

He wasn't sure why he thought he needed to be guarded around her, but he knew for a fact it wouldn't be wise to let emotion come into play with her now. Not when she was about to impersonate his soon-to-be sister-in-law for two weeks. And Jenna herself had made it clear that what she wanted from him was a purely sexual relationship, nothing more.

She sat up again and continued his massage, managing to go straight to his sorest spot. If he could stay in this bed forever with this woman, he wasn't sure he'd ever want to leave.

And yet they had to leave Monday morning. The thought ruined his good mood and brought harsh reality crashing back in on an otherwise perfect day.

"Is it my turn yet?"

Travis rolled over, simultaneously flipping Jenna onto her back. He pinned her to the bed and smiled a lazy smile. "Your turn for what?"

"A massage. You've gotten a full twenty minutes' worth."

"You timed it?"

"Only so I could make sure you don't cheat me when it's my turn."

"I never said I'd give you one, did I?"

She narrowed her eyes at him. "You can't breach massage etiquette!"

"Massage etiquette? Is there really such a thing?" He settled himself between her legs, ready for a good, long stay there. She parted her thighs in response and wrapped her legs around his. As exhausted as he was, he still felt himself stir.

"In my book there is."

"But that's probably the same book that tells you it's okay to lure unsuspecting men onto the sides of cliffs."

"It's my book. I get to decide what's in it."

Travis slid his hands under her shirt and found her erect nipples through the lace of her bra. "There's more than one way to give a massage, you know."

Jenna's breath caught in her throat as he squeezed her sensitive flesh. "I'm open to experimentation," she whispered.

"Good, because this massage will require you to take your clothes off."

She smiled. "Clothes only get in the way of a good massage anyway."

He tried to put out of his mind the fact that this was one of their few nights together—that tomorrow would be the last night. No need to ruin a good thing, but a pang shot through him nonetheless. He never wanted this weekend to end. And he wanted to capture the way Jenna made him feel and bottle it.

He removed his body from hers long enough to get her undressed, and once he'd rid her of her bra and panties, he settled back in to savor her.

"I hope you don't mind if I stretch the definition of massage a bit," he said.

Jenna tugged at his shirt. "I'm open to that, but I personally think the masseur should also be unhindered by clothing."

"I agree completely, but not quite yet." If he didn't have a barrier of clothing, he knew damn well that a slow and deliberate exploration of Jenna's body would be out of the question.

She trailed her fingertips across his buttocks and kissed him softly, making him forget for a moment why he wanted to hold out for a while.

"No fair trying to move things along at your pace."

"Oh, is that what I was doing?" she whispered, then traced his lips with her tongue.

"You're a shameless vixen, you know that?"

She smiled, and Travis knew he was in trouble. "Take off your clothes, and I'll show you exactly how shameless I can be."

Trouble, he decided, had never felt so good.

7

After spending a lazy Sunday exploring the Napa Valley countryside on bicycles Travis had found in the Roths' garage, then spending an even lazier evening making love and talking for hours, Jenna should have felt more relaxed than she had in years.

Instead, she was terrified.

It was Monday morning, and she sat frozen in the chair at the upscale San Francisco salon—a place Kathryn had recommended Travis bring her for "the transformation"—marveling at the odd sensation of her head feeling lighter. Not only that, but there was a breeze on her neck. She was afraid to look in the mirror.

She and Travis had left Napa Valley earlier that morning to head toward Carmel, but they'd stopped back in the city to visit the salon and do some shopping to complete her makeover. She'd already been treated to a manicure, pedicure and facial, and now that her hair had been restored to its natural blonde by a colorist, all she had to do was look in the mirror to see the haircut that would make the metamorphosis complete.

"What do you think of the fabulous new you?" The stylist, a man named Javier who had a buzz cut and wore all black, spun Jenna around in the chair and smiled triumphantly.

Jenna looked into the mirror and saw her sister. It wasn't Kathryn, though. She was looking at a reflection of herself, but gone was her long auburn hair and her makeup-free face. She blinked at the new image of herself and fought the nausea rising up in her stomach.

Her pale blond hair lay in thick, elegantly coiffed chunks around her face and jaw, and then there was nothing. No long, wild tresses draping her shoulders, because those tresses had fallen to the floor and had been efficiently swept up by a salon assistant. Makeup had transformed her into a polished china doll, a transformation Kathryn probably got up an hour early to make every day.

She was an identical twin again, all her uniqueness wiped away with a few hours at the salon. The nausea grew.

She just needed to focus on the money. She was doing it for the money. Twenty-five grand was enough to eliminate her constant feelings of financial insecurity. Her hair would grow back out. The makeup could be washed off.

This was no big deal.

Really, it wasn't.

Then why did she still feel like losing her breakfast?

"Well?" Javier was beginning to look nervous.

"It looks...great."

She heard footsteps and saw in the mirror that Travis had come back from making his business phone calls and was walking toward her, staring at her as if he were looking at a ghost. When he reached the side of her chair, he stopped and smiled at Javier.

"Could you excuse us for a minute, please?"

"Of course." The stylist disappeared, and Travis turned back to Jenna.

He stared for another moment in silence. "Amazing. You look exactly like her."

Jenna held up the photo of Kathryn with her latest haircut up next to her face. "He got the haircut right?"

"It's perfect. I'm sorry you had to have your hair cut off."

She shrugged. "It'll grow."

"I'm going to miss it."

Jenna stood up from the chair and removed the black smock she'd been given by the stylist. Her chest tightened inexplicably at Travis's comment.

"I'm sure this will just make our transition easier. No worries about keeping your hands off of a woman who looks identical to your brother's fiancée, right?"

"Except I know you're not her."

Jenna looked into the mirror again, turning her head left and right, marveling at the makeup job that reminded her all too much of her beauty-pageant days. "I might as well be."

"Why don't we get out of here? I've already paid, and I just saw a boutique down the street that looks like a place where Kathryn would shop."

A change of clothes would be the final step. She'd be able to waltz right into her sister's life and no one would be the wiser. But the closer she came to that moment, the more her mind and body rebelled at the idea.

"Maybe we should have lunch first. I'm getting hungry."

"Are you having second thoughts?"

"I've been having second thoughts since the moment I met you. Best not to linger on them, okay?"

Travis frowned but said nothing as he led the way out of the salon and into the bright sunshine. They walked side by side along the sidewalk of the upscale business district full of stores where only people with money to waste would shop. Jewelry shops, boutiques, cafés filled with uniformly well-dressed people...

They rounded a corner and Jenna spotted a women's clothing boutique on the left, an upscale designer shop whose name brought to mind Beverley Hills and Hollywood starlets. Jenna had never even bothered to set foot in one, and to know her sister shopped there regularly brought home just how far her path had diverged from Kathryn's.

Travis held the door for her, and she stepped into the artificially cool air, her sandal landing with a click on pristine white tile. A saleswoman who was nearly as tall as Travis hovered nearby. She looked as if she hadn't eaten more than a salad in weeks, and a shiny curtain of dark hair hung on her gaunt shoulders. Her name tag announced that her name was Allegra.

She produced something that Jenna guessed was supposed to be a smile and asked, "May I help you?"

"We're looking for a few things for the lady," Travis said.

Jenna wandered over to a rack of dresses, feeling a bit too much like Julia Roberts's character in *Pretty Woman*, and began scanning them for something Kathryn might choose.

"Of course. Any special occasion in mind?"

"No, just casual wear," Jenna said without giving the matter much thought. No way did she plan on squeezing herself into any of the stiff-necked wool suits Kathryn favored.

"I can set up a dressing room if you see anything you'd like to try on," she said, and Jenna nodded.

Ten minutes later they'd picked out some Kathrynesque pieces and were following Allegra to a dressing room equipped with a starkly modern bench seat, a matching clothes tree and walls of mirrors.

"If you need any assistance, just call for me," the saleswoman said before closing the door, leaving Jenna and Travis alone.

Jenna started to remove her shirt, but stopped.

"Don't you think this is an odd way to begin our hands-off pact?"

Travis repressed a smile. "Oh, right. Guess I forgot. I'll wait outside."

He made a move toward the door, and Jenna tugged her shirt the rest of the way off, then unsnapped her bra and let it fall to the floor. "Unless you want to postpone the pact by a few hours."

Travis's gaze dropped to her bare breasts and moved slowly back up to meet her eyes. "You love to play the temptress, don't you?"

"You're such an easy target, I can't resist."

"I should feel insulted," he said with a little smirk.

"But you don't." She slipped off her sandals, then unfastened her pants and slid them down her hips. A moment later, she stood before him in nothing but her black lace G-string. "Maybe you're a little freaked out that I look so much like Kathryn now."

"Honey, in those panties, you look nothing like your sister." He crossed the room and placed his hands on her waist, then pulled her to him.

"I don't?"

"It doesn't matter how your hair is cut or how much makeup you wear. What makes you Jenna is inside, and a few outward changes don't alter who you are one bit."

Her insides warmed up.

"Ever done it in a dressing room?"

He flashed a devilish smile. "Depends on what you mean by 'it.'"

"This could be your chance. One last time, before I take over Kathryn's life?"

He dipped his head down and covered her mouth with his. Jenna pulled out his shirttail and slid her hands up the hot flesh of his back as he thrust his tongue into her mouth, responding to her with a hunger she hadn't expected. Smooth, always-in-control Travis, she suspected, loved to lose control with her.

She pulled back and nipped at his lip with her teeth, then traced his lips with the tip of her tongue. His erection strained against her lower belly, and Jenna wondered how much time they'd have before Allegra came tapping on the door.

"All these mirrors could be fun," she whispered.

Travis pulled her over to the bench, and she unfastened his pants and took him out. He was hot and ready in her palm, and Jenna felt the urge to take him into her mouth, let him watch in the mirrors as she did it. She pulled him down onto the bench and then knelt between his legs.

When he tried to pull her up, she stayed her ground and dipped her head down, ran her tongue along the length of his erection. He let his head fall back to rest on the mirrored wall and gasped as Jenna took him into her mouth.

She licked and teased and worked him toward the edge, savoring the intimate power she had over his body, enjoying the pulsing heat of him in her mouth. Gently, she dragged her teeth along his rigid length, thrilling at his shudder of pleasure.

She continued to pleasure him with her mouth until his breath was fast and shallow, but just as he was about to reach climax, he stilled her with his hand.

"I want to be inside you," he whispered.

Standing up, she slid her panties down and kicked them aside, then crawled on his lap as he withdrew a condom from his wallet and slipped it on. Without wasting another second, she mounted him and forced his erection as far inside her as it would go. And she began to rock her hips.

"We shouldn't be doing this," he managed to say between gasps.

She stilled her hips and kissed him on the mouth, then trailed her lips to his ear, where she nipped at his earlobe. "You want to stop?"

"Hell no."

"Because I can," she said as she tightened her inner muscles around him.

He grasped her hips and began thrusting into her, fast and hard. Jenna bit her lip to keep her moans silent. She rested her weight on her hands against the mirrored wall, then let her gaze wander to one of the angled mirrors that provided a view of their lovemaking. Watching it was just as hot as experiencing it.

Travis took her breast into his mouth and teased her nipple with his tongue, then made his way to the other one. "You should watch," she whispered.

He stopped and looked at her, his eyes glazed over with arousal, then looked at the mirror she nodded toward. Jenna began to move on him again, rocking her hips in a seductive show, giving him his own impromptu home movie.

But she felt herself coming closer to the edge, felt the tension building inside, and slow and seductive would no longer cut it. She increased the pace again, and in a few moments waves of pleasure washed through her, blinding and unstoppable. Her muscles contracted again and again, and she went limp against Travis just as he came, too.

He muffled their release with a long, deep kiss as he thrust into her one final time, their bodies tensing and then relaxing together.

After a moment, Jenna sat back and looked at him, curious if she would see regret in his gaze. Instead, when he opened his eyes, she saw an emotion she couldn't name. Maybe just desire. Or something more.

"Guess I should try on those clothes."

"Or we could just lock ourselves in here for the rest of the day."

"I think Allegra might call the police."

"Maybe you're right." He kissed her again, and Jenna removed herself from his lap and went in search of her panties and bra.

A knock on the door sounded just as Travis was buckling his belt. "Excuse me? Do you need any help in there?"

"No thanks, just trying to make up our minds," Jenna called out.

"Do you need any other sizes?"

"Um, yes," she improvised, "Maybe a larger size of the flower-print sundress."

"I'll be right back with it," Allegra called through the door.

Jenna smiled at Travis as she tugged a dress off its hanger. By the time the saleswoman was back at the door, Jenna was looking at her sister's image in the mirror again. She opened the door and took the dress.

"That looks lovely on you."

"Thanks, but I'm not sure if I like it." She closed the door again quickly, before Allegra could get a look at their flushed appearances and figure out what they'd really been doing.

Jenna turned back to Travis. "What do you think?"

"It looks like something Kathryn would wear."

She tried on three more outfits, and they picked out the dress and pants and sweater set that fit best, then hurried out of the dressing room with her wearing the summer dress they'd agreed she would meet the Roths in at the family's Independence Day party. It was likely she and Kathryn still wore the exact same size and she'd be able to wear her sister's wardrobe, but Travis wanted her to have a few backup outfits in case Kathryn's clothes didn't fit her perfectly.

After he'd paid a ridiculous amount of money for the two outfits—all the while enduring Allegra's suspicious gaze—they made their way back out into the bright afternoon and looked up and down the street for a restaurant.

"I spotted a place that looked like it had good sandwiches when I was using the phone earlier."

"We're there."

She followed him a block down to a trendy little bistro that had outdoor tables on the sidewalk. They sat down outside, and a waiter quickly brought menus and took their drinks order.

Jenna opened her menu, saw a club sandwich and decided without looking any further that that's what she wanted. She turned her attention to Travis, who closed his menu and looked back at her.

He smiled sheepishly. "We can't let that happen again."

"But you were sort of hoping it would happen, or you wouldn't have followed me into the dressing room."

The waiter set down their drinks and hovered beside the table, waiting for them to order. When they'd placed their orders, he left again, and Jenna pinned Travis with an expectant gaze.

"I'll admit, I was hoping we'd have one more chance to be together before we arrive in Carmel."

"Because once we're there, no more fun, right?"

"Right."

A breeze brushed Jenna's back and neck, reminding her again that her hair had been chopped off. One hand wandered self-consciously up to her bare neck, and she forced it back to her lap.

"So, did the relaxation-weekend plan work for you?" she asked, before taking a sip of her soft drink.

Travis stretched out in his chair and smiled. "I'm feeling more relaxed than I have in months."

"I told you it would work. What about going back to the real world—lots of stress waiting there for you?"

A mysterious look crossed his face. "Maybe I've been inspired to do things a bit differently now."

"How so?"

"I'm not sure. Maybe take a few more risks, spend a little less time trying to please my family."

"Why the change of heart?" Though she had a strong suspicion that one weekend of risk taking had showed him what he'd been missing out on by always playing it safe.

"Let's just say you've given me a different perspective."

"I can't take all the credit. I think things started changing for you with that bar fight."

He shrugged and flashed a sheepish smile. "I felt a little like a caveman defending his territory that night."

Jenna recalled the wild abandon with which they'd made love after the bar fight, and her insides heated. She was going to miss Travis—miss having him in her bed, that is. She had a distinct feeling that once they were back in his everyday world, he'd forget all about her being anything more than the woman he was paying to impersonate Kathryn.

She pushed away a little pang of regret and smiled. "Maybe we should go over the important details for the next two weeks again and make sure I'm not forgetting anything."

"Okay, there's the meeting Wednesday with Paul and Rowena Williams to discuss the land they're considering donating to Kathryn's project. I don't have photos of them, but Blake will be there to introduce you, and I'll try to be there, too, if I can find a good reason…"

Jenna listened, nodding occasionally, as Travis recounted everything they'd gone over in the past two days. Her greatest fear was meeting Blake and having to somehow behave with him as if they were two people deeply in love and about to marry. If she could fool Blake into believing she was Kathryn, she could fool anyone.

But the last thing she wanted was to find herself in a compromising position with her sister's fiancé. Travis had assured her he'd endured listening to countless complaints from Blake in the past weeks about Kathryn's insistence that they not have sex until the wedding, but that wasn't much comfort. She had to somehow get Blake to agree that for the next two weeks, they could have no more physical contact than a chaste kiss on the cheek.

Surely, promises of wild sex to come on the wedding night would be enough to convince him. If there was one thing she knew about her sister, it was that she had pitifully conservative ideas about sex. She probably hadn't even gotten out of the missionary position with Blake, so Jenna had every intention of convincing him that his sex life would get really wild as soon as a ring was on her finger.

Travis continued to drill her with review questions as they ate their lunch and left the restaurant, then began the long drive to Carmel. In the passenger seat, she flipped through her file full of facts about her sister one last time, until it felt as if her head would explode.

Finally, she settled back and watched the scenery of the coastal mountain ranges roll past while distracting Travis from details about Kathryn by asking him about his investment firm. As he explained the workings of it, she was surprised to find herself interested, even fascinated.

When they reached Carmel, they drove through town and then made their way to the outskirts of it along a winding road. When they turned off of the road into a gated driveway, Travis hit a remote control that opened the gate, and they pulled through. After a minute, the house came into view amidst rolling hills. It was a Spanish-style mansion that Jenna was pretty sure she'd seen featured on some California architecture documentary a few years back, and it was even grander than she'd expected.

She glanced over at Travis, who was unfazed by the sight of such an ostentatious home—a mansion he took for granted as just a house where people lived—and she knew in that moment that their fling was truly over. They were in his world now, and she absolutely, positively did not belong.

8

TRAVIS GLANCED at the clock on the dash as he pulled into the driveway of the Roth family estate. They were right on time to slip into the Fourth of July picnic without being noticed. Cars crowded the circular driveway, and a valet dressed in a white coat and white shorts lazed against the short stone wall that lined sections of the garden.

"If anyone asks, I've picked you up from the airport. You just got back into town and couldn't reach anyone else for a ride."

Jenna stared at the house. "You didn't tell me your family lives in one of California's great landmark homes."

"You didn't ask," he joked, but her expression made it clear she wasn't in the mood for joking.

"I don't think I can do this."

Travis did a double take at the uncertainty in her voice. He'd quickly come to take it for granted that Jenna was certain about everything, that she had the sort of unshakable confidence that made her comfortable in any situation.

"If most everyone can do it, you can. You've

seen pictures of anyone you'll need to recognize, you've gone over all the facts you need to know— you'll be fine."

"But—"

"I'll be staying close by and watching in case you get into any sticky situations. Just use our signal."

"I'm supposed to make eye contact with you and scratch my nose?"

"Right."

"What if I can't get your attention?"

"I don't think you'll have to worry about that." The bigger worry was if he'd ever be able to take his eyes *off* Jenna, whether anyone else would see the hunger in his gaze when he looked at her.

Travis pulled up to the curb and the valet opened the door for Jenna. Once they were both out of the car and the valet was pulling it away, Travis showed her the way through the house, taking advantage of the fact that everyone was outside to acquaint her with what her sister already knew about the house.

Once they'd finished the quick tour, Travis led the way to the rear lawn where the party was in full swing. His parents had been throwing this Fourth of July celebration every year for as long as he could remember, and some things about it never changed. There was always a quartet playing big band tunes, there was always an array of striped tents throughout the yard shading guests from the harsh sun and there was always his mother drinking a little too much champagne.

"Don't forget," he whispered as they stepped out onto the rear veranda, "my mother could be a little tipsy. Take whatever she says in stride."

Jenna nodded as she surveyed the crowd. "I'm mainly worried about your brother. What if he tries to cram his tongue down my throat the moment he sees me?"

"I've never seen your sister indulge in a public display of affection, so this is the best possible place for you to meet Blake. Just do what we rehearsed."

She took a deep breath and exhaled. "Right."

"We'd better start mingling."

He figured the best bet was to introduce Jenna to Blake right away and get the worst over with, so he scanned the crowd until he spotted his brother chatting up an old business associate.

They wandered across the lawn, and Blake cut off his conversation as soon as he spotted Jenna.

"There's my lovely fiancée!" He embraced his faux fiancée with the enthusiasm of a guy who had no clue he was hugging the wrong woman, then made an attempt to kiss her. Jenna offered up her cheek, then gave him a chaste peck on the cheek, as well.

Blake smiled at her playfully, undaunted by the lack of a mouth kiss. Travis's theory that Kathryn didn't like public affection had been solid, thank God.

"How was the flight home?" Blake asked.

Jenna flashed a charming smile. "Uneventful. I spent the whole time thinking about seeing you again."

Yep, she had her sister pegged. She knew her speech patterns and mannerisms even better than Travis had hoped. He relaxed by another degree and turned his attention to the business associate Blake had been talking to, letting the fake love-birds have a little time together.

After a few minutes, Blake led Jenna off to mingle, and Travis found himself almost completely relaxed. Until he spotted his mother headed straight for them, half-empty champagne glass in hand.

Even under the influence of alcohol, Georgina Roth had a keen radar for bullshit. She was Jenna's biggest test, especially considering how she was always looking for something wrong with Kathryn anyway. Travis excused himself from his business associate and made his way toward Blake and Jenna, arriving just as their mother did.

"Kathryn, it's so good to see you could make it back in time for the party," Georgina said in a tone that made it clear she wasn't all that happy to see her future daughter-in-law.

"Hello, Mrs. Roth."

"Do tell me all about your stay at the spa. You're looking quite relaxed, I must say."

Jenna cast a glance at Travis, and he quickly

looked down at his shoes. "It *was* very relaxing," she said.

"I trust you feel all rested up for the wedding festivities."

"Absolutely."

"Because you know, once you're married, you won't be able to flit away for little solo retreats."

"*Mom.*" Blake intervened. "Kathryn can do whatever she pleases when we're married."

Georgina cast him a withering glance. "Careful what you say now, son."

Jenna seemed at a loss for words, but then she smiled sweetly and gave Blake's arm a pat. "I can't imagine wanting to leave my husband's side. This vacation was only to help me look my best for Blake at the wedding."

"You already looked perfect," Blake said.

Their mother downed the remainder of her champagne and daintily placed the glass on a nearby table. When she turned back to them, Travis could tell by the smug look in her eyes she wasn't finished with Kathryn.

"I do hope you've rethought that whole women's shelter idea. I simply don't see how you'll have the time or the know-how to oversee it."

"I've quit my job at the, um, gallery," Jenna said, her cheeks coloring at her stumble. "And I'll learn as I go."

Georgina couldn't have had any real objection to the women's shelter, but she liked to put up a good front. It wasn't like his mother to be so uncharitable, and Travis suspected her reservations stemmed more from a fear of Blake and Kathryn flaking out on the project once it lost its luster, thereby tarnishing the precious Roth name.

One good thing about their mother was that, unlike their father, Georgina knew the capabilities of her sons.

"Perhaps all your pageant training will help you relate better to the women at the shelters," his mother said in her most vitriolic tone.

Jenna blinked. Travis realized he hadn't quite done an adequate job of preparing her for how condescending his mother could be to Kathryn. It was a testament to Kathryn's love for Blake that she put up with such crap.

And then Jenna flashed a sly smile that was all vixen, not her sister's smile at all. Travis steeled himself for impending disaster. "Absolutely. I can show them how to tape their breasts together for maximum cleavage during job interviews."

It wasn't like Kathryn to make sarcastic jokes, but Blake apparently didn't notice. He laughed, then Jenna joined in, and Travis forced himself to laugh, too. Their mother looked at the three of them as if they'd grown horns.

"That's exactly the sort of attitude that makes it clear to me this project will be a disaster with you running it." She snatched a new glass of champagne from a passing waiter and turned on her heel, then marched off.

Jenna sobered when she realized the damage

she'd done slipping out of character. "Sorry," she said, "I shouldn't have taunted your mother like that."

"She was asking for it. I'm glad to see you finally put her in her place like I've told you to do," Blake said.

Travis tried to pass Jenna a silent look that said all was okay, but before she could see him, he was accosted by Natalie Wentworth, whose timing could not have been worse.

He'd dated Natalie on and off over the years, theirs being a relationship based more on the convenience of sex without commitment than anything else. She was driven to make it to the top of her law firm unhindered by marriage and family obligations, and she had a great set of legs.

He'd been avoiding her recently, though, growing tired of the lack of emotional involvement, but she slipped her arm around his waist and kissed him as if they were still lovers.

When he'd finally untangled himself from her, he caught Jenna's look of confusion.

"Um, Natalie, you remember Blake and his fiancée Kathryn, right?"

"Of course. I'm sure you two won't mind if I steal Travis away for a short while."

Blake flashed his most charming smile. "Of course not. He's just being a third wheel anyway."

Jenna forced a smile, but for all her talk of no-strings-attached sex for the weekend, Travis had the distinct feeling there were strings. Hell, he knew there were, because he felt them tugging him toward her every minute of the day.

IF THIS PARTY DIDN'T END SOON, Jenna feared she'd succumb to the urge to drown herself in the Roth's gigantic Italianate water fountain. She'd slipped away from Blake with the excuse that she wanted to chat with a friend, and then she'd managed to avoid conversation with anyone for a good while by wandering around, snacking on finger foods and trying to look as if she were searching for someone.

Ever since Travis had been lured away by the Nicole Kidman look-alike, Jenna had been fighting a battle inside herself not to care that he was involved with another woman. She had absolutely no reason to care, after all. She wasn't interested in him in anything more than a sexual way, and she certainly wasn't foolish enough to think their weekend of sex was going to blossom into a real love affair.

Hell, she didn't even want a real love affair.... Did she? Her philosophy about men had always been to take advantage of opportunities as they came along, but never to go looking for love. If it found her, then it was meant to be.

And for her entire adult life, that philosophy had worked out just fine. She'd never encountered a man like Travis before, though, a man who lingered in her thoughts constantly, whose body fit with hers as if it had been made to please her—

and a man who was so altogether wrong for her
that she'd be a fool to let her heart get involved.

As Jenna made her way around the lawn and
garden, admiring the Roth family's stunning estate, she willed herself not to look for Travis. Instead, she spotted Blake wandering nearby, clearly
looking for his fiancée, and she ducked behind
the ice sculpture.

This charade was even worse than she'd feared
it would be. Every time Blake came near, she felt
like a sleaze and a fraud, and she wanted to scream
that she wasn't at all who he thought she was.

"Kathryn! It's so lovely to see you."

Jenna turned to find a woman standing beside
her, a woman she had the distinct feeling she was
supposed to recognize. She plastered on a smile
and said, "Isn't this a beautiful party?"

"Oh, absolutely. The Roths always hold such
fabulous shindigs."

Shindigs? Did people really talk that way?

"So how have you been?" Jenna asked, figuring
it was about as benign a question as there was.

"You *know* I've been absolutely horrid ever
since that awful incident with Ryan."

Jenna produced what she hoped was a vague
look of sympathy and nodded.

Her Chanel-clad companion frowned. "Is
something wrong, Kathryn? You seem distracted."

"I'm sorry. You actually caught me on my way
to the ladies' room."

"By all means, don't let me hold you up. I just

have one quick question—do you think I should tell him the truth?"

Uh-oh. "Um, Ryan, you mean?"

"Of course. Who else?"

The truth was rarely a bad thing, right? Could she go wrong advising honesty?

"Yes, I…definitely think you should."

The woman's eyes widened. "Are you *sure*?"

"Well…" Jenna glanced around, wishing Travis would magically appear and keep her from having to answer.

"No, you're right. I will tell him. Right now. The sooner, the better."

Jenna wasn't sure if the decision required a smile or a solemn nod. The woman seemed nervous, so she opted for a nod and excused herself. On her way to the bathroom, Blake spotted her and made a beeline in her direction. Jenna considered dodging and running, but she figured she'd have to face her sister's fiancé again sooner or later, so she stopped and produced a smile.

"Darling, I've been looking all over for you." Blake slid his arm around her waist and pulled her close. "I don't want to let you out of my sight for another minute."

Jenna offered her cheek when he leaned in for a kiss, and he pulled back and eyed her as if she'd just suggested they go shopping at a discount store. "What's with the cheek thing. Is something the matter?"

"There are just so many people here."

"Forget about them. We're nearly newlyweds. They expect us not to be able to keep our hands off of each other."

Okay, this was her opportunity. "Blakey," she said, using the term of endearment Travis had mentioned was her sister's favorite, "Speaking of keeping our hands off of each other…"

"Tell me you've come to your senses," he said, lowering his voice.

"This period of waiting is just as hard for me as it is for you, but I was thinking during my visit to the spa, we could make our honeymoon night even more exciting…"

He smiled, slid his hand down to her hip, and Jenna resisted the urge to slap it away.

"Oh yeah?"

"If we don't have any sort of physical contact for the next two weeks."

Blake's expression went from flirtatious to horrified. He turned to face her and took her hands in his. "Are you crazy?"

It did sound pretty crazy when spoken out loud. Okay, so she could improvise. "I read a book, a sort of sex manual, at the spa, in preparation," she said, lowering her voice to a seductive purr. "And I learned quite a bit, including the effects of a period of complete physical abstinence on the following sexual experience."

Blake's frown disappeared. "A sex manual, hmm? What else did you learn from it?"

"Oh, lots of things, lots of naughty, naughty

things that I cannot wait to try out with you. On our wedding night."

"Like what?" he whispered, smiling and nodding at a middle-aged couple passing by.

"I learned things too scandalous to say out loud in a public place, but once I have you alone in our honeymoon suite, you'll never want to leave."

Blake's eyes dilated, and his breathing grew shallow. "Can't we at least do a little premarital kissing?"

"Not for the effect to be complete." She paused and licked her lips slowly. "Trust me, you won't regret practicing some restraint. It's only two short weeks."

"Maybe I should read that book, too. In preparation."

Oops. Jenna frowned, trying to remember if she'd ever actually read such a book. She had been exposed to plenty of sex manuals in her freelance research, but she had no idea if any of them prescribed strict periods of abstinence.

"I might have left it at the spa by accident. But I'll double-check. Maybe I can find a copy for you at a local bookstore."

Blake tilted his head to the side and offered her a puppy-dog frown. "I don't know if I can survive all that waiting."

"It's not even two weeks—really just a week and five days."

"Can't I get one last little kiss on the mouth to hold me over?"

"No cheating." She flashed her most seductive smile. "I promise, I'll make it worth the wait." She leaned in and gave Blake a brief peck on the cheek, then withdrew her hands from his.

He expelled a ragged sigh but made no further protest.

"I need to make a trip to the little girls' room," Jenna said, spouting the cutesy language her sister favored.

Blake smiled. "Don't be gone long. If I can't touch you, I at least want to be able to see you."

Jenna wiggled her fingers at him and hurried off toward the main house. Rest room signs designated the pool house as the place for guests to go, but she needed to get as far away from the crowd as possible.

Once inside, she wandered down the hallway trying to remember where she'd seen the bathroom earlier, but the sound of Travis's voice coming from a nearby room caught her attention.

"Yes, that sounds like the way to go. First thing, as soon as the market opens tomorrow," he was saying as Jenna followed the sound to the open door of a study.

Travis sat at a cherry executive desk talking on the phone. Relieved to see the one person who didn't think she was Kathryn, Jenna hovered in the doorway, not wanting to interrupt but unable to leave. When he hung up the phone, Travis swiveled around in the black leather office chair and spotted her.

"Sorry, I didn't mean to interrupt your work," she said. "No day off on the Fourth of July?"

"Just one phone call."

"Mind if I hide out in here for a few minutes?" she asked, forcing herself not to inquire about the whereabouts of his female friend.

Travis stood up and came to the door, where he peered out and down the hallway. "Did anyone see you come in here?"

"No."

"We have to be careful," he said, closing the door to the study.

Jenna felt as if her body temperature rose several degrees in such close proximity to Travis, alone. He turned to face her, and she knew by his expression that he was suffering from a bit of over-heating himself.

"I should leave," she said half-heartedly.

"Yes."

"But you don't want me to."

Travis turned the lock on the doorknob, then crossed the room and closed the shades.

Jenna lowered her voice to a whisper as she walked to the desk. "Blake cornered me, but I think I've got him under control."

"So he knows that you don't want any physical contact before the wedding?"

"He thinks I got the idea from a sex manual."

Travis smiled. "Good thinking. I'm sorry I haven't been able to stick close to you like I promised."

"It's okay, you have other obligations."

"Please don't get the wrong idea about Natalie. She and I used to be involved, but we haven't been together in months."

"It's none of my business, but you looked pretty obviously together an hour ago," Jenna said, hating the tone of her voice.

"I made it clear to her that I no longer want to be anything more than friends. She understands where I'm coming from, and she's okay with it."

"I hope you didn't do that on my account."

"I did it because I wanted to." He came to her side and leaned against the desk, letting his gaze travel down the length of her and back up.

His nearness made her forget about everything but the heat between them, and Jenna knew he felt it, too. Otherwise, he wouldn't have been coming so close to violating his own hands-off rules.

"Too bad I'm off limits for you, too," she said, her voice sounding more breathless than she'd intended.

"I didn't realize how hard this would be."

Jenna imagined inching herself closer, demanding one last kiss, but she knew one kiss would never be enough. If she kissed him, she'd have to touch him, and if she touched him, she'd have to make love to him, too.

"Me, either," she whispered.

"I should get back out to the party. I've been away too long."

"I do have one question first. Do you know anything about a man named Ryan and his blond significant other?"

He frowned. "Ryan Case and his fiancée, Madeline. I forgot to give you a photo of them."

"I may have caused a bit of trouble. She asked me some advice about 'telling Ryan the truth,' and I told her she definitely should. Any idea what she was talking about?"

Travis winced. "I'm afraid so. I believe she plans on admitting to him that she's a lesbian."

"Oh. She made some comment about an incident with him recently."

"He caught her with another woman, but she somehow managed to explain it away."

"Like, 'Oh my, I just accidentally fell on this naked woman lying on my bed'?"

Travis smiled. "Something like that."

"Maybe you should talk to her, at least keep her from causing a scene here at your parents' party."

Travis stood up from the edge of the desk and ran one hand through his hair. "Good idea," he said, but he lingered at her side.

"If you stay here, I'm going to kiss you."

His gaze lingered on her, and she could almost see the battle raging inside him. Just when she thought he was going to leave, he closed the distance between them and slipped one hand around her waist. With the other, he cupped the back of her head.

When his gaze locked on her mouth, she knew he'd kiss her, and it was exactly what she'd been aching for him to do.

9

TRAVIS COVERED Jenna's mouth with his, then lingered there. She snaked her arms around his neck and savored the taste and feel of him, slipped her tongue inside his mouth and reminded herself of why she loved kissing him so much.

A moment later, he pulled back. "Damn it."

"Yeah. Damn it."

"We can't be alone anymore together, if this is what's going to happen."

"Right," she said, resisting the urge to rip his shirt open and lick his chest.

"I'm sorry I let my control slip. I know that only makes this harder." He stepped back, and Jenna let her arms fall to her sides.

Travis went to the door and opened it, looked out into the hallway, then turned and nodded for her to go.

Out of nowhere, her desire turned into a sense of violation. Maybe Travis wasn't just concerned about ruining their charade, or getting caught having an affair with his brother's "fiancée." Maybe it was just her. Maybe she'd been right all along that he might have considered her worthy of a few nights in the sack, but that once they were in his world, he couldn't lower himself to her level.

Okay, she could suck it up. She wasn't going to let some arrogant, spoiled rich guy get under her skin. She left the office without giving him a second glance, but she'd only made it as far as the back door when Blake found her again.

"Hey sweetheart, I thought you might have fallen in."

Jenna smiled at his lame joke as if he were brilliant. "I just needed a little quiet. I guess all the noise and heat are getting to me."

"What do you say we skip the fireworks display and have a little intimate fireworks show of our own?"

Ugh, this guy was a broken record, *and* he couldn't take no for an answer.

"I'm not sure intimate is a good idea if we want to keep our pact," she said in her best coy female imitation.

"Hmm, I guess you're not going to change your mind." He frowned. "How about dinner instead? If we're in a restaurant, we'll be forced to behave ourselves, right?"

Jenna groaned inwardly. She'd have to be alone for an evening with Blake sooner or later, so she supposed it made sense to get it over with as soon as possible.

"Sure, you name the place, and I'll meet you there, okay?"

"But what about slipping out of here early with me? You're my excuse to leave."

"Just tell anyone who asks that you need to freshen up for our big date."

He smiled and tugged her close. "Okay then, we'll behave, and I'll see you, say, around seven at Sylvio's?"

Sure, she'd just have to figure out where the heck Sylvio's was. No problem. "It's a plan."

Jenna gave him a quick peck on the cheek and tried to slip out of his grasp, but he held on. "It's odd, but I feel like something is different about you today."

Jenna shrugged. "It's amazing what a little relaxation can do for a girl."

He clearly wasn't convinced that she was simply more relaxed, but he shrugged. "Maybe. I can't put my finger on what seems different."

Her heart pounded in her ears, but he mercifully let her go. She could feel his gaze following her as she went out onto the back lawn again. She wandered around trying to look occupied with a glass of seltzer water, until she got the distinct feeling she was being watched.

Glancing around, her gaze finally settled on a woman sitting alone at a nearby table. She wore sunglasses and what Jenna would have bet money was a wig, and something about her looked oddly familiar. She studied the woman for a moment as she hailed a waiter for another drink, but she had no idea where she might have seen her before.

Jenna did a mental shrug and decided she was letting the stress get to her.

Then she spotted Travis outside again. Jenna made her way over to him and tried to act as if he wasn't someone she'd had sex with in a dressing room earlier that day.

"I've got a date with Blake for tonight."

He winced. "I guess that was inevitable. Maybe I can load him down with work this week to keep him away from you as much as possible."

"I think I can handle him for tonight. We're supposed to meet at a place called Sylvio's."

"I can give you directions, but first we'll need to slip out of here so I can show you the way to Kathryn's place."

"How about you make your excuses and I'll meet you out front in another ten minutes?"

"It could be harder leaving together than it was showing up. Why don't I call you a cab to Kathryn's place, and then I'll leave at the same time and follow you there?"

Jenna nodded, and they parted ways. She wandered around the party a bit more, aware of the sensation of someone watching her. She scanned the crowd and didn't see anyone. Probably it was Travis keeping tabs on her whereabouts.

But then she spotted Travis with his back to her as he talked to his father. Jenna surveyed the crowd again, and her gaze landed on the woman in the wig and sunglasses. She seemed to be staring straight at Jenna, her expression neutral. Jenna watched her for a few moments, and the woman looked away.

Maybe the woman recognized her from some-where, or maybe she could tell she was a fraud. Maybe she knew Kathryn was still at the spa… No, impossible.

If Blake couldn't tell his own fiancée from an imposter, then it wasn't likely anyone else could, either. Kathryn had sworn to Travis that no one else knew about her not coming back from the spa, and Jenna couldn't imagine her sister having spilled the secret to anyone that she'd had a botched plastic surgery.

Jenna managed to slip out of the party without any questions, saying an awkward goodbye to Mr. and Mrs. Roth without enduring any more abuse from the latter.

Fifteen minutes later her cab was pulling into the driveway of an oceanside postmodern con-coction of windows and redwood that Jenna imag-ined her sister planned to transform into a showplace that would lure the likes of *Architec-tural Digest* to do a feature. It wasn't exactly Jen-na's taste, but it was impressive. Kathryn Calvert had certainly moved up in the world.

She paid the driver and wandered up to the front entrance, noting the equally stark-looking landscape design Blake had probably paid some landscape architect a horrifying sum to plant. Be-fore she reached the door, Travis pulled into the drive, and she couldn't help but catch her breath at the sight of him, a vision of male perfection, driving the sleek little Mercedes.

When he reached the top of the steps, he said, "Nice view, huh?"

Jenna had been so caught up marveling at the house and landscaping that she'd failed to look out beyond the surrounding trees to the ocean. She followed the sound of crashing waves to see that her sister's house had a stunning view of the Pacific from every front window. The view alone probably cost as much as most houses.

"Blake bought this place?" she asked.

He nodded. "They didn't want to start out in something that had belonged to either of them when they were single. Kathryn has been living here for a few months, getting it all set up."

"How about a grand tour then?"

Travis withdrew a key from his pocket and handed it to her. "You wouldn't believe what I had to go through to get this. Blake spent an entire day ranting about having lost his keys while I made a copy."

She opened the door and went inside with Travis following. "I guess you shouldn't stay long."

"I'll just give you a quick tour and get out of here before someone spots my car."

He led the way through the house, giving explanations of whatever he knew about. Jenna recognized her sister in almost every detail. It felt weird walking around Kathryn's house without her there, as if she were trespassing. By the time

Travis had finished the tour, Jenna had the vague feeling of having been reacquainted with Kathryn by snooping—even if it was approved snooping.

"Thanks for showing me around," she said.

"I have to admit, it was just an excuse to get you alone again."

"You love temptation," she said, looking out the window at a ship passing far in the distance.

"I can think of worse kinds of torture." He leaned against the window ledge, smiling a weary smile.

"You look tired."

"I didn't get much sleep last night."

"Oh, right." She smiled at the memory of their lovemaking, which had lasted well into the early morning hours. "I know how you feel—being my sister is exhausting."

"Let's hope Kathryn shows up sooner rather than later. Next time she calls I'll make sure she understands what a hard time you're having putting off Blake. That ought to convince her to come home."

Jenna frowned at the thought of Kathryn not showing up until the last minute. The prospect was just too much to dwell on. "I guess you'd better go, huh?"

Travis was watching her mouth, as if transfixed. "That kiss at my parents' house? I don't regret it."

"But it can't happen again."

"I guess not."

"You don't sound very convinced."

"I don't seem to have much self-control when you're around."

Jenna shrugged. "Sometimes a little indulgence is just what you need."

"But not right now."

"No. So I promise I'll try not to tempt you, okay?" She couldn't help but smile at the idea of turning off the chemistry between them. It was impossible.

"Good luck with the dinner tonight. Call me when you get home and let me know how it went."

"You think I'll survive?" she asked, suddenly realizing what a miserable evening she had to look forward to, nothing like the previous few nights of bliss she'd spent with Travis.

"I think you'll do great. And if something goes wrong, it's not the end of the world."

Jenna quirked an eyebrow. "That's a pretty cavalier attitude you've suddenly developed."

"Another one of your effects on me."

He should have left then, but he lingered by her side at the window, watching her through half-lidded eyes.

What she would have given to drag him over to the sofa and make love to him again, but it would be a huge mistake now. And so would kissing him. Yep, big mistake.

Big, big mistake.

Travis finally broke their strange standoff, pushing himself away from the window. He found his keys in his pocket and headed for the door, and a minute later Jenna was watching through the window as he drove away.

She turned around to face the house and sighed into the silence. This was her sister's home, a place she would have been completely unwelcome a week ago, a place she wouldn't even have imagined setting foot in last week.

Jenna wandered through each room again, spotting photos of Kathryn and Blake looking blissfully happy, Kathryn and Blake looking amused, Kathryn and Blake posing for stylish black-and-white engagement photos. There were also a few photos of each set of parents, a few shots here and there of people Jenna recognized as Kathryn's friends.

The entire house was painstakingly organized, obsessively neat, hardly marred by a speck of dust. In the kitchen, she opened the cabinets to confirm her suspicion that Kathryn had organized the dry and canned goods alphabetically and by category.

Typical. In their younger years when they'd been forced to share a room, Kathryn's side had always been perfectly kept, while Jenna's side was always a little messy, a little cluttered—and always a point of contention between the two.

Jenna laughed at a long-forgotten memory of a fight they'd had some time in their preteen years over the state of Jenna's side of the room that had resulted in each of them scalping the other's favorite Barbie doll.

She had the sudden and foreign urge to see Kathryn at that moment, to reminisce with her about old times, to just hang out like normal sisters would. It must have been all the stress of the afternoon getting to her. Clearly, she needed a stiff drink and a good night's sleep, and she'd wake up tomorrow free of any misguided sisterly feelings.

A clock on the wall reminded her that she had less than an hour to get ready for her intimate evening with her sister's fiancé. Jenna decided that was an even better excuse for a stiff drink, but she needed a clear head for the evening's acting session. If she could survive tonight, she told herself as she climbed the stairs to Kathryn's bedroom, she could survive the next two weeks no problem.

Yep, right. No problem.

JENNA SAT IN KATHRYN'S CAR in the parking lot of Roth Investments, strumming her fingers on the steering wheel and trying not to hyperventilate.

It was only her fifth day impersonating Kathryn, and already she was ready to forget the money and run for the hills. She'd barely survived the Fourth of July dinner with Blake, and she'd narrowly avoided disaster at a family dinner yesterday night when Blake's parents started asking her questions about the women and children's shelter project—questions she'd been forced to make up answers to.

Jenna had miraculously managed to dodge Blake for most of the week, thanks in part to Travis inventing extra tasks to keep his brother busy at work, and when she wasn't being Kathryn, she'd found plenty of time to start reconstructing her research and her outline of the pageant-industry article. Travis had loaned her a laptop to work on, but she hadn't felt as much zeal for the project as she'd expected. Her mind was frequently occupied with other thoughts.

Thoughts of one particularly delicious guy in a suit whom she'd also not seen much of this week. Mentally she understood their need to avoid each other, but physically, his absence was more painful than she'd expected. The nights since last weekend had been especially long.

But even in her most passionate love affairs, she'd always been able to keep her mind on the job when it was necessary. It drove Jenna mad to feel so scatterbrained, to find herself staring out the window and daydreaming of Travis whenever she should have been working. She was behaving more like a lovesick schoolgirl than a grown woman, and she'd resolved to put him out of her mind for good.

That should have been no problem, except that she'd be seeing him again in a matter of minutes, and her every nerve ending was on alert. He'd expressed an interest in the women and children's shelter project in order to be present for Jenna and Blake's meeting with Paul and Rowena Williams, the couple with the land to donate.

Jenna glanced at her watch, cursed herself for arriving so early and decided to go in. She entered the gleaming glass office building and found out from the receptionist where the meeting would be held, then followed the directions given to a large, meticulously clean meeting room, complete with a huge conference table and chairs for everyone.

She selected a chair and sat down with her folder of notes, prepared to study the information Travis had given her about Kathryn's charity project in the twenty minutes before the meeting was to begin. But then the sound of the door opening caught her attention, and she looked up to see Travis fill the doorway.

"Hey," was the wittiest thing she could think to say as her body responded to him with all the heat of a blazing inferno. She resisted the urge to fan herself.

"Hey, yourself." He smiled and closed the door, then took a seat next to her.

"How did you know I was here?"

"I asked the receptionist to call me when you arrived."

"Shouldn't we be worried about someone walking in and wondering why we're here alone?" Jenna asked, glancing at the door.

"We're just the first two people to arrive for the meeting. I was hoping you'd get here early."

"Because?"

"Because this has been a long week."

Jenna suppressed a smile. So, he'd felt the same agony she had. The thought was inexplicably satisfying. "Which is exactly why we shouldn't be here alone."

He flashed her a devilish look. "Afraid you can't control yourself around me?"

She wet her lips and leaned forward, placing a hand on his thigh under the table. "Is it *my* self-control we really have to worry about?"

It was a cruel, cruel trick, but she couldn't help toying with him just a little to see if she could make his cool, polished facade disappear.

He shifted in his seat. "Point taken." Jenna removed her hand from his thigh, and he seemed to relax by a degree. "I actually wanted to tell you I heard back from the private investigator today."

"Oh?"

"He hasn't found anything suspicious, other than what has gone on between us."

"I told you there was no reason to worry about us being followed, but what about this guy? Would he tell anyone that you're messing around with your brother's woman?"

"He knows you're not Kathryn. It was the only way to make sure he could do his job."

Jenna nodded, flattered that he'd risk ruining his and Kathryn's scheme for her safety. Again she found herself savoring the feeling of someone looking out for her. It was nice to feel as if she wasn't alone, as if it wasn't just her against the world, even if her guardian angel was only a temporary one.

She was also aware now of the strange sensation of being near Travis when he was not available to her. She couldn't touch him, couldn't confess secrets to him, couldn't share private smiles with him once anyone else was present. She hadn't realized how badly she'd want to continue where they'd left off Monday or how frustrated she'd feel now that they could be no more than casual acquaintances.

This kind of turmoil was *so* not what she'd had in mind when she'd made her deal with Travis.

The sound of the turning doorknob caught their attention, and Jenna looked up to see Blake enter the room.

"Hey, am I actually early for the first time in my life?" Blake said as he went to Jenna and placed a kiss on her forehead.

"It appears so," Travis said.

Jenna quelled her disappointment that she'd lost her chance to be alone with Travis, reminding herself that the situation could only have led to more trouble. It was a good thing Blake had showed up. Really, it was.

Blake gave Travis a curious look. "There's been something strange about you this week. You aren't your usual uptight self. What gives?"

Jenna watched the battle of emotions in Travis's eyes. She couldn't have said exactly what he was feeling, but he was definitely conflicted.

"I don't know what you're talking about."

"You haven't given me a single stern lecture this week, and you keep bebopping around the office like a kid on the day before summer break."

"I haven't been *bebopping*."

Jenna bit her lip to keep from laughing.

"And what's with the decision to buy all that stock in Yoshiro Electronics? That's the riskiest move you've ever made."

Travis shrugged. "I believe in the company."

"See what I mean? You hardly sound like yourself. You never make a big move like that without spouting a long list of statistics and research."

Jenna felt a self-satisfied smile settle on her lips. She'd had an impact on Travis, and a positive one, by the sounds of it.

"I decided to go with my gut this time," Travis said without offering any further explanation.

"If I didn't know better, I'd say you were getting seriously laid."

"What do you mean 'if you didn't know better'? What do you know about my sex life?"

"I know it has cobwebs growing on it," Blake said as he leaned back in his chair and propped his feet on the table.

Jenna couldn't help it—she laughed out loud—and Blake smiled at her as if they were sharing a favorite joke.

"Believe that if you want," Travis said with a shrug, and Jenna saw in Blake's expression disappointment that he couldn't get a rise out of his brother.

"See what I mean? You're being way too casual. You *are* getting laid, aren't you? Are you and Natalie doing the nasty again?"

Jenna recalled the elegant woman who'd accosted Travis at the Fourth of July party. She looked like the kind of woman he belonged with, and Jenna wondered if Travis had told her the whole story on Natalie.

Not that it was any of her business.

The receptionist who'd directed Jenna to the meeting room earlier stuck her head inside the door, then opened it wide for a middle-aged couple Jenna assumed were the Williamses.

Jenna took a deep breath and willed herself to relax and think Kathryn thoughts. No more fantasizing about Travis, and no more chuckling about his sex life.

This was it, the most important part of her job, making sure Kathryn's charity project got the land it needed. She may not have cared for helping her sister, but she wanted the women and children's shelter to be a success.

And if she had her way, it would be.

10

IF TRAVIS HAD TO ENDURE one more minute of pretending Jenna was his brother's fiancée, he was going to hit something. He stood up from the arm of the sofa and stalked across the room, tension coiled inside him. He felt ready to spring at the nearest object in his path.

His parents had thrown a cocktail party tonight to welcome Jenna's parents to Carmel, and Jenna had survived the ultimate test—convincing her own mother that she was Kathryn. But Travis wasn't entirely sure *he* was going to survive the rest of the evening.

For the past week and a half, they'd managed to avoid any major incidents, and no one had guessed that "Kathryn" was a fraud. Maybe a few people had noticed she wasn't quite behaving like herself, but they had no reason to question the issue.

Jenna even seemed to have relaxed into the role. But Travis, on the other hand, was a mess. He was barely sleeping at night, taking cold showers at odd hours and generally not giving a damn about work. Actually, that last change was pretty refresh-

ing. It felt liberating not to be worried about the
countless details of running the business.

He should have been happy with the way the
whole scheme had worked out. Not only had
Jenna done a good job, she'd been fabulous at convincing the Williamses to donate their land to
Kathryn's charity project, and that alone should
have been enough to put Travis at ease.

But it wasn't. Because what he really wanted
was Jenna, all to himself.

And then there was the whole issue of the real
Kathryn, who still hadn't shown up and had been
very noncommittal when he'd spoken to her yesterday. In spite of her insistence that she wouldn't
miss the wedding, she wouldn't say when she'd
be back in town. The swelling, she claimed, was
still too noticeable.

"I'd like to propose a toast," Blake was saying for
the tenth time—his words slurring so that propose
came out "proposh"—"to my lovely Kathryn."

Travis halted at the door, unable to look away
from the spectacle. Blake never could handle his
liquor.

People standing close by looked at each other,
apparently wondering if they really would be
forced to toast Kathryn yet again, but then Blake
raised his martini glass to the Tiffany lamp next to
him and clinked it against the shade.

Jenna managed to look affectionately tolerant
standing at Blake's side, but when he reached out
and placed one hand on her backside, she slipped

away from his grasp. Her gaze sought Travis out, and she gave him a pleading look.

He nodded as discreetly as he could toward the door, and after a moment, he turned and walked out, furious with himself for jumping at another opportunity to be alone with her. He practically ran down the hallway to the foyer and stood there stiff with tension. Was he really about to do something as tawdry as slip into the coat closet with his brother's fake fiancée?

A moment later, Jenna stepped out into the hallway and spotted him. The delicate lavender dress she wore draped her curves in a way that suggested both innocence and raw sexuality. He could see the outline of her breasts and hips, the delicious hint of cleavage at her bodice. He probably never would have noticed Kathryn in the dress, but on Jenna, knowing the vixen the dress concealed...

Yes. Yes, he was.

Jenna cast a glance toward the parlor and then came toward him. Before anyone could spot him, Travis opened the coat-closet door and slipped inside—not a difficult task considering this wasn't the coat-wearing season. Closing the door all but a crack, he found himself surrounded by ladies' shawls and a few sportcoats, the scents of cedar and unidentifiable perfumes and colognes mingling in the air.

He'd just cleared a spot for both of them to stand in when Jenna opened the door and stepped inside, then closed it behind her. Heat flooded his body in that instant, just as darkness closed in around them. After a few moments, he could see Jenna by the light under the door.

"We shouldn't be here," she whispered, taking a step closer and pressing her body against him, pinning him to the wall.

He slid his hands down over her hips and savored the feel of her. "Right. We should go back to the party before someone notices we're both missing."

"I'm going to murder Blake if I have to spend another minute with him."

"He's not your type?" he joked.

"He's like a young, WASP version of Homer Simpson."

Travis warned himself not to feel flattered. After all, he wasn't her type, either. He was just her temporary stress reliever.

He didn't have to worry about a response, because she kissed him then—a long, deep kiss that made him forget for the duration of it that they were in his parents' coat closet. It was only when she pulled away that he remembered.

"What if I go back in and tell everyone I'm not feeling well, then bow out early?" she whispered, breathless.

"We'd be breaking our no-contact rule."

"We already are," she said and slid her hand down, grasping his erection to make her point.

Travis closed his eyes and groaned down low in his throat. The past week and a half hadn't gone at all the way he'd planned, and now he wanted nothing more than to take Jenna home and make love to her all night.

In spite of his better judgment warning him that someone could decide to leave early and open the coat closet at any moment, he cupped her face in his hand and kissed her again, then let his other hand find her rigid nipple through the thin fabric of her dress.

"What the—"

Light flooded the closet, and Travis looked up to see his father standing in the doorway, red-faced and working up to what he knew was going to be an earsplitting bellow if he didn't intervene fast.

"Dad, wait. Let me explain—"

"Both of you, upstairs, now!" Roland Roth nearly growled.

His father turned and stormed up the stairs. Jenna gave Travis a wide-eyed look.

"I'm so sorry," she whispered as she straightened her dress, then slipped out of his grasp and peered into the foyer. "All's clear."

Travis followed her up the stairs, surprised at the lack of fear in his gut. He felt, oddly, almost relieved at his dad's discovery. Maybe even a little victorious in some perverse way, as if he'd finally been found out as a man of his own choosing.

At the top of the stairs, they could see Roland standing in the hallway outside his den. He stood with his arms crossed and an angry glare plastered on his face as they entered the room. Once they were inside, he closed the door behind them with a gentle firmness that expressed his wrath more clearly than a slam ever could. Travis knew his father's moods well, and he'd wager this was the darkest of dark.

Travis positioned himself between his father and Jenna instinctively. His father would not have hurt her, but he wanted to protect her from something, maybe the embarrassment that was soon to follow.

"You two disgust me," Roland said, glaring at Travis as if he were something slimy he'd just found under a rock.

"Dad, this isn't as bad as it looks." He wanted to blurt out the truth, let his father know he wasn't the scumbag he seemed to be and that Kathryn wasn't cheating on his brother, but he held back. They'd come this far, and he couldn't ruin their plan now, even if it meant letting Kathryn look bad to his father. So long as he didn't tell Travis's mother what he'd seen, the situation could be salvaged.

He glanced over his shoulder at Jenna, whose lipstick was smudged—and probably on his face, too. There wasn't going to be any explaining away what they'd been doing in the closet. He'd simply have to bear the brunt of his father's wrath until after the wedding.

"We were just—" Jenna started, but Travis held up a hand to silence her.

"I don't want to hear your excuses."

"Dad, wait—"

"Even if I hadn't witnessed this filthy behavior, I could have guessed what's been going on. You two look at each other like a couple of dogs in heat every time you're in the same room. You could at least have the decency to be discreet."

Damn it. Travis hadn't realized how much their attraction had shown on their faces. No telling how many members of the family now considered him a no-good sleaze.

As much as his dutiful-son side wanted to protest, he kept quiet. What was the worst that could happen? Okay, his father could tell Blake what was going on and Blake could cancel the wedding. That was the consequence he had to prevent.

Jenna spoke up first, though. "I don't love Travis, Mr. Roth. I love Blake. I'm ashamed of what's happened here, and I swear it won't ever happen again."

"You're damn right it won't. I've got a mind to remove you as head of Roth Investments, Travis. Any man who behaves this way isn't fit to run a company, as far as I'm concerned."

Travis's stomach clenched into a knot. But when he tried to muster the energy to argue, nothing happened. Even stranger, the knot began to relax, as if being removed as head of Roth Investments simply wasn't that big a deal to him.

"No, you can't do that!" Jenna said. "Whatever you want—"'

"What I want is a promise from both of you that you won't go near each other again."

"Then you have my promise."

His father looked at Jenna as if her promise was about as valuable as an old shoe, but she kept her gaze leveled on him without flinching. He had to admire her courage.

"Mine, too," Travis said. "Does this mean you won't tell Blake?"

His father aimed his look of disgust at Travis again. "I should, but as far as I can tell, Blake's finally settling down with Kathryn, and I don't see any point in ruining his happiness if you two can straighten up."

Travis shouldn't have been surprised. His father would do just about anything to protect Blake. It struck him in that moment that his father's protectiveness was a big factor in Blake's irresponsibility, that having someone always looking out for him so closely had made Blake too lazy to look out for himself like an adult.

Gritting his teeth, Travis produced his most humble expression. "Thank you, Dad. I appreciate your discretion, and I don't deserve it."

"Damn right you don't. I haven't decided yet what the repercussions for you should be."

Travis glanced at Jenna and caught her stricken expression. She seemed about to protest again, but he gave her a warning look and shook his head.

So what if he had to give up Roth Investments? Was that really such a bad thing? Couldn't he find a job anywhere, doing anything he wanted? Of course he could. If his time building the family legacy had passed, Travis realized, he was okay with that. He could build his own legacy.

Roland looked back and forth between the two of them. "If I ever catch the two of you together again, you can be damn sure I'll make your lives miserable. Understand?"

They nodded simultaneously, and his father turned and stalked out of the room. Jenna exhaled and smoothed an errant curl behind her ear.

"That was fun," she whispered.

"Fun like a train wreck."

"I'm surprised he left us here alone. Do you think he's hovering in the hallway eavesdropping?"

"Anything's possible. We'd better get back to the party before anyone else comes looking for us."

"I'm so sorry, Travis."

"I'm not." He blinked at his own admission. Was it true? Yeah, it was.

Not only wasn't he sorry for letting things get out of hand with Jenna, he was damn happy that he'd finally found a woman he could feel so passionately about. If it meant losing his position at Roth Investments, screwing up his brother's wedding, failing to meet his family's expectations, so be it. He was having a hard time giving a damn.

In fact, if he had to label his predominant emotion at that moment, he'd call it…thrilled. He was falling in love with Jenna Calvert, for better or worse, and he couldn't be anything but thrilled about it.

Whether he was her type or not, he decided the

newly discovered risk taker in him would speak up and let Jenna know exactly how he felt.

But then she spoke up first.

"We have to stop. No more private encounters, no more anything."

"Because of my father?"

"Because I don't see this going anywhere, and it's only going to create more trouble the longer we mess around."

Travis absorbed the blow to his pride without flinching. Okay, so she wasn't feeling quite as adventurous as he was. That didn't mean she couldn't be persuaded. After all, he knew exactly the kind of persuasion she liked best.

"Jenna, I think what we have here is worth pursuing."

She glared at him as if he'd lost his mind. "What we have is just a sex thing."

Just a sex thing? Could he really expect her to see it as anything more when she'd entered into the relationship wanting it to be purely sexual?

No, he couldn't. And as much as he felt inspired to take a risk with her, he knew better than to push their relationship further than she wanted it to go.

"If that's the way you feel, then I guess there's nothing more to say."

"I'm sure Blake is wondering where I am by now," Jenna said, edging her way toward the door.

"Right." Travis watched as she walked out the

door, and for the first time in his life, he experienced the sensation of wanting something he couldn't have.

JENNA FLOPPED DOWN on the sofa, kicked off her heels and exhaled. She'd survived the rehearsal dinner and bachelorette party with a minimum of awkwardness. Although an alarming number of Kathryn's friends were difficult to tell apart with their identically tasteful but bland outfits and identically neutral good looks, she'd managed to keep them straight by having studied their photos.

Jenna sighed with relief. She'd survived two weeks impersonating Kathryn, and she hadn't been discovered. If it wasn't for the fact that her sister still hadn't shown up, she'd feel thrilled that tomorrow was the final day of the charade. She'd be able to take her money and go.... But then, the thought of going put a hollow feeling in her gut, as if she were leaving something behind.

Or someone.

But she couldn't leave behind a man she didn't really have any claim on, so she needed to just put that idea out of her head. She knew how to walk away with her last shed of dignity intact, and she'd do exactly that as soon as she had a check in hand.

She was just contemplating hunting down a package of chocolate chip cookies in the kitchen when her cell phone rang from inside her purse, startling her into a state of alertness. A glance at the wall clock told her it was almost midnight, and she wasn't expecting any calls. She dug the phone out of her purse.

"Hello?"

"I'm watching you," an oddly distorted voice said—the sort of voice serial killers and stalkers always used in the movies.

Jenna's stomach flip-flopped, and she glanced nervously toward the wall of windows that looked out on the ocean. Could it be that someone was lurking on the front lawn, waiting for her?

"Who is this?" she demanded.

"You'd better watch out," the voice said ominously.

It sounded like a man but could have been a woman using some kind of voice distortion device. Jenna tried to ignore the panic rising in her chest and think what she should do next.

"Watch out for what?"

And then she heard nothing but silence. The caller had hung up. Jenna's mouth went dry, and she hit the end call button and dropped the phone as if it had caught fire.

Had her stalker caught up with her in Carmel? If so, how? Was he watching her from outside?

The thought made her grab the phone again to call 911. But then she remembered the detective who was working on her case in the city. Should she call him first?

No, she decided. She needed to call the local police first, have someone come out and look around. But rather than find the phone book to look up the nonemergency police number, she could only think of Travis's number, which she'd already managed to memorize in the short time she'd known him.

She was just about to dial it when the doorbell rang.

Jenna's breath caught in her throat. She glanced around for a weapon and realized she had nothing. She'd let her guard down since coming to Carmel; she'd felt safe.

A small, abstract marble sculpture sat on a nearby table. Jenna picked it up and felt the weight of it in her hands. It could do serious damage if it made contact with the right body part.

She crept to the door and peered out the peephole, half expecting to see a thug in a ski mask.

Instead, she saw Blake, which was almost as bad as a thug in a ski mask. It occurred to her only then that a criminal probably wouldn't have bothered to ring the doorbell. Tension drained from her body, and she expelled a pent-up breath she hadn't realized she'd been holding in.

Jenna considered just not opening the door, but no sooner did the thought form in her head than Blake peered in the window beside the door and saw her standing there.

Damn it.

She turned the lock and slowly opened the door. "Hey, baby. I just had to see you again tonight," he said, but "just" came out sounding like "jush," and his eyes looked bleary.

"Have you been drinking?"

"Jush a little bit. Are you gonna make me stand out here in the cold all night?"

Jenna peered out at the driveway. No car. "How did you get here?"

"I got a ride with a couple of guys from the bachelor party."

She didn't see any choice but to step aside and let him in. He gave her a crooked smile and shuffled into the living room.

"They wanted to go to a strip club," he continued, "but I told them that if I saw any naked women tonight, it was going to be my own woman."

"Oh. How…sweet." Jenna's mouth went dry, and she tried to produce on a nonpanicked smile. "But don't forget our agreement."

"It's less than a day until the wedding. I'm dying here!"

"Exactly—less than a day. By tomorrow night, we'll be…" What? If Kathryn failed to show up, would they be married and stuck in conjugal bliss? Jenna forced herself not to shudder. "Married."

Blake flashed another bleary smile and weaved toward her, his arms extended in a clumsy hug. He nearly toppled Jenna. "Come on baby, please?"

He found her ear and jammed his tongue into it, and the overture made her think of being assaulted by a slug.

Jenna untangled herself from his embrace and stepped back, resisting the urge to rub her ear. "Blakey, you've clearly had too much to drink, and if you don't sleep it off, you're going to feel awful for our wedding."

"Can I sleep here?"

"If I see you in the morning, it will be bad luck."

"But I don't have a way home."

So she'd call him a cab—but that sounded like a pretty coldhearted thing for Kathryn to offer. Jenna just wanted to get out of this place, away from this man, out of her sister's life.

"I'll drive you home."

Blake seemed to be trying to figure out how his plan to get laid had gone wrong. He frowned. "But…"

"Don't worry, darling," she forced out, "we'll be together tomorrow. Tonight, we both need our rest."

"Um…"

Jenna found her shoes and grabbed her keys and purse. "Come on, let's go before we change our minds and do something stupid."

Like ditch Blake on the side of the road.

She brushed past him and marched out to Kathryn's car, then climbed into the driver's seat and watched as her faux fiancé shuffled to the car like a forlorn puppy.

He was just acting like a typical guy who couldn't understand why his fiancée was behaving so strangely. She was directing her anger at the wrong person. Truly, the only person she had to

be angry with was herself for agreeing to impersonate her sister. She needed to cut Blake some
slack. Aside from his inability to hold his alcohol
and his generally airheaded view of life, he was a
decent guy, a good match for Kathryn.

Why that suddenly mattered to her, she
couldn't say, but it struck her then how oddly close
to her twin she felt after walking around in her life
for a few weeks. It was almost as if she were starting to miss Kathryn.

Miss Kathryn? No way.

Blake settled into the passenger seat and emitted periodic yawns as Jenna drove. She reached for
the radio to avoid any further conversation, but as
soon as she found a station, Blake turned it off.

"It's kinda strange. Sometimes I feel like you're
becoming a different person."

Jenna stiffened, and her palms grew damp on
the steering wheel. "How so?"

"Like that radio station. You never used to like
talk radio. You said it made your head hurt."

Oh, right. "I'm just trying to expand my hori-
zons—that's all." She tilted her head in that cutesy way Kathryn always did. "I want to be able to
impress your friends with my knowledge of world
events and stuff."

"Honey, you don't need to worry about im-
pressing my friends."

"Well, if you say so…"

"It's not just the radio thing. It's the way you've

seemed a little standoffish in the past few weeks, and you've had this look in your eyes."

"What kind of look?"

He seemed to search for the right words. "Like you're always thinking of the punch line to a dirty joke."

Jenna glanced at herself in the rearview mirror. *Did* she always have that look in her eyes?

"I guess it's just prewedding jitters."

"It's almost like you're a whole new woman since you came back from that spa."

Jenna focused on the road ahead and did her best to keep from steering off into a ditch. Travis would have choked to hear his little brother making such astute observations.

"Well, my week there had quite an impact on me." In a manner of speaking.

"You haven't had any second thoughts about the wedding, have you?"

"Don't be silly, darling. I can't wait until tomorrow." At least that much was true. Come Saturday night, she hoped to be long gone from Carmel, no longer walking around in Kathryn's life.

Or she could be stuck in a fake marriage with her sister's intended.

Jenna steered into Blake's driveway and left the engine idling, waiting for Blake to get the heck out of her car. She looked at him expectantly, but he didn't budge.

"Only a matter of hours, and we'll be married!" She forced a smile and an affectionate pat on the arm.

Blake leaned over to kiss her, and she offered up her right cheek.

"Well, see you at the wedding tomorrow, then."

When he'd stumbled inside his front door, Jenna backed out of the driveway and found herself dreading the thought of returning to Kathryn's place again. She made a left instead of a right at the first intersection she came to, taking her away from Kathryn's house and toward…what?

She wanted the fastest escape route out of Kathryn's life, and the only person in Carmel who knew her as Jenna and therefore could provide that escape wasn't likely to welcome her with open arms. Ever since their encounter in the coat closet and subsequent confrontation with Roland Roth, Travis had been cool and distant, and she couldn't blame him.

She felt horrible that his relationship with his father and his entire plan to help her sister was in jeopardy just because she couldn't keep her hands off him, and she didn't want to make matters any worse than they already were. She'd sworn to herself that night that she wouldn't touch Travis again, that she wouldn't so much as look in his direction.

But as she steered Kathryn's convertible onto the main road through town, her destination became clear. She needed to talk to him, to see him, ⸱e she needed air and water. It was surely just the ⸱ of dealing with Blake again so late at night, but a magnetic force pulled her toward the one destination she should have avoided at all costs.

Travis may not welcome her, but she had to try. She had to have someone look at her and see her true self, even if it was only long enough to tell her to get lost. If she could just be Jenna, even for only a few minutes, then maybe she could sleep tonight.

Ten minutes later, she parked in the space next to Travis's Mercedes. When she reached his door, her hands grew clammy, and she had to wipe them off on her dress. At this late hour, a few lights were still on in Travis's condo. She took a deep breath and rang the doorbell.

When he opened the door, his expression was neutral. "Is something wrong?"

"Blake came by tonight drunk to beg his fiancée to come to her senses and sleep with him."

"What did you do?"

"I drove him home. What did you think? I'd invite him in for a roll in the hay?"

"I didn't say that. Are you okay?"

"It just shook me up a little. I'm not even sure why I'm here."

His expression still blank, he stepped aside. "Come in."

Jenna stopped in the foyer, wondering what the hell she was doing. Hoping for another night with him? In spite of their differences, in spite of the fact that they couldn't be caught together, in spite of the fact that they had no basis for a real relationship?

Had she gotten that desperate? She took one look at the expanse of his shoulders in a white oxford and knew that she had. She wanted him, regardless of everything else.

She hugged herself, suddenly feeling chilly. A rush of emotion hit her in the chest, and she felt her eyes welling up with tears.

What the hell was going on here? Jenna Calvert didn't burst into tears at the slightest sign of stress.

That was the sort of thing her sister would do. Was she turning into Kathryn after spending two weeks in her life?

Hell no. She blinked away the tears and forced herself to smile. "I'm fine," she said, but her voice broke on "fine."

Travis took her into his arms and held her close, letting the heat of his chest warm her. She slid her arms around his waist and allowed herself to sink in and savor the feel of him. So what if she was crying like a helpless damsel in distress?

Travis pulled back and tilted her face up to his. "I've missed this."

This, as in their physical relationship. Not her. Still, it was something.

"So have I."

She watched his internal struggle reveal itself in his eyes. She'd have bet anything he was trying to decide how far he would allow himself to go.

"You know the first time we kissed, in the parking of that biker bar?"

"I felt like a new man that night. How is it that you have such a strong effect on me?"

"I don't know. Is that a good thing or a bad thing?"

"I don't know, either."

"I guess you have to decide if you want to be the kind of guy who makes out in the parking lot of a biker bar," she said, only half joking.

"I guess so," he murmured right before placing a soft kiss on her lips.

Jenna held back, letting him decide how far to take it. And he did nothing more than brush his lips on hers. But that barely there sensation was like electricity, bringing all her nerve endings to life.

"I didn't come here for this," she whispered.

"Then why did you come here?"

"Because you know I'm not Kathryn."

"It will all be over with tomorrow." He brushed a strand of hair off her cheek.

"Will it? What if Kathryn doesn't show up? Have you even heard from her?"

He paled. "Not since Monday. I was sure I'd convinced her she can't miss her own wedding."

"But I know Kathryn. If she doesn't look perfect, she's not going to show. Was her face still swollen on Monday?"

Travis nodded, his expression grim.

Jenna shuddered. The thought of really having to go through with a fraudulent wedding was something she hadn't allowed herself to consider much. "Does the minister know he might not be performing a legal ceremony?"

Travis exhaled and walked over to the couch, where he collapsed and raked his fingers through his hair. He looked exhausted. "I explained to him that the bride and groom might not be prepared to sign the marriage certificate tomorrow."

That still didn't eliminate the problem of standing at a church altar and making false vows. Jenna knew without a doubt that, regardless of the twenty-five grand, she couldn't do *that*. Masquerading as her sister for the sake of a good cause was one thing, but playing games with the divine was more than Jenna was willing to do.

"Travis, if she doesn't show up—"

He held up a hand. "Let's don't cross that bridge unless we have to."

Right. She didn't have the energy to push the issue now, so she'd just keep blindly hoping, at least until morning, that Kathryn would show.

Jenna slipped off her sandals and went to the couch, then sat down beside Travis, releasing a sigh she hadn't realized had built up inside her. He reached out and ran his thumb along the edge of her jaw, a gentle caress that said more than words could have.

All her good intentions melted away, and she ˡᵗed him with a fierceness that wouldn't be

"You look like you're in need of some stress relief," she whispered.

His weary expression transformed into a slow smile. "You'd better believe it."

That was all the invitation she needed. She climbed onto his lap, well aware that the maneuver pushed the skirt of her dress up to the tops of her thighs. If he wanted, he'd get a prime view of her hot pink lace panties.

His hands found her bare thighs, and he slid them up until his fingertips brushed the seam of her panties. "I was hoping you'd come over here."

"What else are you hoping for?"

"You probably know that better than I do."

Jenna leaned in and brushed his lips with the lightest of kisses. "I think I've got a pretty good idea."

11

THERE WAS NO DENYING how much Travis wanted Jenna. No more playing games, no more ignoring the electricity that surged between them. At least not tonight.

The moment he'd seen her on his doorstep, he knew he had to have her one more time. Maybe the morning light would reveal all the ugly truths that kept them apart, but for tonight, there was no further will left in him to resist her wild sex appeal. Even all polished up as a duplicate of Kathryn, Jenna was still an untamable vixen. He'd been a fool to think he could change that—a fool to have ever wanted to change her.

She began to unbuckle his belt, and a moment later her hand slipped inside his pants and found him hard and ready. He lifted her up from the couch ___ ill but dragged her to the bedroom, where he ___ her on the bed and pushed her dress up to ___ suddenly feeling that same caveman ___ st experienced at the biker bar.

___ he wasn't Travis Roth the CEO, or ___ or the wealthy catch. He was someone entirely different—someone he wasn't quite sure he recognized as himself, at least not before two weeks ago. Jenna seemed oblivious to his money, unimpressed with his status, interested in him purely as a man.

Travis trailed hungry kisses up her leg until he found the sensitive flesh of her inner thigh. He took a gentle bite, then moved up to her panties and tugged at them with his teeth. Once he'd rid her of the hot pink scrap of lace, he buried his face in her honey-colored curls and plunged his tongue inside her.

She bucked and gasped, but he held her hips still as he began to massage and explore with his tongue. Soon, she settled in and let him do as he pleased.

When her breathing became rapid and shallow, he pulled back, not wanting her to leave satisfied too soon—not when he had so many other things he wanted to do with her yet. He crawled up onto her and settled his hips between her legs, then began to grind through the fabric of his underwear. She was wet and ready for him, and the sensation of it, even through cotton, was amazing.

He didn't want any barriers now, though. He wanted to feel her hot flesh warming his whole body, so he stood and pulled her up by her hands, then freed her of her dress and bra. It only took another few moments for him to get undressed himself and reposition himself between her legs. He wanted so badly to be buried in the wet heat of her that he nearly forgot himself, but just in time, he remembered the need for a condom and reached for his nightstand drawer to find one.

Once he'd tugged it on, Jenna wrapped her legs tight around his waist and with a shift of her hips, he slid inside of her. He pushed himself deeper until their bodies were completely joined, and then he paused and buried his face in her neck, savoring the feel of her.

Jenna slid her hands down his back and grasped his buttocks as she sank her teeth into his shoulder, and he could no longer lie still. He raised up on his elbows and thrust into her with growing intensity, watching pleasure transform her face as she gasped and cried out.

This was where he belonged, where he fit perfectly, where he never wanted to leave. Here with Jenna, just the two of them, Travis felt as if he'd found his place in the world—or at least his place in bed.

He paused long enough to taste her breasts, savoring the heavy, perfect weight of them, her tight nipples begging for his attention. He inhaled her soft, female scent and committed it to memory, because he knew he'd need something to cling to after she walked out of his life.

Wrapping his arms around her, he rolled onto his back and pulled Jenna on top of him. When she sat up and began rocking her hips, the sensation brought him instantly to the edge of climax, until he willed his body to slow down. He grasped her hips and slowed her pace, savoring each shift of her body against him.

She watched him as they made love, her gaze as bold as everything else about her, but for the first time, watching her, too, Travis noticed something in her gaze he'd never seen before—vulnerability. Peering out from behind the untamable temptress, he saw a woman who wasn't totally sure of something.

But then she grasped his wrists and pinned them over his head, increasing their pace on her own, driving them quickly toward release. And when she began to cry out, her contractions brought him his release, too. He broke free from the binds of her hands and pulled her against him, kissed her long and hard until the waves of pleasure passed.

In that moment, with Jenna in his arms, Travis knew that what they had was a once-in-a-lifetime kind of connection, and he could not imagine letting her go.

JENNA AWOKE to the sensation of a man's warm body against hers, and she realized with a start that she'd allowed herself to fall asleep in Travis's bed. She looked around for a clock and saw one on the nightstand that said it was 5:00 a.m.

Damn it, she'd never intended to stay here all night, and she wanted to leave before anyone might stop by and see Kathryn's car parked in Travis's driveway.

She sat up and watched Travis for a moment as he slept. Heat radiated out from his body, warming her, reminding her of the heat they'd generated earlier. Together, they were combustible, and she couldn't imagine recreating such chemistry with another man.

But there would be no more nights like this with Travis. He'd hired her to impersonate her sister, and the fact that she'd slept with him, too, was just a perk to him. An unexpected benefit.

So, that was life. She wasn't going to get all bent out of shape just because some millionaire bachelor wanted her sexually.

That's all she'd wanted from him, too, wasn't it?

Absolutely.

"Something wrong?" Travis said, his voice gravelly from sleep.

"I'd better go. I've got an early day today, and so do you."

"The wedding," he groaned. "Don't remind me." He rolled toward her and draped his arm across her lap. "You don't have to leave."

"What if Blake shows up here in a few hours— what if anyone does?"

"Oh, right." His voice was stronger now. He'd been jarred wide awake at the thought of their getting caught, apparently.

Jenna slipped out from under the weight of his arm and stood up from the bed, oddly uncomfortable with her nakedness for the first time in front of Travis. She groped around on the floor for her clothes and fumbled to dress quickly in the half darkness.

"I guess we'll see each other at the wedding, then."

He sat up in bed and exhaled a frustrated sigh. "I'm sure it won't come to that."

"How can you be so sure when you haven't even heard from Kathryn?"

"If she doesn't show up, the wedding is off."

Jenna paused in the middle of zipping her dress. "After all the trouble you've gone through, you'd really let it be called off?"

"I won't let you participate in a fraudulent wedding."

"Oh." She'd never expected him to put her above his family now, after they'd gone through so much trouble to cover for Kathryn.

He slipped out of bed himself and tugged on a pair of pants, then went to his dresser. "In case I don't get a chance later, I should pay you now."

Jenna watched, her throat and mouth going dry as he withdrew a check from his wallet and strode over to her.

"Twenty-five thousand dollars, as we agreed upon."

She stared at the check, at his small, neat handwriting that spelled out the numbers to more money than she'd ever been given at one time. She should have been happy to have her money and a one-way ticket out of Kathryn's life, but instead, she finally saw exactly what she'd gotten herself into.

Standing there with her dress half-zipped in Travis's bedroom, with his scent still lingering on her skin, she understood what she was to him.

A whore.

She'd been his paid distraction for a few stressful weeks, and she'd walked right into the job willingly. She'd even volunteered her services—made them a part of the deal.

Her voice caught in her throat, and she couldn't lift her hand to take the check. Wouldn't take it. She still had one last scrap of her pride, at least, and she could use it to walk out of Travis's life now and for good.

Blinking back tears, she shook her head. "Keep your damn money."

Jenna turned and hurried from the room, grabbed her bag in the living room and found her shoes. Travis stopped her at the front door.

"What's the matter?"

"Your timing couldn't be more clear. You don't have to pay me off to make sure I get lost."

He looked at her as if she were speaking a foreign language. "You held up your end of the deal, and you earned the money."

"I'm not a prostitute."

"I never said you were." He reached out for her, but she skirted his touch. "You were the one who suggested we bring sex into the deal."

"Right. It was the stupidest idea I've ever had." She opened the door and ran out, determined not to let him see her tears.

"Jenna, wait!"

But she didn't. She climbed into Kathryn's car and slammed the door, tossing Travis a look that let him know exactly how bad an idea it would be to follow her.

Of all the wild stunts she'd ever pulled in the face of stress, sleeping with Travis Roth had been, by far, the dumbest, and now she only wanted to get as far away from him as possible. Maybe distance would ease her sense of foolishness. Or not. At the very least, running away gave her something to do.

Jenna was halfway back to Kathryn's house when she glanced into the rearview mirror and noted the pair of headlights that had been with her, she was almost sure, nearly since she'd left Travis's condo. If she hadn't been so focused on making sure he didn't follow her, she might not have noticed this car.

As she navigated the roads through town, tension coiled inside her the longer the car stayed on her tail. It would have been an amazing coincidence for someone to be out driving so early in the morning, taking the exact same path through town that Jenna was taking.

But why would anyone follow her? Could it have been Blake, suspicious of his fiancée having an affair, now ready to confront her with proof? Jenna chewed her lip, imagining what she might say if confronted. Now that she'd turned down Travis's money, would she just tell Blake the truth, or would she leave that for Travis and Kathryn to explain? Maybe they were the ones who deserved to face Blake's wrath.

But what if it wasn't Blake? What if the person or persons who'd been after her in San Francisco *had* tracked her down in sleepy little Carmel? What if they were just waiting for the opportunity to run her off the road—or worse?

To test the theory, she took a few unnecessary turns and watched as the car followed her. Her heart raced, and she began scanning the street for a police station, a fire station—anyplace safe. All she spotted was a twenty-four hour gas station lit up in the fading early morning darkness. It would have to do. Jenna pulled into it and parked, then watched as the car slowed in front of the station and continued on down the road. Jenna couldn't see more than an outline of the driver, but if she'd had to guess, she would have said it was a woman.

The car was a sedan bland enough that she couldn't tell the make or model, definitely not Blake's splashy red Porsche.

Maybe she was just letting paranoia get the best of her. Who could have tracked her down here? Really, the notion of someone following her all the way to Carmel, lurking in the shadows undetected the entire time, was preposterous.

Inch by inch the tension drained from her body as she watched the car's taillights travel farther and farther away, then disappear completely. It really had just been an odd coincidence that the car had made all the same turns as Jenna. Maybe the person had been lost and was just following the only other car on the road hoping to find his or her way back to the center of town.

Yes, that had to be it. Jenna exhaled a ragged breath and pulled out of the gas station lot.

12

JENNA AWOKE WITH A START, her brain groggy from too little sleep. The alarm clock confirmed that it was only 9:00 a.m.—three hours since she'd collapsed in bed.

She was aware of the sensation of someone's presence in the room. But she wasn't at Travis's house anymore, so she should have been alone. She sat up in bed, her heart pounding, and nearly screamed when she saw a figure sitting at the foot of the bed.

It took her a split second to realize it was her twin sister. "Kathryn!"

"Hey, sis. Nice hair." Kathryn smiled, and Jenna noted that there were no unsightly bulges on her lips or cheeks.

"Your face is normal," she muttered, pushing herself up in bed and squinting at her sister in the morning sunlight.

Perfectly normal, if slightly more inflated than what nature had given them.

Kathryn lifted a hand to her cheek self-consciously. "The swelling only went down completely yesterday."

"You could have called to let us know you were coming back."

"I'm sorry. I tried, but I couldn't reach Travis. I figured you would know I wouldn't miss my own wedding."

"We couldn't be sure about that."

"I missed my flight home last night because of traffic on the way to the airport, so I had to catch the red-eye this morning."

"I'm just glad you're back. I couldn't have gone through with a sham wedding," she said, remembering only after she spoke that Travis had relieved her of that responsibility.

She forced the memory of early morning out of her head.

"Thank you…for everything. I know it probably seems ridiculous to you, but—"

"But you want your in-laws and everyone else to think well of you."

Kathryn blinked at her lack of hostility. "Yes."

"That's understandable."

"Um, thanks."

It struck Jenna that this was possibly the longest and most civil conversation she'd had with her sister in years. Strangely, she didn't even feel like throttling Kathryn for nearly missing her own wedding and putting Jenna through two weeks of the most bizarre sort of torture.

She yawned and stretched. Time to start getting ready for the wedding—that is, it would be if she were still the bride. Which she wasn't, thank God.

The thought thrilled her so much, she nearly leaped out of bed to give her sister a big hug. Instead, she swung her legs over the edge and sat there until the fog lifted from her brain.

"It must have been strange for you, pretending to be me, walking around in my life."

Jenna tried to muster some righteous anger, or at least a sense of annoyance, but nothing came. Walking around in her sister's life for two weeks had made her...what? Want Kathryn back in her life, she realized with a start.

She didn't want them to be separated by petty differences anymore. She wanted a sister. The Roths, for all their problems, clearly benefited from having such a close family, and Jenna had started to understand what she'd been missing out on by letting her differences with her twin get in the way of their relationship.

"It was definitely strange..." she said, staring across the room at the little music box Kathryn had had since they were kids. Jenna knew that if she opened it, a ballerina would pop up and start spinning around as tinkling music played. She'd had an identical one long ago.

"Travis said you were able to handle Blake without any incidents." Jenna looked over at Kathryn to see her staring at her hopefully.

"Don't worry, there was no hanky-panky. He thinks you read a sex manual at the spa that convinced you of the value of no physical contact for the two weeks leading up to the wedding."

Kathryn laughed. "Poor guy. I wish Travis would have let me tell him what was going on, but he was convinced Blake wouldn't be able to keep up the act if he knew you weren't me. He was probably right."

"Blake showed up here last night, drunk and ready for action. You drove him home."

"Oh. Thanks."

"Are you going to tell him about this whole thing?"

"Of course. I think I'll wait until the honeymoon, though, so the news doesn't upset our wedding day."

"How do you think he'll take it?"

Kathryn smiled. "I'm sure he'll take the news just fine if I time it well—say, when he's basking in the afterglow of reunion sex."

"That's all the detail I need."

"I feel awful getting married with a lie between us, though."

"Maybe you should tell him now." Jenna stood up and stretched her back, feeling the tension drain away bit by bit as the reality that she no longer had to be Kathryn sunk in.

"I don't know...."

"I think he'll take it okay. So long as you tell him why you did what you did, he'll understand."

"You think?"

"I'm sure. Maybe you could bring him some breakfast and coffee to help him with his hangover."

Kathryn stood up from the bed. "I'd better get

going then. I don't have much time before I have to be at the salon."

"I guess I'll hang out here if you don't mind. I don't have a way home—"

"You'll come to the wedding, won't you?"

"I'm invited?"

Jenna imagined having to see Travis again, and her stomach grew queasy.

"Of course." Kathryn gave her an odd look. "I was hoping the fact that you were willing to help me meant we could stop being mad at each other."

"Yeah, me, too."

"I'm sorry, Jen. I didn't treat you well in high school, and it's only gotten worse since then."

"I didn't make it easy to be nice."

"I guess I had my own resentments for the way you wanted to be different from me. I'd always loved the way things were when we were 'the twins.'"

"I know you did." Jenna had a sudden and uncontrollable urge to hug her sister for the first time in more years than she could remember. Maybe she'd never enjoyed being one of an inseparable pair the way Kathryn had, but she could understand her sister's longings, at least.

She went to Kathryn and gave her an awkward squeeze. Her sister smiled when they parted, and Jenna felt silly for having to blink back the sudden dampness in her eyes.

"Now go talk to that fiancé of yours. I'll be here when you get back."

"You promise?"

"I promise."

Jenna watched as Kathryn hurried out the door, her designer sundress swishing as she walked, and she realized for once that she was looking at her sister and not just her identical twin.

TRAVIS DOUBLE-CHECKED his pocket for the wedding ring, then headed out into the church lobby to greet the guests who were beginning to trickle in. Kathryn had said Jenna was going to attend the wedding, but that didn't mean she'd even give him a cold glance.

Not that he could blame her. His timing had been lousy, trying to offer her a check right after she'd climbed out of his bed, but he wouldn't feel right until he knew she was compensated for all the trouble she'd gone through.

Travis smiled and nodded at distant relations and acquaintances as he wandered through the lobby. It wasn't until the church was half-full that he spotted the tall, slender blonde he'd been looking for. She wore a racy red dress that set her apart from her sister, and she'd done something to her hair that had transformed it from Kathryn's classic, tasteful style to a wild, sexy mop of waves and spikes. Her lips were painted vixen-red to match her dress, and her high-heeled sandals were the exact same shade.

Here was the woman who'd invited him into her shower, who'd seduced him in a biker bar, who'd turned him from an uptight bore into a man he could hardly recognize as himself. A man who took risks at work and in his personal life and felt exhilarated by each and every one of them.

But seeing Jenna gave him a stab of regret, as if he'd failed in taking a risk where it mattered most.

She climbed the steps of the church and entered the front doors without so much as glancing at him.

"Jenna?"

She shot him a look of pure animosity, her eyes icy blue. And then she kept walking, straight into the sanctuary, where she found a seat in one of the rear pews.

Others had noticed her, too, and were staring after her in disbelief. "Was that—" a man standing next to Travis began.

"That was Kathryn's twin sister, Jenna."

"I had no idea she had a twin."

"They're not very close," Travis said before wandering away.

His father caught up with him. "Travis, was that Kathryn's sister?"

"Yes," he said, trying to make his way back to the sanctuary where it was almost time for him to take his place at the altar next to Blake.

"Something strange is going on here." His father eyed him with interest, giving the matter serious thought. "Why do I get the feeling you have some explaining to do?"

"I have to go, Dad."

"There's been something odd about Kathryn these past few weeks, hasn't there?"

"In what way?"

"She just hasn't seemed like herself. And I never would have pegged her as an adulterer until I saw it with my own eyes...."

It took all his willpower not to confess the truth.

"Do you have something you need to tell me, son?"

"I'm not sure what you're talking about," he lied.

"Whatever it is, you've got my word I'll keep quiet about it."

Travis exhaled all of his frustration and pulled his dad to the side. "Kathryn disappeared, okay? She went off to a spa and had some botched lip enhancements done, then refused to come home. I hired her twin sister to impersonate her."

There. Now Roland Roth would know exactly how big a control freak his elder son really was.

But instead of looking disgusted, his father grinned. "You went to all that trouble to keep this wedding on track?"

He nodded.

"Blake couldn't have been in on this—he's too lousy at keeping a secret."

"He had no idea."

"But how did you keep him from coming on to the wrong woman?"

"Jenna took care of that. She kept him at arm's length the entire time."

And then a look of understanding dawned on

his father's face. "So I didn't catch you and *Kathryn* fooling around—it was you and her sister!"

In spite of himself, Travis felt a huge burden lifted from his shoulders. He realized then that no matter how badly he wanted not to care what his father thought of him, he did.

"Exactly."

"I'll make sure your mother never hears about this."

"Thanks, Dad. Now we'd better find our places."

The lobby had emptied, and everyone was seated inside the church now. He was supposed to be at the front of the sanctuary with Blake.

Travis found Blake in the rest room, adjusting his bow tie and patting nervously at his hair in a mirror. "It's time for us to go out."

"Kathryn talked to me today."

"About?"

Blake tossed him a look through the mirror. "You know what about. You could have told me."

"Could I? You're sure you could have kept quiet?"

Blake's expression turned sheepish. "Okay, probably not. But still, it weirds me out to know I was hitting on Kathryn's sister."

"Sorry."

Blake turned away from the mirror and gave Travis a friendly clap on the shoulder. "Thank you for helping Kathryn out the way you did. I know how important it was to her to keep Mom and

Dad and everyone else from thinking badly of her, and you kept the charity project on track."

Travis glanced at his watch again. "We'd better get going."

A few moments later they were positioned at the altar, and as Travis looked out over the crowd, he couldn't help letting his gaze settle on Jenna. She, however, never looked back at him.

And then his attention was drawn away from Jenna to a woman who entered the back of the church and looked around nervously. She was wearing a blue dress and clutching a matching blue handbag to her side as if it contained the crown jewels. Something about her seemed…off. Not quite right. Travis felt himself tense as he watched her.

She scanned the crowd from left to right, then took a seat near the end of the last pew. Jenna noticed the woman then, too, and stared at her with a look of recognition before looking away.

Travis relaxed then. The woman must have been someone Jenna and Kathryn knew.

Music began to play, and Kathryn's maid of honor started down the aisle. Next came the procession of identically lavender-satin-clad bridesmaids, then the flower girl. Finally, the music transitioned into the bridal march, and everyone in the church stood and turned to watch the bride enter.

Kathryn started down the aisle with her stepfather accompanying her, but again Travis found his gaze wandering away from the bride to her sister. Jenna was staring at the woman in the blue dress again, and he watched in what felt like slow motion as the woman reached into her handbag and withdrew a small handgun, then aimed it at Kathryn with shaking hands.

"Stop! A gun!" he yelled as his feet sprang into motion and carried him down the aisle.

But Jenna had seen the gun, too, and she pushed her way past people until there was no one between her and the woman with the weapon. She tackled the woman, and they were scrambling on the ground when Travis reached the back of the church and pushed his way through the gathering crowd.

The gun fired, and it felt as if his heart stopped beating. There was a collective pause, and then an uproar as someone shouted, "She's been shot! Call an ambulance!"

When Travis spotted Jenna on the floor, she was curled up in a fetal position with blood oozing from her side. His pulse kicked into overdrive, and he raced to her and dropped to his knees beside her.

He was vaguely aware of several men subduing the woman in the blue dress while she howled for them to let go of her. As he gently placed a hand on Jenna's shoulder, the crowd milled about them, and someone called out for a doctor.

"Jenna? Can you hear me?"

She said nothing. He felt for a pulse in her neck and was relieved to feel a faint but steady one. His throat tightened up, then his chest. He didn't want to lose her. Doing the only thing he could think of, he took off his jacket and pressed it to the wound on her side.

More than anything else in the world, he wanted her safe and well. He would have done anything to see her well again.

The sound of a woman's hysterical sobbing caught his attention, and he looked up to see Kathryn nearby, Blake restraining her, trying to console her.

"I'll take a look at her," a familiar voice said.

Travis looked up to see Bob Jensen, a surgeon and an old family friend, kneeling beside Jenna. He began examining her as she lay limp and unconscious, the bloodstain on her dress growing in spite of Travis's efforts.

"Is she going to be okay?"

"I don't know."

His eyes stung as he tried not to think about what "I don't know" might mean.

If he had the chance, he would make things right between them. And if he didn't have the chance, he'd spend the rest of his life regretting it.

JENNA STRUGGLED to climb out of the hazy nothingness. She heard voices, and images flashed in her mind. The woman in the brown wig, the gun, the explosive sound, the searing pain in her side. She didn't want to die.

Her eyes opened, and there was light, but she

couldn't focus. Her mind couldn't wrap itself around one thought for more than a moment. Was this what dying felt like?

"Jenna?" A voice sliced through her fear and gave her something to struggle toward.

Travis. She wanted to cry out with relief that he was there, but the haze wouldn't lift. She listened for his voice and fought to form complete thoughts. At least, she understood, she was alive.

Her last memory was of the woman in the brown wig, the woman who'd seemed oddly familiar until she aimed the gun at Kathryn, and then Jenna had known who she was.

Finally, she could open her eyes again, and she saw Travis. He looked as if he'd been awake for days, with dark half moons under his eyes and a five o'clock shadow coloring his jaw. His bow tie was gone, his tuxedo shirtsleeves rolled up, the formerly pristine white fabric splattered with blood.

Her blood.

His gaze was locked on Jenna, and she felt all the air whoosh out of her lungs. She hadn't realized how badly she'd wanted to see him, how much of the aching inside her had been a longing for him to be at her side. So much for her resolve not to let emotions get involved.

She struggled to clear her mind of the fog, to keep her eyes focused and thoughts coherent. Slowly, the fog lifted.

"Do you feel up to having a visitor?"

She tried to produce a smile. "Maybe just one,"

she said and was surprised when the words came out fully formed.

"Good." He stood up from his chair and gingerly sat down on the edge of her bed. "I was afraid you'd kick me out as soon as you saw me."

Jenna tried to sit up in bed, but the pain in her side convinced her that a horizontal position wasn't so bad. Then she noticed the buttons that raised and lowered the bed, and in a matter of seconds she'd adjusted the bed to a gentle angle just short of causing the pain to worsen.

He took her hand in his. "Hey, you. How are you feeling?"

"I've been better. I guess I ruined Kathryn's wedding."

"You didn't ruin anything. Everyone's waiting to hear that you're okay. They're planning to finish the ceremony tonight."

"The woman who shot me—was she caught?"

He nodded. "She's in police custody now. Apparently she's someone you interviewed during your research of the pageant industry?"

"I recognized her when I saw her in the church, but it took me a little too long to put two and two together. She'd been at your parents' Fourth of July party, too, but the wig she was wearing threw me."

"She's the one who's been harassing you, isn't she?"

"That's my guess. She seemed a little disturbed by my questions when I interviewed her, but I wrote it off as her not wanting to cast the pageant

industry in a bad light. Today she must have gotten Kathryn mixed up with me."

"I don't understand how she could have confused the two of you, unless she knew about your
impersonating Kathryn."

Jenna thought of the car that had followed her
the night before. "Maybe she's been following us
ever since you picked me up in San Francisco."

"Why wait until the wedding to make her
move?"

Jenna shrugged, feeling just as perplexed as
Travis looked.

"I'll call the police station later to see what they
can tell us about her motives, if anything. But for
now," he took her hand in his, "we have more important matters to discuss."

Jenna remembered then how her life had become condensed into a ten-second movie in the
short time between her being shot and passing
out. Everything that had been confusing and uncertain prior to the bullet entering her torso had
suddenly become simple issues of black and
white. She understood that whatever petty
differences had created a rift between herself
and Travis, she should have worked to get past
them.

She should have known that the most powerful attraction to any man she'd ever felt was something not to be ignored. And she should have
recognized the emotions Travis evoked in her as
exactly what they were—love.

If getting shot in the side had convinced her of anything, it was never to let a chance for true love slip through her fingers.

"Yes, we do," she said.

Jenna struggled to move herself closer to Travis, wincing at the pain that throbbed in her side.

"You shouldn't try to move yet."

She crooked her finger at him. "Come a little closer then."

Travis carefully stretched out in the bed beside her and propped his head on his elbow next to her. "Close enough?"

"I love you," she whispered.

He traced a fingertip along her jawline. "I never want to feel like I've lost you again."

"And?" Jenna was going to muster her last ounce of strength to kick him out of her bed if he didn't return her feelings.

He smiled. "I love you, Jenna. I love everything about you—your wildness, your intelligence, your beauty, your strength…. I love the way you make me feel like a more adventurous man, and I don't ever want to go back to the way I used to feel."

She blinked at the dampness in her eyes. Her throat constricted, and she couldn't think of a single reply that would do his words justice.

"I've got a proposition for you," he said before she could speak.

"I think I've had more than one lifetime's worth of your business propositions," she said, her stomach turning queasy at the thought of what he might say next.

"This isn't business, it's personal, and don't worry, I've learned my lesson."

"What lesson, exactly, did you learn?" Jenna asked.

"To never, ever try to tame a wild vixen like you into a proper society lady."

"Ah, that's probably good for you to know."

"So do you want to hear my proposal?"

"I'm listening."

"What do you say the next wedding we attend be our own?"

Jenna's heart got stuck in her throat, but after a moment she managed to say, "Are you asking me to marry you?"

"I am."

Nothing had ever been so clear to her as the fact that she and Travis belonged together, that she was complete with him in a way that she could never be without him. None of their external differences mattered.

"I'll do it on one condition...."

"If it's anything like the condition you placed on our last deal, I think I can accommodate you."

"Oh yeah? You want to have another weekend of sensual stress relief with me?"

"No."

"How about a week, then?"

"Definitely not acceptable."

"A month?"

"Not even close."

Jenna pulled him closer and silenced him with a kiss.

He pulled back just enough to say, "I want an unlimited, lifetime guarantee of Jenna Calvert-style stress relief."

She smiled at her future husband. "I think you've got yourself a deal."

Epilogue

Maui, three months later…

Travis squinted as his eyes adjusted to the dimly lit little tourist shop. Beyond the shelves of tanning lotions and the racks of beach gear and swimsuits, he spotted the magazine stand. While Jenna headed for the refrigerated display of bottled water that they'd come in search of after a not-so-leisurely afternoon hike, Travis wandered over to the stand and felt his pulse quicken as he saw that *Chloe* magazine's October issue was on the shelves, complete with Jenna's article headlined on the cover.

Sure, he'd seen the complimentary copies of the magazine that Jenna had received, but there was something special about seeing it in a store, knowing her story was now out there in the world, being read by people everywhere.

He grabbed an issue from the rack and thumbed through until he found the right page— "Kill the Competition: Behind the Scenes in America's Not-So-Pretty Pageant Industry." No sooner had he read the title than the magazine was snatched from his hands.

"Hey, let me see that." Travis reached for the magazine, but Jenna evaded his grasp as she laughed and scanned the pages.

"Wait your turn."

"Better yet, you can share." He snaked his arm around her waist and pulled her against him as he read over her shoulder.

Her cocoa-butter scent reminded him of the adventures they'd had with tanning oil earlier that morning in their private garden. They were only in Maui for a quick stay before continuing on to Tahiti, but already he was considering extending the month-long trip by a week. Or two. Or six.

Images of Jenna frolicking on the beaches of the South Pacific wearing nothing but a sarong around her hips were making him think he was in for more fun than any one man should be allowed to have.

He spotted Jenna's byline, and his chest swelled with pride. Not even a gunshot wound had deterred her from her goal, and in the end, she'd written what he considered an article worthy of a Pulitzer. News of her ordeal had created a buzz about the article, and now Jenna had the luxury of picking and choosing the publications for whom she wanted to write.

"I still can't believe the story I stumbled into," Jenna said, shaking her head as she read.

"You didn't stumble—it just took you a while to figure out how big a story it really was."

The woman who'd shot Jenna had gotten away

with murder five years earlier and was convinced that Jenna was onto her. Andrea Patton, former Miss Golden State, had murdered the woman she'd considered her biggest competition by feeding her low-fat brownies laced with ground-up peanuts after she'd heard about the woman's severe peanut allergy. Andrea confessed to everything in an emotional breakdown at the police station, and Jenna had gotten a whole new angle for her story.

Not only had her career taken a turn for the better recently, but her relationship with Kathryn had blossomed, too. Travis couldn't help feeling partly responsible for the sisters' newfound friendship, and while he suspected they'd never be as close as many twins were, they seemed to have accepted their differences and learned to appreciate each other for the individuals they were.

Their families, on the other hand, were still coming to terms with everything. Kathryn and Jenna's parents had been rightly disturbed by the shooting. Jenna had resisted all her mother's efforts to baby her during her weeks of recovery, and she'd bristled at her mother's sudden shower of affection.

Travis's mother and father were still acting a little shell-shocked. First having their dreams of a perfect family wedding explode in a burst of gunfire, and then having not only Kathryn but also her twin sister, Jenna, join the family—Travis suspected it was a bit more than his mother could take without a good, stiff drink.

They'd been civil enough to Jenna, though, and she was much less concerned than Kathryn about his parents' approval. Travis didn't give a damn what the Roths thought, not now when he had found more happiness than he'd ever dared to imagine.

Jenna paid for the magazine and water, and they wandered hand in hand back out into the late-afternoon sunshine.

"Want to look into those windsurfing lessons now?" she asked when they passed an athletic shop with ads for lessons in the window. She'd been teasing him all week about his aversion to water sports.

"Tomorrow. We'll definitely do it tomorrow. After such a strenuous hike, I had something a little more intimate in mind for right now."

"Hmm. Intimate, you say?"

"You, me, the hot tub, a little sensual stress relief—for old times' sake?"

"It wouldn't be complete without a bottle of wine."

"I spotted a nice California red in the minibar this morning."

Jenna pulled him close and smiled a wicked smile. "Did I ever show you the *other* thing I know how to do with a good bottle of wine?"

The Cowboy's Mistress

Cathy Gillen Thacker

Beth –
This one's for you, sis.
When you read it, you'll know why.

Chapter One

"It's six o'clock. Do you know where your children are?"

Rachel Westcott looked up at the sound of the low masculine voice, and Travis Westcott had the satisfaction of watching his former sister-in-law's face pale with the shock of seeing him again after nearly seventeen years.

When her shock faded, he saw her confusion. Was it true? Did she have no clue as to what the twins were up to, as they had claimed? Well, there was one way to find out. Travis sauntered into her spacious office at the Tradewinds Travel Agency and shut the door behind him.

"Well, do you?" he provoked lazily. He wished she weren't so damn beautiful and that he wasn't so distracted by her incredibly good looks.

"Of course I know." Her chin lifted a haughty notch and she fastened her wide golden-brown eyes on his. "They're at home."

"Guess again," he said tightly, aware that though she was just a year younger than him, which made her thirty-four, she had the poise of an older woman and the stunningly perfect physique of a younger one. More disturbing than that was his discovery that she still had what she'd always had, even at the tender age of seventeen—an elusive striking quality that always caused a man to look twice. Rachel couldn't go anywhere without heads turning. Some called it charisma. Some called it magic.

Rachel was silent. He could see the pulse beating in her throat, but she held whatever she was feeling about him at that moment firmly in check. "No, I don't think I will guess," she said.

Because he knew it would irritate her, he let his gaze drift over her fair translucent skin and wildly curling shoulder-length flame-red hair. "I think you'd better."

Her soft bow-shaped lips tightened into an irritated pout. "I don't want to play games with you, Travis."

"Believe me, this isn't fun for me, either."

She viewed him with utter condescension. "You've obviously come here to tell me something, so why don't you get on with it?"

Travis saw no reason to make it easy for her. "I thought you might want to explain yourself first," he drawled as he took a seat on the corner of her desk and cocked his head to one side. "Or perhaps I should say, explain your children."

Keeping the bulk of the desk between them like a protective shield, she drew herself up to her full five foot five. "How do you even know I *have* children?"

Travis shrugged, watching her toss her hair out of her face. He wished he could think of another way, besides kissing her, to quickly extinguish the cool challenge in her eyes. "I don't really. At this point, I'm just going on what the twins claim."

At the mention of the word twins, her face turned

very white. She gripped the edge of her desk with both hands.

"They're at the ranch now," Travis continued, taking some satisfaction in the way she was beginning to shake. "With my mother."

Rachel sat down because she knew if she didn't she was going to fall down. "What do you mean the twins are at the ranch?" she repeated in a low tight voice.

"Just what I said," Travis returned impatiently, looking older and more savvy now, but no kinder. He was no less the quintessential Texas bad boy than he had been years before. "They're there."

"At the ranch?" she repeated shakily, taking in his ruggedly carved face and slate-blue eyes. "That's impossible. They don't even know... I never told them."

Travis lifted a thick black brow. His mouth curved cynically. "It seems there were quite a few people you neglected to tell."

Guilt flooded Rachel. Then fear. This was her worst nightmare come true.

"How did they get to the ranch?" she asked finally. She should have seen this coming. Now that Brett and Gretchen were older, they were bound to try to find out more about their father. But fool that she was, she'd thought she could stave them off with a few vague replies about a marriage that just wasn't meant to be and an early death....

Travis's supercilious look made her want to deck him. "They drove out to the Bar W."

"Drove!"

"Evidently they took off early this morning and got to the ranch about four this afternoon. Walked right up to the front door, introduced themselves to my mother and 'explained' they were doing some 'research' into their roots.''

"Oh, my God,'' Rachel whispered.

"That's right,'' he thundered, unfolding his frame to stand before her desk. Hands flat on the polished chrome-and-glass surface, he leaned forward until he literally towered over her, all six-foot-four muscle-packed inch of him. He muttered something beneath his breath about crazy, unpredictable women and their gold-digging schemes. "What are you trying to pull here, Rachel?''

"Nothing.'' She stood and reached for her purse. Her plan set, she strode past him.

He caught her arm as she passed, and reeled her back to his side. "Just where do you think you're going?''

Rachel tried unsuccessfully to shake free of his grip. "Where do you think? To get the twins, of course.''

His jaw hardened to the consistency of granite. "I agree that'd be best, and the sooner the better.''

Trying hard not to inhale the sexy male scent of him, or notice how thick and glossy and utterly touchable his black hair was, Rachel cast a denigrating look at the hand still curled around her arm. "It'd be a lot easier for me to get out of here if you'd let go.''

"Not until we get a few things settled.''

"I hardly think—''

"It's an eight-hour drive to the ranch.''

Rachel fought the tingles of awareness radiating outward from where he touched her. Using her other hand to pry his fingers from her arm she twisted her body lithely and wiggled out of his grasp. Travis might be wearing a silk tie, but there was still something dangerous and almost disreputable about him. "I remember very well where the ranch is.'' Her pulse racing, she stalked away from him. "I'll drive all night if I have to."

Travis folded both arms close to his chest. "I have a private jet waiting at the airport. I can get you there in a little over an hour."

The idea of the short travel time appealed to her. The idea of being cooped up with Travis for any length of time, for any reason, did not.

He shrugged his broad shoulders. "Of course if you're afraid to be alone with me..."

She shot him a drop-dead look as they headed for the exit simultaneously. "Don't flatter yourself."

He reached the door first, then stopped and blocked her exit. She backed up and glared up at him, hating his cool superiority almost as much as she hated all the misconceptions she knew he harbored about her.

"So what's your choice, Rachel?" he asked with predatory grace. "Are you going with me or leaving the kids at the ranch for the night?"

Her heart was suddenly beating very fast. And it was all his fault. "That's not a choice," she snapped. "It's a nightmare."

Resting a shoulder against the door frame, he laughed softly. "At least about that much we agree."

As she scanned his face, the bitter memories of her past difficulties with the powerful Westcott family overwhelmed her. And her children, unsuspecting though they might be, were at the center of a newly brewing family storm!

"All right," she said finally, holding his intense blue-gray gaze. She swallowed hard, knowing she had no other choice. "I'll go with you."

THE JET TRAVIS had waiting at the Beaumont airport was small, new and expensive-looking. It was also painted white and red and bore the Texas West Airlines logo. To Rachel, it was the symbol of Travis's almost overwhelming success. In the years since she had known him, he had started his own Texas-based commuter airline and was now a multimillionaire with a national reputation. So the jet itself was no surprise. What she hadn't expected was that Travis was going to pilot it himself.

"Were you at the ranch, too?" Rachel asked as she settled into the seat beside Travis and fastened her seat belt.

"No. I was at my office in Fort Worth when my mother phoned me."

He hadn't lost any time in getting to her, Rachel thought. "Was Jaclyn very upset?"

Travis shrugged. "Not half as upset as she'd be if my father were still alive."

Rachel stared at the instrument panel. "I read about Zeke's death," she said softly. "I'm sorry."

"Are you?" Travis's voice dripped with sarcasm.

Once they took off, Rachel stared out at the fluffy white clouds and sapphire-blue Texas sky. She twisted her hands together in her lap, wishing now as always that Travis wasn't so blunt. Or so hell-bent on calling out the truth, as he saw it, anyway. "You know there was no love between Zeke and me...."

Travis slanted her an aggrieved glance and gave her no chance to continue. "Should there have been?"

"Maybe," Rachel acknowledged tightly. "If he'd ever seen fit to give me a chance."

Travis gripped the controls with both hands. "You proved *your* character the day you eloped with my brother."

His thinly veiled barb was meant to get a reaction and it did. Rachel whirled on him as much as her seat belt would allow. "Did you ever happen to think our marrying might have been Austin's idea?"

"I don't doubt it was." He gave her a scornful once-over, pausing to linger on her breasts, before returning his glance to her eyes. "You were a pretty hot little number even then."

"If you weren't piloting this jet," Rachel fumed, balling her hands into fists, "I'd deck you for that."

One side of his mouth lifted in a taunting smile. "You'll have your chance if you still want it, once we hit the ground. But I warn you—" his silky soft voice sent shivers rolling up and down her spine "—unlike Austin, I fight dirty and I fight to win."

Cheeks flaming, she stared at him in smoldering anger. "I don't doubt that, either," she said.

But the reply she expected never came. He seemed relaxed and completely unperturbed by their argument.

Had she been able to bear the silence, she would have said nothing more the entire rest of the flight. Unfortunately she found the silence worse than their previous repartee. Needing to do something to get her mind off Travis and her potent reaction to him, she said finally, "So, how is your mother?"

Travis continued to concentrate on piloting the small sleek jet. "Happy as a nursing calf now that she thinks she's got a couple of grandchildren. 'Course," he drawled, ignoring Rachel's soft indrawn breath, "I don't know how long that happiness will last." He peered at her contemplatively through twin fringes of narrowed dark lashes. "How long do you think it'll take, Rachel?"

Rachel could tell by the smug look on his face that

he was trying to get a rise out of her, but curiosity made her unable to resist taking the bait. "How long for what?" she asked warily.

Both corners of his mouth lifted in a crocodile grin. "For me to expose you."

Rachel shook her head in silent mounting fury. She clamped her arms beneath her breasts and stared straight ahead, damning everyone—the twins, who'd gotten her into this hopelessly untenable position, herself, for foolishly accepting this ride to San Angelo, and Travis, for being so typically rude and insulting. "You're just like your father," she finally said.

"Thanks." He nodded happily, as if she'd just crowned him Prince of Wales. "I appreciate the compliment."

Rachel stared straight ahead. "It wasn't a compliment."

"How come?" he asked innocently.

"You know damn well how come!"

"Tell me, anyway. We've got time to kill."

"Because your father wrecked my marriage to your brother."

"He disapproved," Travis countered argumentatively. "I wouldn't say wrecked."

"Well, I would!" Rachel shot back hotly.

"You're saying you would've stayed married to Austin had my father not disinherited him?"

He took Rachel's silence as a *no*. "Then what are you saying, Rachel?"

Rachel straightened indignantly. "That Zeke's disapproval hurt Austin very much."

"His hasty ill-thought-out marriage to *you* hurt *my father* very much."

"Can we drop this?" she inquired stiffly.

"Sure," he said.

Again, the silence was nearly unbearable. Feeling as wrung out as if she'd just participated in an iron women competition, Rachel sighed. "Whose idea was it for you to come and get me, anyway?" The culprit should be shot at dawn.

"Mine." He grinned at her, enjoying her discomfiture to the hilt. "Regrets?"

Rachel rolled her eyes. "Too numerous to count."

"You'll pardon me if I don't sympathize with you. After all, this scam was not my idea."

"Nor mine," Rachel muttered. He slanted her a doubtful glance. Even though she hated to give it, Rachel knew she owed Travis, indeed the whole Westcott family, an apology for what had happened. "I really am sorry about this," she said.

"Right. And that's supposed to make everything better?" Travis said cynically.

The edge in his voice prompted Rachel to turn and look at him and be confronted almost immediately with how intimate a setting the cockpit of the two-seater jet was.

He had taken off his suit jacket the moment they'd stepped onto the plane, and the striped cotton shirt he wore delineated the muscles of his arms and shoulders, and the washboard flatness of his stomach. She turned her eyes away from the splendid masculinity of his body and back to his face. "This shouldn't have happened," she said firmly.

"I agree with you," Travis said grimly. "The kids never should have driven out to the ranch."

"It's not as if I suggested this to them, Travis!" she retorted.

"Maybe not, but if you had more control over your children, then it wouldn't have happened."

"They're curious about their father."

I am, too, Travis thought, feeling both troubled and irritated. *Was* Austin the twins' father? Or was this all just another one of Rachel's scams? God knew, his mother seemed convinced. They were Austin's spitting image, she'd said. But his mother would have accepted any children claiming to be the offspring of her long-dead eldest son, Travis feared. She wanted Austin back that much. And if not Austin, then some small living part of him. Worse, Travis wanted that, too. Which meant they could both easily be taken for a ride.

"What did you tell the twins about their father?" Travis asked gruffly.

"Only that he died before they were born," she replied in a soft haunted voice.

"And that's it?" Travis asked incredulously. He wished that Rachel had taken the time to change into something less feminine and alluring than the dress she'd worn to work. After all, he had taken her back to her house for an overnight bag.

He wasn't sure what the dress was made of—rayon, maybe—but she couldn't have selected one that would've done a better job of showing off her considerable physical assets had she tried. Both elegant and exotic, the wrap dress molded to her breasts and tied at the side. The full skirt fell almost to her ankles and swirled out from her slim waist when she moved. Even the short cap sleeves revealed the shapely lines of her upper arms. She looked so good in it that whenever Travis looked at her, he felt his mouth water. "In sixteen years, that's all you told them?" he finally managed to say.

"I more or less intimated we had no extended family living. And on my side, anyway, it's true. My dad died a long time ago."

Travis understood why she would've wanted to lie about her own father. In his view, Rachel had plenty to be ashamed of in that regard. What he didn't understand was why she hadn't come to his family. She must have know all along that she could hit on them for financial help. "Why did you lie to them about us?" he asked.

Rachel looked at him as if he were missing a major section of his brain. "Considering the way I was treated by you and your father, like some odious piece of white trash, do you even have to ask?" she snapped.

No, Travis thought, on reflection, he didn't. Had his father known about the twins, had Zeke had even a hint, he would have fought Rachel for custody of Austin's children.

The jet descended through the clouds, and the ranch came into view. Rachel sucked in her breath at the sprawling acreage, with its gentle hills, streams, groves of trees and sprawling pastureland. She had always loved the Bar W Ranch. As a kid, she'd spent hours dreaming about what it would be like to grow up on such majestic land and to command the respect and admiration the Westcotts did. Later, when she and Austin had begun dating, they'd dreamed of living there together. But it wasn't to be.

Travis guided the jet onto the runway. It jolted slightly as the wheels hit, then glided smoothly to a halt. "This wasn't here before, was it?" Rachel asked as they climbed down onto the tarmac.

"No. I had it built after my father died, so I could come home more easily."

Rachel nodded her acknowledgement.

Travis told himself he didn't need her approval as she followed his lead and headed for the pickup truck in the hangar. And yet, irritatingly, it felt good, anyway.

They were both silent as he drove the short distance to the sprawling two-story plantation-style ranch house. Travis could only imagine what Rachel was remembering as she looked at the white stone mansion, with its one-story wings that sprouted on either side of the main house. From an architectural standpoint, the house was perfect in every detail, from the dormer windows on the fashionable gray hip roof to the black shutters that graced both sides of the French doors that doubled as windows for nearly every room. Six white columns supported the wide graceful front porch, and a black wrought-iron railing encompassed the perimeter of the second-floor balcony.

There was a detached ten-car garage. Beyond that was the bunkhouse, the neatly maintained barns and miles of white fence. The house alone was 14,000 square feet. And that didn't count the pool or patios or gardens at the rear.

Most visitors marveled at the sheer beauty of the place. Not Rachel. She seemed to be regarding the sprawling mansion with a mixture of loathing and trepidation. But perhaps that, too, was to be expected, Travis thought. Her single prior visit to the ranch had hardly been a happy one.

Rachel's legs were shaking but she climbed down from the truck as gracefully as she was able and started up the front walk toward the double beveled-glass doors.

She had been to the ranch only one other time, the

night Austin had taken her home to announce they had just eloped. She couldn't help but remember now how hurt, humiliated and ashamed she had been that night when she realized she would never be accepted by Zeke Westcott, Austin's father. He had been so opposed to their marriage he hadn't even let them get past the front hall. He'd thrown them out, telling Austin not to bother to come back until he'd rid himself of his white-trash wife. And Travis, damn him, had sided with his father. Only Jaclyn Westcott had ever wanted to give her a chance....

The front doors opened and the welcoming committee dashed out. "Hey, Mom!" Brett and Gretchen said simultaneously, hanging back, sheepish looks on their faces.

Rachel checked them over visually and to her relief found them none the worse for wear after their unauthorized expedition into their past.

"Hello, Rachel," a soft cultured voice said.

Rachel looked up into the eyes of Jaclyn Westcott. At sixty-two, she seemed frailer, softer. "I hope, now that we've found one another again, we won't ever lose touch."

Not sure she knew what the older woman meant and not sure she wanted to know, Rachel turned to her children. They might have set out only to satisfy their curiosity, but now Rachel feared a custody battle, at the very least a demand for court-dictated visitations from her late husband's family. She said as pleasantly but as firmly as possible, "Brett, Gretchen, get your things together. It's time to go."

"No," Brett said stubbornly, crossing both his arms over his chest. "Gretchen and I have already talked about it. We aren't leaving."

Chapter Two

"It's really nice up here," Rachel said.

Yes, it was, Travis thought resentfully. Thanks to Jaclyn's determined housekeeping, the attic area was spacious, clean and neatly organized. Intrigued with the row of window seats at the dormer windows, Rachel made a beeline for one of them. It was already dark, so she couldn't see much of the ranch below except for the lights lining the front drive. But it was enough to hold her as spellbound as a kid in a candy store, Travis noticed, as he strolled closer.

She turned, nervous now at the idea of being alone with him. Her eyes darted past him to the softly lit attic with its carpeted floor and abundance of storage cabinets and chests. And then back to his motionless form. He knew she was thinking about their errand, which was to bring down slides of the ranch to show the twins, but all he could think about was the irritating intimacy of sitting down to a family-style dinner with Rachel, his mother and the twins. The formal dining room hadn't heard such laughter or activity in years, he realized, not since he and his brother had been kids. Worse, he could see his mother's enchantment with Rachel and her children, and he wasn't one bit comfortable with it. Fortunately the twins weren't interested in the ranch, just in meeting relatives, so they'd be gone soon.

"Can't find the projector?" she asked coolly.

Travis braced a shoulder against the wall, enjoying the way the pulse was beginning to throb at the base of her throat. He let his gaze lazily rove the softness of her lips and tried not to think about how those same lips would feel under his. "I know exactly where it is," he said softly.

Rachel took an uneasy step back. "So what's the problem?" The hollows beneath her cheeks created shadows beneath the paleness of her fair skin.

"No problem," Travis countered laconically, wishing that her hair didn't look so touchable and soft and that she didn't smell quite so good. "I just have a few things to say to you."

"I don't think I want to hear this," she said tersely, starting for the stairs. He moved to block her way. Three steps later, her back was to the attic wall, and he hadn't so much as laid a hand on her. Trapped but not defeated, she lifted her hands to cover her ears. "I'm not going to listen to this," she asserted stubbornly.

"Yes, you will, unless you want my mother to hear it, too."

She evidently knew he meant what he said because she slowly dropped her hands and sent him a murderous look.

"I know what you're up to, Rachel," he informed her flatly. "You're not going to get away with it. Not as long as I have a single breath left in my body."

She smiled at him sarcastically. "I think your death by suffocation could be arranged."

"You wish."

At a stalemate, they stared at one another for long seconds. Long enough for him to see how smooth her mouth was even without lipstick. Long enough for him to see the hot embarrassed color pour back into her cheeks. Their staring match continued. As the moments drew out, he became even more aware of her. His body tightened with pleasure that was almost pain. It was all he could do not to lean in and kiss her smart mouth into stunned silence, just for the sheer hell of seeing her lose her cool.

Rachel's golden eyes widened as if she knew exactly what he was thinking. She tensed, averted her gaze and heaved a bored-sounding sigh. "Okay, Travis," she said, anger giving her voice a taut sexy edge. "You win." She clamped both arms together at her waist and stared at him determinedly. "I'll play your little game. Just what is it you think I'm trying to get away with now?"

"As if you don't know," he said sourly.

"I told you," she said with exaggerated patience. "I don't."

He gave her another long look, letting her know he wasn't fooled for an instant by her innocent act. He stepped closer, so they were mere inches apart now, instead of a foot. "It's very clever, the way you worked it out." Travis dropped his voice to a low predatory whisper and went on with grim admiration, "Sending the kids in first."

"I haven't the slightest idea what you're talking about."

Damn, but she could lie as if it was the truth, he thought. "Don't you?" he asked curtly.

"No." A warning flashed in her golden eyes.

"Then let me enlighten you," he said roughly, advancing closer. The hurt that had been bottled up inside him for years threatened to pour out. His arms shot out to either side of her and he sandwiched her between him and the wall. "You married my brother for his money. After he was disinherited, you left him."

Her expression grew stonier as she elbowed him aside. "His disinheritance had nothing to do with our break-up. I left him because I *wanted* him to reconcile with his family—"

"What a load of bull!" Travis cut her off furiously, not about to let her smooth over what had happened. "You only loved him when you thought you would share in his trust fund and live on this ranch." Didn't Rachel have any idea how much her betrayal of his brother had affected not just Austin, but himself? For years now Travis had doubted the motives of every woman with whom he came in contact.

"I married Austin because I loved him," Rachel retorted hotly, stepping past him. "And I left him for exactly the same reason."

Travis turned and continued to regard her with contempt. "Some love," he said softly, wondering if Rachel knew how much he had wanted her to prove his father wrong about her, how much he had wanted her to stand by his brother through thick and thin. "The marriage lasted four months."

Rachel held her arms akimbo, as if beseeching him to understand. "We were young. And foolish."

"And selfish," Travis added. His mouth taut, he continued, "Austin was devastated when you walked out on him, so much so that he never recovered." Dammit, his brother had *died*, wanting her back.

"I didn't cause him to drink," she said bitterly. "I didn't put him behind the wheel of that car."

"Didn't you? Funny, I don't remember him ever hitting the bottle *before* he married you."

Tears glistened in her eyes as she whirled on him. "Your family put too much pressure on us—"

"And my mother paid you handsomely to get out—"

"That was after I had left him," she whispered miserably, covering her face with her hands.

"Right," Travis snapped back, irritated that she was actually making him feel some sympathy for her. "It was your reward for a job well done!"

He caught her wrist before she could deliver a stinging blow.

"This is getting us nowhere," she said, twisting free of his grasp.

But there was one more thing Travis had to know. He caught her by the shoulders when she tried to move away. "Answer me this," he demanded roughly as her chest rose and fell with every quick frantic breath. "Did you know you were pregnant with his children when you left him?"

She confronted him with a head-on glare. "No. I never would have left."

He wanted to believe her. He just didn't know if he could or should. She'd duped his family once with her lies. With both his father and his brother gone now, he knew it was up to him to see that she didn't do it again.

TRAVIS WAS in the front hall the following morning when the sound of voices reached him. "Brett and Gretchen may well want to take over the ranch one day," his mother was saying. "Perhaps work it together. But in the meantime, Rachel, I need someone to take over the day-to-day running of it. Since you're the children's mother and Austin's widow, it should be you.''

His heart pounding, Travis stayed right where he was.

"I don't know anything about ranching," Rachel protested.

"Neither did I when I married Zeke," his mother countered calmly. "I learned. And I want this ranch to stay in the family."

Deciding this ludicrous conversation had gone far enough, Travis stepped into the room, his temper soaring. He leveled a censuring look at his mother. "Rachel's right, Mother." He cast Rachel a disparaging glance. "She could no more run this ranch than I could sew a dress."

His mother's blue eyes flashed a warning. "You don't know that," Jaclyn countered.

"The hell I don't," Travis retorted sharply. Forcing himself to calm down, he said much more quietly, "Mother, please, stop and think about what you're doing."

"I already have, and my mind is made up. I am deeding the ranch over to Rachel and her children."

"Just like that?" Travis stared at Jaclyn incredulously, wondering if he had ever really known his mother at all.

"Of course not," his mother said. "Rachel will have to prove herself capable of running the ranch first. She'll have three months. If she can keep the ranch running in the black, then the ranch will be hers."

Travis pictured the family wealth going down the

drain faster than it could ever hope to be recouped. "And if it's in the red? Then what?" Travis demanded.

"Then I'll figure I'm not cut out for ranching," Rachel cut in.

Travis wheeled on her. To his amazement, she had gotten over her shock and was now siding with his mother. "You can't seriously be thinking of accepting this offer?"

"Only under very specific terms," Rachel replied, looking like the thoughtful competent businesswoman she was.

"Which are?" Jaclyn asked, looking pleased.

Rachel folded her arms at her waist and continued in a crisp tone, "One, I be given carte blanche in the running of the ranch. If I'm going to do it, I'll need to do it my way. Two, you'll have to give me time to get everything squared away in Beaumont. Summer vacation is coming up, so it will be no problem to bring the kids out here for the summer. Three, I'll have to take a leave of absence from my job at the travel agency."

Travis stared at her. She was as crazy as his mother. "You're not serious?"

Rachel smiled with deadly calm. Whatever reluctance she had exhibited earlier was gone. "I've never been more serious about anything in my life."

"DON'T LOOK SO SURPRISED to see me," Rachel said.

It had been weeks since she'd accepted Jaclyn's offer. Now she faced an obviously angry Travis.

"Can't help it. I was hoping you'd change your mind," he drawled without apology. He watched her lift a suitcase from her car.

Rachel's jaw set. She was in no mood for this. The

drive west had been long and arduous. Fortunately the twins had already gone inside with their grandmother, so they didn't have to witness this. "If you think you're going to spend the next three months haranguing me every single moment we're alone—"

"Gee, Miss Rachel," Travis said sarcastically, "you must read minds because—"

"—you've got another think coming," Rachel continued, oblivious to his interruption.

"—because that's exactly what I planned."

They finished speaking at exactly the same time and stared at one another in silence.

"Keep this up and I'll go to your mother," Rachel seethed.

"Oooh." He spread both his hands and shook them in a parody of a tremble. "I'm a-shaking in my boots."

She swiftly gave him her back and busied herself unloading the car. "You wouldn't want to upset her," Rachel said.

He moved so she could see him. "As far as I'm concerned," he drawled, "*this* is upsetting her."

Rachel set the cardboard box containing her makeup mirror and hot rollers on the hood of the car with a loud thud. "She didn't look upset."

"Give her time." Travis plowed through her belongings, frowning as he looked into the canvas bag containing her electric razor. "I'm sure with you around, she'll get there."

"Look." Rachel slapped his hand away from her toiletries and swung around to face him. "Can't we just give this a chance?" She planted both hands on her slender hips.

He shrugged, slouched against the car and regarded her insolently. "Give me one reason why I should."

His goading brought a warm flush to her face and a burst of adrenaline to her veins. "Family harmony, for one."

Travis rested one elbow on the hood of her car and leisurely crossed his ankles, seeming as relaxed as she was tense. "As far as I'm concerned, you're not family and haven't been for some time," he said pleasantly.

The way he let his eyes rove over her flame-red hair made Rachel wish fervently she could brush her hair so she could restore some order to the wind-tossed curls. "My children are family," she countered, refusing to let him rattle her.

"So?" Travis shrugged indolently before he straightened to his full six-four. "Does that mean you have to be here too?"

She drew a deep breath, fought the flare of her temper and tried one last time to reason with him. "You don't know me very well," she said quietly, the accusation in her voice plain. "But then," she said ever so quietly, "you never did, Travis." She expected him to flinch with guilt at her reprimand. To her disappointment, he didn't move a muscle. "We could change that now," she continued evenly.

"Why would I want to do that?"

She reminded herself that years ago, when she would have welcomed his support, he had sided with his father and stubbornly refused to so much as try to get to know her.

"Because you want things to be different this time," Rachel continued persuasively. "Because you're fair-minded. Or at least you could be..." She knew it in her heart!

He compressed his lips grimly, his conscience remaining unaffected by her impassioned speech. "I also don't want to get burned."

Rachel blew out a long exasperated breath. "You really are just like your father, aren't you?" It wasn't a compliment.

But he took it like one. "To the bone." Travis smiled.

"An advanced chauvinist?"

"And proud of it." He turned back to the car. "Looks like you brought half the house," Travis remarked, moving to help Rachel lift a particularly heavy box from the back seat.

With effort, Rachel turned her glance from his flat stomach. Telling herself it didn't matter how sexy or attractive he was, she kept her voice casually neutral. "Don't tell me that bothers you, too?"

Travis shrugged, and easily pulled out another box she could barely lift. "You're just going to have to take it all back."

"At summer's end?"

He flashed her an unrepentant bad-boy grin. "Or sooner."

Her whole body thrumming with pent-up emotion, she watched him carry a box to the front porch. Striding back to her, his slate-blue eyes boring into hers, he finished in a silken voice that rippled across her skin, warming everywhere it touched. "I don't think you know what you're getting into."

"Being here with you?" she snapped. "I have an idea."

"Sheer hell, huh?" His playful grin said it was otherwise for him. For him, it was beginning to be fun.

"Couldn't get much closer," Rachel affirmed.

His glance swept over her hair, lingered pointedly

on her mouth, then returned with lustful abandon to her golden-brown eyes. "You are catching on. But that's not what I was talking about."

"Oh?" She arched a delicate brow.

His handsome face became abruptly serious. "Ranching is a hard life, Rachel."

No, she thought, dealing with Travis was hard. In comparison, ranching would be easy. She sent him a composed smile. "No harder than working for a travel agency or the airlines, I'm sure. Just different. Besides," she said with a wry twist of her mouth, amused he was being so obvious about trying to get rid of her, "it's not as if I'll be taking care of the herd single-handedly, you know."

He didn't find her remark amusing. Stalking closer, he braced his hands on his hips, the movement pushing aside the edges of his suit jacket. "You don't even know how to ride."

"So I'll learn." No matter what Travis did or said in the next few days—and she was sure he would give just about anything a try—he wasn't going to scare her away or stop her from trying to secure her late husband's inheritance for her children.

Travis rubbed a hand along the clean-shaven lines of his jaw. His eyes were intense, and his sensual mouth was mobilized into an even deeper frown. "There's a lot more to it than knowing how to sit a horse," he said as if speaking to a virtual idiot.

He was patronizing her again. "I expect so," Rachel said, mocking his tone to a T.

Their glances did battle silently. "Look," he said reasonably after a moment as he smoothed the thick black hair that grew sleekly down the nape of his neck. "All orneriness aside, I have an idea what this must seem like to you. It's beautiful country out here. And there's no denying the Westcott name carries a lot of clout in this part of Texas. But there the fantasy ends, Rachel,'' he continued with gruff indifference to her feelings. ''You can't just play rancher the way a kid plays house.''

Rachel drew a deep breath. Maybe it was good they were getting this all out in the open now. ''Are you trying to insult me, Travis, 'cause if you are,'' she said, making no effort to mask the warning in her low velvet tone, ''you're making a good start.''

His gaze hardened, letting her know he wouldn't apologize. ''I'm trying to be honest with you, Rachel. I thought that was what you'd want.''

Rachel walked a distance away, so she wouldn't be inhaling the brisk masculine scent of his hair and skin. ''What I want, Travis,'' she said slowly, enunciating each word and looking directly into his eyes, ''is for you to stay the hell out of my way.''

Rachel thought but couldn't be sure she saw a glimmer of respect in his eyes.

''I imagine you'll want a few days to settle in before getting involved in the ranch,'' he said.

''Where are the hired hands?'' she asked, the model of polite efficiency. ''I'd like to meet them.'' Maybe if Travis saw she was serious about working hard, he would ease up on her.

Travis grimaced. ''This time of day they're all over the place, tending to their chores.''

Rachel wasn't buying that. He had to know where someone was. ''The chief hired hand, then.''

''Our cow boss is Rowdy Haynes,'' Travis answered carefully.

''You must know where he is,'' Rachel persisted

when no further information was immediately forth-
coming.

Again, Travis was silent. He knew but wasn't willing
to tell.

"I'd like to meet Mr. Haynes," she continued firmly
with a defiant lift of her chin. "The sooner the better."
She wished she didn't have to tilt her head so far back
to look into Travis's eyes. And wished his black hair
wasn't so agreeably tousled by the wind.

Travis shrugged after a moment, his powerful shoulders shadowing her from the worst of the late-afternoon
sun. "Have it your way," he said with soft indifference. "As soon as you change I'll—"

Rachel didn't know what Travis had up his sleeve
this time, but she wasn't about to give him time to do
it, while she was off—just like a woman!—changing
her clothes. "That won't be necessary," she interrupted stiffly.

She knew she looked fine in her tailored city shorts
and matching pale lemon blazer. She didn't need to put
on fresh lipstick to do business. In fact, she felt it
would be better if she didn't. Nor would she conde-
scend to the help by putting on jeans and trying to be
one of them when undoubtedly they already knew or
would soon know, she was not. It would be better just
to be herself and let matters progress from there.

Rachel didn't know what to expect when she entered
the bunkhouse. A one-room dormitory, maybe. Instead,
she saw a dining hall to the left and an office to the
right. Straight ahead was a hallway with rooms off to
either side.

"The men bunk in the back, two to a room," Travis
said. "The showers are at the rear. I wouldn't go back
there without an all clear if I were you."

Rachel didn't intend to. Pausing outside the open office door, she glanced in and saw a blond man who couldn't have been more than twenty-five or -six, sitting behind a computer terminal.

"Rowdy, I'd like you to meet my former sister-in-law, Rachel Westcott. She's going to be running the ranch for my mother this summer."

Rowdy's eyes widened speculatively as Travis continued with the quiet authority of a man long accustomed to giving orders, "Starting at 6 a.m. tomorrow, you don't make a move without first consulting her. Mrs. Westcott's to be clued in on every aspect of this ranch. I mean it, Rowdy. You don't make a move before talking to her."

Rowdy absorbed that with a nod. Rachel wasn't quite sure what Travis meant, she only knew she was in trouble. Deep trouble. She swore silently to herself, wishing all the while Rowdy didn't look quite so much as if he was about to burst out laughing.

"Ma'am." Rowdy stood and extended his hand. His brown eyes both questioned Travis and challenged her. "Pleased to meet you."

"I'll be getting settled in today, but first thing tomorrow I expect a tour of the facilities. I also want to see an up-to-date report on every aspect of this ranch."

"Yes, ma'am." Rowdy tried, but didn't quite suppress a smirk before he turned his glance to Travis in a way that was strictly, confidentially, man-to-man. A way that said no matter how well-intentioned Rachel was or how much authority she had she couldn't possibly hope to manage the vast Bar W Ranch.

"You told him not to cooperate with me," Rachel accused the moment she and Travis left the bunkhouse.

Travis shook his head, his mouth grim, and looked

at her attentively. "Dream on," he said, the pleasure he felt at his ability to get to her evident.

Rachel reined in her feelings and informed him with icy disdain, "I have a news flash for you, Travis."

He rolled his eyes. "I can't wait."

"I don't care how hard a time he or anyone else gives me. And that includes you. *I'm going to do this. I'm going to succeed!*"

He didn't bother to argue with her, merely lifted a skeptical brow. And although his expression remained disturbingly inscrutable, she had the feeling he was laughing; it rankled, more than she expected.

"Well, don't worry about it. Like my mama said—" Travis rocked back on his heels and stuck his thumbs through the belt loops on either side of his zipper "—you'll get your chance to prove yourself capable. Starting at 6 a.m. tomorrow, Rachel, this ranch is all yours."

"Thank you," she said primly, satisfied he'd finally conceded her this much, however reluctantly.

"What happens after that," he concluded, grinning, "is your problem."

Chapter Three

The alarm went off at five. Rachel slipped out of bed and into the shower. Minutes later, she put on a pair of jeans, boots and a plain blue chambray shirt. She had no idea what a female ranch manager should wear; she only knew she wasn't going back to the bunkhouse dressed in city shorts again.

Slipping silently out of her bedroom, she headed down the hall and out the door. The yard was quiet as she walked over to the bunkhouse. The aroma of coffee wafted out the door.

She knocked briskly on the outer door, then stepped inside. Rowdy's office was empty, but the spacious dining room was not. All conversation ceased the moment she stepped inside. Roughly twenty men sat at the two long tables. It was clear from the empty plates that they'd just finished breakfast

Seeing her, Rowdy stood up. "Boys, this is Miz Westcott," he drawled in a voice as thick and smooth as molasses. "She's going to be running the ranch this summer." To Rachel's relief, there was nothing save the respect due her in his quiet inflection. Apparently he'd had second thoughts since his borderline-rude treatment of her yesterday. Rachel's confidence grew when among the men, there was a murmur of hello.

"I expect she'll want to say a few words," Rowdy said, then sat down.

Actually, Rachel corrected Rowdy silently, she didn't want to speak to the hands, not until she'd had a tour of the ranch and read the reports she'd asked for. But knowing the men were bound to be curious about her, perhaps even nervous about working for someone new, she smiled. "As you all probably have heard by now, this is all new to me, but I expect to get acclimated very quickly. Once I do, I'll undoubtedly be making some changes. I'll expect everyone's full cooperation. In the meantime, if you have any problems or suggestions, please feel free to come to me." She made eye contact with several of the men. "Carry on." She pivoted, intending to head back out the door.

"Uh, whoa, Miz Westcott," Rowdy said, halting her progress.

The undertone of insolent mirth in his voice sent a chill of remorse up her spine. Why, oh why, she thought miserably, had she ever allowed herself to think this was going to be easy?

"What would you like us to work on today?" Rowdy continued in that voice, which was so subservient and overly polite it was rude.

Rachel turned slowly. She had no choice but to play along with Rowdy, but she wouldn't make it easy for him. "Work on?" she repeated mildly.

"Yeah." Rowdy made a great show of trying and failing to suppress a grin before turning abruptly serious. "You want us to move the herds, start branding the new calves or start repairing the fence in pasture forty-one?"

Every man was looking at her, waiting for her to make a mistake. "Split up," she said sternly, giving him a look that said he should be able to figure out some things for himself. "Do all three."

"Can't," Rowdy informed her lazily, shoving his hands deep into the pockets of his jeans. "It'll take every man to move the herds to alternate pastureland."

"Then do that," Rachel said, beginning to feel a little flustered.

"Move them where?" Rowdy asked. "Pasture forty-one is inoperable at the moment." Chagrined, Rachel realized she didn't even know how many pastures the Bar W had.

Drawing on all her inner strength, she regarded Rowdy patiently and willed the embarrassed blush that crept up her neck to stay out of her cheeks. "Where do you usually move them?" she asked.

"Wherever we're told," Rowdy said, beginning to sound as exasperated as Rachel felt.

Rachel took a breath. Fighting panic, she worked on slowing the erratic beat of her pulse. "What other pasturelands are available?" she asked, keeping her gaze locked on Rowdy.

"She's running this ranch and she doesn't know?" one of the hands muttered incredulously.

"Look, I ain't working for no woman." One of the men in the back stood up, disgruntled. "'Specially not one who doesn't know what the devil she's talking about."

"I agree." Another stood up, then another and another.

"Wait a minute," Rachel said, desperately trying to stave off disaster. "All of you worked for Jaclyn Westcott."

"That's different," another man in the back spoke up. "*She* knows what the hell's going on."

"Well, I will, too," Rachel asserted bravely.

"When?" one of the hands, a grizzled-looking man with three days' growth of beard, asked in disgust. "I vote we strike. Or at least put Rowdy in charge."

Rachel looked at Rowdy, expecting him to help her out, now that the joke was over and they had indeed initiated her by fire, but all he did was shrug. He looked at her as if to say, *what the hell did you expect, lady?*

The men started filing out the door.

Rachel was so angry she was tempted to just let them quit, but she knew she couldn't. Jaclyn had already told her the Bar W had the best hands for miles around. Rachel *might* be able to succeed without them, but having them quit on her first day was the kind of start she didn't need. Besides, she knew that the only way she could learn the business was if they were there to help her.

"Hold it," Rachel said. When that didn't stop them, she put two fingers in her mouth and whistled shrilly. The men stopped walking but continued to talk. She stepped up on a bench and regarded them from a position of physical superiority.

The dissenting voices of the men slowly quieted and silence reined in the room. "Let's talk about this," she said, her years of negotiating difficult travel packages for individuals and corporations coming to her aid. "Exactly what would get you to stay?" she asked flatly.

"More money," the grizzled cowpoke said.

Then money it was, Rachel thought, not daring to think how this was likely to be received by Travis when he found out. If he found out. "How about a ten percent raise, effective immediately?"

The men no longer looked ready to walk, neither did they look ready to give in. "And another ten percent for every man who's still here, working hard, at the end of the summer."

She had them. She knew it by the slow smiles that spread across their faces.

"All right then, that's settled. Now, I need someone to help me determine the daily schedule. If not Rowdy, then—"

Rowdy interrupted. "I can do that."

Rachel knew Rowdy was only volunteering to avoid giving up power. He was still going to be trouble. Like Travis, he just didn't want her here. Still, she'd succeeded where she wasn't wanted before. Maybe not when she was married to Austin, but plenty of times since. "You think you can handle things for today?" she said curtly, making it clear she wasn't awarding him the job indefinitely, not unless his attitude changed.

Rowdy was cooperative but not defeated. "Yes, ma'am, I reckon I can," he responded tersely.

This once, Rachel decided she could ignore the insolence in Rowdy's brown eyes. But she'd be damned if she'd do so three days from now. She'd fire the son of a gun, rather than work with a thorn in her side. "Fine. I'll see you all tomorrow." She stepped down from the bench unassisted, turned on her heel and left.

Rachel was still shaking with the emotional ordeal of the narrowly averted strike as she slipped in the front door of the ranch house and saw Jaclyn fussing over the sideboard in the dining room. Travis was beside her, helping himself to a cup of coffee. For someone who didn't live at the ranch anymore, Rachel thought sourly, he was sure around a lot. Worse, he was dressed in a pair of jeans that did amazing things for his rear end and a cotton shirt that outlined the contours of his chest to mouth-watering effect, which meant he probably was not planning to go to his airlines office in Fort Worth today.

"Rachel, where have you been so early?" Jaclyn asked.

"Speaking with the hands." Rachel helped herself to a plate and steadfastly avoided Travis's gaze. She began helping herself to ham and eggs. What did it matter to her how wickedly attractive he looked in jeans? "We were going over their work assignments for the day."

Jaclyn started. "Already? I didn't know you intended to get started so soon, or else we would have talked!"

Rachel smelled a rat. Jaclyn turned to her son, her displeasure with him evident. "I told you I wanted Rachel to wait until next week before she dealt with the hands."

"It wasn't up to me." Travis shrugged. "Rachel wanted to get started right away."

More likely I was pushed into it, Rachel thought.

Jaclyn shook her head in regret. "I'm sorry, Rachel," she said, as she took a seat at the head of the table. "This is my fault. I was so preoccupied helping the twins get settled in yesterday, I didn't think to discuss my plans for the transition with you."

You mean there were some? Rachel thought, weak with relief. Maybe this wouldn't be such an impossible task, after all. "That's all right," Rachel soothed, grateful she had Jaclyn on her side. "Travis was more than helpful.'' She turned so only he could see her dagger-filled look. *I'll pay you back for this, Travis,* she thought, and felt a jolt of satisfaction when he had the conscience to look uncomfortable.

''It went well?'' Jaclyn asked hopefully.

Rachel would tell Jaclyn about the threatened strike, but not with Travis sitting there so smugly. ''It went fine,'' she lied. ''But I can see I've got my work cut out for me.'' She turned so she couldn't see Travis at all. ''You'll help me get situated?''

''Of course, dear. I wouldn't dream of throwing you into this with no preparation,'' Jaclyn said.

But Travis would, Rachel thought grimly, which pointed up sharply the difference between the Westcott men and the Westcott women.

HOURS LATER, Travis was driving around the ranch, checking on both the property and the herd and making notes about things to tell Rowdy on the sly. Fortunately he'd had the foresight to arrange to take the whole week off. And it was a good thing, too, considering the way things were shaping up. He'd half expected Rachel to back out of her agreement by now. She hadn't.

Needing a break, he cut the engine on the pickup and got out to look at the rolling green hills and acres of painted white fence. Funny, he hadn't actually lived on the ranch for years, yet the idea it would not be his made his gut twist painfully. For as long as he could remember, this had been his home, his center. He ate and slept in a condo in Fort Worth, but this was still where his heart was and always would be. And dammit, his mother knew that.

There wasn't an acre of land here that didn't hold some memory for him. He could hardly drive half a mile without seeing where he'd first learned to ride, or first been thrown, or where he and Austin had played and fought. Brothers. Heart and soul.

Oh, he knew why his mother was doing this. She felt guilty. So did he. Because neither of them had been able to stand up to Zeke. He certainly hadn't been able to get his stubborn cuss of a father to stop riding Austin so hard, though God knew he had tried to divert Zeke's attention from his older brother. But Austin was all his father had ever been able to focus on. It had been Austin upon whom Zeke had pinned all his dreams. Travis didn't know if it was because Austin was his firstborn, or if Zeke just liked him better. He only knew that he had paled in comparison to his brother, at least in his father's estimation. And if he let his mother hand over the ranch to Rachel, he would've failed again. Miserably.

He just wished it wasn't going to be so tough to take the place away from her. Because he knew now, if he hadn't before, just how hard and long she intended to fight him.

Unfortunately, no sooner had Travis returned to the ranch house than he was confronted by his mother. One look at her face and he knew she was furious with him.

"You get those hands in line, Travis, or I swear I'll fire every one of them."

Travis felt a flicker of hope. He'd been wondering all day what had happened down at the bunkhouse. It seemed he was about to find out. "Did Rachel tell you they gave her a hard time?" he asked innocently.

"She didn't have to," his mother stormed. "I saw how pale and defeated she looked this morning."

Travis had seen it, too. Remembering, he was overcome with guilt. He could have smoothed the way by

introducing Rachel in such a way that she would have
been accepted, but he hadn't. Because he knew, as
surely as Rowdy and the others hands did, that Rachel
didn't belong there. She would never be able to run the
ranch, not the way his father had, or his mother after
Zeke died.

Travis went to the refrigerator and helped himself to
a long-necked beer. "I can't fire Rowdy. We need him
too badly."

"Another cow boss could be found. A former daughter-in-law and twin grandchildren cannot."

Travis studied his mother. "You're doing this for
Austin, aren't you?" But Rachel had left Austin, and
Travis didn't intend to let her disgrace or hurt the fam-
ily again.

"And myself. Every time I look at them, it's like
having a second chance with your brother." She came
toward him and touched her hand to his arm. "Don't
you understand that, Travis?"

Travis was beginning to.

His mother shook an admonishing finger at him. "If
you can't help Rachel, at the very least stay out of her
way. I mean it, Travis. I lost my eldest son because
Zeke wouldn't welcome Rachel into his heart and his
home. I will not lose my grandchildren because of
you."

HOURS LATER, an exhausted Rachel slumped over the
desk in the study that had once belonged to Zeke. Running the Bar W was a bigger job than she had ever
imagined, but Jaclyn had gone overboard to help her,
giving her a computer-generated list of things that had
to be done daily, such as the feeding. Weekly, she had
the payroll. Monthly, ordering food for the bunkhouse

and arranging visits from the vet. Quarterly, filing income-tax returns. Now Rachel not only knew what to do, but when to do it.

In addition, she had read the personnel files on every hand, as well as a brief overview of the various problems they'd had since Jaclyn had taken over management. Next on her list was a stack of ranching journals that explained current breeding practices. She would not return to the bunkhouse until she had a handle on that. As soon as she did, and she was coming closer with every hour that passed, she would ask to be taken on a tour. From there, she would—

Rachel's thoughts were rudely interrupted. The door to Zeke's study was flung open and Travis stormed in. "Who the hell authorized you to give the hands a twenty percent raise?"

She had known this was coming. Rachel stood so she could face him on eye level. "Your mother did."

Travis wasn't the slightest bit appeased. He stalked forward. "Does she *know* about it?" he asked, his blue-gray eyes as hard as glass.

"As a matter of fact," she said proudly, "she does, Travis. In fact, we had a long talk about it this afternoon. *She* thought I should have fired the hands outright for insubordination, but I didn't want to do that, not until I'd given them a chance to get to know me and correct their behavior."

"We'll go broke before that happens," Travis fumed.

"I don't think so. I've looked at the books, Travis. This ranch operates in the black by a wide margin."

"Not for long," Travis predicted direly. He slouched in one of the leather wing chairs in front of Zeke's old mahogany desk. "Not the way you do business."

Just as Travis's attitude was entirely too bleak and forbidding, this room was entirely too dark and gloomy, Rachel thought, getting up to move around.

She turned toward him, sending him her most censorious look. "You're right," she said smoothly. "I shouldn't have had to give the hands a ten percent raise to stay on, or another ten as incentive to last out the summer, and it probably wouldn't have been necessary if you'd done a better job handing over the reins. Instead you treated me like some interloper—"

"Which you are," he interrupted crudely.

"—who has no business being here," Rachel continued, ignoring his interruption. She stalked close, her heels moving soundlessly across the faded red Persian carpet. "The hands merely responded in kind—"

Travis swore virulently. He got up and sent his black Stetson hat sailing across the room. It hit the heavy red velvet draperies and fell to the floor with a muffled thud. "You gave them a raise for that?" he countered furiously.

Rachel turned and gave the hat a lengthy perusal, letting him know without saying a word how childish she found that particular gesture. She turned back to him, her composure intact. He had rattled her but good the day before, almost ruining her relationship with the hired hands before it began. She wouldn't give him license to do so again. "I gave them a raise to stop them from going on strike," she said plainly, holding his lancing gaze with very little effort, so virulent was her own anger.

Knowing she was going to lose her temper, too, if she didn't rein in her feelings, she lowered her voice. "I had to give them a raise. The ranch can't afford to be without good help, and I don't yet have the expertise to be able to hire replacement hands. *Yet,*'' she said with icy determination. ''In three months, if they're still giving me a hard time, they'll be out on their butts.'' *You, too.*

Travis swore again. He stomped over to retrieve his Stetson, as if he had no idea how it got there. ''I knew this was going to cost us.'' He whacked the hat against his thigh before shoving it back on his head. ''I just didn't know how much.''

She wasn't sure if he was talking about the past or the present. But it didn't matter what he thought of her then, and it didn't matter what he thought of her now. ''Is that all?'' she asked coolly, more anxious for him to leave than he would ever know.

''No, it's not all.'' Tipping his hat back on his head with an index finger, he came toward her, not pausing until they were a scant twelve inches apart. ''Before you do something like this again, you clear it with me.''

''When, may I ask?'' she countered, and had the pleasure of seeing his eyes darken. ''On one of your infrequent visits to the ranch?''

Travis stepped nearer, until the distance between them had completely closed and they stood toe-to-toe. She inhaled the rich masculine scent of him, felt the warmth of his body and saw the muted desire in his eyes.

''As it happens,'' he said ever so softly, his well-thought-out words sending chills of sensual awareness racing up and down her spine, ''you'll have plenty of time to see me. I'm moving back in.''

Chapter Four

"You can't do that," Rachel said.

"The hell I can't!" Travis shot back smugly.

"You have a business in Fort Worth."

"Yes, I know," he retorted dryly.

"And a condo."

"And a fax and a phone and a computer," he finished her recitation for her impatiently. His eyes narrowed beneath the shelf of his thick black brows. "I'll be bringing them all here." Seeing her displeasure at the news, one side of his mouth lifted in a taunting grin. "Which isn't to say I won't occasionally have to fly into Fort Worth for the day," he admitted with comically exaggerated regret, "but the rest of the time, Rachel darling, I'm going to be here. What do you think about that?"

"You don't want to know."

"Maybe I do," he returned smoothly. In an effort to avoid physical contact with him, she stepped back. Her hips hit the edge of the desk with an unexpected thud, knocking books and papers every which way. Travis reacted with damnable swiftness, reaching forward to keep her ranching books from sliding to the floor with his right hand and catching a wealth of computer print-

outs with his left. He shoved them back onto the desk,
then instead of stepping back, as any gentleman would
have, he planted his hands on either side of her, the
warm sides of his palms and his thumbs touching the
sides of her hips.

"I'm waiting," he provoked softly.

And I'm determined not to play. Her head tilted back.
Refusing to let him badger her into compliance, or harass her off the ranch, she merely lifted an unimpressed
brow. "Is this really necessary?"

"I don't know," he replied, his gaze roving her face.
"Suppose you tell me."

"I'm not telling you anything except to buzz off,"
Rachel muttered, planting a hand in the middle of his
chest. She pushed. He went nowhere. Not about to engage in an undignified struggle with him, she merely
glared at him stonily and prepared to wait him out.
Surely he would tire of this intimidation routine soon.
"And that you're incorrigible," Rachel couldn't help
but add as the seconds ticked by.

"Thanks." He grinned.

"Not to mention rude—"

"Don't forget opinionated—" he drawled.

"Chauvinistic—"

"And determined," he added, shifting his weight so
his knees nudged hers. Seductively. Unbearably.
"Don't forget that."

"I won't," Rachel muttered, moving her legs
slightly to avoid further contact with the warm solidness of his. It was a mistake. No sooner had she shifted
than he used her momentary imbalance to wedge a
space between her jean-clad legs and push even closer.
To her mortification and fury, he didn't stop until the
outsides of his thighs nudged the insides of hers.

Streamers of electricity sparked everywhere they touched, adding to the weightless feel in her tummy. And though they still weren't touching *there,* she could imagine all too potently what it would feel like if they were.

And that was when he did it. Simply lowered his mouth to hers. Fit his lips over hers. And kissed her.

Lord, could the man kiss. She'd never felt such a swirling of emotion. She was consumed with heat as he kissed her long and hard and deep. Her head was swimming. Her heart soaring. Her conscience...

Her conscience! Oh, hell! she thought as she regained her senses.

Drawing back, she slapped him. Hard. He wasn't the least deterred.

Palms flat on the desk on either side of her, he leaned even closer, the faint rasp of his evening beard briefly scoring her cheek. "So what do you think, Miss Rachel?" he whispered, his warm breath fanning her hair. "Are you going to enjoy being so close to me day and night, night and day?"

Rachel held perfectly still. He was dauntingly close to her, close enough to easily turn this confrontation into either a wrestling match she was bound to lose or yet another searing soul-numbing kiss. "You know I won't," she predicted darkly, glaring at him, daring him to give her another reason to slap him. "But you should also know I don't plan to capitulate no matter how unpleasant you try to make my stay."

"Is that so?"

"Yes." She was determined not to let him know how disturbing she found his continued closeness, but she could do nothing about the frantic beating of her heart. "And just for the record..." she continued silkily.

"Yes?"

She smiled and looked straight into his eyes. "I think you're a woman-chasing chauvinistic jerk."

He laughed, soft and low. Too late, Rachel realized that by losing her temper, even slightly, she had fallen into his velvet-lined trap. But not for long, she vowed silently.

"Not that it matters to me what you do," she continued coolly. Palm to his chest, she shoved him out of her way and continued around to the other side of her desk. Her golden eyes radiated a warning. "So long as you stay out of my way."

"Think again, sweetheart." Travis waited until she'd sat down again, then sent her a crocodile smile. "I plan to be underfoot all the time. In fact, I'll be around so much it'll probably be downright aggravating."

"Suit yourself." Rachel went back to the papers on her desk. She had tons of literature from the Texas A&M University extension service to go through. It didn't matter to her if he wanted to stay and watch. She just hoped he wouldn't try to kiss her again.

"And I'll be taking back this office, too," Travis said.

Her head snapped up. Her full attention captured once again, she stared at him, seething. He knew damn well this office was the main symbol of power at the ranch and had been for years. Whoever occupied it was deemed to be in charge. If he took it over, then the men, Rowdy especially, would assume that Travis was still in charge, regardless of Jaclyn's decision.

"We'll see about that," she said.

He tipped his hat at her in a way that promised only

more devilment. "We certainly will," he promised smoothly.

IT WAS AFTER MIDNIGHT the next evening when Travis came into the house carrying his fax machine. Pausing only to turn on the hall light, he nudged one of the double oak doors open with the toe of his boot and strode into the study. He'd intended to set the fax down on the top of the desk, but the desk wasn't where it should have been. Swearing, he set the machine on the floor, then backed cautiously to his left and reached for the light switch.

He was still swearing two minutes later when a smug-looking Rachel sauntered in. "Back already?" she asked sweetly.

"What the hell have you done?" he thundered, looking at the sleek ultramodern office furniture. The room was done over in pearl gray and pale peach.

"What does it look like I've done?" Rachel glanced around as proudly as an interior decorator. "I've made this office my own."

He curtailed the urge to cross the room, toss her over his shoulder and haul her upside down to her car. "Where's the furniture that used to be here? That's *always* been here?"

"In the sewing room off the kitchen. Your mother said you could set up shop there. She thought you'd prefer it to one of the upstairs bedrooms but—"

"What I would prefer," he interrupted through clenched teeth, "is this room. With everything as it was."

"Sorry." Rachel paraded past him. Taking a seat behind her new desk, she crossed her legs demurely at the ankle and tugged at the hem of her trim ladylike skirt. "But I've taken over in here."

"So I see," he said grimly. "But not for long."

Her chin went up. She shot him a victorious smirk. "That's what you think."

He studied her, searching for a raw nerve, a way to recapture his advantage. But all he saw was a hauntingly beautiful face, a nose that was as slim and straight and impertinent as the rest of her, golden eyes that radiated intelligence, and lips that were so sensual and compelling they bordered on being downright voluptuous. Worse, she harbored an innate determination to have her own way and an inner drive and ambition every bit as strong as his own.

But he couldn't let any of that sway him from what he had to do. His gaze swept the sexy disarray of her flame-red curls. "I'm not going to make this easy for you, Rachel. I'm not just giving you the ranch."

She rolled her eyes in a parody of surprise. "Honestly, Trav, I never would have guessed."

"You may have conned my mother and made her feel guilty for the family's actions years ago—"

"But not you," Rachel guessed. She rested her chin on her hand.

"No, not me," he confirmed flatly, not about to let his head be turned by a pretty face and an even prettier body. "I know your marriage to my brother was a mistake."

Her eyes flashed and she leapt to her feet, closing the distance between them. "Maybe it was," she asserted, her temper flaring. "Maybe we weren't strong enough then, either of us. But I'm strong enough now, Travis." She shook her index finger at him like a teacher chastising an errant student. "Strong enough to stand up to you and Rowdy and anyone else who might get in the way of my doing what is best for my kids.''

He caught her hand and pushed it down between them. ''And what's that?'' he asked silkily.

She wrested her hand from his light grip and stepped back, her breasts heaving. ''Giving them a sense of their father and the heritage he would've wanted them to have.''

Travis tore his eyes from her chest. ''And the Westcott money has nothing to do with it,'' he said sarcastically.

''Wrong again!'' Rachel snapped. ''The Westcott money has everything to do with it. Because you see, Travis, I learned long ago, that without money, there is very little freedom.'' Her voice dripped to a compelling whisper. ''And what I want most for my children is the freedom to choose…to be anything they want to be.''

Looking at her, he could almost believe it. Almost.

Dammit. Hadn't he promised himself he wouldn't let her con his family again? And here he was, almost falling for her latest scam.

He looked around the office again. ''I'll get even with you for this,'' he swore. And it was a promise he meant to keep.

''YOU'RE SWINGING the rope too low. You need to hold it higher. Over your head, not level with it.''

Rachel turned to see Travis propped up negligently against the corral fence. His powerful body was silhouetted against the midmorning sun. The temperature was already ninety and inching higher. She had started perspiring hours ago, but Travis looked cool and relaxed. His jeans cloaked his powerful calves and thighs and pinpointed his abundant sex with disturbing accuracy. Her resentment of him upped another notch. "Go away."

He laughed at her low succinct tone and sauntered nearer, his boots rhythmically kicking up clouds of dust. "Can't take a little friendly criticism?"

"I can't take you," Rachel corrected, refusing to notice that he smelled like soap, leather and expensive cologne and that his eyes lazily cataloged the sweat-stained fabric of her shirt. Irritated by the way her clothes kept sticking damply to her chest, Rachel lifted the lasso and took another practice swing. "Now, goodbye, Travis."

"Who's been teaching you?" he asked curiously.

"Why do you care?" Rachel asked as the rope circled overhead once, twice, then caught on her hair.

"'Cause I do." Wordlessly he extricated the loop of rope from her hair. His teeth flashed white in his suntanned face. "Cowboying isn't as easy as it looks, is it?" he taunted.

Rachel tossed her head impatiently. "Easier than dealing with the likes of you."

The impact of her insult didn't register on his face. "Try it again," he instructed inscrutably.

"Not until you leave."

He hooked his thumbs through his belt loops and rocked back on his heels. "Afraid you'll miss in front of me again, huh?"

"No. Afraid I won't be able to quell the impulse to lasso *you*."

"Yeah?" To her mounting fury, he looked intrigued by the thought.

"And," Rachel continued archly, wishing just once she could get the better of him, "tighten the noose."

Rather than be infuriated with her as she had wanted, he threw back his head and laughed. The sound of his rich masculine voice echoing in the stillness infuriated her even more than his irksome presence. Determined to show him she was more of a rancher that he thought, she aimed her lasso. It swung high and wide and landed, with miraculous accuracy, on the target she'd sought.

"Okay. So now you've managed to lasso a fence post," Travis drawled from close behind her. "Let's try something harder. Something that moves," he said as she marched forward to extricate her rope from the post.

"Fine." Rachel pushed the word between gritted teeth and shot him a deadpan look meant to provoke. "Go get me a cow, Travis, and I'll lasso it."

"One of those new organically raised Brahma ones you just bought?"

Rachel stopped dead in her tracks. Was there anything he didn't know about her actions? "How'd you hear about that?" she ground out suspiciously.

"Oh, it's the talk of the ranch," he assured her confidently. "Not to mention the entire county."

She surveyed him grimly. "Why?"

"'Cause they're more expensive to purchase and to raise, for starters." Travis sauntered closer. He pushed his hat back, so she could better see his face. "I don't know what they taught you at the ranch-management seminar you just took over at Texas A&M, sugar, but there's very little market for organically raised beef. In fact, I know of only two supermarkets in the entire state that even carry it."

She sent him a haughty look. "On the contrary, Travis, there's a big demand, but there are only two major *sources* to supply it. I intend to make our ranch the third.''

Travis braced his legs apart and crossed his arms over his chest like a bandit about to embark on a raid. His eyes narrowed. ''Have you discussed any of this with my mother?''

''Yes.'' Rachel smiled at him sweetly. ''She thinks it's a great idea.''

Travis's jaw clenched in a way that filled Rachel with satisfaction. ''I suppose you told her how much harder it will be to raise this beef?''

Telling herself it was only fair to give him as much grief as he was giving her, Rachel busied herself rewinding her rope and shrugged off his cautionary words. ''It's not that much harder,'' she replied. ''I just have to see that they're fed organically grown grain, and water that's free of any pesticides, fertilizers and herbicide runoff.''

''The calves can't be fed any growth hormones—''

''The Bar W doesn't use steroids to begin with.''

''—or antibiotics or parasiticides,'' Travis said, anticipating her side of the argument lazily as he followed her back toward the center of the corral. ''What are you going to do if one of the calves gets sick?''

''I'll call Doc Harvey and have him promptly remove it from the herd. It can still be treated, Travis.''

''But no longer sold as organic,'' Travis argued, wondering if she had any idea just how good she looked in those jeans. They hugged her fanny just right and made the most of her long slim thighs, clinging until they disappeared into the half-moon tops of her calf-high red boots.

''True, but then it could be put in with the rest of

the herd and sold on the commercial market,'' Rachel said, lifting her face to his.

"Not at a profit,'' he said, staring down into her golden-brown eyes. He shouldn't have kissed her the other night. He knew it. It had just been a power play on his part, meant to startle or scare or goad her into packing up and leaving. It hadn't worked. And ever since, he'd not been able to get her out of his mind or forget how sweet her lips had tasted. He hadn't been able to stop himself from wanting more. And that left him with only one recourse. He had to do everything in his power to get her off this damn ranch before he started something and before she surrendered. Because that would make their current harassment of each other seem penny-ante.

"So, yes, it'll be more expensive to raise cattle this way,'' Rachel continued, "but we'll get more for our money in the end.''

Travis put a hand on her elbow and turned her toward him. "You really think you know what you're doing,'' he said grimly, knowing even if she thought she did that she didn't.

"Yes,'' she said confidently, her head high. "I do. Your mother and I both think this is the way to go. We're starting small, of course, to work out the kinks, but if it's successful, we'll be changing the whole operation over the next three years, until the Bar W is raising only organic beef.''

Travis knew Rachel's plan sounded good on paper. But in reality there was much that could go wrong. He shrugged. "It's your funeral.''

"Thanks,'' she said, extricating her elbow from his grasp. "I appreciate that.''

He paused.

"Something else on your mind?" she prodded. "As long as we're having this discussion, we might as well get it all out in the open." When he didn't respond, she strode away from him.

It wasn't his job to protect her. Travis fought the reflexive chivalrous need to step in. Wasn't this exactly what he wanted? For her to make so many mistakes so quickly that his mother would have no choice but to take back control?

It was and it wasn't. Oddly enough, he didn't want to see her hurt. Not that way, anyway. Not when he knew she was trying so hard. He hadn't expected that. He wasn't quite sure what he had expected. Maybe for her to be some sort of behind-the-desk ranch manager who'd taken on airs. Instead, she was out with the men more often than not. She'd made no secret that she was learning the business and she welcomed all help. And because she was so pretty and sociable, she got plenty from some of the younger men.

Of course most of the men still resented her. But he had the uncomfortable feeling that would pass, given time and continued hard work on her part. It was her feelings for him that were harder to deal with.

She detested him. That was never clearer than now, with her glaring feistily at him from across the corral. Of course maybe he deserved that, considering the way he'd treated her. But she was an interloper, he reminded himself sternly.

Still, he shouldn't have kissed her. He'd just done it to get a rise out of her, to shut her up and watch her eyes light up with fiery temper. But it had been so good he hadn't even minded the slap. So good he was still thinking about it, wishing he could haul her into his arms and do it again right now. And that, he knew, wouldn't do. Not if he wanted her off this ranch.

Travis followed her. "There's nothing on my mind but lassoing," he said, picking up their earlier discussion. "Now that you've mastered the fine art of capturing fence posts, you really should try something harder."

"I said I'd be happy to lasso you," she returned.

He grinned, liking the way the color flooded her fair cheeks. "Go ahead and try it."

Looking at him standing there so arrogantly with his arms over his chest, his legs braced apart, his black Stetson low over his brow, Rachel wanted nothing more than to put him in his place once and for all. She shot him a dark look. "My pleasure, cowboy," she drawled.

She swung the rope, aimed it and threw. He moved. The rope landed in the dirt.

"Missed," he pointed out cheerfully, looking as contrarily pleased with her ineptness as she was frustrated by it.

"You moved," she accused angrily, reeling in her rope with swift jerky motions.

"So do cows," he pointed out affably.

She swung again, fast and hard, hoping to catch him off guard. He caught the rope with one hand and with a light yank reeled *her* in, fast and hard. "Like to play rough, huh?" he taunted. "So do I."

Her breath was coming in quick shallow pants. "It doesn't matter how much you harass or belittle me, Travis. I'm not leaving."

He caught her to him, so their legs and stomachs were aligned. "It can get very hot out here in the summer,'' he warned softly as his eyes drifted over her face. ''Too hot for some.''

Her breasts rose and fell with each agitated breath. ''Then you better head for the air-conditioning, Travis,'' she countered just as softly, dimly aware that she had never felt more alive in her life than she did at that very moment. '''Cause I love the heat.''

His eyes darkened. His head lowered. His lips parted. For one long moment she had the oddest sensation he was going to kiss her again. She told herself firmly to lean back, but instead found herself leaning toward him....

He released her so swiftly she nearly lost her balance. ''I love the heat, too, sugar.'' His low voice vibrated with promise and passion. His eyes sparkled with mischief and desire. ''So watch out.'' On that note, he grinned at her, tipped his hat and sauntered away.

Fuming silently, the lasso clutched tightly in her gloved palm, she watched him swagger toward the gate. It wasn't fair, she thought, that one man should have so much. He was handsome, intelligent, irksome as all get out and arrogant to a fault. Plus, he had a will and inner determination that was surely as strong as hers.

But he was wrong about her.

She did belong on this ranch. And so did her children. And one day soon she would prove it to him.

Chapter Five

"Planning a ride?" Travis asked from the other end of the stables, several days later.

"No, I'm just practicing saddling this horse," Rachel responded ironically. Since the lassoing "lesson" she had avoided him steadfastly, seeing him only at family dinners. But it seemed her luck had run out, as she had known in her heart, it eventually would. No matter how much Travis swore he detested her, he just couldn't stay away from her for long.

"Where're you going?"

Unable to help but note how ruggedly fit and handsome he looked in his faded jeans and dark blue denim shirt with the pearl snap buttons, his Stetson pulled low across his brow, Rachel leaned beneath the horse and finished tightening the cinch. Initially, she had no plans of answering him. But it seemed he wasn't going to budge until she satisfied his curiosity, at least marginally. "Out," she said.

He grinned, as if knowing just how much he annoyed her.

"Out where?" he prodded.

"Out to check on my new Brahma calves."

"Right." He gave a mock serious nod. "The organically raised folly."

"Very funny."

"I doubt you'll think so when you see what effect raising them has on the ranch books. Especially when you add that to the raise you already gave the hired hands. There's going to be one big addition in the debit column."

Rachel was already uneasily aware of that. She'd initially done too much too fast, but as it was too late to go back and undo anything, she knew she would just have to muddle through and find a way to make everything work. She knew she could. She just had to apply herself and not let Travis's constant taunting and chaperoning get the better of her. "Must you constantly interfere?" she asked, regarding him as if he were a loathsome snake.

He straightened with an indolent shrug. "I thought I was trying to help."

Rachel swung herself up into the saddle. It took her only a moment to get her weight situated in the middle, but she could have sworn he was laughing at her from behind the palm he speculatively ran across his jaw. To his credit, however, his blue eyes were serious as he met hers.

His dark brows drew together. "You sure you know what you're doing?" he asked, unable to completely mask his worry over her safety.

"I think I can ride a mile to the pasture without getting lost," Rachel retorted stiffly, trying not to notice just how far she was from the ground, now that she was sitting astride her mount. Or let on how much that still bothered her.

Travis's eyes sized her up. "You ever been out entirely on your own?" he pressed.

"Of course I have," Rachel replied, ignoring the real thrust of his question. "I drive around the ranch in my pickup all the time. In fact, I have now not only memorized most of the pastures, but I know where all the gates for each are located, too."

"I meant on the back of the horse," Travis persisted.

Rachel was miffed he was still dwelling on what she had yet to learn, rather than what she had already accomplished. "I'll be fine." It was time she went out without Rowdy anyway.

Rachel put a rein in each of her hands. She tapped her horse lightly in the sides with the heels of her boots. To her humiliation, the horse refused to move. She tried again, a little harder this time. Still no luck.

Travis rolled his eyes and shook his head. "Given that demonstration of your expertise, there's no way you're going out alone," he muttered.

Ignoring her prompt protests, he grabbed a saddle and threw it on the back of his own horse. In a tenth the time it had taken her to saddle up, he was finished and leading his horse by the reins out into the walkway in the center of the stables beside hers.

"This really isn't necessary," Rachel said.

"The hell it isn't," Travis said roughly, halting his horse right next to hers. He held her eyes for a breath-stealing moment before continuing in a low soft penitent voice, "My mother'd have my hide if I let anything happen to you. Besides—" he grinned, leaning over and taking her reins "—this horse is a valuable animal. Don't want anything happening to it."

Rachel resisted the urge to call him a few colorful names as, astride his horse, he led hers out of the barn.

"How did you do that?" Rachel asked, frowning, as she began to bump along in the saddle with an uneven rhythm. Beside her, Travis moved smoothly, one with his horse.

"Do what?" he retorted.

"Get my horse to go?" Rachel asked, frowning again, wondering what she'd forgotten. She was sure she'd done everything Rowdy'd taught her to do.

"You were holding the reins too tight," Travis supplied, telling both horses, "Whoa." He swung himself out of the saddle and opened the corral gate. "Pulling on the reins means stop."

"Yes, I know that," Rachel grumbled, wishing he didn't make everything she found so difficult about riding, beginning with getting on and off a horse, look so darned easy, as easy as breathing.

"Figured you did." He grinned at her from beneath the brim of his hat, and once they had cleared the corrals and were headed off toward the pasture and her young Brahma herd, he bent over and handed the reins back to her. Leaning back so that his weight was situated squarely in his saddle, he glanced at her speculatively. "You always bounce around in the saddle like that?"

Rachel rolled her eyes. If he'd been any kind of gentleman at all, he wouldn't have commented on her lack of expertise. "I'm still learning." She jerked up and down, up and down, her bottom smartly hitting the saddle with every step.

"Yeah. I can see that," Travis said dryly. "Who taught you?"

"Rowdy."

Travis's glance swept down her body, starting at her shoulders, moving past her waist, lingering on her thighs and knees, before returning to her face. He looked very unhappy, Rachel noted, but she wasn't sure he was unhappy with her.

"Didn't Rowdy teach you how to sit a horse properly?" Travis asked.

Rachel blinked. "Sit a horse?" she repeated dumbly.

"You know. You put your feet in the stirrups and use your knees to keep your legs against the horse," he explained impatiently. "That's it. Yeah, put 'em in. Like this." He demonstrated, pressing his knees lightly against his horse's belly. He smiled as she awkwardly mimicked what he'd done. "Now, as you ride, move with the horse in rhythm. Think of yourself as being one with the horse, instead of bouncing along on top of his back."

To Rachel's delight, his suggestions worked. Riding that way was infinitely more comfortable. And since she no longer had the feeling she was going to tumble off at any given moment, it wasn't as frightening to her, either. "Thanks," she said with a relieved sigh, knowing he hadn't had to help her, but had done so out of the goodness of his heart.

"Now, about the reins," Travis continued, ignoring her demonstrated relief. "How come you're holding one in each hand?"

Rachel shrugged. "That's what Rowdy told me to do. He said this way if I want to turn right, I pull the right rein. If I want to turn left, I pull the left." She studied Travis, who was holding his reins in one hand, effortlessly maneuvering his horse.

"Well, that way will work," Travis allowed, "but it's for beginners."

Travis looked more competent, Rachel had to admit. But it also seemed to her he was splitting hairs. If both ways worked, why not let her use the easy way to get around? "I don't see the difference," Rachel said.

"There isn't any, unless you need one hand free to lasso a stray calf. 'Course—" he winked at her '—considering the way you lasso and the fact you can barely sit a horse…" He ducked as she swatted her hat at him and nearly lost her balance and seat in the bargain. "I guess there's not much chance of that."

Rachel plopped her hat back on her head and, grasping the saddle horn with one hand, grumbled, "Okay. You might as well show me how to ride with my reins in one hand."

"The same as you do with one in each hand, only now you have one hand free."

"What happens if I want my horse to go left?"

"Then you bring the reins to the right side of the horse," he explained simply. "That will automatically tauten the reins on the left, and bring the horse's head around."

"And the horse will go in whatever direction you point its head," Rachel finished.

"Right." Travis grinned at her. "Let's try it."

For the next several minutes, they rode around the pasture they were in. Rachel was confused at first, because it was opposite from the way she had learned, but Travis was an excellent teacher.

"Well, it's not second nature yet, but you've definitely almost got the hang of it," Travis finally allowed after she had successfully completed several tricky maneuvers.

"Thanks for the lofty praise," she said dryly as they continued on in the direction they'd started.

His eyes glimmered. "No false praise on this

ranch,'' he countered flatly. ''You either earn it or you don't.''

''Double thanks.''

''''Course, if you're out here all summer, you'll probably be riding like a tourist by summer's end. And actually that's kind of fitting, since you do work as a travel agent,'' he teased.

Rachel thought about reaching over and swatting him, then decided it wasn't worth the effort.

''Exactly when is your leave of absence at the travel agency up, anyway?'' he asked.

Rachel rode on, enjoying the bright blue sky overhead and the warmth of the fair summer morning. She kept her eyes on the thick green grass and said, ''I didn't take a leave of absence.'' Travis's brow arched speculatively and Rachel continued, ''They wouldn't give me one. So I resigned.''

His mouth thinned. And yet, Rachel mused, the action did nothing to detract from the sheer sensuality of his mouth.

''That was quite a gamble, wasn't it?''

''Not really.'' Rachel smiled, enjoying the one-upmanship between them almost as much as she enjoyed running the ranch. ''As I don't intend to fail.''

''Yeah, well, supposing you do?'' he pressed, his head twisted and his eyes remaining unswervingly on hers as he moved his horse a little ahead. ''Then what?''

Rachel felt her heartbeat pick up as she struggled to keep pace with him. And there was a definite heat wave starting up her neck, moving into her face. ''Then I start over, come fall,'' she said defiantly.

They reached the pasture where her new herd was quartered. Travis swung himself out of his saddle. Before she could react, he was reaching up to give her a hand down. "You don't seem very concerned about the prospect of being unemployed," he said as soon as he had her on the ground. His hands tightened around her waist. "Unless, of course, you're planning to use your situation to pressure my mother into letting you and the twins stay on no matter what."

Rachel slipped out of his light grasp and tried not to think about how warm his hands had felt. Gentle, and yet resolute.

"I don't care what you think of me, Travis," she informed him as she had many times before. Turning her back on him, she strode over to the pasture fence and stared out at the scrawny-looking herd of Brahma calves. Most were about the size of large dogs, weighing no more than fifty pounds. It would be a year or more before they were ready to send to market. "I know, had it been up to him, that Austin would've wanted his children to share in his heritage," Rachel continued.

"Austin isn't here any longer," Travis pointed out as he positioned himself next to her.

"No, he isn't, but I still owe him. And this time, I'm not going to let him down," Rachel said grimly.

"This time? What do you mean this time?" Travis reached over and caught her arm.

"Nothing," Rachel said, ducking her head. She wasn't about to get into any of this with him. Not now. Maybe not ever.

"Rachel. You can't just leave it at—" Travis broke off abruptly as a low-flying helicopter swooped in overhead. It was white and had a red cross on the side. And it seemed to be headed for a landing on Westcott land.

Suddenly Travis was all action. "Come on. Someone must've been hurt."

Minutes later, they were at the site of the commotion. "What happened?" Travis asked, jumping off his horse.

Rowdy wiped the sweat from his brow and pointed to a half-grown steer trussed up in a corner of the field. "Damned cow attacked one of my men."

Heart pounding, Rachel led the way to the stretcher, with Travis and Rowdy close on her heels. Rachel recognized the injured as being one of the newest hired hands, Bobby Ray Johnson.

She hunkered down beside him while the paramedics worked to immobilize his left shoulder and arm. "What happened?"

"I was out here working on the fence," Bobby Ray said weakly as the paramedic put the finishing touches on an air splint.

"You were working on it while the cows were in the field?" Rachel asked.

A shadow fell over her. "We always do that," Rowdy intervened.

"It's usually not a problem, Rachel," Travis said. "The pounding scares them off. They usually give us wide berth."

Concerned, Rachel turned back to Bobby Ray. "Did the cows leave you alone?"

"At first," Bobby Ray admitted. "Then I don't know what happened. I was just hammering the last new board when that crazy cow came up behind me and nudged me into the post. I turned around and gave him a hard slap on the side and yelled at him to get away, like I always do when one of 'em misbehaves or gets to crowding me. And that was when he charged me. If Rowdy hadn't been out here..." Bobby Ray shuddered, then grimaced in renewed pain. "I swear, Ms. Westcott, that cow's dangerous! I thought he was going to kill me!"

"I say we get rid of it," Rowdy said as soon as the helicopter had taken off with Bobby Ray toward the hospital in San Angelo.

Rachel strode toward the cow. Like all the cows on the ranch he had an ear tag that identified him by number for their records. His read #2021. At the moment, with his feet tied together, lying quietly on his side, the half-grown steer wasn't a danger to anyone. In fact, she thought, as she looked down into the big black eyes, he looked perfectly harmless. But appearances could be deceiving. "Has anyone called the vet?" she asked over her shoulder.

"Not yet," Rowdy said.

"Fine. I'll do that. Rowdy," Rachel directed, "you get this steer in quarantine in one of the pens next to the barn."

Rowdy touched a hand to the brim of his hat. "Yes, ma'am."

Travis followed Rachel to the pickup. He stuck his hands into the back pockets of his form-fitting jeans. "Mind filling me in on what you're doing?"

She shot him an impatient look. "I'm going to get Doc Harvey out here right away and have him take a look at that steer."

"What for?"

"To see if he's sick."

Travis shook his head disagreeably, their earlier camaraderie forgotten. "I can tell you right now that cow wasn't rabid."

"I wasn't necessarily thinking of rabies. He may

have eaten some potato weed or western horse net-
tle—''

''Then the cow would've been acting drunk,'' Travis
cut in, exasperated, ''not mean.''

''Unless he's a mean drunk,'' she corrected. She
whirled to face him, wishing she could recapture the
spirit of cooperativeness they had enjoyed earlier.
''Look, we don't know what's going on with that
cow,'' she said as she attempted to reason with him.
''For all we know he could be sick with some conta-
gious disease. But one thing is certain,'' she said
firmly, refusing to let Travis's expertise sway her. ''I
am not going to make any decision on what to do with
him until I have all the facts.''

''ANY WORD ON BOBBY RAY?'' Travis asked hours
later as an exhausted Rachel walked in the back door
to the ranch-house kitchen.

''He's resting comfortably at the hospital and due to
be released tomorrow. He has a broken arm and a dis-
located shoulder, though, so it'll be at least three
months before he can work again at full speed.''

''And in the meantime?'' Travis asked, pouring Rachel a glass of lemonade.

She accepted the cold drink with thanks. ''I told him
we'd give him two weeks' paid sick leave and then he
can come back to work on lighter chores after that.''

''What about the cow?''

''Doc Harvey examined him and found no evidence
that the cow had been into anything poisonous. Nor is
#2021 sick.''

Travis frowned. ''I was afraid that would be the
case.''

To set Travis's mind at ease, Rachel told him her

plans. "I'm going to continue to keep him under quarantine for another week or so."

"Why not just get rid of him now?" Travis persisted.

"Because he's only half-grown."

"You heard Bobby Ray. He thinks the animal's crazy."

Rachel set her glass down on the table with a thud. "Doc Harvey disagrees."

Wordlessly Travis reached into the drawer where the clean kitchen cloths were stored. He pulled out a tea towel and held it under the cool water. Then he wrung out the excess water and handed it wordlessly to Rachel, who rubbed it over her flushed face and neck.

"Look, I like Doc Harvey," Travis continued, propelling Rachel into the nearest chair, "but let's face it. He didn't grow up on a ranch and he hasn't been out of vet school all that long. He's still wet behind the ears when it comes to something like this."

"So is Bobby Ray, for that matter," Rachel countered calmly. She slouched down, propped up her feet on the seat of another chair and let her head fall back until it rested against the top rung. "So am I. What's your point?"

Travis stood with his legs braced apart and crossed his arms. "I really think you should get rid of the cow."

Rachel tore her eyes from his powerful frame and set her jaw stubbornly. She would not think about what being so close to him, so often, did to her. Or about how kind and thoughtful he could be when he was not trying to provoke her or actively get her off the ranch. "In another six months, that cow will be worth twice as much," she argued.

"In six months someone else could be hurt. Listen to me, Rachel." Travis's voice dropped a compelling notch. He dropped into the chair beside her, so that they were sitting face-to-face. "I've been around animals all my life. They're not that different from people. They've got personalities, too, and some of them are just plain mean."

Rachel lifted the heavy length of her hair off her neck. "Schizophrenic?"

"Yes."

Her feet hit the floor with a bang. She pushed away from the table, away from the by-now achingly familiar scent of his cologne. "That's an old wives' tale, Travis." She resented the fact he was so close, so concerned. And always, always underfoot!

"If someone else gets hurt…" he warned, coming around grimly to face her.

"It'll be on my conscience," Rachel said, tilting her head back and pulling in a deep breath. "But it's not going to happen, Travis."

Just as a real friendship between them probably wasn't going to happen. Despite his surface civility now, prompted by their mutual concern over the ranch and the safety of the men, she knew he didn't trust her any further than he could see her. And that, unfortunately, might never change, no matter what she said or did.

Chapter Six

"You've been awfully quiet this evening, Rachel," Jaclyn observed as the dessert dishes were being cleared away. "Any particular reason?"

Travis had been wondering the same thing. Used to Rachel's vivacity, he'd found her silence vaguely disturbing, too.

"I just can't believe that steer attacked Bobby Ray. Number 2021."

Jaclyn set down her coffee in alarm. "You haven't had any more trouble with him, have you?"

"No, but I think I'll go down and check on him, anyway, if you don't mind."

"Certainly you're excused," Jaclyn said graciously.

Travis stood up, too. "I'll go with you." He ignored the flash of dismay on her face. "I'm curious about how he's doing, too."

No sooner had the two of them left the dining room than Rachel extricated herself, rather pointedly, Travis thought, from his light guiding grasp.

"This really isn't necessary," she said through stiff lips.

He paused to get a flashlight from the shelf above the back door, and as he did so he took in the new

style of her hair. She'd done something different tonight. Instead of wearing it loose, she'd pulled it off
her neck and twisted it into an elegant figure eight.
White and jade-green silk ribbons were threaded
through it. He wasn't sure how she'd done it—it
seemed complicated as all hell to him—but he liked it.
It really looked elegant. And the pearl earrings she was
wearing were another nice touch; they drew attention
to the delicate lines of her face and made her seem all
the more feminine.

"Save it. I'm going," Travis said. He glanced down
at her slender legs and the two-inch heels that encased
her feet. The jade-green pumps were perfect for showing off her slim legs during a semiformal dinner at
home. Not so good for walking out in the yard. He
sighed impatiently. "I'll wait while you put on a pair
of boots."

"These shoes are fine," Rachel retorted.

"Suit yourself." Travis thrust an arm in front of her
and held open the back door. "It's your ankle you'll
be spraining."

"Don't you wish."

Travis could tell by the contentious gleam in her
eyes that she was spoiling for another fight about what
she'd done, or neglected to do, about the crazy cow.
Feeling his own temper rise, he followed her to the
corral. Unlike the yard surrounding the house, the corral was shadowed by the barns. The darkness was as
soothing as the chirp of the cicadas in the trees, but
there was enough moonlight for him to see even the
slightest change in her face.

Her back to him, Rachel moved around to the left,
until she could see steer #2021, standing alone at the

far side of the pen. "You see," she said in a low victorious voice. "He's fine now."

"Sure he's fine," Travis agreed. "While he's by himself, penned up and eating the best grain the ranch has to offer."

"There is no reason to destroy him."

Travis rested both elbows on the top of the corral fence. He wished Rachel would stop being so stubborn. "We weren't talking about destroying him," he corrected. "We were talking about sending him off to be slaughtered, which I might point out, is going to happen sooner or later, anyway."

"He'll bring more money when he's fully grown."

Travis studied her, seeing a new way to tease her. "Are you sure you have what it takes to be a rancher? You're not going to cry when it comes time to slaughter the beef you're raising?"

Rachel tossed her head and looked down her nose at him. "No, I am not going to cry. I am well aware that ranching is a business, Travis. Which is exactly why I refused to let that cow go until he is grown and we can get a full return on our investment."

"You're right," Travis drawled provokingly. "There is no reason to get rid of him now, except of course for the fact that he attacked one of our hands without provocation."

Rachel's expression softened sympathetically, and for a moment she forgot to be angry with him. "I'm sorry about what happened to Bobby Ray." One hand gripping the top rail, she leaned toward him earnestly. "But I can't help but think there must have been a reason for what happened. Maybe the vet was wrong. Maybe Number 2021 did ingest some minute amount of potato weed that didn't show up in the tests. Maybe something *made* him act crazy.''

Travis raised a skeptical brow.

Rachel finished stonily, ''All I know is that cows, like people, deserve a second chance.''

''Are we talking about the cow now or you?'' he wondered aloud, knowing full well his question was likely to annoy her. Still, he wanted her to say literally everything that was on her mind, and if the only way to get her to do so was to provoke her, then so be it.

''Maybe a little of both.''

He studied her, watching the moonlight play on her hair. She looked guilty and upset. And so vulnerable he was tempted to forget the havoc she'd once caused his family and start fresh with her. ''What did you ever do wrong?'' he asked, curious about what she would admit to in her current frame of mind.

Shoulders slumping slightly, she moved away from him and stared out into the starry Texas night. ''You remember the day you came to tell us your father was disinheriting Austin?''

''Yes, I do.'' In fact, he remembered that day as if it was yesterday. He'd gone to their trailer early one morning, so early he'd gotten his brother and Rachel out of bed. She'd looked gorgeous, wrapped in a robe, her glorious red hair all tousled, her skin flushed with the warm glow of sleep. Austin had looked happy, too, despite the dismal poverty of their surroundings. Travis had felt guilty about being there, about doing his father's dirty work, yet he'd known, for his brother's sake, that Austin had to be told what their father was up to. Travis had delivered the blow. Rachel had left the room crying. Austin had cussed him and thrown him out....

Rachel sighed now, and stared down at her clasped hands. "I was so sure that we were doing the right thing by staying married, Travis," she reported sadly. "I was so sure that we didn't need money and that we could be happy without it."

Seeing his brother and his new wife together for the first time, Travis had thought so, too. At least until he'd delivered the news.

"How did Austin feel?" Travis asked, wishing everything had been different, that the rift in his family hadn't occurred. And that Rachel and Austin had been given a chance to make it on their own without Westcott family interference.

Rachel shrugged listlessly, and when she spoke her voice sounded thick and unsteady, as if her throat was clogged with tears. "He tried to act like it didn't matter, but he was devastated, not just by Zeke's rejection of me, but of him, too. Oh, Travis," she said, blinking furiously, "he wanted to come back to the ranch so badly."

At that moment it was all Travis could do not to take Rachel into his arms and offer her the comfort he ached to give. "Why didn't he?"

"Pride. He knew if he brought me, Zeke would toss him out, and he wouldn't go without me."

"So he was stuck."

Rachel nodded affirmatively. Her voice gathered strength. "I tried to comfort him. But when weeks passed and he only got more depressed, I knew he'd never be happy without his family and his home. I couldn't take that away from him. Because I was standing in the way of any reconciliation, I did what I knew I had to do. I packed my bags and I told him it was over, that the marriage had been a mistake from the beginning, and I left.''

Travis saw the sacrifice. It hadn't come easily to her. It hadn't been a whim, but a deliberate action, calculated to help his brother, not hurt and betray him. He studied her, realizing she was a much more complicated woman than he had ever given her credit for being. A much more compassionate woman. ''Did he ever try to contact you after that?'' He studied her upturned face.

''Yes.'' Rachel dropped her head forward. She rubbed at her temples with the fingertips of both hands. ''I was very cruel, but I knew I had to be.'' She shook her head in obvious regret, shut her eyes and swallowed hard. ''I didn't want him yearning after what could never be.''

''And my mother?'' Travis regarded Rachel sternly, telling himself not to let her beauty mislead him. He couldn't let himself forget that Rachel had taken money from his mother in the past, just as she was trying to take the ranch from Jaclyn, and from him, now. ''How does my mother figure into this?''

Her arms hugging her chest, Rachel began to pace. ''I don't know how she found me. Maybe Austin told her where I'd gone. But I got a letter from her, telling me how sorry she was things had worked out the way they had, and she praised me for doing what I felt I had to. I think she knew what it was costing me to give Austin up. At the time, he was all I had.

''Anyway—'' she ducked her head, embarrassed ''—there was a check enclosed, to help me make a fresh start. A week later, Austin was dead. And all I had,'' she said softly, ''were my regrets.''

''You didn't come to the funeral,'' Travis accused,

remembering how stunned and hurt he'd been about that.

"I couldn't," she said sadly. "I didn't want to upset Zeke."

She'd been right, Travis thought. Her coming to the funeral would have made his father crazy with rage and hurt.

"But later," Rachel continued, "I visited Austin's grave and said goodbye in my own way."

Travis wanted to believe she had loved his brother and wanted only what was best for him. Still, there was much he had to ask, much he had to examine about her character. "If Austin hadn't died," he said slowly, "would you and he have gotten back together because of the twins?" He discovered, to his surprise, that he wanted her to say no as much as he wanted her to say yes. It was painful for him to think of her with Austin, and yet painful for him to think of her hurting Austin, too.

Rachel shrugged again. "That I just can't say, Travis," she said, her chin lifting a defiant notch.

He admired her honesty. "Why didn't you ever tell me any of this?" Why hadn't she just leveled with him from day one?

"Because you weren't ready to listen."

Travis almost ducked his head in shame. He knew that was true. He also knew his feelings had changed in the weeks she'd been on the ranch. Initially, he had wanted nothing more than to make her leave. But that was before he had started to get to know her. Now, that wasn't what he wanted at all. He still didn't want her running the ranch, though. He never would. The ranch was his rightful inheritance, not hers. And yet the thought of her leaving, of rarely if ever seeing her again, bothered him more than he wanted to admit.

She glanced over her shoulder. "They'll be wondering what's keeping us."

Yes, Travis thought, they certainly would.

"We better go back in."

"Look, Miz Westcott, I've been talking to the men and we're all in agreement. We want that crazy cow to go."

Rachel squared off with Rowdy in the bunkhouse while the men listened. "If the cow were still acting up, I'd be tempted to agree with you, but he's not."

"He wasn't acting up before he attacked me, either," Bobby Ray said from his place at one of the long plank tables.

Guilt pushed at Rachel as she recalled Bobby Ray in the back of the helicopter. Even now, he would be weeks recovering. "I'm sorry about what happened to you, Bobby Ray. But I've talked to Doc Harvey—"

"Who just happens to be as green as a kid fresh out of high school," Rowdy harrumphed.

"That's enough, Rowdy," Rachel said tightly. "Doc Harvey is extremely well qualified and you know it."

"Going to school doesn't mean he knows anything about range work," Rowdy spat back. "And I know that crazy cow's mama. She was as mean as her calf is now. Ornery and ill-tempered."

Rachel faced Rowdy stubbornly. She was so tired of him challenging her. Worse, she knew the rest of the men took their cues from their foreman. If she couldn't get him on her side, or at least make him respect her, she would never be able to run the Bar W smoothly. Making no effort to conceal the exasperation in her voice, she volleyed back, "We're not looking for Mr. Congeniality, Rowdy, just a full-grown steer to take to market."

Rowdy shot her a challenging look. "I still say we get rid of him."

"When it's time," Rachel qualified. "Now, we'll continue to keep the cow isolated and under observation."

"And if there's any more trouble?" Bobby Ray challenged, looking just a bit fearful.

"Then I'll make a decision at that time," Rachel said gently, surer than ever she was doing the right thing in refusing to let either of the men, or one slightly crazy cow, intimidate her. "Now, about the pesticide-free feed for the organically raised herd. I noticed we're getting a little low." She glanced at Rowdy. "Have you ordered more?"

"Not yet. I think they're ripping us off, price-wise. I was looking around for a cheaper supplier."

"Keep trying to find one. In the meantime, order another week's supply of pesticide-free grain from the current source."

"It costs double the ordinary grain," Rowdy protested.

"I'm aware of that," Rachel said quietly. "But if we feed them anything else the herd won't be organically raised. And then it will all have been for naught, won't it?"

Rowdy met her stare for stare. "Suit yourself," he said. He turned and headed for his adjacent office. "It's the Westcott's money."

And not mine, Rachel supposed he meant.

Realizing the gauntlet had been thrown down and that all the men were watching for her reaction Rachel said, with deadly calm, "Rowdy, I understand things are being run differently now. If you're having trouble doing the job..." She left the words hanging, but the threat in her voice was implicit. And real.

Jaw set, he whirled back to face her. "I can do the job," he retorted tersely. His eyes, full of resentment, bore into hers.

Too late, Rachel realized she had made a mistake by crossing him in front of the men. She had a brief uneasy feeling her cow boss was going to extract some sort of revenge for this public dressing-down.

"Fine," she said.

Rowdy's chest rose and fell with the effort it was taking to control his temper. He removed his hat and slapped it against his thigh. "About the mesquite in pasture forty-one. What do you want us to do about that?"

TRAVIS WAS IN HIS OFFICE when Rachel found him. Observing his tall frame in the converted sewing room, Rachel felt another pang of guilt. The heavy furniture from his father's office had been crammed into a room that was barely a quarter the size. Computer listings and manila files were stacked on every available surface. His computer, fax, copier, phone and answering machine covered the rest. Travis barely had room for the swivel chair behind the desk. Worse, the Cape Cod curtains and sunshine-yellow color scheme added a ludicrously frilly touch to what should have been a businesslike domain.

But he didn't have to work here, she reminded herself sternly when her guilt threatened to get the better of her. He had an undoubtedly spacious office in Fort Worth. She did have to work here. She wouldn't waste any time worrying about a situation he had created for himself. She had enough to do just trying to solve the problems on the ranch.

Rachel rapped on the door frame. "Got a minute?" she asked casually.

Travis leaned back in his father's old swivel chair. His black hair mussed, his eyes clear and vibrantly alive, he looked handsome, self-assured, and very male. He tossed the computer printout he'd been studying onto a pile of papers on his cluttered desk. "What's up?"

Rachel tore her eyes from the long legs propped on one corner of the desk and the way his jeans fit those legs snugly from the top of his boots to his waist, and every point in between. She lounged against the door frame. "Rowdy and some of the other hands want me to cut down the mesquite in pasture forty-one. I know they hog water and the grass there is drying out, but the trees also provide shade. I'm hesitant to take away what little relief from the heat the cattle have."

"Yeah, so?" He leaned farther back in his chair.

"So..." Rachel took a deep breath, put aside her considerable pride and prepared to ask for help. "I'm wondering what you would do if you were in my place."

Travis's eyes stayed on hers a reflective moment.

She felt the jolt of his intent assessing look all the way down to her toes. Like an ongoing electrical current, it had every inch of her thrumming and alive.

His sexy smile widened to a taunting depth. "Ah, but Rachel, I'm not in your place, remember?" he reminded her lazily. His gaze roved her face with contemplative pleasure. "My mother and you saw to that."

Rachel fought the heat creeping up her neck and the urge to throttle him. Damn him, she thought, for enjoying every second of her discomfiture. Her voice choking with suppressed indignation, she surmised grimly, "You're not going to give me any advice, are you?"

He took his clasped hands, lifted them high above his head, stretched every muscle in his brawny arms and chest, then moved them to the back of his neck. His eyes on hers, he tipped his chair back even farther. "It'd kind of spoil the fun if I told you what to do, wouldn't it?" he taunted in a soft provoking voice that sent shivers up and down her spine. He studied her intently, then shrugged. "You're running the ranch now. You decide."

So much for expecting him to be decent, kind, caring or helpful in any way. She swore and turned smartly on her heel. "You're a selfish bastard."

His laughter was low and enticing, and it filled the sewing room to overflowing. Then he made a *tsk*ing sound. "Rachel, Rachel. I'm surprised at your language."

Rachel kept going and didn't look back. The only surprise she had was her own stupidity for expecting him to help her in the first place. Just because he'd been nice to her once the other night, just because they'd actually had one civil adult conversation and he had seemed to come away from it with a better understanding of what she'd been through with his brother, didn't alter anything. He still wanted her off the ranch. And no matter how tense, unhappy or unwelcome that made her feel, she reflected sorrowfully, his attitude wasn't going to change.

Chapter Seven

"Where the devil have you been?" Travis asked hours later when Rachel strode into the house, her red cowboy boots clicking authoritatively on the tile floor. "Dinner was over an hour ago."

Rachel was still stinging from the way he had dismissed her request for advice, but her pride compelled her not to let him know it. All too aware that his eyes assessed every inch of her, she shoved her dust-covered, flat-brimmed hat off her head and let it fall down her back, held around her neck by the long leather string. "Careful, cowboy, you're beginning to sound like you actually care about me."

He watched her wipe the sweat from her face with her sleeve. His expression was grim. "That's not funny."

"Neither was missing dinner," Rachel retorted. She deeply inhaled the scents of freshly baked bread and mesquite-smoked turkey. "And it smells like it was delicious." Turning to the Westcott's cook, Maria, she said, "I have to eat on the run tonight, so would you mind fixing me a couple of sandwiches and a thermos of iced tea?"

"It's no problem, Rachel," Maria said. "I'd be

happy to do it. And I'll put in some fruit and cookies for you, too.'' Maria moved off, her bulky figure bustling into action.

"You still haven't answered my question,'' Travis prodded. "Where have you been?''

Her glance trailed down his tall form. Instead of the usual coat and tie he wore for dinner, he, too, was dressed in jeans. "You're not exactly dressed for dinner, either.''

"I was.''

"And?''

"And what?''

Rachel tore her eyes from the crisp dark hair curling out of the open V of his collar. "And where are *you* going now?''

"I *was* going out to look for you. Which brings me back to my original question,'' he countered. "What's going on? Where've you been?''

Pointedly ignoring his request for further information the way he had ignored her plea for help earlier, she turned to Maria. "Give my apologies to Jaclyn and the children and tell them I'll be back in a few hours.''

"Wait a minute,'' Travis said. He followed her as she picked up the paper bag containing her food and a box of garden tools, then strode out the back door and into the driveway. "Where are you going?''

"Where does it look like?'' Rachel tossed the words dryly over her shoulder. "Back out to the range.''

"To do what?''

Rachel stood on tiptoe and put the tools into the bed of the pickup. "Wouldn't you like to know?'' she shot back almost flirtatiously.

"Believe it or not—'' he stepped in front of her, blocking her way ''—that is why I asked.''

Rachel elbowed him aside and yanked open the door of the driver's side. "Well, forgive me if I don't see any reason I should tell you."

He watched as Rachel tossed her lunch in, then climbed into the pickup and slid behind the wheel.

He slammed the door shut for her and leaned in through the open window. "I'm trying to be helpful," he explained patiently.

"You were anything but helpful this morning." Rachel tried to shove the key into the ignition, frowned when she realized it wasn't the right one and put in another, wiggling it until it fit.

"That was different," Travis countered defensively.

Rachel turned her head and sent him a long cold look. "Why?"

He leaned in closer. His smile was mischievous and provoking. "*That* involved basic decision making. *This* involves tools."

"Chauvinist." She turned the ignition key, floored the accelerator and gunned the engine.

He cut around the front and hopped into the passenger side before she could stop him. "Now that we've established that, how about letting me drive?"

"Forget it!"

"That's what I thought," he sighed. "So where are *we* going?" he asked.

"Back out to pasture fifty-three!"

"What's happening there?"

Rachel adjusted the rearview mirror and tried not to notice how the alluring scent of him filled the cab. "Broken windmill."

"Why don't you have one of the hands look at it?"

"Because they're all out thinning the mesquite by

half in pasture forty-one right now. Besides," she continued confidently, "I figured I could do it myself."

His eyes roved her face, her shoulders, her arms, her hands, before returning with laser accuracy to her eyes. "What do you know about windmills?"

"Nothing," Rachel responded blithely, infuriated that for some strange reason she couldn't seem to take anything but shallow breaths. Maybe it was the lack of food, combined with the heat, doing her in. Certainly, she thought, it had nothing to do with him! Holding the wheel with one hand, she rummaged with her right into the sack. The truck hit a rut and lurched hard to the right. "Now what are you doing?" he asked.

Rachel grimaced and put both hands on the wheel again. "Trying to get a sandwich out for myself. Guess dinner will have to wait."

The truck hit another rut.

Travis swore as his elbow collided with the passenger door. "If you'd let me drive—"

"What? And let it be said I'm leaning on you?" She laughed bitterly and kept her eyes on the road. "No thanks, cowboy."

"Rachel, you don't have to carry it this far," he advised with brotherly exasperation.

"The heck I don't!" She turned the truck into the entrance to pasture fifty-three and jerked it to a halt just short of the motionless windmill. She cut the engine and ticked off her list of grievances. "Every time I turn around, my authority is being questioned. You're letting me know, one way or another, I don't belong here. Rowdy and the men are doing the same thing."

Travis's eyes narrowed. "Rowdy's still giving you a hard time?"

"Careful, you're beginning to sound protective, and

we wouldn't want that, would we?'' She slammed out of the truck, not knowing why she was so upset. Only that every time she was around him she was tense and on edge, expectant almost, as if she was waiting, no wanting, something to happen, the way it had that night in her office when he'd kissed her.

Travis got out quietly. He picked up her food sack, closed the door firmly and strode to her side. "Is Rowdy still giving you a hard time?" he repeated.

Rachel shrugged, sorry she'd said anything. "No more than you. Forget I said anything, okay?"

He handed her the sack. Though she'd been incredibly hungry just moments before, she found her appetite was all but gone now. Nonetheless, she sat down on the front bumper of the truck, pulled out a sandwich and began to eat.

When she'd finished, she joined Travis in inspecting the windmill. "I noticed right away what the trouble was," she said, between gulps of iced tea. "Weeds have grown up and around the wheel. I think once I cut through that garbage and clean it out, it'll start turning again and we'll get some water moving from the irrigation pond into the creek bed."

"How long has it been this way?" Travis asked with a disapproving frown.

Rachel shrugged, feeling pleased that he seemed to agree with her assessment of the situation. "I'm not sure. We haven't had any cattle out here since the first week I was on the ranch." She capped her thermos and headed back to the pickup for the tools, her strides long and purposeful. "But we're fixing to move some out tomorrow morning, so it's got to be fixed before then."

She cast a dubious glance at the falling sun. It slid, a bright red ball, toward the crimson-and-pink horizon.

She tried not to worry. "Hopefully I've got enough daylight," she said when she returned to Travis's side.

It was still hotter than blazes. Sweat dotted her forehead. Figuring her hat would get in the way more than it would help, she took it off. Taking the bandanna from her neck, she tied it around her forehead and caught the ends of her hair in a coated elastic band. Travis began to pace as she surveyed her tools. "Something bothering you?" she asked.

"Like what?" he challenged.

"I don't know. You've got a funny look on your face." *As if you want to help me out and you don't.*

Wordlessly he followed her down to the base of the windmill. Dropping to his haunches, he examined the tangled undergrowth in the thick wooden cog more closely. "Is that supposed to be a compliment?"

"Take it however you want," Rachel said as she hopped down into the empty dirt-and-gravel-lined canal where the water should have been flowing.

"You know..." Travis began thoughtfully as she started to hack away at the undergrowth with a pair of shears.

"What?"

"Never mind." He stalked away. Rachel shot a glance at his retreating back, so broad and masculine, then turned her attention to the task. There wasn't much daylight left, she warned herself sternly. She couldn't afford to dally, never mind concentrate on his sexy loose-boned walk. Besides, if she fixed this windmill by herself, it would improve her standing with the men. After her last blowup with Rowdy, she needed every bit of credibility she could get. Above her, Travis had resumed his pacing to distracting effect.

Suddenly Travis's shadow was looming over her,

blocking out the dwindling sun. "I'm surprised at your expertise," he commented as she dug out a handful of thick reeds and tossed them up on the bank beside her with a gloved hand.

"You're telling me you couldn't easily do the same?" she returned lightly.

"No. As it happens, there isn't a job on this ranch I couldn't, or maybe I should say haven't done." He jumped down into the empty irrigation ditch beside her.

"Wait a minute." She planted a dusty glove in the center of his chest and held him away from the wheel. "I thought I told you I wanted to do this alone."

"So you said," Travis retorted, "but I'm tired of standing around."

Rachel told herself her sudden breathlessness was from the exertion, nothing else.

"If you're worried about anyone finding out," Travis bartered, "we won't tell them I gave you a hand, okay?"

Rachel continued to hold him off, the flat of her hand against his hard flexed muscles. Beneath her palm, she could feel the strong quick beat of his heart. "Why are you being so nice?" she asked.

"Because it's damned hard not to be. I was raised to always help a lady," he explained tersely, sounding irritated with himself.

She arched a brow and sent him a disbelieving look. "Could've fooled me lately," she drawled.

"Yeah, well, your taking over the ranch is different," he growled. His hand swung up to catch her wrist. His grip light but firm, he forced her hand down between them, held it one long breath-stealing moment, then let it go.

Rachel ignored the frantic beating of her heart. "Because the ranch is territory?"

"And then some," he agreed.

"And we all know how males are about their territory," she baited.

"Of any kind."

She shook her head at him. He wasn't talking about anything specific. It was her fault she was thinking about *romantic* territory, and how fiercely Travis would guard a woman he considered his. "So why are you suddenly being so nice?"

He reached behind her for a scythe. "I'm not doing it for you. I'm doing it for the cattle."

"Right," she said wryly.

He crouched down beside her and began hacking at the lowermost tangle of plants. Three strokes and he'd completely cleared one cog of the big wooden wheel. Rachel watched, amazed at his physical expertise. "You've done this before," she guessed.

"As it happens, plenty of times." He stood and pointed to a cog at the top. "Your turn."

Aware her own motions were much less powerful than his, Rachel began cutting through the growth. "I always thought you were more an executive, a manager," she commented, reasoning that idle talk would make their job go faster.

"At my airlines, yeah. Here at the ranch, though, I've always been an able hand." He grunted with the force behind his swings of the scythe. His mouth compressed grimly. "My dad saw to that."

Rachel marveled that his mouth could look so sensual and appealing even when he was frowning. "What do you mean?"

Travis continued to hack away rhythmically while

she snipped and tugged with equal ferocity. "Dad didn't want either of his sons turning into sissified city slickers," Travis confided. "So from the time we were old enough to walk he kept us busy doing all the dirtiest jobs on the ranch. He made us learn the ranch from the bottom up, and even so—" Travis's voice faded "—I had the feeling, in Dad's eyes, that neither of us ever *quite* measured up."

Rachel heard the hurt in Travis's voice. She, too, knew what it was like to have a less than satisfactory relationship with a parent. Angry at Zeke for what he'd put them all through, she tore out another handful of weeds. "Your dad was pretty rough on both you guys, wasn't he?"

Travis nodded. "More so Austin than me, though." He exhaled and continued reflectively, "I'm not sure if it was just because Austin was the oldest, or because he planned from the beginning for Austin to take over the ranch, but Dad was on Austin's back constantly." Travis shook his head.

"But you?"

Travis shrugged his powerful shoulders. "He prodded me, too, incessantly I sometimes felt, but it was never as bad for me, because I was the second son and hence less important in my Dad's eyes. Or...I don't know. Maybe it was just because he spent so much time trying to make Austin grow up right that he didn't have as much time for me."

Rachel tore her eyes from the trim fit of his jeans. "I know how being second feels. It's not a good feeling."

"But you were an only child," Travis protested, turning toward her.

"And second-best to my daddy's gin." She sat back

on her heels, her chest heaving with exertion. Their eyes met in a moment of understanding. ''It's hard when, for whatever reason, you don't quite measure up in your parent's eyes.''

''And harder still when your parent lets you down,'' Travis added with a stern look, letting her know he considered her father's drinking to be her father's problem and not hers.

Rachel went back to the few weeds that were left. Travis tossed his scythe aside. With a tremendous creak and a groan, the huge wheel began to turn. And once it had started to move, there was no holding anything back. Water came rushing out, splashing down, the sheer force of it sending them back against the bank. Knocked off balance, Rachel slipped and would have fallen had Travis's strong arm not anchored around her waist. He pulled her swiftly against him and held her there, the strength in his powerful body an easy match for the force of rushing water.

One hand beneath her hip, he shoved her up and toward the bank. ''Climb on out,'' he said above the noise of the wheel and the water.

She did as directed, water streaming out of her pants and down her legs. He followed shortly thereafter, looking as wet and uncomfortable as she was. ''Are you okay?'' he asked.

Rachel nodded, but her legs had the consistency of putty. Wordlessly he slid his arm about her waist and held her against him. He got her steadied again, but his eyes never left hers. Before she knew what was happening, his mouth was covering hers, bringing with it the salty taste of his skin and the fragrant scent of his cologne, and then the whole world exploded in myriad sensations. She was aware of so many things. The heat of the warm summer night and the greater heat of his body. The descending darkness. The rock solidness of his chest teasing the growing tightness of her breasts. The strength of his thighs, the burgeoning proof of his desire.

Most of all, she was aware of his kiss. It was hot and delicious and steaming with the prospect of so much more. There was something inevitable between them, something she no longer seemed to have the strength or will to fight. She went limp as a rag doll as his tongue entered her mouth and swept the insides with luxurious abandon. She sighed when he brought her tongue into play with his. And she arched against him when he withdrew his tongue, only to coax her lips apart and slide it inside her mouth once again. Over, around, inside, out. She wanted more of him, wanted more of this, she thought dizzily, as her fingertips threaded through the thatch of hair curling against his nape and her mouth clung to his with riveting abandon. She didn't care if it was crazy. It felt too good.

And still he kissed her, long and hard and deep. An ache started in her chest and drifted inexorably lower, to her middle, then lower still, to her thighs. His mastery was riveting, and far too wonderful to try to stop. Giving in to the moment completely, she angled her body up and into his, softness to hardness. The fierceness of his desire against her middle ignited her senses like a match to dry tinder. Gratification and desire combined and swept through her in compelling waves.

She hadn't known it could be like this. Hadn't guessed at her own reaction to him, but now that it was happening, she seemed powerless. She couldn't protest when he hooked his arms around her waist and lowered her slowly to the ground.

His body stretched out beside hers. "Hot damn, Rachel," he whispered almost prayerfully, raining kisses across her face before once again settling on her lips. "You're sweet...so good."

And he was, too, she thought, as his knee parted hers. Nimbly, he unbuttoned her blouse. His head dipped lower. His tongue lashed damp fire across the swell of her breasts. She held her breath in expectation as he unfastened the front clasp of her lacy bra and parted the edges. The warm summer air tickled her skin. He cupped her breast with the base of his hand, lifting the taut nipple, rubbing it tenderly with his thumb. She cried out as his mouth covered the aching crown and arched her back yet again as he increased the sweet pressure with his mouth, wanting completion.

Just when she thought she couldn't stand it any longer, he moved to her other breast and gave it the same loving treatment. "Travis," she whispered urgently, curling her hands into his hair.

"I know, sugar," he whispered as she squirmed impatiently beneath him. Lifting his head, he gazed down at her as if she were the most beautiful woman on earth. He slid over, so he was between her thighs.

Mindless with need, Rachel unsnapped his shirt and yanked the edges apart. His eyes still on hers, he reached for the snap of her jeans. She sucked in her breath as he slid the zipper down and slipped his hand inside. His mouth covered hers as his hand dipped even lower, diving through the soft downy curls to the apex of her thighs. Rachel whimpered helplessly as he found and stroked the most sensitive part of her. Again and again. Until every inch of her was on fire, aching for more.

Both hands on her hips, he slid her jeans lower. She helped him with the unfastening of his jeans. As her hands and eyes found him, she again sucked in her breath. And then there was no more time to think. He was kneeling over her, his hands beneath her hips. Lifting her. Sliding inside.

The impact of their joining was electric. Reveling in it, he went deep and held her tight. She clung to him as they kissed, a thousand conflicting emotions whirling inside her. Desire, despair, shame, hunger and wanton abandon. But most of all, she thought, as he began to move once again, slowly at first, then more and more confidently, she wanted this. Needed this. She needed, heaven help her, him.

"Travis…" Her hands curled into the muscled firmness of his back. "Oh, Travis. I…please…"

"Not yet," he murmured, as he slid a hand between them, stroking, lower and lower. Again, he found her. The last tiny vestiges of her restraint fled. She went tumbling over the edge, mind and body spinning. He joined her, and together they catapulted heedlessly toward oblivion.

Minutes—or was it hours or just seconds?—later, Rachel's breath had slowed. And it was then, only then, that her common sense returned. *Dear Lord, what had she done?*

Hand to his chest, Rachel shoved him off her and jerked from the warm tempting circle of his arms. It didn't matter that he kissed like no one else, that he made her feel as no one else ever had, not even Austin. It didn't matter that what they'd just shared had felt like love. She *knew* it wasn't.

She yanked her jeans up and struggled to her feet, swearing vituperatively all the while. Scalding tears stung her eyes. "I can't believe I just did that," she cried, yanking the edges of her blouse together.

Travis struggled to his feet, too. His shirt open, his jeans up but unzipped, he looked sexy, tousled, dazed at first and then dangerous. "I've heard of regrets," he drawled. "But isn't this a little soon?"

She wasn't in the mood for any of his lazy humor. "Shut up!" She aimed a killer blow at his chest.

He caught her wrist before it connected and yanked her against him, the action not exactly ungentle, but not one that could be resisted, either. "You're beautiful, you know that?" he whispered compellingly, raining soft tempting kisses down her face. "And I want you again."

At his touch, Rachel's insides turned to hot liquid. Her thighs turned to butter. But her resolve not to make the same mistake twice remained strong. "No," she said, stepping back as far as his grip on her would allow. She drew in a harsh panting breath. *"No!"*

Reluctantly he let go of her wrist, studied her silently. If he had any regrets at all, Rachel thought sourly as she observed him, he was hiding them well. "Okay," he acceded finally. "Maybe it was a little fast."

"A little!" she echoed, incensed.

"It still happened," he insisted.

Rachel drove her hands through her hair, pushing it off her face. "Not again, Travis. We can't and won't do this ever again."

"Why the hell not?" He advanced on her. His hands rested on her shoulders, warm and compelling. "It was good for you. I know it was," he persisted softly, his eyes tenderly searching her face. "I felt your climax, Rachel." His voice dropped another seductive notch. "You were like a tight, hot glove, wrapped around me like wet velvet—"

She jerked away from him and put her hands over her ears, hating the vivid memories his words evoked almost as much as she hated herself for melting inside like a giddy teenager whenever she was near him. "Don't," she moaned. *Don't make me want you again!*

"Why not?" Hand in the waist of her jeans, he swung her around to face him. His other hand slid under her chin, forcing her head up. "Does it hurt that much for you to face the truth?" he whispered hoarsely, something suspiciously like hurt glimmering in his eyes. "To admit to me that we might actually want each other, be good for each other?"

She laughed bitterly. He was making this sound simple. And it wasn't. What they had shared was lust, plain and simple, not love. The depth of her shame sent heat into her cheeks as she remembered how wantonly, how irresponsibly, she had just behaved. Never had she done anything so foolish and shortsighted, so guaranteed to bring embarrassment and heartache. Maybe it was de rigueur for him, confirmed bachelor that he was, but it wasn't for her! Furiously she sputtered back, "The only thing our, uh…"

"Lovemaking?" he supplied dryly. His look hardened accusingly. "You can't even say it, can you?"

She took a deep breath, refusing to let him suck her into another pointless argument. Granted, what they had just done was reckless, but it didn't mean they had to continue acting that way. Drawing the lacy halves of cloth together, she reclasped the front of her bra. "Obviously our physical needs took precedent tonight,'' she said, forcing calm into her voice as she rebuttoned her shirt. "But it will never happen again, Travis. Never." She wouldn't let it.

"Why not?" he challenged, watching as she refastened her belt.

Rachel steadfastly avoided his eyes as she stared at the ground where they'd just made love. "Because there's too much at stake."

"Like what?" He towered over her. "The ranch?" he taunted softly, wickedly. "Or your own ambition and greed?"

"All that and my children's future," Rachel acknowledged with a regal nod, denying nothing because she wanted him to think the very worst of her. "I won't risk their inheritance, Travis. Not for any man. And certainly not for another ill-advised roll in the hay with you!"

He stared at her as if seeing her for the very first time. "You're really cold-blooded, aren't you?" he ground out.

"Yes," Rachel lied, "I am." Knowing it was her best defense against his passion, she finished aloofly, "Remember that the next time you're tempted to do—" she inclined her head toward the ground where they had just lain "—that."

She turned on her heel and marched defiantly toward the pickup. As she walked away from him, Travis swore virulently through his teeth. But whatever he said about her—and he said plenty—couldn't begin to top what she was saying about herself. She had never felt lower in her life.

Chapter Eight

"Travis, I want to know what's going on," Jaclyn insisted over the long-distance phone line. "You haven't been home for three days now. Is there some problem with your airlines?"

"Just the usual overload of summer business, resultant equipment failures and rescheduling crises," Travis said dryly.

"Then why aren't you home?" Jaclyn persisted.

Because of Rachel and what happened between us the other night, Travis thought. He was still steamed by the way she had reacted after they'd made love. Like it was the crime of the century or something, instead of something that was...well, inevitable.

"The children, Brett in particular, both miss you," Jaclyn continued.

"They have you and Rachel," Travis argued gruffly.

"True, but it's not the same as having a man around the house, Travis, and Brett is at an age where he needs a male role model in his life."

Travis leaned back in his swivel chair. His secretary stood in the doorway, a sheaf of papers in her hands. Travis waved her in wordlessly and took the papers. He smiled his thanks before she retreated.

"How is everything at the ranch?" Travis asked, aware that he missed being there. He missed being at the heart of things. And he missed seeing Rachel. He'd never been so sexually attracted to a woman in his life. And it wasn't just that. He liked being with her, even when they were fighting. He liked seeing her get all feisty. He liked the fact that she was not only strong enough to do battle with him, but refused to back down, no matter what she felt the odds of her winning. He liked seeing her eyes light up with temper. And even better, he liked seeing them grow all misty and soft with desire....

"I'll tell you how it is around here. It's lonely," Jaclyn finally said.

Well, Travis thought, it wasn't his fault Rachel couldn't handle having a short-term love affair. If he were smart, he'd avoid her entirely. And yet how could he do that and still watch over his family's interests in the ranch?

"Rachel and I both want you home," Jaclyn continued.

Hope flared briefly, like a match in the dark. "She said that?" Travis asked, sitting forward. He rested his elbows on his desk and tried not to think about the heat that filled his lower body at just the thought of Rachel. And how she'd felt against him, so soft and womanly, when they'd made love.

"No, but I know she's thinking it," Jaclyn replied.

Travis closed his eyes and let out a beleaguered breath. Much as he didn't want to, he could recall all too clearly the look in Rachel's eyes the last time he'd seen her. She'd been fiercely angry.

"Travis," his mother demanded impatiently. "Are you paying attention to anything I'm saying?"

Travis sighed. Normally he tried to help his mother, but in this instance she had no idea what she was asking of him. Especially when his brain was telling him he needed to forget about the passion that had flared between him and Rachel and stay on his original course. He'd give Rachel enough rope to hang herself, and she'd prove she was incompetent to run the Bar W.

Unfortunately he was having a hell of a time doing that. The gentler side of him wanted to encourage and help and protect her. The gentler side kept urging him to forget that she was out to steal his rightful inheritance.

"Look, Mom…" he began irritably, wishing he could tell his mother the truth. But he could hardly reveal how tempted he was by Rachel's beauty, her style, her gutsiness and temper and strength.

"Say you'll come to dinner tonight, Travis. Please."

His guilt at disappointing and hurting his mother held him motionless. Whether he wanted to admit it or not, he did have a responsibility to his family and to the ranch. And he couldn't keep running from his desire. The only way to deal with it was to face it, and then not act on it.

"All right," Travis promised reluctantly. "You've talked me into it. I'll be home for dinner tonight."

Two HUNDRED AND FIFTY miles away, Rachel knelt in the searing noonday heat and surveyed the damage in pasture forty-nine. It was one of the best sources of grass and water they had, but almost overnight, it seemed, the pasture was full of holes and long mysterious furrows. "What's causing this?"

"Jackalopes," Rowdy said, surveying the yellowing summer grass. "Definitely jackalopes."

Rachel swore silently to herself. Great, she thought. Something else she didn't know about, and there was no use pretending she did. She straightened slowly and turned to face him, glad that her flat-brimmed hat shielded her face from both the scorching summer sun and him. "What's a jackalope?"

Rowdy kicked the toe of his boot into the opening of one of the shallow furrowlike burrows, approximately six feet in length. "It's kind of a cross between a prairie jackrabbit and a gopher. They burrow down to get away from the heat. When it's as hot as it has been, well, you can see how quickly they do damage." He kicked at the burrow again.

Rachel counted fifty or sixty such holes in the pasture. It was easy to see they were more than just a nuisance. A cow could easily turn an ankle or break a leg. "How do we get rid of them?"

Rowdy scowled. "Can't put out any poison. The cattle might get ahold of it."

"Of course."

"Only solution is traps. But you can't set 'em up in the daytime 'cause the jackalopes are smart enough to see them and run away. You have to do it at night." Frustrated, he strode back and forth, muttering a string of curses. "These are all over the ranch. It's going to take every man available and we'll still be short."

He turned to her. "In the heat, they burrow constantly, searching for water, cool earth. Another week this hot, without rain, and there's no telling the amount of damage they'll do to the ranch." A grim yet challenging look flared in his eyes. "I don't suppose you'd want to help?"

"Of course I'll help," Rachel said, wanting him and the men to know she wasn't above getting her hands dirty. "What kind of traps are we going to use?"

"EXACTLY HOW OFTEN is Rachel not showing up for dinner?" Travis asked his mother. It was nine-thirty. The twins had retired to the game room to watch a movie.

"She's been out on some ranch-related calamity or another all week," his mother confessed, pouring herself a cup of coffee from the silver service on the coffee table. "Frankly, I'm tempted to interfere. On the other hand, I did give her free rein. And now that the men are beginning to accept her as their boss, I fear if I try to step in and tell her to slow down that she might take it the wrong way."

"And assume you're telling her that because you think she's not capable?"

His mother nodded. "Exactly. I know how much she's had to struggle and study. I know how hard she's trying to prove herself. I only want to support her." Jaclyn sighed. "It means not interfering in how she chooses to run the family business, even if she is running herself into the ground to do it."

Travis frowned. He had never wanted Rachel to succeed at running the ranch and he still didn't but he didn't want her ruining her health, either. "What does Rowdy have to say about all this?"

"I don't know. I haven't seen much of him, either. Travis." Alarm colored her low tone as he strode toward the door. "Where are you going?"

"To see what's going on." He had a hunch something was. And whatever it was, it wasn't good for Rachel.

The lights were ablaze in the bunkhouse when Travis stepped outside the ranch house and started across the yard. A glance in the sprawling multivehicle garage showed that all but one of the ranch pickups were there. Which meant one of two things, he thought. Either Rachel wasn't sharing with the men whatever problem she was having and hence the men weren't helping her solve it, or she was up to something else. Something she didn't want any of them to know about. Neither option was palatable.

Fighting his increasing feelings of unease, Travis strode swiftly to the bunkhouse. From the porch he could hear the loud raucous laughter. And the mention of Rachel's name.

"We sure fixed her, didn't we, Rowdy?"

"She'll be out there all night!"

"Stupid woman—Travis!" Rowdy pushed back his chair with a scrape. "What are you doing here?"

"Where's Rachel?" he ground out.

The hands exchanged uneasy looks. Rowdy said, "She's being initiated tonight, Travis. We, uh, well, we sent her out to look for jackalopes."

Imagining Rachel out alone, in the darkness of night, was more than Travis could take. The next thing he knew he'd crashed into the table, grabbed Rowdy by the shirtfront and was an inch from slamming a fist into his jaw. "If she's even the slightest bit hurt," he said between his teeth, "the slightest bit upset by all of this, I'm coming after you personally, you understand me?"

Rowdy's face turned beet red. He nodded.

Travis released him so hard and fast he nearly slammed into the wall. "Get this room cleaned up!" Travis ordered, his voice echoing like a thunderclap in the sudden stillness of the room. "Put the beer and the cards away."

The hands scurried to do as they were told.

Bobby Ray looked upset. "Uh, look, Travis," he said in a shaking voice, "we were just having a little bit of fun, trying to help her be one of us. We really didn't think she'd mind, 'cause she's always seemed like a good sport, at least to me, but if you want, a couple of us can go get her—"

"No." *No one was going after Rachel. No one was going to be alone with her but him.* "She's been humiliated enough. Where is she?"

"Pasture fifty-three," Bobby Ray said.

Travis turned on his heel and stormed out of the bunkhouse, the door slamming behind him. He strode to his pickup and climbed in.

His mouth set grimly, he started the engine. He didn't relish the idea of facing Rachel again after they'd recklessly made love. Never mind telling her she'd been duped.

RACHEL KNELT in the darkness, her only illumination the stars and moon. Even though the sun had gone down more than two hours ago, it was still warm and steamy, with only a hot Texas breeze to cool her. Using the back of her hand to wipe the perspiration from her brow, she finished setting the last of the thick animal nets over the burrow holes dotting the pasture, then moved back slightly, standing beside her open metal animal trap to wait.

Fifteen minutes passed. Twenty. Thirty. A half hour faded into an hour, then two, and still nothing. Only the sound of the cicadas in the trees, and the occasional hoot of an owl. Reminding herself she wasn't the only one waiting for the damned jackalopes, Rachel rubbed at the aching muscles in her shoulders and back and fought off her drowsiness.

The sound of an engine in the distance cut through the night silence and jerked Rachel back into full wakefulness. Swearing, she got to her feet. If she had to do all this again tomorrow night because some driver had made too much noise, she was really going to be ticked off.

To her surprise, it was Travis who got out of the truck. Her breath caught in her throat. Every inch of her tingled. She told herself it was because she hadn't seen him for days, and the last time she had, he'd been soaking wet, holding her against him.... No! She wouldn't think about the way they'd made love! Or the fact that he apparently had no regrets about it, while she had plenty.

His shirt gleaming in the moonlight, he came toward her. She motioned him to silence, holding an index finger to her lips. "Keep your voice down or you're going to ruin everything."

A peculiar, almost apologetic look crossed his handsome features. He drew nearer. Looking suddenly reluctant to face her, he rubbed at the back of his neck and avoided her eyes. "Rachel," he began in a near normal voice. "I've got something important to tell you."

Irritated by the way his deep sexy voice was carrying in the starlit night, Rachel stomped nearer. "Well, whatever it is can't be anywhere near as important as trapping the damned jackalopes in this pasture," she hissed. "You ought to see the damage they've done. There are holes everywhere. Watch out!" She grasped his arm above the elbow and pulled him sideways. "You almost stepped on a trap."

"So I see." He glanced down at his feet, the peculiar look still on his face. Suddenly, to her further consternation, he seemed to be fighting...laughter! "You set up fishing nets all over this field?" he asked in a strangled voice.

"They're super-strength nylon animal nets, and yes, I did," Rachel shot back impatiently. "One over every hole, along with a little bit of raw bacon for bait."

"Why?" Travis asked, his voice sounding even more strangled than it had before.

"Because if I don't catch the little critters who're doing all the burrowing, the cattle are going to fall and go lame," she explained in exasperation, surprised she would have to spell it out for him. Then again, maybe he was testing her again, to see if she really knew what she was doing.

Travis glanced back out at the empty pasture, the moonlight spilling down onto the thick dry summer grass.

She followed his glance. "Can you believe animals did all this damage?" she continued, trying hard not to notice how good he smelled, like soap and after-shave and man. Or think about how everyone else on the ranch would react if they knew she'd had sex with him. Wasn't it bad enough the two of them were fighting constantly? And yet the first time he'd actually been helpful, she'd fallen into his arms and let him make love to her as if there were no tomorrow.

"Rachel," he stated calmly. "About the other night—"

"Don't even think it. I'm not one of your little cowgirls who's just going to fall into your arms again."

"Oh, no?" He quirked a brow.

"The only thing I'm concerned about is the damned jackalopes. I'm determined to get every last one of them, even if I'm here all night!" She frowned as Travis doubled over at the waist, chuckles welling up from deep inside him.

Rachel glanced back at the nets. She was certain she'd put them out correctly, just as Rowdy and Bobby Ray had showed her. "What?" she demanded of Travis. When he didn't respond, she brushed a hand through her hair and commanded bad temperedly, "Stop laughing."

"I can't help it, Rachel..." he said, shaking his head in helpless laughter as he clutched at his abdomen and wiped the tears from his eyes.

Too late, Rachel knew what she should have sensed all along. The sick, embarrassed feeling inside her doubled. She didn't know whether to laugh or cry. She only knew she'd never felt more humiliated in her life. "I've been duped, haven't I?" she said slowly.

Travis nodded. His laughter had stopped, but the smile was still on his face, although to his credit he was trying hard to erase it completely. "I'm afraid so."

Rachel felt the blood rush from her chest, to her neck, to her face. Even her ears were hot! "About which part?" she asked dully, shame and disbelief quickly following the initial flood of embarrassment. "About how you catch a jackalope or—"

Travis put up a hand to cut her off. "There is no such thing as a jackalope."

Rachel glanced back at the rutted pasture. "Then what caused the holes?" she asked, perplexed. "Gophers?"

Again Travis shook his head. "Armadillos," he said,

coming nearer. Now his laughter had stopped. "And they do need to be gotten rid of, not only because of the holes they dig and the risk that presents to any cattle, but also because they carry disease."

Rachel stared out at the pasture, not daring to look at his face for fear she'd see how stupid he really thought her. Tears stung her eyes. She told herself they were caused by sheer fatigue and not any loss of face she might feel. "You don't get rid of them using nets?" she asked.

"No," Travis said, his voice deep and soft and soothing as he moved so close to her she could feel the heat emanating from his tall body. "You put out an application of blood meal. It's an organic fertilizer available at any nursery. The stuff smells awful, but it'll work at running off the armadillos until the next rain. And the cattle won't bother it."

"Do we have any blood meal?"

Travis shrugged. "Probably not, unless Rowdy has already gone to the nursery and picked up some and spread it over the other pastures. It's not the kind of thing we keep around, because of the rancid smell, but it'll be easy enough to get. I suggest you have the men who were the most active in this prank spread it."

Rachel let out a wavering breath, glad Travis hadn't taken the opportunity to humiliate her further, but rather had seemed to try to curtail any embarrassment she felt over her own gullibility. "I'll do that," she said grimly, feeling her voice thicken as tears threatened once again. "Thanks."

Head down, she started to brush by him.

He caught her arm, his warm fingers closing over her flesh. "Rachel, I'm sorry."

So was she. More than he could ever know.

She glanced up at the moon and stars, aware the tears were running down her face now, knowing she was powerless to stop them. "The hands expected me to sit out here all night, didn't they?"

Travis didn't sugarcoat the situation. Nor did he refrain from grinning, just a bit. His hand gentling on her arm, he said softly, "They probably would have come and got you at some point."

Imagining what a joke she was to the hands, Rachel's anger flared anew and she swore, soft and low. "But in the meantime, I'm the laughingstock of the ranch," she said, then followed that with a swear word worthy of the men.

Travis let her go and leaned back against the side of the pickup. "Not the whole ranch," he reassured her, tucking his hands in the back pockets of his slacks. "My mother and the twins have no idea what they did."

"Great. That makes me feel ever so much better." Rachel shoved past him and reached blindly for the door of her pickup. She had yanked it all the way open when the next thought hit. She whirled to face him. "Were you in on this, too?"

"No." Reaching out, he grabbed her wrist, reeled her in to his side and shut the truck door. "I came out to get you as soon as I found out about it."

Rachel yanked free of him. "Thank God for small miracles," she said sarcastically.

Travis straightened until he towered over her. "Why are you mad at *me?*"

"Why not?" she ground out, turning away.

"Wait a minute." His hand shot out to grab her shoulder. "Where are you going?"

Hair flying, she spun around to face him. "Where do you think?" she railed. "The bunkhouse."

"Don't."

"Why the hell not?"

"Because we've already had one scene tonight in the bunkhouse," Travis said roughly, pulling her near again. "We don't need another."

"We've already had one scene in the bunkhouse?" she repeated, aware that when she touched him like this, body to body, her whole being still filled with tingling electrical charges. "What happened?" And why was her breathing suddenly so shallow? Why were her hands trembling? Her lips parting? Why was she wishing he'd just do what they both wanted and kiss her?

Travis's grip on her released. Reluctantly he set her slightly apart from him. His tone was gruff and somewhat apologetic. "I read Rowdy the riot act when I found out what he and the other guys had done."

She glared at him, her indignation flaming as she pictured them all standing around the bunkhouse, laughing at her. The idea of Travis storming in there like some hero rescuing a damsel in distress made it all the worse. "How dare you!"

He stared at her in consternation. "How dare I what?"

She'd been pushed over the edge once too often by all the stupid men on this stupid ranch! "It isn't enough you refuse to help me when I come to you for advice," she said. "But now, you insist on helping me when I don't want your help! And you've already seduced me into making love with you like some crazy hormone-driven teenager! Now you've undermined my authority with the men!"

He caught her arms above the elbow and held them tight. "Calm down!" he ordered, shaking her slightly.

"Don't you tell me to calm down!" Rachel shouted.

"Rachel..." he said gently.

Rachel felt a touch of panic as he continued to look at her in that kind and tender way. When he was so strong and welcoming, she was tempted to be weak and yielding.

Abruptly coming to her senses, she jerked from the warm tempting circle of his arms. It didn't matter that he kissed like no one else. She couldn't be sidetracked into making love with him again. She had her future to think about, and if she didn't find a way to make the hired hands respect her, she would never earn the right to run this ranch permanently. She would never acquire her dream!

"Just leave me alone!" she said. She'd been humiliated enough. Having him witness her downfall only made her feel worse. She regarded him coldly. "I don't need your help, and I certainly don't need your pity."

Chapter Nine

"We missed you at dinner," Travis said.

Rachel glanced up from the stack of papers in her hand. Travis was framed in the doorway of the tiny office at the front of the barn. His eyes were friendly and alert, and he looked more handsome and ruggedly appealing than ever. "I explained to your mother, and Brett and Gretchen why I couldn't be there."

"Yeah, I heard. You had to work." He sauntered into the room. "What's so critical you couldn't spare an hour to have a meal with the family?"

"We're branding the new herd tomorrow."

"So?" Travis shrugged his broad shoulders. "That's nothing the men don't already know how to do. There's no reason for you to be involved."

"I beg to differ," she said lightly, as her stomach fluttered and dropped another notch. "I think it's very important I be there."

"To assert your authority over the men?"

"Yes. Although I might add if someone on this ranch who shall go nameless set a better example, it might not be necessary."

He grinned, appearing to enjoy the obvious warmth creeping into her face. He paused and looked over her shoulder at the papers on the scarred wooden equipment table. "What are you up to?"

Rachel stared at his genuinely curious expression. She sighed heavily, letting him know she was not enjoying the unsolicited attention. "If you must know, I'm reading up on cryo-branding."

He rested one lean hip on the edge of the table. "How come?"

Unable and unwilling to be that physically close to him, she stalked over to a table of ranch gear in the corner. "Because I plan to switch to it in the near future."

Travis stalked her lazily. He braced a shoulder against the wall and slipped his hands into the back pockets of his jeans. "Isn't freeze-branding more expensive?"

"So what if it is?"

"Then why do it?" he continued as if she had answered him as politely as he had asked the question. "Unless you're trying to make this ranch go broke in record time, that is."

"It's more humane." She glared at him. "Don't you have something else to do?"

He grinned again, exerting all his charm this time. "Nope. I'm all yours for the evening, as they say."

"Great," Rachel muttered.

He watched as she tugged off her cowboy boots and pulled on high-topped barn boots. She reached for her leather gloves.

"So what are you going to use for the freeze-branding?" he asked, straightening indolently. "Liquid nitrogen, or dry ice and alcohol?"

"Liquid nitrogen," Rachel said, then paused. "Have you ever done it?"

"Nope." Travis shrugged. "I've read about it, though. Have you?"

"No, but I've seen a demonstration. I was going to go get Rowdy and ask him to assist me—you need two people to do this—but since you're already here," she decided reluctantly, "you may as well help me out."

He touched the brim of his hat, amused by her long-suffering attitude. "I'd be glad to be of service, Miss Rachel," he drawled.

Her color heightened even more. She tossed him a pair of leather gloves and protective eye wear. "Put these on," she ordered in a clipped voice. "And get a pair of barn boots. I'll meet you down at the other end of the barn."

Booted feet planted a foot apart, arms folded tightly at her waist, she was waiting for him when he appeared. "Took you long enough," she said.

"Getting dressed always does. Now, getting undressed, that's another matter entirely. I can do that pretty quick," he confided, drawing inexorably nearer, as if they were about to have a very interesting tête-à-tête. "Must have to do with—"

"Spare me the details of your love life," she interrupted.

He placed a hand flat on his chest. "Why, Rachel, I'm shocked! Who said anything about making love?"

Refusing to let him fluster her, Rachel retorted heatedly, "You're the one who mentioned getting undress— Never mind." Deciding there was no way she could benefit from furthering this conversation, she changed subjects swiftly. "Let's get down to work. Okay?"

Travis grinned as if he knew he had gotten to her. He held his gloved hands wide. "You're the boss."

She sent him a plaintive look, then handed him the leather restraint. "Would you do the honors?"

He slipped into the stall with a calf. Kneeling, he quickly restrained the frightened animal. "I thought this was so *you* could learn the ropes," he said, slipping on his protective eye wear.

"I *am* learning how to brand," Rachel retorted irritably. Still she had no desire to get into the stall and wrestle with a calf.

"I see," he said.

Ignoring his demonstrated disbelief, Rachel slipped on her own eye wear, uncapped an insulated container of liquid nitrogen, poured a small amount into a small plastic-foam cooler, then recapped the first container. "Please. No fooling around once we get started," she said.

"I'm with you there," Travis said quietly, all seriousness now as he used his gloved hand to stroke the calf into trembling submission. "That stuff is dangerous."

Rachel carried the cooler just inside the stall. "This won't hurt a bit," she soothed as she turned on the electric clippers and sheared a three-inch square on the calf's left hip. Using room-temperature alcohol and a grooming brush, she swiftly and thoroughly cleaned the area they intended to brand.

"Now what?" Travis asked, holding the calf perfectly still.

"We wet the area once more with alcohol—it's important the skin be wet when the brand is applied—and then dip the iron into the nitrogen." She moved forward to do so. "Then we apply the brand to the skin." She pressed it firmly, making sure all portions of the Bar W brand were in contact with the hide, then held it for fifty seconds. "Done," Rachel said, removing the brand.

"The skin looks frozen," Travis remarked, studying the brand.

"In a couple hours it'll become swollen and look like frostbite," Rachel said. Rising carefully, she exited the stall, carrying the brand and cooler of liquid nitrogen.

"Then what?" Travis asked, unbuckling the trembling calf from the leather restraint. With the back of his hand, he stroked the side of the calf's face gently, lovingly.

Rachel forced her eyes away from the tender ministrations of his hands and back to his face, trying not to think about how good it had felt to have those same hands sensuously stroking her body. "In about twenty days, the hair around the brand will have completely fallen out. When it comes back in again, it'll come in white, because the nitrogen will have destroyed the pigment cells in the skin," she explained. She held what remained of the liquid nitrogen in the cooler carefully away from her chest.

"And that's it, huh?" Travis shoved back his protective eye wear, so it rested on top of his head.

"Yeah." Rachel nodded. She stepped back in the aisleway, allowing him room to open the door of the stall and slip out, too. "The cow will be branded for life."

Suddenly, as Rachel watched in stunned surprise, the calf bolted. It tried to dart between Travis's legs. Travis simultaneously tripped over the calf and pushed the animal. In a split second, Travis lunged forward, then attempted to regain his balance. His shoulder banged the stall door. And the stall door hit Rachel. The next thing she knew the liquid nitrogen had splashed up and hit the front of her blouse.

Knowing there was no time to spare, Rachel quickly put down the container and with one fierce yanking motion ripped her blouse open. Buttons flew. Travis slammed the stall door shut behind him and leapt forward to help her struggle out of the splattered cloth. "Are you hurt?" he demanded as her ripped shirt fluttered to the barn floor.

"No. I...I don't think so," Rachel said shakily, glancing down. None of the ninety-degree-below-zero liquid had touched her skin.

She shoved her own eye wear up to get a better look at her chest. Her transparent bra would hardly have afforded her much protection.

Beside her, Travis let out a ragged breath. "Thank God," he said.

Suddenly Rachel became aware, as did he, that she was standing there half-naked.

Thinking quickly, he shrugged out of his shirt. Next thing she knew the denim fabric was wrapped around her, enclosing her in the warm male scent of him. As heady as the scent assaulting her nostrils was the gallant way he held the edges of the cloth together, closing off her trembling body from view. "That was close," he said. "Too close."

Rachel's head tipped back. She'd come very near to being scarred for life. She trembled. "I agree."

He looked down at her. "Rachel..." he said, his voice low, hoarse, raw.

The next thing she knew his arms were around her, holding her against him, and they were kissing. Only this time wasn't like the first time or the second. This time there was even less restraint...and more hot searing passion. He was so utterly male, so strong, so insistent. He made her want to open up, to absorb him and take in every nuance.

Her hands moved to his neck, then lower, to the smooth skin and endless muscles of his bare back. She hadn't known she could be so greedy, but she was. She hadn't known anything could feel this good, but it did. She moved against him, up and into him, not caring that with her movements his shirt fell down around her shoulders, not caring that all that stood between them from the waist up was one thin transparent scrap of cloth.

His hand swept to her breast, cupped it. The crown raised against his hot seeking flesh. His hand moved to her other breast, sweetly exploring. And still they kissed, until she no longer knew where her mouth ended and his began. Only that she had waited all of her adult life for someone, something like this, to happen to her.

He groaned as she let her fingertips work down his spine and pressed her into him all the more urgently, until her breasts were flattened against the hard planes of his chest and she ached to know more fully the hot ridge of his desire. The yearning pressure of his mouth increased, so alluring and wonderfully evocative, until all the strength sapped out of her legs and she trembled with the promise of more.

He paused long enough to glance over his shoulder at the emptiness of the barn. One arm slid beneath her knees. He swept her up into his arms, crumpled shirt and all, and carried her the short distance to the tack room. And it was then, as he set her down in front of the scarred table, that she fully realized what was happening.

The heat of her embarrassment flooded her face. She couldn't believe they'd been about to do this again. They were in a barn, for pity's sake. She was the manager of this ranch! She couldn't—especially not in the barn. Sweet heaven, what had she been thinking?

"No, Travis, stop," she gasped, flattening a palm against his chest.

"What do you mean, no?" he rasped, his hands resting on her bare shoulders. "That didn't feel like any no I've ever experienced!"

She pushed away from him and struggled into his shirt. "We can't do this, Travis." She tried to fasten the buttons despite her trembling.

"Why not?"

"Because it's a mistake, that's why," Rachel said. "Just like the last time was a mistake." She tried to make a cool controlled move toward the door.

He was quicker, cooler still, moving just as resolutely to block her way. "I don't play games, Rachel."

"Neither do I."

"Oh?"

"I'm not playing games," she protested. "I just came to my senses." *Thank heaven!*

"But not before you kissed me like that. Like—!"

She shoved the hair from her eyes with both hands. "I made a mistake, okay?"

"No, it's not okay," he said softly. His slate-blue eyes were fierce. "Whether you want to admit it or not, what we did just now was right." His glance skimmed her mouth lovingly before returning to her eyes. "Nothing in this world ever felt so right to me."

Nor to me, Rachel thought. But she also knew that wasn't the point. "So we acted impulsively!" How could she have let herself be so vulnerable with him?

"But how will you feel about this tomorrow, Travis, in the cold light of day?" Tears sparkled in her eyes. "What will people say when they find out you've taken up with your late brother's wife?"

His jaw clenched. "They won't find out."

Recognition dawned, making her feel even more bitter and self-righteous. "Oh, I get it now. You want me to be your secret and oh-so-convenient, live-in, close-mouthed mistress."

"You don't have to be so crude!" he said without an ounce of his previous tenderness.

"Why not?" Rachel shot back. "It's the truth. You want me to be with you and keep my mouth shut."

His eyes pierced hers. Rachel gulped, knowing she'd gone too far. Too late, he was already focusing on her mouth and yanking her against him. Though Rachel struggled against it, she could feel the fierceness of his desire against her middle.

"Not necessarily," he replied in a soft sarcastic voice. "I can think of plenty of things—" he touched his lips to hers lightly "—to do with that beautiful mouth of yours, besides shut it."

"*You're* crude!"

"And you're a liar if you're trying to tell me you don't enjoy my lovemaking," he whispered. "Or that you don't want me again tonight!"

Fighting the charges of electricity that arrowed through her, Rachel twisted out of his grasp. "I won't be your secret mistress."

Travis leaned against the door frame and folded his arms across his chest. "To call you my mistress would be to believe you're less than my equal, Rachel," he said gently. "And you're not."

Their eyes met. Rachel's throat ached.

"And I want you to be my lover, my equal-in-every-way lover," he said. He moved to take her tenderly in his arms once again. "I want that very much."

Rachel rested her head against his chest, hating to admit how close she was to giving in. There were times when she detested him, but there were also times, like now, when she knew she'd never felt more drawn to any man. "Mistress. Lover," she said bitterly, as his hand gently stroked her back. "It all boils down to the same thing." *I may be falling in love with you. And you, Travis, want me.*

"Not in my mind, it doesn't," Travis whispered. "A mistress is a kept woman. A lover is someone who pulls her own weight, and that, Rachel," he said softly, "you do very nicely."

Although that was the closest Travis had ever come to giving her a compliment about the way she ran the ranch, she refused to let his soft seductive soothing words sway her. Pushing away from him, she gathered up her ruined shirt.

He caught her around the waist. They were aligned firmly hip to hip, torso to torso. His body was hard and unyielding, but his voice was soft and soothing. "I understand you're scared," he said sympathetically. "I didn't expect the passion, either. But we can work it out."

"Come to an agreement," she paraphrased dryly, sensing another deal in the making. What would he offer her to be his lover? she wondered. A permanent home on the ranch as long as they were together? Or just a room in town?

"Exactly," Travis agreed practically. "We can find some way to be with each other that's comfortable for both of us."

The only thing that would make Rachel comfortable was marriage. And that, he wasn't offering. She stared at him, wishing they'd met some other time, some other way, and that she had never had her reputation compromised by her hasty ill-thought-out marriage to his brother. "Assuming we could deal with a scandal should one—"

"We could."

"And my kids and your mother?"

"We could manage them, too."

"And find a way to be together—"

"Yes."

"Just how 'comfortable' will any of this be if I earn the right to run this ranch from now on?"

His face whitened. He said nothing. But then he didn't have to. She could see how he felt. "You'd never forgive me, would you?"

Still, he said nothing.

"Don't you see, Travis?" Inside, she felt as if her heart was breaking. "The ranch will always be between us, and even if it wasn't, there's always the ghost of Austin."

He was quiet. "Why are you so quick to write us off?"

"Because there is no 'us,' Travis," she said. "Only a temporary lapse in judgment."

Travis's mouth thinned. "As you see it..."

"I'm determined not to repeat it."

His jaw clenched with the effort it took to rein in his temper. "Right. I forgot," he said with deliberate cruelty. "A romance with me might get in the way of your ultimate goals."

"Travis..." she began, feeling weary to her soul.

But it was too late—he was already stalking out of the barn. And this time, he didn't look back.

RACHEL SNEAKED into the kitchen the back way. Jaclyn gasped, her gaze moving from Rachel's oversized shirt to the ruined one in her hand. "Goodness, darling, what happened?"

Rachel stopped dead in her tracks, an embarrassed flush heating her cheeks. "I spilled some liquid nitrogen on my shirt. So Travis lent me his."

Jaclyn paled. "Were you hurt?"

"No, thank goodness," Rachel replied with genuine relief. "But I know I should have been more careful. I will be in the future." And would have been tonight had she not been concentrating so much on Travis and his sexy handsome presence, instead of what she was doing, Rachel scolded herself silently.

"Was Travis helping you?"

"Yes." Rachel prayed she didn't look as if she had just been thoroughly kissed. So thoroughly she was still feeling the tingles. She forced herself to turn around and meet Jaclyn's concerned gaze. "He wanted to see how cryo-branding was done."

"Oh. That sounds interesting," Jaclyn said. "Do you think it will work out?"

"Oh, yes." Rachel smiled, then realized Jaclyn was watching her. "Something on your mind?"

"I just wondered if you and Travis had another quarrel."

"Not exactly," Rachel hedged. "Why?"

"He seemed rather upset."

So am I, Rachel thought. She and Travis couldn't continue like this. Yet it was impossible to be so close to him and not desire him. "Where is he?" she asked casually, turning her thoughts away from the passionate kisses they had shared. Had they been anywhere else but the barn...no, she wouldn't think about what might have happened.

"That's just it. I don't know." Jaclyn frowned. "He stormed in like a heathen, went upstairs, grabbed a clean shirt, came back down and announced he was going out for the evening."

Rachel swore silently. It was clear she was going to have to find some way to talk to him and smooth things over. "Oh. Well, he deserves an evening out."

"And you deserve a hot meal, as hard as you've been working," Jaclyn said with maternal concern. "Sit down and let me fix you a plate."

Rachel forced another smile as her inner turmoil grew. "I really should change..." She gestured at Travis's denim shirt, still warm and scented with the fragrance of his cologne and the heady masculine smell of his skin.

"Nonsense. You look fine. Beside, there's something I wanted to ask you about Brett and Gretchen." Jaclyn put a plate of steaming food in front of Rachel. "You know Maria is taking a week off to visit her daughter in California, starting Monday."

Rachel glanced up from her chicken-fried steak and mashed potatoes. "She mentioned it to me this morning, yes."

"I usually take time away from the ranch during Maria's vacation, too. But this year, instead of going to Galveston to visit friends, I'd like to take the twins to Florida to visit Disney World, Busch Gardens, maybe even the Keys. What do you think?"

"I think that would be wonderful," she said slowly, meaning it. If only she could have a change of pace, too. But as Travis had reminded her so many times, she had a ranch to run.

Chapter Ten

"Bye!"

"Have a wonderful time!" Rachel and Travis shouted as they waved. They stood shoulder to shoulder in front of the Bar W airstrip, watching the chartered Texas West Airlines jet taxi and take off.

As soon as the jet disappeared from view, Travis spun on his heel and swaggered back to the Cadillac they'd driven out to the airstrip. He jerked open the door in a way that let Rachel know he hadn't completely forgiven her for calling a halt that night in the barn. Not yet. Nor was she sure she wanted him to. Maybe it was safer for both of them if he stayed angry with her.

Travis started the Cadillac with a vengeance and backed out of the shade next to the hangar. "You don't have to look so thrilled," he finally grumbled. "Besides—" he jabbed a thumb at the center of his chest, while continuing to steer the smooth-riding luxury car with the other hand "—I'm the one who should be upset."

Rachel turned to face him, thinking that, as angry as she was with him, she still liked the way he looked in jeans. Like a real cowboy. "You?" she demanded. "Why?"

His lower jaw jutted forward. He slanted her an aggrieved glance, then finished in a low grim thoroughly exasperated tone, "Because I know what my mother is up to, even if you don't."

Rachel shot him a confused look.

"My mother saw me come in without my shirt a couple of nights ago."

"So? She saw me come in wearing it!" And probably, Rachel thought morosely, knowing Jaclyn's keen eye and superb people-sense, she had also realized that Travis had steadfastly avoided being alone with Rachel ever since.

"Which probably also means she figured out for herself what happened," Travis said.

Rachel didn't like being reminded of the way she'd responded to his kiss or how close they had come to making love again. If they'd been anywhere but the barn, if the ranch hadn't been standing between them... But it was, she reminded herself firmly, then and now! And so was Travis's continued resentment of her. "How do you know that?"

"I just do."

Hating his confidence in the face of such an indelicate situation, Rachel stared at him through narrowed eyes. "You didn't tell her that you kissed me, did you?"

Travis guided the car around the circular drive and halted it in front of the house. He cut the engine and turned to her. "What we shared was a heck of a lot more than a simple kiss." Merriment tugged at the corners of his mouth and his teeth flashed white. "At least the way I recall it."

Unfortunately, that was the way Rachel recalled it, too. She quelled the urge to fidget in the plush leather seat and decided to have this out with him, in the car, in broad daylight, in front of the ranch house rather than inside it. "Go on," she instructed flatly.

"So I'm not playing her game." Travis shrugged.

"Which is?"

He gave her a droll look. "You really haven't figured this out?"

"What?" Rachel's pulse quickened.

Travis studied her intimately. "Okay. She knows you're unhappy here."

"I am *not* unhappy!" Rachel protested. "I love running the ranch."

"Unhappy with me," he specified, his exasperated voice overriding hers. "And that you're lonely and isolated."

Rachel couldn't deny she missed the company of other adults. Since the jackalope fiasco, the ranch hands had been increasingly nicer to her and more respectful, maybe because she hadn't punished anyone, but they still weren't exactly her friends. Yet. "And?"

Travis rubbed at his thigh with the flat of his palm. "And she wants me to make you feel better."

Rachel tossed her head. "The only way you could possibly do that is if you went back to Fort Worth."

Travis slammed out of the car, circled around the front and opened the passenger door. "First of all, there's no way that'll happen as long as you're here," he drawled.

Rachel propelled herself into the hot sun. "How nice to know you trust me," she shot back sweetly, heading for the shade of the front porch.

"Second, she has no intention of my leaving."

Travis ate up the distance between them. "In fact," he continued, thrusting his key into the lock on the front door, "my leaving you is the farthest thing from her mind."

Rachel rolled her eyes, exasperated. "I still haven't the foggiest idea what you're talking about." He swung open the door and she went inside.

"She's matchmaking!"

Rachel whirled to face him. She planted her hands on her hips. "Now I know you're crazy!"

Travis studied her grimly. "We both only wish. The truth is she loves you like a daughter and she's crazy about the kids."

Heat and panic combined sent strange vibrations through her entire body. She inhaled a short gasping breath. "I was married to your brother!"

"And my brother is dead," Travis replied gruffly. "In a few years, the twins'll be off to college. You'll be alone. And she figures you'll probably marry again. If it's to someone outside the family, Mom knows chances are she'll lose you again. She doesn't want that to happen."

"I still don't see where you come into all this," Rachel said, telling herself sternly that what he was intimating couldn't be true.

"Don't you?" Travis gave her a steady look that robbed every drop of moisture from her mouth.

Deciding too much had been said, she tried to exit the front hall. He put his hand over hers, preventing her escape.

Knowing from experience that this conversation was not going to be over until he'd said all he had to say, Rachel stilled.

"She wants me to step in and personally fill that

husbandly void in your life. Fortunately for both of us—'' Travis released his hold on her abruptly ''—I'm just not interested in marriage. Period. Nor do I have any intention of putting myself in Austin's shadow. I spent far too much time doing that as a kid.''

He strode in the direction of his office. Rachel stared after him, then decided as far as she was concerned, their conversation wasn't finished. When she caught up with him, he was seated in front of his computer.

''I don't understand. Did you do that out of hero worship? Out of choice?'' Rachel tried to soften her voice, wanting to understand just what it was that had driven Travis to live in Austin's shadow.

Travis typed in a command on the keyboard and didn't look at her. ''More like obligation. And parental expectation.'' He hit the Enter key with more than necessary force, then swiveled to face her. ''For as long as I can recall, I was expected to do the same extra-curricular activities, take the same kind of lessons, enroll in the same business, economic and agricultural classes at the same university. After Austin's death, I even picked up the slack by helping run the ranch.'' He pushed away from the chair and began to pace the tiny room. ''But I am not,'' he warned as he clamped both powerful forearms over his chest, ''repeat, *am not,* going to do this, too.''

''How reassuring,'' she said dryly, determined to cover her hurt, ''to know my virtue is safe with you.''

''Now that, I didn't say.''

For a moment her lungs stopped functioning.

''Your heart is safe with me, as is your single-woman status,'' he corrected. ''About the rest—'' he grinned at her with bad-boy panache ''—we'll have to see.''

"Get this through your head, Travis. I'm not going to become your lover."

"Time will tell, won't it?" he assured her confidently. "Should I expect you for dinner?"

Rachel glowered and gave him a brief parody of a smile. "Not on your life, cowboy."

BECAUSE SHE KNEW he normally liked to eat at seven, Rachel barricaded herself in her office, then went out to supervise the work of the hands. She waited until nine to journey to the kitchen.

To her dismay, Travis was still there, slouched low in his chair, his booted feet propped up on the seat of another chair, a long-necked bottle of beer in his hand. The aroma of simmering spices and beef filled the air.

He tipped his hat at her, drawling, "Don't you look surprised."

"I thought you'd be done by now," Rachel responded tartly.

"Would've been, if I hadn't had to cook," Travis said, taking another sip of beer. He looked at her and grinned, enjoying every ounce of her discomfiture. She ignored the pot simmering on the stove and looked inside the refrigerator.

"Actually," Travis continued lazily, watching as she took a frozen microwave dinner from the freezer compartment, "I was hoping you'd cook for me."

Rachel set the frozen dinner down with a thud. "Dream on."

He watched her pull the makings of a salad from the well-stocked fridge. "I tell you what. I'll make you a deal."

"Oh, yeah?" Rachel had to climb over his legs to get to the sink.

"I'll share my chili, if you share your salad."

Rachel wasn't of a mind to cooperate with him. Unfortunately she was starving, and his chili was much more tempting than the frozen entrée she'd just gotten out of the freezer. "Is it edible?"

"Cross my heart." He gave her his best choirboy look. "Come on, Rachel. I'm trying to declare a cease-fire. After all, we're going to be alone here all week."

He had a point, Rachel admitted grudgingly. She hated arguing. This was a chance for them to become friends and for her to persuade him she not only could but should run the ranch. "I suppose it would be okay," she relented. "This once."

Having gotten his way, he sent her a tantalizing grin and his feet hit the floor with an energetic thud. He went to the pantry and began rummaging around, finally emerging with a yellow package of cornmeal, which he tossed from palm to palm. "You know how to make corn bread?"

"Yes." She drew out the word carefully, not about to start waiting on him hand and foot, truce or no.

His dark brows lifted hopefully. "The old-fashioned, cooked-in-a-cast-iron-skillet kind? You know, that you make on top of the stove?"

"Yes."

He took off his hat and set it aside, then approached her in all seriousness. "Will you show me how? After you finish the salad, of course."

The thought of corn bread spread with butter was too good to pass up. Rachel left the greens on the sideboard. "The corn bread will take a while," she warned. "We better start it first."

Together they got out the ingredients.

"You sure are good at this," Travis remarked, as he

watched her mix the ingredients. "How come you never married again?"

Rachel put some butter into the microwave to melt. "Who says I didn't?" she asked contrarily.

"Did you?" When the microwave dinged, Travis reached in to get the dish.

"No." Rachel added the melted butter to the dry ingredients in the bowl.

"Why not?"

"Because of the twins. I would never marry someone unless he loved them as much as I do."

"Surely there are men out there who'd love the twins?"

Yes, but they don't love me. Not the way I want and need to be loved. "What about you?" Rachel asked as she broke an egg. "You've never married."

"Says who?"

She turned with a start, irritated to find how jealous she felt at just the thought of Travis's marrying someone else. "Have you?"

He grinned at her and reached over to add the buttermilk to the bowl. "No."

"Why not?" She told herself the acceleration of her heartbeat and the dampness of her palms was just due to the challenge of matching wits with him.

Travis took the bowl from her and began to stir the batter. "It's not easy finding a woman to love you for you alone, when she sees all this. And then," he sighed, "there's my airlines, too."

Rachel buttered the bottom of a cast-iron skillet. "You're more than the sum total of your financial assets."

"That's what I keep telling the ladies." Travis smiled. "How did we get onto this subject, anyway?"

"You were nosing around in my private life, as usual." Rachel poured the batter into the skillet and then placed it on the burner.

"And you weren't nosing around in mine?"

She handed him a carrot to peel. "Can we drop this?"

"Sure. What do you want to talk about?"

What's safe? She couldn't think about his looks or the way he kissed or the desire that kept surging within her every time she was close to him. If she didn't know better, she'd think… No. She was not foolish enough to actually let herself fall in love with a confirmed bachelor. It was just desire she was feeling. The forbidden element of their infatuation.

"Oh, well, at least my mother got what she wanted."

Afraid he could read the direction of her not-so-innocent thoughts, Rachel flushed guiltily.

"The two of us alone," Travis continued affably. "She probably figures in a week we'll either kill each other, start a romance or declare a permanent truce."

She wouldn't even consider a romance with him. As for the truce, he didn't know how good it sounded to her. And yet, a truce would deprive her of the prickliness that had served as her emotional armor. A truce might open the way to…their previous recklessness.

"Or don't you want a permanent cease-fire?"

She shrugged and kept her face inscrutable. "Maybe."

He gave her one of his Texas bad-boy grins. "Like to tangle with me, don't you?" he prodded in a low sexy tone.

Rachel ignored the chill that chased down her spine. "It breaks up the monotony."

He touched a hand to the side of her face. "The monotony or the loneliness?" he asked softly.

He was too close for comfort. "Maybe a little of both," Rachel allowed.

His hand slid around to the nape of her neck. He drew nearer still.

Her heart pounding, Rachel stepped back.

"Aw, come on, Rachel. Don't run from me." His other hand came up to rub her back tenderly. "Don't run from this."

"Travis, I…" She tried to move away from the hand on her spine, but she succeeded only in bringing her breasts into contact with the hard muscles of his chest. It was all she could do to suppress the moan welling up in her throat.

His eyes darkened. Fire raged through her. He brought her up on tiptoe, and then his mouth touched hers. He gave her a kiss that was so gentle, so reverent, so coaxing, it left her weak. Her breath whispered out unevenly. They kissed again, this time with much more courage, her lips yielding to the hard demanding pressure of his.

He released her but didn't step back. "I won't push you. I won't lie to you, either." His eyes probed hers, searching for understanding. "I want to make love to you," he whispered. "I want it so bad I lie awake nights imagining how your body would tremble beneath my hands. And I want you to make love to me." He tangled his fingers in her hair and leaned forward to give her one last, soft, kiss. She was trembling when he drew back. And she trembled even more as he said, "And that, Rachel, is not going to change. No matter how much you ignore it, no matter how much you ignore me, the passion between us is not going to go away.''

RACHEL PUNCHED her pillow for the hundredth time and tried to get comfortable in the four-poster bed, but it was no use. She couldn't stop thinking of Travis, in his own bed, just down the hall.

Damn him, anyway. Every time she started to think they might be friends, Travis went and pulled something like that. Why did he have to be so relentless about going after what he wanted?

His relentless desire intrigued her and scared her. She wanted him to court her. She wanted to please him. She wanted them to be friends. Maybe more than friends. And at the same time, she knew he was only interested in an affair at best.

Besides, he was her ex-brother-in-law, for pity's sake. The only problem was she couldn't think of him that way any longer. She knew, as sad as it was, after the way he'd kissed her tonight, so sweetly, lingeringly and persuasively, that she never would again.

''THIS IS UNDOUBTEDLY going to be the longest week of my life,'' Rachel muttered the next morning as she began to fix herself some toast for breakfast. It didn't help, of course, that it had seemed to take forever for her to fall asleep and when she finally did she'd dreamed of Travis, of the heat of his kisses and the fervency of his desire. She awoke near dawn, drenched in sweat and aching in places she would much have preferred not to ache.

''Do you always talk to yourself when you're alone? And why is it going to be the longest week of your life?'' Travis asked as he strolled into the kitchen.

"No, I don't always talk to myself although maybe I should," Rachel said gruffly, catching a whiff of his freshly showered body as he brushed past her to get to the coffee.

He looked askance at her empty plate. "No eggs?" He looked disappointed.

"There are plenty," she bit out. "In the refrigerator."

"That's a thought. A Rocky-style breakfast, downed raw. Shall I get you a couple and break them into a glass?"

Rachel thought she would be ill if she had to look at a couple of raw eggs sitting in a glass, never mind watching anyone actually drink them. Worse, she felt Travis might just do that if he thought it would get a rise out of her. She gave him her back. "Suit yourself."

"You sure are prickly in the morning," he observed.

She glowered at him over her shoulder, irritated she couldn't get a moment's peace. "Maybe it's the company."

He grinned unrepentantly. "Maybe." Still grinning, he removed a carton of orange juice from the refrigerator. "You know, you don't look as if you slept too well."

"Yeah, well, you look like you slept incredibly well," she grumbled.

"Yep, as a matter of fact, I did. Want to know what I dreamed about?"

"No!"

His eyes gleamed with mischief. "I could tell you—"

"I'm sure you have better things to do," she interrupted.

"Not really. The summer airfare wars are winding down, and we already have our travel rates set for fall. Plus, travel is up in general in late August and September, mostly because of all the kids going back to college, so..."

"I'm glad you're doing so well," she said.

He leaned against the counter and sipped his juice. "What about you? How are things going?"

That, Rachel would rather not talk about. "Things are about as I expected them to be."

"Given up on raising organic beef yet?"

"No."

"Find a buyer for the herd you already have?"

I'm working on it, Rachel thought. "I will," she assured him.

He grinned.

If she didn't know better, Rachel thought, she'd think Travis was actually beginning to root for her, despite his own interests in the matter. But that couldn't be happening, could it? Not when he was so determined to hold on to the ranch.

Her toast popped up. Eager to be out of his way, she grabbed the two pieces and flipped them onto her plate, burning her fingers slightly in the process.

Before she could react, he grabbed her fingers and blew on them. "You know, some say butter is the best thing for a burn, smoothed on nice and slick, but it's actually the worst thing to use. What you need is ice-cold water." He dragged her hand over to the tap and pushed it beneath the running faucet. "See how that cools the skin?"

And how his touch heated it just as quickly, she thought.

She jerked her hand away from his and attempted to

look as calm and collected and faintly mocking as he did. "Thanks for the first-aid lesson," she said dryly.

"We aim to please." His eyes held hers for a long moment before he looked at her plate and frowned. "Is that really all you're having?"

"And coffee."

"I thought you'd know how to cook, having kids and all."

Rachel carried her plate to the table and sat down. "I do know how to cook," she reminded him in exasperation. Realizing she'd forgotten the jam, she got up and headed for the cupboards over the counter, making sure to give him wide berth. "I made the salad and taught you how to make corn bread last night, remember?"

"Oh, yeah," Travis drawled, as he watched her search the shelves. "Guess that slipped my mind in light of all the *other* important things that went on."

Refusing to dignify his innuendo with either a reply or a blush, Rachel carried the jam, when she found it, back to the table. Unfortunately the jar was brand-new and wouldn't open, no matter how she tried.

"You're not doing so well opening that jam, either."

"That's because it won't open," Rachel said between gritted teeth.

He swaggered closer. "You forgot to take off the plastic safety seal around the lid. Gotta do that first, Rachel. Then you can open it."

"I know that," she said irritably, picking at the seal with her third finger.

"Getting a headache?"

"No!"

Suddenly, he was massaging her shoulders and neck. "Sure you're feeling all right?"

"Yes. Wonderful. Or at least I was before you showed up and *invaded my space.*"

He laughed. Using the pressure he exerted on her shoulders, he whirled her around to face him. "Lady, I haven't even begun to invade your space." He leaned down until their eyes were level. "And trust me, you'll *know* when I have."

She knew he wanted her to fight with him. He wanted her to haul off and hit him. He wanted her emotions to be out of control, so he'd have an excuse to drag her into his arms and kiss her thoroughly. Well, she wasn't going to play his game. Fighting for calm Rachel closed her eyes and took a deep breath. "Travis, I have not yet had my coffee and—"

"Oh. One of those." He clucked sympathetically. "Just stay right where you are. I'll get you a cup. How do you like it? Cream only, right?"

Rachel buried her face in her hands. This week was going to seem like a year! "Right," she said weakly.

He set it in front of her. It was just the way she liked it, with double cream.

Travis poured himself a cup and strolled over to open the kitchen blinds. Sunlight streamed into the room. "You know, I always felt sorry for people who couldn't wake up until they'd had their coffee. Seems like a waste of a good half hour or so, you know?"

Rachel sipped her coffee and closed her eyes, still groggy from lack of sleep. "I have a feeling you'd wake anyone up."

"Right about that. When I set my mind to it, that is." His voice dropped a seductive notch. Although she hadn't yet opened her eyes, she could feel him studying her. "Are you sure you're feeling all right?"

No, she wasn't feeling all right, she thought. He'd

turned her life upside down. And she had the feeling that his campaign to get her into his bed had just begun.

"I'm fine," she said. "I just...I miss the twins." And that was the truth! She hadn't been spending nearly enough time with them. But that would change, too, just as soon as she secured their inheritance for them.

"I know," Travis sympathized gently. "I miss them, too. But I'm sure they're having a wonderful time."

Rachel finished her coffee, got up and placed her cup in the sink. "I know." If only her life were as serene and well-ordered as her children's seemed to be at this moment.

Travis, mistaking her glum look, joined her at the sink and started to console her by taking her in his arms. Rachel jumped back.

"Now what?"

Rachel ran her hands through her hair, wishing she'd had the foresight to tie the freshly shampooed strands back in some tight unappealing fashion, rather than leaving her hair down around her shoulders. "Look, Travis, despite the window of opportunity you undoubtedly see here, I am not going to allow myself to be seduced again," she began heatedly. "I'm not a foolish kid anymore. I don't confuse physical desire with the reality of making my everyday life work. I am not going to fall into the same trap twice."

"Meaning what?"

"Meaning I am not going to have an affair with you just to make my life easier!"

He stomped nearer, blazing with anger. "You think that's all this is? Convenience? You think that's what I want? Just the first piece of, er, available woman?"

Rachel lifted her chin and glared at him stormily. "I

don't think you've gotten much past easing the ache in your groin!''

He flinched.

As his eyes darkened with hurt, she was filled with guilt. "I'm sorry," she apologized. She held up both hands in a gesture of surrender. "I'm insulting you and I don't mean to. You're a very handsome and sexy and appealing man, okay? But I am not, I repeat, *not,* in the market for an affair!"

He sent her a hot amused look. "You don't kiss like you're not in the market for an affair."

"I fail to see how—"

"You kiss like you're a woman who needs to be loved well and often, by a man who knows what he's doing."

Her heart pounding, Rachel stood her ground. "And I suppose that's you."

He inclined his head and lowered his mouth to hers, so their lips were but a millimeter away. "I think I'm in the running."

Rachel jerked her head back and stepped away. "And I think you have an ego the size of a Mack truck!"

He shrugged. "At least I'm honest."

"I'm trying to be honest with you!" she said.

He stepped back and clamped his arms across his powerful chest. "No," he corrected. "You're trying to ignore what's happening between us. And you're furious because *I* won't let you."

Rachel pretended little interest. "All right. You're right about this much. I do find you desirable, Travis. But I'm not going to act on that desire. Your family means too much to me. Jaclyn has become the loving mother I never had. I care about her."

"So what does that have to do with us and the fireworks we feel when we kiss? Why do we have to drag the kids or my mother or even the ownership of the ranch into that?"

She took a deep breath, wanting more than anything to fashion some sort of workable truce with him. "Because passion fades. We both know that."

His brow lifted in obvious disagreement. "The hell we do!"

Rachel set her chin stubbornly. "I won't risk the happiness I've found here at the ranch for a love affair with you."

His face changed. He looked away for a long moment, then back at her. Too late, she saw she'd hurt him—badly.

"Fine. Have it your way. Be alone the rest of your life for all I care."

Chapter Eleven

That afternoon, Travis sat in his Fort Worth office. His secretary had left hours ago, but he was reluctant to follow suit. The condo he'd called home for the past seven years no longer had much appeal for him. And he couldn't go back to the ranch. Rachel was there. Rachel...

She'd become such a large part of his life. Such an important part. He'd told himself initially that he was just protecting his own interests by keeping such close tabs on her. But somehow, as the summer had progressed, all that had changed. He'd started to enjoy her company and feel he could confide in her. Their familial connection aside, he had started to *like* her and want her as a friend. And that disturbed him greatly.

He still wasn't sure he should trust her. And yet, he knew deep down that he did. She would never deliberately hurt his family or the ranch, though she might do so without meaning to. And as for her being cut out to run the ranch, a person only had to be with her for five minutes to know that she was so enamored of the Bar W, and indeed every nitty-gritty detail of ranching, that she could run it. A strong independent businesswoman, she was feisty, hardheaded and possessed too much gumption for her own good. Of course, some of her experiments, like organically raised cattle, were bound to fail. But others like freeze-branding might succeed.

He couldn't fault her work habits. She was up early and went to bed late almost every day. She loved his mother and was an excellent mother to her own children. She seemed to revel in the extended family— having three generations under one roof. She belonged there. Sometimes, to his immense irritation, more than he did himself.

Heat radiated through him as he recalled how Rachel's lips had felt under his—sweet, giving and inventive. And he knew he'd had just a taste of her ability to surrender. But he might never be given the chance to make love to her again, or to find out more about her most private thoughts and feelings.

What would have happened had he and Rachel not been in the barn the night she'd spilled the liquid nitrogen on her shirt? What if they'd been somewhere else, somewhere private, with a bed? Would she have let him make love to her, as he'd sensed she yearned to do? Would she have said to hell with everything else and given in to her feelings, or would she have continued to hold him at arm's length? And why did the thought of either possibility leave him in such a vaguely disgruntled mood? Hadn't he already made a decision to cut her out of his life, at least the romantic part?

Even now, when he was upset with her for putting on the brakes, he still wanted her in bed with him, where she belonged, her body warm and pliant and giving beneath his, her fiery red hair spread out like silk on his pillow. He still wanted to sleep with her wrapped in his arms all night. He wanted, he admitted with gut-wrenching honesty, what he could never have, what he had no right to want—his late brother's wife.

Was he falling into the same trap he had in his youth? Was he unconsciously, dutifully, molding his life into the shape of his brother's? Travis knew it might seem that way to outsiders. But after much reflection, he knew it wasn't true. He knew it was time to put all that aside, to stop worrying about what Austin had done or not and start working on his own future.

And like it or not, he had changed since Rachel had entered his life. His business was no longer enough to keep him happy. He needed more. And he thought now he would get it.

"It can't be that bad. *Can* it?"

The sound of the low sexy voice brought Rachel's head up. The joy she felt at seeing Travis again after his absence was muted by the despair she felt over her work. One thing was certain, though. Rachel couldn't deal with another seduction attempt. She lowered her head to the cluttered surface of her desk again and moaned, "Go away, Travis."

"Hey there," he chided good-naturedly, not bothering to disguise the sensuality that smoldered beneath his gaze. "Is that any way to greet a person you haven't seen in five days?"

"It's the only way I'm going to," Rachel said stubbornly. Her bad temper, she knew, was her only defense against him. "Now go away."

"Sorry. No can do." He crossed to her desk and scooping up a handful of papers, he cleared a space and sat on it. "You don't look too good, you know that?"

"Thanks for telling me." Inhaling his scent was like receiving an injection of adrenaline.

"Matter of fact, you haven't been getting a whole lot of sleep lately."

And he looked disgustingly rested, Rachel thought.

The truth was, she *hadn't* been getting a whole lot of sleep. For a variety of reasons. She kept thinking about Travis and what they could have if only so many things didn't stand between them. Not wanting him to know how vulnerable she was where he was concerned, she propped her feet casually on the edge of her desk. "What brings you back to the Bar W? I thought you were going to stay in Fort Worth until Jaclyn and the twins returned."

"They're coming back early this afternoon instead of late tonight. Apparently the twins miss you desperately. They said they tried to call you, but the phone was busy."

"I have been on the phone since early this morning," she said.

He scrutinized her carefully. "Are you sure you're okay? You look like you've been through the wringer."

Rachel kneaded the knotted muscles in the back of her neck with both hands. "Maybe because sending five hundred head of cattle to market is no easy task."

"Yeah. I heard you've been doing that this week," he said sympathetically. "I saw Rowdy on the way in."

Rachel frowned, wishing she didn't have to tell him how things had turned out. "Then you undoubtedly know what a poor price the herd commanded," she said tightly, wishing like hell she had better news to relate to him.

Travis shrugged, unconcerned. "Supply and demand. That's the way it goes."

"Thanks for the financial analysis," she countered dryly.

"Speaking of financial analyses...is that what you've been doing?" His eyes skimmed her legs and hips as he watched her get up and walk over to the file cabinet to replace a sheaf of papers.

Deciding finally she'd rather give him the news when no one else was there to witness him rub it in, she said tiredly, "I doubt I'm telling you anything you haven't already guessed, but for the record, the financial margin I thought I had is gone. I'm in the red. I haven't given up, but with the price of beef still plummeting, I doubt there's any way I can turn things around before summer's end. Not unless I can find a buyer for the Brahma calves."

"No luck so far?"

He didn't look as happy as Rachel would've expected him to. "Not yet," Rachel said calmly. "I do have several prospective buyers coming out to the ranch later this week. One nearly every day, as a matter of fact. That's why I was on the phone all morning."

"Well, maybe that'll do it," he said.

"Maybe," Rachel allowed. She tried not to look too surprised at his sympathetic attitude. "Does your showing up here mean you've decided we're friends again?" The truth was, she had missed him terribly. Why, she didn't know. It should have been peaceful without him to badger her, but it had been lonely. She'd come to count on his disrupting presence to make her forget her troubles with the ranch and goad her into doing better, just for the pleasure of showing him she could.

Travis shrugged. "I've made it pretty clear a simple friendship isn't what I want from you, but I'll take it over nothing any day. I've come to like having you around."

Rachel stared at him, amazed. Realizing how open he was to compromise now, she was filled with a warm glow. Trying, however, not to let herself take his change of heart too seriously lest she get hurt in the bargain, she teased wryly, "I bet you say that to all the girls."

"No," he said softly, his eyes as serious as hers were merry. "I don't."

Their eyes held. Her mouth went dry. Rachel had the oddest feeling she was teetering on the edge....

"Look, I've been thinking," Travis continued genially, plopping his Stetson down on his bent knee and idly fingering the brim. "Regardless of how all this turns out, maybe you and the kids could stay on, anyway, just live here. My mother loves the company. You could be assistant ranch manager or something."

His certainty that she would fail struck an angry chord. "Don't patronize me, Travis. And don't assume just because I haven't found a buyer for the Brahma calves thus far that I won't. I still have another month left."

"I wasn't patronizing you."

Rachel swallowed the knot of emotion in her throat. Whether he'd meant to or not, he had hurt her feelings and her pride. "The hell you weren't!" she shot back. "You're secretly glad I haven't succeeded as I'd hoped."

Travis studied her boldly. "I won't deny I expected this to happen," he began honestly, "considering your lack of ranching experience and the magnitude of the job you took on. But so what?'' He shrugged as if the outcome were no big deal. ''You gave it your best.'' He gave her a hard look. ''Meant what I said earlier, about your staying on regardless of the outcome.''

''No,'' Rachel said stiffly. Her pride wouldn't allow it.

''Why not?'' His voice lowered another soothing persuasive notch. ''You can't deny you like it here.''

Too much. ''I've already imposed enough.''

''You're family, Rachel.''

''Is that really the way you see me, Travis?'' Rachel asked bitterly.

He drew away, alert to the anger in her gaze. ''I don't know what you mean.''

''I think you do.''

''Well, I don't,'' he said tightly. ''So you'll have to elaborate.''

''I'd rather ask a question, instead. Are you figuring yourself into the equation?''

''In what way?'' he bit back.

''Will *you* be staying on at the ranch?''

''That depends.''

''On what? On whether I give in to your constant attempts at seduction and become your live-in lover?''

She'd expected him to be insulted by her cruel remarks. He only smiled, his face inscrutable. ''You make it sound sordid,'' he said casually, getting off the desk and coming closer.

Only pride kept her from back-stepping as he approached. ''That's because it is,'' Rachel said flatly.

He wrapped his arms around her suddenly. ''That's where you're wrong, Rachel,'' he said softly, threading his fingers through the riot of curls at the nape of her neck. His gaze scanned her face tenderly. ''Our making love could never be sordid. Enlivening. Entertaining. Fulfilling, yes. Sordid, never.''

She turned away, willing him to let her go, but he didn't release her. Now they were standing, with her back to him, his arms locked about her waist, his chin in her hair.

Despite herself, Rachel almost melted into the warmth of his chest and the strength of his welcoming arms. Only the knowledge of what he really wanted from her kept her from furthering the embrace.

She uncrossed her arms and used her elbows to propel herself away from him. "I won't run around, sneak, lie or cheat," Rachel said. "I won't be with someone who's ashamed to be with me. Not again." She spun around in time to see the shock registered on Travis's face.

"Austin was ashamed of you?"

Humiliated and angry with herself for having revealed so much, she said coolly, "I never said that!"

Travis closed the distance between them swiftly and held her in front of him. "The truth, Rachel. What did my brother do?"

Rachel stared at him, her pulse racing. She'd never heard him sound so fiercely protective. "He didn't mean to do anything."

"But he did just the same, didn't he?" Travis bent his knees slightly, so he could better see into her eyes.

She turned away, irritated to find herself in the position of defending a man who had hurt her and let her down. "You don't know how hard it was for him," Rachel said, wishing she didn't feel so humiliated. "He wasn't used to dating anyone from my background."

"So?"

"So it was difficult for him, and it didn't help any

that my father was usually drunk and abusive when
Austin arrived to pick me up for dates.'' She gestured
helplessly. ''His friends didn't understand. Nor did his
family.'' She paused to give Travis a pointed look that
let him know how much he'd hurt her in the past.
''Everyone thought he was with me for only one reason, but it wasn't true. We never made love then, although he really wanted to—'' Again, realizing she had
said far too much, she stopped speaking abruptly.

''Is that why he married you? Because you refused
to put out?''

Rachel sighed miserably, taking no offense because
none was meant. ''In retrospect, I think that probably
was part of it. And I think subconsciously he wanted
to get back at your father for putting so much pressure
on him to run the ranch.''

He studied her quietly. ''And you, Rachel? What
about you?'' he asked softly. ''What were you thinking?''

Rachel figured she'd been foolishly honest so far.
She might as well tell him the rest. ''I knew I came
from an ill-thought-of home. I wasn't going to be labeled a tramp, too.''

''But to actually marry someone, Rachel, to commit
to them for life…'' Travis said, aghast.

''You have to understand,'' she said, her humiliation
fading as she saw the understanding in his eyes. ''We
may have had very different views about the nature and
course of our relationship, but we also thought we were
very much in love. We were both so young, Travis,
and so very naive. We really thought we could make
it work. We thought getting married would legitimize
our relationship, make it more acceptable to family and
community.''

"But it had just the opposite effect," Travis recalled sadly.

"Yes. Everyone resented me even more."

"Including Austin?"

Rachel knew there was no point in denying it and she nodded. "Yes," she said simply. "He was hurt when his family wouldn't accept our relationship and hurt when my father didn't even seem to care what happened to me. And I think, whether he meant to or not, that deep inside he blamed me for all of it."

Travis was silent for a long time. "I don't see what any of that has to do with us," he said finally.

"I won't hurt your mother that way. And I won't set a poor example for my teenage children."

"My mother wants us to get together."

"She wants us to declare a truce and be friends," Rachel corrected. "That's not the same thing."

"It could be," he said quietly.

"No, Travis."

Silence fell between them. He looked at her tenderly. She had the oddest impression that at that moment he would have a hard time denying her anything. She knew she wanted to please him, as well, to win his approval and his understanding, if only for the sake of knowing she had done it.

"I still want you, Rachel," he said quietly.

And I still want you. But she also knew their circumstances were far too complicated ever to let a love between them flourish. Travis knew it, too. Otherwise, he'd be talking permanent relationship, not temporary love affair.

Her eyes still riveted to his, she shook her head sadly. "I won't be your mistress, Travis." The edges of her mouth curved up in a bitter smile. "Not even if doing so allowed me to continue on as assistant manager of this ranch. And that's final.''

"IT'S SO GOOD to be home!'' Jaclyn said a mere four hours later.

"It's so good to have you all home again!'' Rachel said, embracing all three weary travelers in turn. *And not to be alone with Travis anymore.*

Every time she looked at him, she heard his low sexy voice ringing in her ear. *I still want you, Rachel.*

But sex wasn't just a physical act to her, like brushing her teeth or working out. It was a commitment to each other and to the future, a blending of heart and soul. To Travis it was apparently just something pleasurable.

Dinner that evening was lively. The twins looked tanned and healthy, content to be back on the ranch again, as was Jaclyn. Travis looked happy, too.

"It sounds like you did everything there was to do in Florida,'' Rachel marveled.

"Just about,'' Gretchen said. ''But we would've had a better time if we hadn't been so worried about you. It wasn't right that we got to take a super vacation and you had to stay here all alone and work.''

"She wasn't alone,'' Brett put in with a yawn. ''Uncle Travis was here.''

"Speaking of work,'' Rachel added lightly. ''I've got some chores in mind for the two of you this week, starting tomorrow.''

The twins groaned in unison. ''We hate ranch work,'' Brett complained.

"Too bad, 'cause you're going to do it, anyway. Besides, it builds character.'' Rachel grinned.

Surveying the twins with a mixture of maternal pride

and exasperation, Rachel wondered if they ever would appreciate all she was doing for them this summer, working her fingers to the bone, just so they would have a secure future. Not that it really mattered. She was going to take care of them, whether they appreciated her efforts or not.

Jaclyn sent a curious look at her son. "How did the two of you get along without us?"

"Fine." Travis smiled at his mother innocently, then turned to her. "Isn't that right, Rachel?"

Depends on what you meant by fine, Rachel thought. If he meant that she was supposed to have been in a perpetual state of excitement, they'd gotten along tremendously. Rachel smiled. "We managed just fine."

Jaclyn looked from Rachel to Travis. There was no masking either the speculation or disappointment in her eyes. Clearly, she'd been hoping for so much more to develop.

Chapter Twelve

"Mix that crazy cow back in with the herd? Are you loco?" Rowdy said incredulously the following morning.

Rachel sat back calmly in her office chair. "That's what I said, Rowdy."

Rowdy looked at the only other person in the room for help. "Travis, tell her she's crazy."

Travis looked up from the copier in Rachel's office, where he was copying a sheaf of papers relating to his airline business. He sent Rachel an ornery grin and parroted, "You're crazy."

Rachel swiveled around to face him. She wished Travis would quit wearing that tantalizing cologne of his. Every time she caught a whiff of sandalwood and spice, she was reminded of the night by the windmill and how it had felt to be so thoroughly, wickedly, close to him. She returned his parody of a grin. "Thanks ever so much, but you have nothing to do with this, Travis."

Travis picked up his papers and swaggered toward her, his hips undulating in a smooth male motion. He deposited his papers on a corner of her desk and sat down in a chair next to Rowdy. He slouched low on his spine, propped his elbows on the chair arms and templed his fingers above the midpoint of his chest. "Why do you want to move the steer, anyway?"

"Because I need that corral next to the barns," Rachel said.

"What for?" Rowdy asked.

"I'm planning to put the organic herd there."

Both Rowdy and Travis did double takes. "All fifty?" they said in unison.

The force of their incredulity sent a blush of warmth to her cheeks that made the blusher she'd put on that morning quite unnecessary. "Just for the day," Rachel qualified. Because they were still both looking at her as though she was from outer space, she continued conversationally, "A prospective buyer is coming out to look at the herd. Which reminds me, Rowdy, as soon as you're done moving the steer, bring all the men to the barn."

Rowdy stood in anticipation of being dismissed, holding his hat in front of his knees. "How come?"

"We're going to groom those calves and give them baths."

Rowdy squinted at her. Rachel refused to even look at Travis.

"You're kidding, right?" Rowdy asked. Beside him Travis remained ominously silent.

"No," Rachel told her cow boss calmly. She looked directly at Rowdy and didn't drop her gaze. "I want those calves looking like they're ready to win a blue ribbon at the county fair."

"Now hold on there, Rachel," Travis said, leaning forward in his chair. "This isn't a 4-H project—"

"You're right. It isn't." Rachel smiled at her cow boss. "Rowdy, you're excused."

The foreman shook his head glumly, plopped his

Stetson on his head and turned to leave. "Keep trying to talk some sense into her, Travis," he muttered on his way out in a voice Rachel knew only Travis was meant to hear. Rowdy sent Travis a brief man-to-man glance. "God knows I can't."

Rowdy left. Travis turned back to Rachel. From the way he looked at her, she knew she was in for a fight.

"I gotta agree with him. This is the dumbest thing you've ever done, assigning the hands to play beauty parlor to a bunch of calves." He stood and moved forward to sit on a corner of her desk.

Rachel's heart pounded at his nearness. He had shaved very closely that morning. His gleaming black hair was agreeably mussed.

"It's not as if I'm going to make them do this every day, Travis. Besides," she continued confidently, "they'll be singing a different tune when I cut the deal with Rob McMillan."

Travis blinked in surprise and fastened his eyes on her like twin lasers. "Who's he?"

"Only the owner of the biggest chain of natural-food stores in the Midwest." Finding the intensity of his gaze as disconcerting as the washboard flatness of his abdomen and the bunched muscles beneath his shirt, Rachel got up to pour herself some coffee from a silver service.

Travis followed her. He picked up a teacup from the tray, frowned at the delicate china pattern, then poured himself some coffee, too. "Then he probably already has a line of organically raised beef," Travis countered.

Rachel smiled and took a seat on the sofa. "Nope. He doesn't. Until now, Rob's only carried fish and poultry in his stores. But he's thinking of getting into organically raised beef."

Travis frowned again. He swallowed his coffee in a single gulp. Avoiding her eyes, he put his cup aside. "Where'd you hear that?"

"The last Southwestern Cattle Raisers Association meeting," Rachel said, then added confidently, "and Travis? I intend to be that supplier."

TRAVIS HAD TO ADMIRE her determination, even if he did think she was going overboard. And he wasn't the only one who shared that opinion.

"Come on, Uncle Travis," the twins complained after lunch as they hauled buckets of sudsy water over to the seventy-five-pound calves. "Get us out of this."

Travis laughed at the twins' aversion to physical labor, remembering he himself had felt exactly the same way at that age. "No can do. Your mama is determined to have every one of those fifty calves washed, rinsed and blow-dried." Even if it was the craziest thing he'd ever heard.

"Towel-dried," Rachel corrected, tossing Brett a towel so he could rub down a just-scrubbed animal and lead him to the pen. "And it'd go a lot faster if *you'd* lend a hand, Travis."

"Yeah, Uncle Travis. If we have to wash these baby cows, you should, too," Gretchen persisted, her hands on her hips.

"One for all and all for one," Brett continued persuasively.

Watching the twins band together and back each other up, Travis was reminded of the camaraderie he'd shared with Austin when they were kids. Now, with Austin's children on the ranch, he felt a sense of family that had been lacking in his life for a long time. And the twins, though clearly no ranchers, seemed to be enjoying living here, too. As far as his mother went, she was in seventh heaven. Not a day went by that she didn't plan and execute some special activity for or with her grandchildren.

"Unless, of course..." Rachel paused archly, refusing to finish her sentence.

Travis couldn't resist when she looked at him that flirtatiously. He edged nearer and captured the other end of the towel she held in her hand. "What?"

Using the towel they were both holding as leverage, she pulled him aside and teased, "You're afraid to get really down and dirty with the rest of us."

He saw the challenge in her eyes, then picked up the water hose, pressed the trigger release on the nozzle and squirted her in the middle. "Watch who you're calling squeamish, Miss Rachel."

Rachel squealed as the spray of cold water hit her. She tossed a soapy sponge. It bounced off his shoulder. Bubbles splashed into his face.

"Okay, that does it," Travis said. "Now you've declared war." He retrieved the sponge from the grass, dunked it in the bucket and lobbed it at her nose. She ducked at the last minute.

"Ugh!" She straightened, hands on her hips. Her face was bright red with embarrassment. Travis thought he'd never seen her look prettier.

"Kill him, Mom!" Brett yelled encouragement from the sidelines as the hands turned around to watch.

"Yeah. Get him good!" Gretchen said. "Don't let him get away with that."

Her beautiful lips pursed with anything but amusement. "No," she said primly, turning her back on him. "I don't think I will."

The corral was dead silent as Rachel walked back to

her bucket and picked up the sponge and the hose. Soapy sponge in one hand, hose in the other, she turned toward a calf. Travis's spirits sagged. What he'd hoped would be a little bit of horseplay had somehow turned into a fight. He gave the twins a guess-we-better-get-back-to-work shrug and turned to locate a sponge.

He'd just bent down to retrieve one, when the water hit him square in the seat of the pants. She had a good aim. He ran toward her, swearing revenge.

Laughing, Rachel backed up and tried to dodge his advance. With a whoop and a holler, Travis wrested the hose from her hands. Or at least tried to, but she held on tight. Before he knew it the trigger nozzle had been pressed down, and they ended up squirting Rowdy.

Rowdy, who was no slouch in the water-fight department, promptly got the both of them back with *his* hose. Gretchen, Brett and the rest of the hands joined in the fun. Soon sponges were flying and hoses were being squirted in every direction. Laughter and shouting and good-natured ribbing filled the air.

It was at least half an hour before anyone got back to work.

"IMPRESSIVE, AREN'T THEY?" Rachel murmured hours later as she and Travis stood alone, admiring the calves in the newly sodded pen.

She was impressive, Travis thought, with her sun-burned nose and her crazy ideas and the way she'd cheerfully organized everyone and gotten the job done. "I gotta admit they do look...better," Travis said.

"Admit it, Travis." She nudged his leg playfully with one of hers. "They looked darned good."

"Like pampered pets." He stood shoulder to shoulder with her at the corral, his foot propped up on the bottom rail of the fence. "But I'm not so sure that's the image you're going for, Rachel."

"It's exactly the image I'm going for." Rachel turned toward him earnestly.

Travis had wanted to kiss her all afternoon. The presence of the hired hands and the kids had prevented it during the water fight. The fact they were in such a public place and it was still broad daylight prevented it even now. But it wouldn't prevent it forever. Because Travis knew he *was* going to kiss her again.

"Trust me, Rob McMillan is going to love it," Rachel continued cheerfully.

Rob McMillan is going to love you, Travis thought.

His good mood souring fast, Travis demanded, "What do you know about this guy, anyway? Have you ever met him?"

Rachel gazed adoringly out at her scrawny spanking-clean Brahma calves, who at this point in their development were not much bigger than large dogs. "Not face-to-face," she admitted. "But I've talked to him on the phone at length."

"Is he young?" Travis asked.

Rachel turned toward him, her golden eyes filled with a suspicious light. "Why?"

Travis shrugged. "I don't know. I just wondered."

"Well, he's young," Rachel replied with a mixture of smugness and resentment as she turned back to her herd. "And single. A real go-getter."

Travis felt his jaw set. "Hopefully, you'll get what you want from the meeting." *A deal on your calves so you'll have more time to spend with me.* Now where had that thought come from? he wondered, perplexed.

"Thanks. I hope it goes well, too." She smiled at

him, looking relaxed again and happy to be with him. Suddenly she gave a little gasp. It was remarkably similar to the soft womanly sounds she made during sex, Travis realized uncomfortably. She glanced at her watch.

"Gosh it's late," Rachel murmured. "Rob will be here soon." Glancing down at her damp jeans and stained shirt, she shook her head ruefully. "I better get cleaned up."

And I'd like to help, Travis thought, easily able to imagine the two of them in a hot steamy shower. "It probably wouldn't hurt to put on a dry pair of jeans."

Rachel laughed softly and sent him a mute reproving glance. "Don't be silly. I'm going to wear a dress."

IT HAD BEEN such a nice day, Rachel thought, as she reclined in the fragrant bubble bath. It hadn't started out that way, of course, with the men grumbling and carrying on. But when the twins had come out to help and Travis had joined in, it had been great. For the first time since she'd been living at the ranch, she'd felt as though she and Travis were connected by more than just the past and the Westcott name. And wrong or not, she would have liked the day to end with her wrapped in his arms.

Closing her eyes, she could easily envision many more days like today. Meals together. Holidays. She could see them playing, fighting, loving and living together, day after wonderful day. But that was fantasy, not reality, she told herself firmly. Travis wasn't interested in running the ranch with her. Or in working by her side. Or in having a family.

So what if they were no longer sworn enemies and were on the verge of being trusted friends? So what if she was still wildly attracted to him and he made love to her the way no other man ever could or would? He was completely charming, disarming, hardworking and successful, but that didn't make him any more marriageable, or an intimate relationship between them any more possible.

Travis was an emotional drifter. He wanted a woman who would love him physically without attaching any emotional strings. As much as Rachel appreciated the exultant abandon of his kisses, the thoroughly satisfied way he had made her feel when he'd made love to her, she could never be with him again. Not knowing he was still as footloose as he had ever been when it came to the women in his life.

She might be able to do without a ring on her finger, if she knew Travis really loved her, and only her. But she couldn't do without commitment. If she was to be with him again, he would have to pledge his heart and soul to her first. He would have to promise her tomorrow, not just today.

TRAVIS HADN'T MEANT to bother Rachel when she was getting ready to greet a guest, but he couldn't help but stop and gape when he passed by the open doorway to her bedroom. He hadn't seen her look so dressed up and pretty since that night the previous spring when he'd first seen her again. The navy blue denim shirt-dress she was wearing looked brand-new and fit her willowy body with unerring sensual accuracy. The bodice snugly hugged her breasts. A wide silver belt drew attention to her slender waist. Beneath the hem of the full skirt he could see the frilly edge of a white lace petticoat and was irritated to see she'd left the bottom two buttons of the skirt undone to further show it off, just as she had left the top two buttons undone.

"You look like you're ready to go on a date, not to a business meeting," Travis remarked, watching as Rachel bent to slip her stocking-clad feet into her dressy cowboy boots, which had been polished to a shine.

"Good." Rachel sighed, satisfied. "Because that's sort of what we're doing."

"What?"

"We're going to dinner in San Angelo as soon as Rob's toured the ranch and seen the herd. I've arranged to have some of our nonorganic Westcott beef prepared for us by one of the chefs in his hotel restaurant. Wasn't that clever of me?"

"Stunningly clever," Travis said dryly, all too aware it *was* a good move on her part. The beef they raised on the ranch was of superior quality. "I still think…"

"What?" Rachel paused in the act of fastening silver hoop earrings in her ears.

You should button up that dress. "Are you sure you shouldn't wear a suit?" Travis asked. *Something not quite so sexy or feminine or flirty.*

"Well, actually, I thought about it," Rachel admitted conversationally as she ran a brush expertly through her springy flame-colored curls. "But I really want to look like a lady rancher, you know?" She put down the brush and used her fingertips to fluff up the ends of her hair. "And maybe it's corny, but this is what I think I should wear. After all, we're selling Texas and the traditions of the Old West, so a Western-style dress seemed perfect."

She spritzed on some delicious-smelling perfume, then paused and looked concerned. "Why? You don't think… I don't look fat in this dress, do I?" Hands on her hips, she rushed to the full-length mirror and pirouetted slowly.

"No." The problem was she looked too beautiful. Travis tried not to groan as she smoothed the fabric of her skirt over her slender hips with the palms of her hands. "No, you don't look fat." He strolled close to her.

"Then what is it?" Perplexed, Rachel whirled to face him.

I'm jealous as hell, that's what's the matter, and I know I have no right to be. No right at all. "Nothing." His desire for her was his problem, and it was something he was just going to have to deal with.

The sound of a car sliced through the silence.

"Oh, my gosh!" Rachel dashed to the window just as a sleek stretch limousine pulled up in front of the house. "He's here!" She raced past Travis, pausing only long enough to give him a quick sisterly kiss on the cheek. "Wish me luck!" she cried excitedly.

With the business deal, Travis wished her all the luck in the world. But not with Rob McMillan personally.

"WHEN WILL YOU LET me know?" Rachel asked as their coffee cups were cleared away.

The handsome entrepreneur grinned at her. Blond, blue-eyed and suntanned, he looked like a California surfer. In the past, she would have been immediately attracted. Now, Rachel realized sadly, in the romance department, he couldn't so much as ignite a match. Romance for her involved tall Texans with black hair, slate-blue eyes and smart oh-so-sensual mouths. Romance for her was filled with as much heartache as it was impossibility. But Travis was the only man who interested her, even if he was all wrong for her.

"I've got a few other avenues to check out first," Rob was saying.

"I understand." Rachel smiled, encouraged by the rapport they'd established. She gathered up the projected figures and reports she had prepared for Rob, handed him his copies and stuck her copies back in her briefcase. "I try to be thorough, too."

"But I'll try and let you know by the end of the month," he promised. "So, now that we've concluded our business, want to go dancing?"

Rachel smiled and thought of Travis back at the ranch waiting for her, curious to know how things had gone. "Thanks," she said pleasantly. "But it's been a long day."

"I understand." Rob stood chivalrously as Rachel gathered her purse and briefcase. "I'll call you with my decision."

Rachel shook his hand firmly and looked square into his eyes. "I'll look forward to hearing from you."

Their goodbyes said, she started for the exit. She was nearly to the door when she saw him, sitting at the end of the bar, nursing what looked to be an untouched beer and a bowl of pretzels.

She sauntered to his side. She grinned, admitting to herself that in his tweed blazer and hat, Travis had never looked sexier. Or more Texan. "Fancy meeting you here," she said.

"Yeah, well, I worried about your getting home all right. Since you rode into town in Barry's limousine and all."

"It's Rob, as in Robert, not Barry. And I planned to

take a cab.'' She softened, oddly touched. ''Did you have dinner?''

''No.'' He slapped a bill onto the counter and stood. He grinned. ''I was too busy watching you eat.'' He took her arm, and by unspoken agreement, they headed out of the restaurant. ''So, how was the Westcott beef?''

''Delicious,'' Rachel said. Yet she couldn't help but think it would have tasted even better had she been sharing the meal with Travis, instead of Rob. ''How come you didn't come and join us?

He looked down at her as if she was the most fascinating woman in the world. ''I didn't want to intrude,'' he said softly.

Rachel's tummy did a little flip-flop. ''Just making sure I made it home okay?''

''Mothers,'' Travis lamented, then shrugged as if it was all Jaclyn's fault. ''Mine instilled me with manners.''

''I've never had a bodyguard before,'' she drawled, as together they stepped out into the warm Texas night.

Travis paused and just gazed at her. The seconds ticked by. As she stared up at him, Rachel realized that the animosity between them was completely gone. They still might disagree, and heatedly when they differed in ideology, but they no longer mistrusted one another.

''How does it feel having a bodyguard?'' he asked softly.

Rachel held his gaze. It had been a long time since she'd been protected by a man. And she knew Travis's devotion was something she could not only manage to get used to, but something she was beginning to covet. ''Good,'' she almost whispered. ''Damn good.''

"WAS YOUR DAY as hectic as mine?"

"Change that to the last several days, and the answer is yes," Rachel replied as Travis joined her in the kitchen. In fact, they'd both been so busy they hadn't really seen each other since he'd brought her home from San Angelo.

"Everyone else asleep?" Travis asked.

"Everyone except the two of us." Rachel brought a tin of cookies and a carton of milk to the kitchen table. "It's after midnight."

Travis found two glasses and sat down opposite her. It was funny, he thought. Women had come and gone in his life over the years. But with Rachel it was different. More and more these days, his moods were directly linked to her. When they fought, his thoughts were black as thunder. When she smiled at him, he knew a new kind of peace. A new kind of want. One that just wouldn't go away.

"I know why I'm still up." She smiled and turned her golden-brown eyes on him. She poured herself a glass of milk. "I'm wired, because I met with another prospective buyer for the Brahma herd."

Travis took a cookie from the tin and snapped it in two. "How'd it go?"

"Great." Rachel kicked back in her chair. "I know I said the same thing after I met with Rob McMillan, but I think I really might have a buyer this time."

"Bathing the cows really helped, huh?"

She wrinkled her nose at him. "You're making fun of me," she accused.

"Sure am," he admitted with a wink. "How much grumbling did the hands do this time?"

"Just as much as the twins, as usual," Rachel reported. "I didn't care. I still don't." She sat forward earnestly. "I know sprucing those Brahma calves up makes a difference."

Women! "If you say so."

"You're making fun of me again."

"Yep."

They grinned at each other.

"How's *your* business going?" she asked.

"Like gangbusters, at the moment," Travis said. "Our summer ticket sales exceeded all expectations. That's where I was today—in Fort Worth, meeting with my staff, trying to determine the travel dates for the special rates next year."

"Is it hard for you, working out of the ranch?"

"Actually it doesn't seem to make much difference," Travis admitted. "Anyway, I know the business so well now I could run it with my eyes closed."

It was himself that was the problem. Lately everything he'd thought he knew about himself seemed wrong. He'd figured ranching wasn't his passion. Yet he couldn't bear to let the Bar W go to Rachel or anyone else. He'd also been dead certain he would never marry. Now, knowing marriage was what Rachel wanted out of life, he found himself thinking about it, too. In the abstract, anyway.

Struggling to keep his mind on their conversation, instead of on how well her Western dress outlined her breasts when she sat back in her chair that way, he asked casually, "Was your prospective buyer impressed with the ranch?"

"Of course. Who wouldn't be?"

"You really feel it's impressive?"

She held his gaze. "Don't you?"

He nodded, feeling more content than he had in a long time. And it was all because of her. It was hard to remember why he had once resented her. Impossible to stop thinking about one day making love with her again. Even though she kept telling him it would never happen...

"In the years I was away," Rachel confided as she got up to look out the kitchen window, "I used to dream of this place. The way it was when I was a kid."

She turned to face him, her hands braced against the windowsill. Travis joined her at the window and glanced out at the grounds. "Were they happy dreams?" *Were they about Austin?*

"Sometimes. Sometimes not. I envied you so much," she whispered.

"Why?"

"For having grown up here and been part of such a respected family in the community."

"It wasn't that different," Travis asserted.

"Wasn't it?"

His gaze roved over her flowing hair and fair skin. A little too much sun had just colored her nose and cheeks.

"I would've given anything to have this kind of security," Rachel continued. "In my case, appearances were not deceiving," she confirmed sadly. "Like I've said, my father either drank or gambled away everything he made."

"What about when the twins were born?"

She shrugged and, pushing away from the window, strolled about the kitchen. "There's still a great deal of difference between the life we had in Beaumont and this. So much that sometimes I worry about corrupting the twins."

He followed her. "And at other times?"

"I want to give them permanent financial security.

Maybe it's selfish of me in a way, but it's what I want.''

Why couldn't it be like this between them all the time? he wondered. So open and honest. "It's not selfish to want to take care of your children, Rachel," he assured her. "That's why I asked you to consider staying on at summer's end."

"And I told you," she said firmly, tightening her lips in prim disapproval, "I can't do that."

His impatience had him tensing. "Why not?"

She sent him a level look, her mood just as intractable as his. "You know why."

Yeah, Travis thought, he did. But it had nothing to do with finances or the deal with his mother or even her past with his brother and their former animosity, as she would have him believe. It had to do with her feelings, and his, and the fact that neither of them could seem to control them for long, not when they were together. But Rachel still wouldn't face that. The evasion in her eyes now prompted him to act.

"Because of this?" he asked matter-of-factly. He hauled her into his arms and kissed her senseless, until she was trembling, until she was kissing him back, wrapping her arms around his neck and holding him close, her body soft and warm and pliant against the length in his. He threaded his hands through the tangle of curls at her neck and tilted her head back. "That's not a reason to leave, Rachel. That's a reason to stay."

Chapter Thirteen

"Look, Mom, I think it's great that you want to run the ranch, but Gretchen and I don't ever want to run it. So, if that's where this talk is leading…" Brett said as he and Gretchen joined her in her office for a family powwow.

Rachel looked at their faces and thought about how much they looked like their father. And Travis, too. Whether the twins realized it or not, this ranch was not just a link to their past and their father. It was a part of them. "I thought you liked living here," she said.

"We do. We love it. We love Gran and Uncle Travis, too.

"But that doesn't change our plans for the future," Brett continued. "We still want to go to college. And we're not studying agriculture," Brett continued firmly, reading Rachel's mind. "I want to study film-making. Gretchen wants to major in fashion design."

Rachel stared at her children in bewilderment. "This ranch is your legacy from your father," she said. "It's your connection to him."

"Maybe so. But does that mean we have to run it?" Brett complained.

"I think that's what Gran wants," Gretchen interjected practically, her expression glum.

"Well, couldn't we just let you run the ranch, since you like it so much?" Brett asked Rachel hopefully. "And when you get too old—"

"Banish the thought, young man!" Rachel corrected with a loving smile.

Brett grinned. "Well, you can hire someone else to do it."

"Yeah, or train one of *our* kids when we have them," Gretchen added.

Rachel sighed. How could her children not want what she was working so hard to attain for them? "I suppose there's a chance you'll change your mind," she said.

"Don't hold your breath," Brett advised with his customary candor. "But I don't mind *you* running the ranch. In fact we both like it, 'cause we see more of you this way."

That was true, Rachel knew. Working out of an office at home made her instantly accessible.

"So what's up?" Travis said, coming in just as the twins left.

"Brett and Gretchen have told me, as much as they love living here, that neither of them want anything to do with running the ranch."

Travis went to the window. He stood with his back to her, his hands shoved in the pockets of his jeans. "Then why break your back doing it for them?"

"Because I like doing it," Rachel said. "And because they might change their minds."

He shot her an arch look over his shoulder. "From hints I've picked up, I'd say that's doubtful."

She bristled. "Children don't always know what's best for them."

He turned and leaned against the window. "But they have the right to choose their own paths in life."

"Yes, they do," Rachel agreed. She met his glance levelly. "And I would never force them to manage the ranch against their will. I will, however, work diligently to protect their investment. And the income from the ranch will allow them to pursue their dreams, whatever they are."

"Aren't you leaving something out?" He started for her, his strides long and lazy.

"Like what?" Rachel asked, her heart pounding. His closeness was overwhelming. She liked it when they talked intimately about themselves to each other. And yet it was difficult for her, because every time they did, she wound up yearning to be held in his arms again.

"Like the fact that you want this ranch for yourself," Travis said in a flat noncommittal tone.

She flushed at his blunt unexpected attack. "It's not that simple, Travis."

Travis fell silent, but she knew from the way he looked at her that he disagreed. To him, it was simple. The ranch had always been his. Now she was trying her very best to take it away from him, not just on a temporary basis but for all time.

Rachel sighed. She hated the position Jaclyn had put her in. But prior to Rachel's appearance, Travis had rarely been out at the ranch. If she left, Rachel was willing to bet Travis would go straight back to Fort Worth. Rowdy would run the ranch, and it would no longer be cared for on a day-to-day basis by family.

She studied Travis, loving the suntanned hue of his

face and the laugh lines that feathered out around his eyes. "Are you angry with me?"

He shrugged, shoved a hand through the tousled layers of his glossy black hair and said gruffly, "At the moment I don't know how I feel."

One minute he loved her. The next he resented her. Yet through it all she remained constantly on his mind. Rachel was the first thing he thought of every morning, and the last thing he thought of before he went to sleep. Hell, these days, he even dreamed about her. He could no longer imagine the ranch without her. And yet, something in him still rankled at the enormity of what both she and his mother were asking him to give up.

"As much as I wanted to earn the right to run this ranch, I never wanted to take anything from you," Rachel persisted, her golden eyes on his.

"But you have, anyway," Travis countered quietly, his feelings an ambivalent mix as he regarded her gravely. "That's the hell of it, Rachel." His voice dropped a weary notch. "You have, anyway."

Travis was halfway out the door when the phone rang. Rachel picked it up on the first ring, while Travis lingered in the doorway, waiting to see if the call was for him.

"Yes, Sheriff," Rachel said. She listened intently, her expression growing grimmer and more troubled with every second. "I apologize for the inconvenience. Yes. I promise I'll take care of it right away. I'll see to it personally," she promised, then said a swift goodbye.

Travis started for her. As he did so, he realized how much his feelings had changed. Two months ago, he would have relished any calamity Rachel faced. Now he wanted only to protect her. "Bad news?"

Rachel was already reaching for her hat. "We've got cows out on the highway."

"Which means we've got fence down somewhere, too. Who's available to help?"

"No one except you and me."

She slipped on her flat-brimmed hat and pushed the string tie up to her throat to secure it. Her eyes lifted to his. Travis thought he'd never seen her looking so pretty. Or determined to succeed.

"Will you help?" she asked.

Suddenly, who owned the ranch didn't matter. Travis just knew he couldn't let her down. His hand flat on the small of her back, he propelled her through the door. "How's your lassoing coming?" he teased.

Rachel grinned and winked up at him. "Guess we'll find out, won't we, cowboy?"

As it turned out, there were only three cows on the highway, and Rachel and Travis were easily able to herd them back to Westcott land. As they approached the pasture, the going got rougher. Travis swore. "I count twelve, no, fifteen more outside the fence."

"Looks like we've got our work cut out for us," Rachel said grimly. As they approached on horseback, the cows scattered and began to run. Rachel went wide to the left, Travis wide to the right.

As she worked her horse back and forth, most of the cows settled down and went obediently back to the middle, toward the fence. All except one. Frisky and mulish, he tried to outrun her. Rachel picked up her lasso and swung. She missed her target the first time. But not the second. She reeled him in as Travis finished herding the rest of the strays back into the pasture.

"Nice work," he said when Rachel caught up with him. "You've really improved with that lasso."

"You can probably credit my teacher with that," she remarked.

"Oh?"

Her hands on the saddle horn, she shifted forward in the saddle and regarded him with mock seriousness. "He said I was swinging my lasso too low," she confided. "He was right."

Travis thought about how she had transformed herself from city slicker to rancher extraordinaire by sheer grit and a desire to succeed. The resentment he'd been feeling toward her fled completely. He was foolish to resent her for wanting the ranch, because she cared about it in a way he hadn't for years and probably never would again.

His eyes locked with hers as he tugged the brim of his hat lower. "I imagine you taught that teacher of yours a thing or two, as well," Travis said softly.

I hope so, Rachel thought.

And suddenly Travis saw her not taking something he loved from him, but giving him his freedom. It was days just like today that he had always dreaded. Now, he no longer had to deal with inevitable ranch calamities. His first love was still the Texas-based commuter airline he'd started from scratch and turned into a multimillion-dollar business.

He started to tell her about his change of heart, but the air filled with earsplitting bleating. Rachel and Travis turned in unison. A calf had gotten tangled in the downed barbed wire. Two more cows were heading for the fence opening. "Never a dull moment," Rachel murmured. Already swinging herself out of the saddle and down to the ground, she said, "You head off those would-be strays and get the fence back up. I'll get the calf."

"Gotcha." Travis touched two fingers to the brim of his hat and grinned at her. She grinned back at him as he prodded his horse's belly with his heels and took off.

"Come on, baby. Hang on. I'll get you out." Speaking in musical soothing tones, Rachel grabbed the calf around the throat with one arm and straddled his back. Subduing him with her weight, she began to pry the wire from the calf's legs. Then, maintaining the pressure around his throat, she backed the calf away from the offending wire.

"How bad's he hurt?" Travis asked, returning and climbing down from his horse.

Rachel inspected the deep jagged lacerations. "These wounds need to be cleansed and bandaged." Still holding the calf between her legs, Rachel took her scarf off and ripped it in half.

Travis nodded grimly, apparently agreeing with her. "I'll finish the fence. Then we'll head back."

"We're taking this calf with us," Rachel called after his retreating back. She bent over to secure a makeshift bandage. The calf bawled hysterically when she touched him. Startled by the ferocity of the sound, Rachel jumped and backed into another cow, who was grazing nearby. The injured calf bawled again, and without warning the whole herd became excited and took up the complaint. Cows began to scatter every which way, mooing and knocking into one another in their haste.

Rachel struggled to hold on to the calf just long enough to secure another bandage.

"Rachel, watch out!" Travis shouted.

She lifted her head, saw him drop his tools and head for her at a run. At the naked fear on Travis's face, she sucked in an uneven breath. She turned and saw a steer charging at her, his eyes huge and wild. Only it wasn't just any steer. It was the same one that had attacked Bobby Ray. She screamed and dodged. The next thing she knew, the animal had ducked his head and sent another cow flying into the barbed-wired fence Travis had just strung tight. It crashed down under the weight of the cow.

The steer turned around again, a crazed look in his eyes, and took off again, charging wildly down the field into the center of the now stampeding cows. Knowing she had to subdue him, Rachel jumped on her horse and followed him.

She raised her rope above her head, aimed and threw.

She caught him squarely around the neck and tightened the noose. He skidded to a halt, as Rachel's horse closed the distance between them. And it was then, as Rachel came right up on him that the crazed cow jerked like a bucking bronco and took off again, pulling Rachel right along with him.

"Let him go, dammit!" Travis shouted from somewhere behind her, but Rachel held on stubbornly, her horse cutting in and out of the herd of excited cattle. She continued to hold tight even as she was jerked from the saddle and pulled along the ground. Finally the steer ran out of air and collapsed on his haunches in the dust.

Travis rode up, leapt out of his saddle and hunkered down beside her. Around them, the stampede had quieted. The day had been saved.

"Rachel," Travis said, his voice sounding strange and shaky. "Oh, God...Rachel," he whispered. "You're hurt."

"I am?" Rachel asked, dazed. She put her hand to her aching forehead, and when she took it away it was covered in blood.

"YOU CAN SEE HER NOW, Mr. Westcott," the nurse in Emergency said.

Travis sprang to his feet. It had been forty-five minutes since he'd brought Rachel in, but it seemed like days.

He found her lying on a gurney, a sheet drawn up to her chest. Her skin looked as pale as the hospital gown she was wearing. Resisting the urge to haul her into his arms and smother her face with kisses, Travis took her trembling hand in his. She looked so vulnerable it tore at his heart. He hated seeing her this way. And yet he had never been prouder of her than when she had lassoed that crazy cow.

"I had to have a tetanus shot," she complained. "How do you like the bandage?" She forced a weak smile and used her free hand to point to her temple.

"Cute."

"The doctor says it's so close to my hairline the scar'll never show."

"No concussion?" Travis scanned her face worriedly.

She shook her head, then winced, as if in pain. "No. Just a headache from where I was stitched up."

"I thought they numbed you before they started sewing."

"They did. It still hurts." She released a wavering breath and held his hand tightly. "Did you get hold of Rowdy?"

"Sure did. They're finishing the job we started."

"At least they didn't have to tend to that crazy cow."

"No, they didn't. Thanks to your lassoing skill."

"And the way you tied him up," Rachel added.

"He was out of commission. So everything's back to normal now," Travis reassured her. "And they took that little calf that got tangled up in the barbed wire to the vet, too."

"Oh, Travis, I'm so sorry this happened," Rachel whispered.

"You've got nothing to be sorry about. No one could have subdued that steer faster or more expertly than you did, and that includes me."

"But it was all my fault. I never should have instructed Rowdy to mix him back in with the herd."

"You don't have to talk about this now if it's going to upset you," he declared huskily, figuring if *she* cried *he'd* end up crying and embarrassing them both.

"No." Rachel's lips quavered and she lifted her golden eyes to his. "I want to talk about it, Travis. I want you to know if I'd had any idea how vicious that cow could really be, I would have ordered him destroyed. You were right. It wasn't worth the liability to keep him."

Travis sat down beside her on the hospital gurney. "I wish I hadn't been right," he said softly. His eyes searched hers, making sure for the hundredth time since she'd taken the spill from her horse that she really was all right. "I never wanted to see you hurt."

"I know." Her hand softened beneath his, becoming pliant and acquiescent, just as her mouth, her whole body had, when they'd made love. "How did you know something like this would happen?"

He shrugged, wishing he could be with her like this

and not desire her, wishing he could stop wanting to protect her or stop feeling as if she was his top priority now and to hell with the ranch. To hell with everything except her.

"Years of experience," he answered her quietly. "What Rowdy and Bobby Ray said was true. Some cows, like people, are just plain mean and ornery."

They were silent. "Well, next time I'll know better," Rachel said firmly as she pulled herself together. "Next time I'll listen to you and Rowdy when you try to tell me something."

Travis smoothed the tangled auburn curls from her face and smiled at her.

"What's so funny?"

Travis shrugged again. "I was just thinking. When you first came, I wanted nothing more than to be able to tell you what to do and have you do it. Now that you're actually listening to me, though, I wonder if maybe I didn't like you better the other way. You know, kind of feisty and temperamental—"

She aimed a teasing blow at his shoulder.

He caught her fist and unthinkingly pressed a kiss into her knuckles."

"Oh, Travis," she sighed, "are we ever going to come to terms with our situation?"

Travis smiled at her. "I think I already have."

"What do you mean?"

"It's not the ranch that's important to me. You are." He looked up as the doctor jerked back a curtain and entered.

"How is she?" Travis asked.

"Probably sore as all get-out, unless I miss my guess," the doctor said. "But no broken ribs, so she's free to be released. I don't want her up on horseback for a couple of days, though. The best thing for her, if you can get her to stay still, is bed rest for the next twenty-four hours or so.'' He shot Rachel a stern look. ''Give that black-and-blue body of yours a rest. And don't get your stitches wet.''

Rachel made a face. Just the thought of staying in bed for a day made her feel like an invalid. ''Can I wash my hair?''

''If you can do it without getting your stitches wet.''

''When do the stitches come out?'' Rachel asked.

''One week. Think you can handle that?''

''No problem,'' Travis promised before Rachel could reply. ''I'll make sure she gets absolutely everything she needs.''

''BUT I DON'T WANT to stay in bed,'' Rachel argued as Travis drove her home.

''Tough. You heard what the doctor said.''

''Can't we at least drive out to the pasture where the stampede occurred?'' Rachel persisted.

He slanted her a glance. ''You promise me you'll go to bed, as ordered, the moment we get home?''

''Yes.''

''You promise me you won't so much as try and get out of the car when we get there, but will be content to sit and look out the window at your wonderfully behaved cows and repaired fence?''

Rachel was silent a moment. ''I don't see what—''

''Now, Miss Rachel,'' Travis drawled, as if he were her nanny instead of her friend, ''you heard what that doctor said.''

Rachel closed her eyes in defeat. ''I promise,'' she said.

"You see?" he said once they were there. "Everything's fine."

And it was, Rachel noted with relief. "Rowdy and the hands did a good job."

"How about you?" Travis asked quietly, his concern etched in the masculine planes of his face. "You feeling okay?"

Rachel nodded, wanting nothing more at that second than to wrap herself in his strong arms and stay there for the rest of the day. Not making love necessarily, though that would be very nice, but just being held. She wanted only to be close to him again, without any complications or outside matters coming in to separate them.

"I'm fine. Just a little tired, that's all."

When they reached the house, Rachel winced and unfastened her seat belt. "I don't know how rodeo cowboys do it," she lamented.

"They've got grit," Travis said, circling around to help her out of the car. "Just like you do."

"Hey, the boss is back!" Bobby Ray shouted from behind her. Rachel turned to see every hand in the place walking toward her. Tears sprang to her eyes as she saw that Rowdy even had flowers in his hand. He tipped his hat, looking genuinely glad to see her. "Ma'am. We're glad to see you're all right."

"You gave us all a scare," Bobby Ray said. "Not to worry, though. That crazy cow has been sent off to market, just like you asked. And the vet sewed up the calf that got hurt."

"Thank you." Rachel took a deep breath. "I owe you all an apology, though." She visibly searched out each and every hand's eyes. "You told me something like that would happen. It did. I'm sorry I didn't bow to your expertise in the matter. Next time, I promise I will.''

''Yeah, well—'' Rowdy looked abashed ''—we owe you an apology for that jackalope hunt. Guess we're even.''

''Oh, come on,'' Rachel said. ''It was funny. Of course,'' she continued as she ambled slowly and painfully toward the house, ''had you sent me on a snipe hunt, I wouldn't have been nearly as gullible, 'cause I know what snipe are.''

The men chuckled in unison. ''Yeah, well if you want to call a truce and start fresh...?'' Rowdy left the thought hanging.

''I'd like that very much,'' Rachel said graciously. She looked at Rowdy. ''I'm going to be laid up for a few days, so if you'll run the ranch in the meantime, I'd appreciate it.''

Chapter Fourteen

Travis strode into the ranch-house kitchen and skidded to a stop. His sensual mouth curling upward at the corners, he slouched against the counter and regarded Rachel. "What are you doing out of bed?" he demanded.

"What does it look like I'm doing?" she asked, rolling her eyes. "I'm going to wash my hair."

"Without getting your stitches wet?"

"It won't be easy so I thought I'd ask Jaclyn or Gretchen to help me." She looked around as if noticing for the first time how quiet the house was. A flush of pink crept up her cheeks. "Where are they, anyway?"

"Dinner out and a movie. It's the housekeeper's night off, anyway. I'm in charge of feeding you."

Rachel groaned. "I'm not up to your chili today."

"Nothing that spicy, huh?" Glad to see Rachel was feeling more like her old self after a day in bed, he came closer and grabbed her around the waist.

"Not tonight." She tipped her head back and didn't move away. Travis had the sudden urge to kiss her. Not sure he could stop with just that if he did, he let go of her gently.

"Well, you're in luck if it's bland you want," he said as he looked in the refrigerator. "'Cause what I had in mind was either canned soup or scrambled eggs—''

"I'm not hungry, Travis," she interrupted, the patient in her turning a little temperamental and grumpy. "I just want my hair washed."

He exhaled loudly, then scanned her from the top of her red head to her bare toes. She was wearing a pale pink wraparound robe and a white high-necked nightgown that would have suited a nun. The outfit was so chaste, and yet, on her the overall effect was astonishingly sexy. "One-track mind, huh?" he asked, pretending to be exasperated.

"You can feed me later," Rachel allowed petulantly. "After you've washed my hair."

"Me?" Travis echoed in disbelief.

"You." She gave him a dazzling determined smile, and one hand to his shoulder, propelled him toward the kitchen sink.

"Now wait a minute—"

"I know, I know. You ain't no beauty-parlor operator." Rachel put shampoo bottles on one side of the double sink.

"You're damn right I'm not," Travis grumbled. It was hell to be this close to her, to want her so badly he ached, and not be able to touch her.

Dragging over a chair, she climbed onto the kitchen counter. Using a rolled towel as a neck rest, she prepared to stretch out, so that her hair tumbled into the stainless-steel sink.

"We're going to do this here?"

Rachel's eyes sparkled as she lay down. "Unless you can think of a better place. Would you hand me that plastic wrap please? I want to put it over the bandage."

He complied, then helped her secure it. "I've never done this before."

Her eyes met his. "I have faith in you," she said. "And just think how much better you're going to help me to feel."

Unfortunately that was all Travis could think about. About how it would be to make love to her again. Not in a frenzy of passion this time, of pent-up frustration and desire, but tenderly.

"Unless, of course—" Rachel paused "—you want me to get water in my stitches and risk an infection. Then I suppose I could do it by myself, or at least try."

"That's blackmail," he said gravely.

She lifted a shoulder unapologetically. "Yes, but is it working?"

He only grinned in answer. The thought of sinking his hands into her flame-red tresses wasn't nearly as unpalatable as he pretended. In fact, he noted, suppressing a groan of desire, it was damned sexy, too.

Travis adjusted the water temperature and learned how to work the spray nozzle next to the sink. She talked him through the first rinse, the shampoo, the second rinse, conditioner and third rinse with her eyes closed.

It felt good, having his hands in her hair. Intimate and sensual. And Rachel noted, as she peeked and saw the expression on his face, he didn't seem to be minding the chore all that much. Beyond that, though, it was very hard for her to tell what he was thinking. She knew he desired her, had even come to respect her as a woman and a rancher. But would he ever care enough about her for them to have a real future together? Or was their lovemaking a one-time affair that would never again be repeated?

He squeezed the excess water out of her hair. With his help, they wrapped her hair in a towel and left the plastic wrap where it was, over the bandage.

He held out a hand. "Easy does it," he said as he guided her to a sitting position on the countertop.

Without warning, the room spun as if she were riding a merry-go-round, but Travis's strong arm caught her.

"Dizzy, huh?"

"A little."

"Then that does it."

The next thing Rachel knew she'd been swept up in his arms. His strides long and purposeful, he headed for the stairs.

Rachel's pulse pounded in her ears as he carried her to the second floor. In the dark shirt and jeans, his hair rakishly tousled, the shadow of evening beard on his face, he looked a thousand times more tempting and dangerous and alluring than he ever had.

He placed her gently on the bed, then sank down beside her. Rachel leaned against the pillows. The room had long ago stopped spinning. But she had enjoyed being carted off to bed by him so much she'd been loath to stop it.

"Better?" Travis asked.

Rachel nodded. "Much," she whispered.

He put his hand on top of hers and traced the back of it warmly. "You gave me quite a scare, you know."

"I know." She tried hard not to tremble as he traced yet another evocative pattern on her skin.

He gave her a searching look, this one more fraught with emotion than the last. "I don't ever want to be that scared again," he said.

Rachel's heart soared at the revelation he cared

about her deeply and wasn't afraid to show it. "I promise I'll be more careful."

"You damn well better be," he grumbled on a note of genuine relief. "You're important to me, you know. Damn important." His powerful shoulders eclipsed her vision at the same instant his hands framed her face. Rachel had a millisecond to draw a breath, then his mouth came down on hers.

Pleasure sizzled inside her as his tongue swept into her mouth, tasting her until she ached. His hand stroked her body, gentling, arousing. He continued to kiss her until she was drugged with desire, her body rigid and aching with wanting. Rachel wreathed her arms around his neck and held him close. She hadn't realized until just then how much she had yearned for this. She clung to him wholeheartedly, surrendering to the steamy sensuality of his embrace and yet demanding of it at the same time. She couldn't taste him deeply enough. Couldn't feel him close enough. Couldn't get enough.

And even though nothing like this had ever happened to her before, she knew it was dangerous for her to let herself feel this way. Dangerous to let it continue the way he obviously wanted it to continue. "Travis," she moaned, moving her mouth from his, "this isn't fair." He still didn't want marriage.

"I know all the reasons why not, Rachel," he said, his breath coming as fast and hard as hers. His eyes scanned her face tenderly. "I've gone over them myself a million times. But it always comes back to this. You've got something no other woman has ever had for me, something I can't turn away from," he admitted gruffly. "And judging from the way you kiss me, I think I have a hell of a lot to offer you, too."

Then his mouth was on hers again. And there was

no more time to think, only to feel. And feel she did. Her senses were inundated with the touch and taste of him. He was so hard and strong. He smelled so good, so evocatively male. And damn him, he knew just how to kiss her. Just how to wring a response from her. Not that she seemed to be fighting it all that much, she realized, dazed. Their innate differences aside, she knew Travis was right. What they were experiencing was something special. Certainly no one had ever made her feel like this. So soft and feminine and helplessly wanton. No other man had ever made her feel the urgent need to be one with him.

He tilted his head and kissed her from another angle. When he lifted his head again, he stroked his hand down her neck into the open collar of her nightgown.

"Oh, Travis," Rachel murmured, as the last of her resistance crumbled and heat tunneled through her in wave after delicious wave.

He paused. "I love you, Rachel. Before this goes any further, I want you to know that." He looked into her eyes and her heart soared.

"Oh, Travis. I love you, too," she said, her lip trembling with the emotional price of the admission.

"Oh, yeah?"

"Oh, yeah," she murmured sexily, just holding him close for a moment.

"Well, that's good 'cause you're everything I've ever wanted in a woman. Everything. I realized that yesterday when I saw you get dragged off that horse." He buried his face in the fragrant dampness of her hair. "I don't know what I'd ever do without you, Rachel," he confessed, his voice lowering another thoroughly possessive notch. "God knows I sure don't want to find out."

Rachel drew back so she could see the rugged lines of his face. "Staking a claim, cowboy?"

He grinned back at her. "You bet." Deliberately he threaded his fingers through her hair and put pressure at her nape to draw her head up and back, until it was precisely under his. "In the best way I know how," he finished softly. His face as he looked at her, all warm and tender and loving, made her want to cry.

"Oh, Travis," Rachel whispered.

"That's right," he whispered back. "Say my name. Say it over and over and over again."

Nothing had ever felt as good or as right as the touch of his lips on hers. The rest of the world blurred. Again they kissed, until there was only this moment, only the two of them alone, and the love they had professed for one another.

He shifted his hands to her hips and pulled her against him. She welcomed the thrusting pressure just as she welcomed his tongue in her mouth and minutes later, when the kiss finally ended, the feel of his palm warmly caressing the slope of her neck. She could tell by the look in his eyes that this time he wasn't going to stop, not unless she made him. And she knew she wasn't going to make him.

This time...this once, she was simply going to enjoy what life had given her, take all the pleasure and forget the problems that undoubtedly lay ahead.

He bent to kiss her again, deeply and thoroughly. She reached out blindly for him, seeking his love and the tenderness she knew he had to give.

Breathing raggedly, he drew away and rested his forehead against hers. His heart was thundering in his chest, just as hers was. "No regrets this time, Rachel," he vowed.

"No regrets," she promised.

His eyes darkened. "You're sure?" he teased. "You're not delirious with pain, are you?"

Wordlessly she undid the snaps on his shirt and slipped her hand inside. "Make love to me, Travis," Rachel whispered, caressing the solidness of his chest and guiding him close. "Make love to me now."

Groaning, he stretched out beside her. They undressed one another slowly, provocatively.

"You're beautiful."

"So are you."

"I never thought this would happen." Rachel breathed in sharply as he touched her.

He grinned. "I did."

They laughed together, softly, wantonly.

If this wasn't heaven, Rachel thought, it was as close as it got. She closed her eyes, loving the feel of the sandpapery stubble on his face as it brushed against the softness of her breasts. His mouth, hot and rapacious, wetly covered her nipples and urged them to life.

An aching sizzled through her, from breasts to stomach to thighs. "Oh, Travis, I want you," she murmured. Her thighs turned to liquid and fell open even farther, and her hips tilted up and forward.

He let his eyes roam her body. "Then show me."

She touched him. "Like this?"

He moaned and caught her hand. "Yes, like this," he said.

He rolled toward her. For long moments they lay side by side in the pale moonlight washing in through the windows, reveling in the glorious difference of her pliant curves and his silky hardness. They stroked and explored. Their glances met. His eyes filled with love. "Let's do everything, Travis," she persuaded softly, her hand closing around his warm male heat. "Absolutely everything."

And they did.

Kissing without touching. Touching without kissing. Touching and kissing simultaneously. Rachel climaxed once, twice, until at last, impatient, he eased the weight and length of his body over hers. His eyes were both serious and tender as he moved against her, then inside her with excruciating care.

Her senses reeled with pleasure as he began to move, at first with sensual deliberation, then more and more passionately until she was rocking beneath him, aware only of the heat and the building pressure, the mindless urgent need for release.

She felt it all, reveled in it. And still he couldn't, wouldn't, stop, not until they had both given of themselves as never before, until they were both ravished, fulfilled and utterly exhausted.

The quiet that followed the crescendo of their lovemaking was riveting. And anything but relaxing.

Rachel moved slightly so her head was no longer on his chest. She was glad it was dark now. Glad they were alone. Moments ago, embroiled in the heat of their passion, of her urgent need to be with him, of the wonder of their mutually professed love, she'd felt freer than she had in years. Now, with the rush of pleasure fading, she only felt afraid. She didn't want anything to spoil their newfound happiness, and she was desperately afraid something would.

The ringing phone broke the silence.

His arm still around her, Travis reached for the receiver beside the bed. "Hang on a minute, Rowdy," he said, after he'd listened for a moment. "I'll get her."

Rachel flushed guiltily, as she thought about what had happened. She'd done what she'd sworn she would never do. She had become a cowboy's mistress.

Wasn't it ironic, she thought, that Travis looked completely at ease about the compromising nature of their intense attraction and love for one another, while she was now a bundle of conflicted feelings? She wanted to be with Travis. She wanted to make love with him, and be loved by him. And yet she didn't want anyone to know about it, for fear it would undermine her authority. But that wasn't Travis's fault. All he'd ever professed to want was to make wild passionate love to her. She sent Travis a smile as she accepted the phone.

"Hi, Rowdy. What's up?" She listened a moment. "Good. No. Nothing further. All right. I'll see you first thing tomorrow. Thanks."

She handed the phone back to Travis. While he hung up the receiver, she scooted off the bed.

"What'd Rowdy want?"

"Just to tell me how things are going." Needing suddenly to get out of the house, to have time to think, she started for her bureau.

Travis lay back against the pillows, his hands folded behind his head. "Now what are you doing?" he asked.

"Dressing. I'm going down to the stables to check out that calf that got hurt yesterday."

Travis sat up halfway and propped his weight on his elbow. "Why, if he's fine?"

Rachel pulled a shirt from the closet and a handful of undies from her bureau. "I just want to see him myself."

"I thought the doctor told you to stay in bed,"

Travis pointed out. His eyes sparkled suggestively as he patted the place beside him.

"He told me to stay in bed and rest," Rachel corrected. She grinned at Travis as he continued to try to coax her back into bed. "I wasn't resting."

His look immediately turned to one of concern. He caught her hand as she passed him and drew her down, so that she was seated on the edge of the bed. Lifting her hand to his mouth, he gently kissed her fingertips. "I didn't hurt you, did I?"

He looked deep into her eyes, and for a moment it was all Rachel could do not to get lost in the slate-blue depths. "No," she said softly, remembering all too well how wonderful he had been to her. "You made me feel better than I have in a long time, Travis." *More a woman. More loved.*

"Then why the rush to leave?" he asked softly, trailing a hand down her spine.

Was this what it would be like from now on? Rachel wondered, as she tried with all her might to resist him. Would Travis be constantly trying to lure her into bed? Would she be torn between her duty and her desires?

"Why not let the calf wait until tomorrow?"

"Because I have a responsibility," Rachel returned abruptly, irritated she should have to spell this out to Travis when he knew darn well the depth of her commitment to the ranch and to every living thing on it. And she felt most irritated because they would have to be careful to hide their affair. How could she even think of doing that around her children?

Travis's grip on her waist gentled from a persuasive touch to a soft sultry stroking caress that made her insides go to mush. The look he gave her was hot and steamy. She felt the by now familiar languidness between her thighs and just as determinedly ignored her sensual reaction to his nearness. She told herself it didn't matter. She had a business to run.

"Want me to go with you?" He watched as she modestly draped the top sheet around her middle and scooped up a handful of her clothes. He leapt agilely to his feet, then followed her into her adjacent private bathroom.

Rachel glanced yearningly at the huge marble tub, then thought no. Odds were, if she stepped into that even for a second, Travis would follow.

Determinedly she reached for a washcloth and held it under warm running water. She would've preferred to shut the door, but with him standing gloriously naked against the jamb, there wasn't a lot she could do.

"Look, I'll go down to the barn for you, if you want. You don't have to go down there tonight," Travis said.

"Thanks." Rachel cut him off brusquely. "But I want to go."

Rachel knew her motivation for going out went much deeper. The truth, whether she wanted to admit it to Travis or not, was that she still hadn't found a buyer for the organically raised herd, and she was beginning to feel panicky. The only time she could really relax was when she was actively working toward her goals and tending to the ranch. And right now, she didn't want to think about failing—or how complicated her personal life had just become.

Rachel shrugged. "I just think I'll sleep better after I've seen him again."

"Once a softy, always a softy," he teased. "Miss Rachel, you are all heart."

"You make me feel that way," she confessed.

"That's always been my intent."

They exchanged smiles. Glancing up, she caught a glimpse of herself in the mirror and was amazed at how loved she looked. How different, with her mouth all red and swollen and thoroughly kissed. Her cheeks were flushed, and above the tightly wrapped sheet, the uppermost curves of her breasts were pink and tender and tingling.

And right behind her, Travis stood proudly, watching her, as bold as she was shy. And why not? she asked herself on a reluctant sigh as she ran a brush through the damp ends of her hair. He had every right to be proud of his physique. His body was tanned and fit and lightly covered with whorls of dark hair. Lower still was the velvety sight of his burgeoning arousal. Just looking at him made Rachel draw in her breath sharply.

"Here," he said gently, untucking the corners of the sheet where it was snuggled between her breasts. He reached for the warm wet washcloth. "Let me."

Rachel caught the sheet a half second before it fell completely. Deliberately she avoided his eyes. She knew if she looked at him directly, if she kissed him just once, she would be lost. Gloriously lost. "No, Travis. Don't."

"Why not?" he said softly as his playful mood faded.

"Because even though I love you, I've got to pull myself together and get back to managing the ranch."

"Do you?" he asked. When she didn't answer, he rubbed his hands over her bare arms and confessed gently, "Rowdy let me look at the books, Rachel." She tried to turn away, but he held her firmly in place. His voice was gentle but stern. "I know you're still in trouble. But don't you see? It doesn't matter anymore, now that we've got each other."

Rachel stared up at him in disbelief. "It matters terribly, Travis!" she disagreed, more sharply than she had intended. "I can't let your mother and the twins down." And she had so little time left to secure her children's inheritance.

"You haven't let anyone down," Travis argued kindly.

"Haven't I?" Rachel sighed. "I've taken a ranch that was operating in the black and turned it into one that is operating in the red. What do you call that?"

Travis's lips compressed grimly. "No one on this ranch doubts how hard you've tried."

He was speaking as if the gig were up. Rachel's shoulders stiffened defensively. "It's not over yet, Travis," she warned.

"Not even if I want it to be?" Travis challenged, his eyes dark, his voice edged with tension.

Rachel sensed a gauntlet had been thrown down between them. Her heart started pounding.

"I love you, Rachel," Travis whispered, drawing her into his arms and holding her close. His breath whispered across the shampooed freshness of her hair. "I love you with all my heart." He squeezed her tightly. "Regardless of what happens with the ranch, I'll never stop."

"Oh, Travis," Rachel whispered, holding him close. She rested her face against his shoulder. "I love you, too. I really do."

"Then marry me," Travis said passionately. He hooked his finger beneath her chin and lifted her face to his.

And suddenly, for Rachel, it was as if history was repeating itself. She spun away from Travis, aware she had never felt more miserable in her life. "I can't," she said. But wasn't this what she had wanted?

If he was stung by her rejection, he didn't show it. "Why not? You'll still have the ranch."

"But it'll be for all the wrong reasons!" she cried.

He stared at her incredulously. "Because you love me and agreed to be my wife?"

"Because I won't have *earned* it," she explained.

"Oh, I don't know about that," he teased, his wicked grin colored with relief. He pulled her to him and held her against the strong hard length of him. "Being married to me could be hell."

She laughed softly at the exaggeration in his words. "Knowing what a Texas bad boy you are, Travis Westcott, truer words were never spoken." She looked up at him, all the love she felt for him in her eyes. "But I still can't marry you," she said, sticking to her guns. "At least not now. Not yet." *Not until I've accomplished what I set out to do.*

"Because of the ranch?" The tenseness came back into his face.

"I'm not going to marry into it, not this time," Rachel countered intractably.

"Then don't." Travis shrugged. "Go back to work as a travel agent. If you want, you could even start your own agency here in San Angelo. It won't matter what you do. We'll be together."

"I want to ranch," Rachel insisted stubbornly.

"Then do that," he advised, exasperated. "As my wife."

"No."

His jaw set, he stared at her and shook his head. Rachel could tell he was about to lose his temper. "This is stupid. You love me. I love you."

"I'm not discounting any of that," she whispered miserably.

"Then what are you trying to tell me?"

She faced him boldly. "That it's not over yet. That I still have two weeks to make good on my deal with your mother and earn this ranch for the twins."

"Face it, Rachel," he said, making no effort to temper his words this time. "You are never going to sell that herd, at least not at the kind of price that you want and need."

"You don't know that!"

"The hell I don't! I've been in this business a darn sight longer than you have."

"In a peripheral sense, maybe."

His jaw tautened. "And if you don't sell that herd, you'll never get back in the black in time to earn the right to run this ranch."

Rachel flung her washcloth back into the sink and rushed past him. "That's a fine thing to say to me, Travis!"

He stomped after her and yanked on his jeans. "Oh. Now I get it. Now you're saying you want me to lie to spare your feelings. Well, I won't do that!"

Rachel picked up his shirt and his boots and flung them at him. "I should've known you wouldn't believe in me."

Travis ducked as one of his socks came flying past his head. "I never said that." He yanked on his shirt and fastened the pearl snaps. He was halfway done when he realized he'd put the two edges of the shirt together crookedly. Muttering curses through his teeth, he ripped open the snaps and started again. "I just said there's nothing more you can do that you haven't already done."

"Yes, there is," Rachel said as she pulled on her own jeans and boots.

"Yeah?" Travis sat down on the side of the bed and yanked on his boots. "Like what?"

"I'm going to hire a photographer and a publicist!" she announced haughtily.

He gave her a funny look. "To do what?"

"To help me put together a brochure and maybe even a video to help sell my Brahmas. Only this time, instead of trying to sell the merits of those calves I bought, I'm going to sell the whole ranch, instead. I'm going to sell the Westcott reputation for excellence."

Travis's glance narrowed. He stood slowly. "What if it doesn't work?"

His continued lack of faith in her stung. "It will." Fully dressed, she breezed past him.

He followed her out the door and down the stairs. "But what if it doesn't?"

She swallowed hard and held back the hot bitter tears of defeat. "Then I go home to Beaumont," she said thickly. "The twins can start school there in the fall."

Travis sighed. Was he going to have to buy a herd of his own cows in order to keep her? He stepped lithely in front of her, blocking her way. "And we're over?" He snapped his fingers. "Just like that?"

Rachel swallowed. She backed up until her spine grazed a wall. "I didn't say that." Her head lifted proudly as her heart did battle with her pride. "Of course I'd still see you, if...if you want," she finished uncertainly.

Hurt glimmered in Travis's eyes. "As what?" he commanded hoarsely. "My mistress?"

"Your lover," Rachel corrected. "And that isn't

such a bad thing,'' she said persuasively. "You said so yourself. We'd be partners, equal in all respects..."

Travis's breath blew out slowly. "I don't want a lover anymore, someone I see only on occasion, Rachel. I want a wife. A family. And I want to live on this ranch.''

He was offering her everything she had ever wanted. Yet she knew from bitter experience how such a marriage would be received by the community at large. Her motivations would be suspect, and she couldn't go through that again. She couldn't put her children through it, either. Earning her own way was laudable. Sponging off someone else was not. She would not be thought a gold digger. Never again. "I can't do that, Travis,'' she said quietly.

They stared at one another in heated silence for a moment. "Is this ranch really more important to you than I am?''

"Travis—''

"That's the bottom line, isn't it?'' He slammed both his palms against the wall. "Your career—your ultimate goals—come first.''

"You're being unreasonable,'' she asserted angrily. She had expected him to understand her. It infuriated her that he didn't. Using her elbow to push him aside, she stomped off toward the kitchen.

"I'm being unreasonable?'' Travis stormed after her.

"If the situation was reversed, I'd give you a chance to work things out career-wise.''

"I'm giving you the chance,'' Travis said, his voice vibrating with tension. His eyes bored into hers. "I just want you to do it as my wife!''

"Why can't we just be lovers now?'' she pleaded softly. After all, he was the one who had suggested it.

Travis took her in his arms and held her. "Because I love you and I want to be with you." He stroked her hair with his hand. "And we have to set a good example for your kids."

"Now you're talking like a father!" She had never felt more miserable and misunderstood and maligned than she did at that moment. Worse, once again, the Westcott ranch was standing between her and Travis.

"You're telling me you'd be comfortable to continue on as we are, with the two of us having to sneak around? That's why you're going out, isn't it? To make sure you won't get caught in a compromising position when my mom and the kids get back."

Rachel flushed guiltily and wished fervently everything wasn't so confused. "That's part of it," she admitted slowly.

"So how would we see each other? Would I pay my mom a quarter to take the kids somewhere? Would we rendezvous in the attic at high noon or just meet outside at midnight, and pray none of the hands happen to come along and see us?"

"You're not only being ridiculous, you're being crude," Rachel countered.

"Practical," he corrected sternly, still keeping her in his arms. "And it's about time one of us was."

"I need time, Travis."

He studied her sadly. "And I'm telling you, time has run out. We've wasted half our lives, Rachel. Is it so wrong of me not to want to waste another minute and to want to sleep with you in my arms every night? Is it so wrong of me to want to tell the whole world I love you?"

No, it wasn't wrong. It was what she had once longed to hear more than anything in the world. Unfortunately the timing just wasn't right. "I can't marry you when I'm a failure," she said. "Please try and understand."

"What the hell do you think I've been trying to do?" he said. He released her and moved past her.

"Travis—"

He grabbed his hat off the hook next to the door, slapped it on his head and stalked to the door. "Let me know if you change your mind." He went out and the screen door slammed behind him. "If you ever do!" he shouted after a moment. "Until then, I'll be in Fort Worth!"

Chapter Fifteen

"Good news?" Jaclyn asked, as she entered the ranch-house office carrying a silver tea service on a tray.

Rachel nodded. "The best. I found a buyer for my herd. They'll be giving me a down payment when they sign the contract later today, and that money will put the ranch back in the black. Plus, they're interested in a long-term arrangement. I haven't worked out the terms with them yet, but I'm confident we can arrange something."

"I'm impressed. The brochures you had printed really worked," Jaclyn said.

Rachel nodded, satisfied. "I think the video helped, too. The combination of the two was a very effective marketing tool."

"So why don't you look happier?" Jaclyn asked. She poured them both a cup of tea. She paused. Her expression grew troubled. "It's Travis, isn't it?"

"Yes," Rachel admitted on a tremulous sigh. She hadn't seen him in two weeks.

The corners of Jaclyn's mouth edged upward into a reflective smile. "I thought so."

Rachel studied her mother-in-law, wondering if she

was up to hearing the truth. "You may as well know. I'm in love with him," she blurted out.

Jaclyn smiled and sat in a chair opposite Rachel. "I figured that, too."

"You're not upset?"

"Honey, I love you." Jaclyn got up, walked around the desk and hugged her warmly. "Why would I be upset?"

"Because I drove him away."

"No," Jaclyn corrected, giving Rachel another quick spirit-bolstering hug before resuming her seat, "you brought him home."

"For the summer, maybe," Rachel allowed.

"For good," Jaclyn interrupted. "His heart is here now, on the ranch. Travis never would've realized how much his heritage really meant to him, or understood the importance of passing our heritage on to the next generation of Westcotts if you hadn't understood it yourself and been here to show him, Rachel."

Jaclyn's admiration made Rachel feel she had accomplished something important. "I thought earning the right to run the ranch would make me happy," Rachel said slowly. "I thought living here would give me the respectability and sense of family and belonging I've always craved."

Jaclyn studied her, a compassionate look in her blue eyes. "And it hasn't?"

Rachel shrugged. "I thought I'd be delirious with my success. But..."

"You're not."

"No. I just feel empty." She held up both hands before Jaclyn could interrupt. "Don't get me wrong. I'm proud of myself, but I thought it would mean more.

I thought running the ranch was all it would take to make me happy.''

"And it's not?"

"No," Rachel admitted. Tears shimmered in her eyes. "I miss your son desperately."

"Have you told him?"

Rachel let out a shaky laugh and wiped at her eyes. "No."

"Why not?"

"He was so furious with me when we last talked, before he left." And with good reason, Rachel acknowledged silently. He'd said he loved her! He'd actually asked her to marry him! And what had she done? She'd said no. And why? Because she had let her pride get in the way. She saw now how wrong she'd been to put the ranch ahead of everything, including the man she loved.

"My mother had a saying. There's never anything that can't be fixed. If you try hard enough, that is." Jaclyn looked at Rachel long and hard. "Are you willing to try hard enough?"

Rachel knew, given half a chance, she and Travis could be happy together. Happier than either of them had ever dreamed. "You really think Travis will forgive me?"

Jaclyn smiled. "No one ever went wrong following their heart."

TRAVIS WAS in his Fort Worth office. He stood as she entered, his expression one of concern and caution. "Is everything all right at the ranch?"

"Yes." *And no,* she thought, *not without you.*

Her heart pounding, she gestured at a chair in the luxuriously appointed office. It was quite different from the cramped sewing room he had been using. "May I sit down and speak with you a moment?"

"I've always got time for you," he said, his face inscrutable, his eyes intense. "You know that."

Rachel sat down gratefully and clasped her hands in front of her, willing them to stop trembling. "Now that I'm here, I've got so much to say I don't know where to start." *Or even if you are going to want to hear it.*

His eyes held hers. He looked tired, she thought, as if he hadn't been sleeping well, either.

"Take your time."

She tore her eyes from his. "About the ranch."

"I heard about your success with the organically raised herd," he said before she could continue. "Rowdy and my mother both phoned to tell me. Congratulations."

"Thanks," she said awkwardly.

"I didn't think you could do it." He smiled at her and his voice dropped a compelling notch. "You proved me wrong."

She hadn't expected him to be happy for her or look so proud of her success. It made her feel even worse about the way she'd turned her back on him. As if she'd betrayed him.

"About the ranch and the deal I made with your mother..." she began. His mouth tightened unhappily at the mention of the Bar W, and seeing his defenses rise, she had to force herself to go on. "Your mother gave me papers making me conservator of the ranch for the children, but I can't sign them. I've thought about it, and I know now it wouldn't be right."

He studied her tensely, looking no happier than he had before she'd told him she was giving it all up. "You're telling me you're leaving? Now?"

Please, don't let it be too late. "No. At least I don't want to," she replied. Her heart was in her throat. Her eyes locked with his. She took a deep bolstering breath, trying not to let her emotions overcome her. "I'd like to stay on, either in the same capacity as ranch manager, answerable to you and Jaclyn, or as a hired hand, or an assistant to Rowdy."

"Whoa!" Looking as somber and uncertain as she felt, Travis put up an imperious hand to stop her and circled around to the front of his desk. "What brought this on?"

It's now or never. Lose my pride or the man I love forever. "My love for you," she said simply. Mouth trembling, she got to her feet and took his hands in hers. She squeezed them tightly, taking her strength from his. Her mouth trembled as she tilted her head back and looked deep into his eyes. "I realized I was a fool to turn down your offer of marriage. And I'm so very sorry I hurt you. Oh Travis," she whispered. "I do love you."

"I love you, too," he said. He wrapped his arms about her waist and brought her against him. She snuggled against his warmth, aware that nothing had ever felt so right as the two of them together. And nothing ever would.

"Can you forgive me for being so foolish?" she asked.

He kissed her deeply, thoroughly, and with a dangerous lack of restraint. "Of course I can forgive you."

"But—"

"That's over now, Rachel." He squeezed her tightly, so that they were touching everywhere. "We don't have to talk of it again."

Hope for the future flared in her heart, and Rachel

found she suddenly had more courage than she knew. "Does that mean you still want to marry me?"

He bent his head and answered her with a slow searing kiss that curled her toes and weakened her knees. When they were both breathless and aching, he lifted his head. "If you'll have me, hell yes, the offer still stands," he said gruffly. "In fact," he said, further delineating his plans, "I want to marry you as soon as possible."

"Oh, Travis," Rachel cried, joy exploding inside her like fireworks in a Texas sky, "I want that, too."

His hand stroked her hair lovingly, drifted lower, down her back. "And if you'd waited one more day until I cleared my desk of everything urgent, I would've come out to the ranch myself and asked you again," Travis said, squeezing her waist. "In the meantime—" one arm still around her shoulders, he reached behind him for a manila folder with her name on it "—I have an early wedding present for you."

She sent him a puzzled look and then opened it, gasping at what she saw. "Travis!"

"Those are papers stating that I give up all present and future claims to the ranch, whether you marry me or not. I was going to give you those and then propose all over again."

She couldn't help it, she started to laugh. He stared bemusedly into her flushed face. "Is the idea of marrying me that hilarious?"

"No. It's just that I'm trying to give up the ranch. And you're trying to give it to me." She shook her head in rueful contemplation.

"And we both want to get married," he finished, a satisfied gleam in his eyes.

"Yes." She sobered briefly. "I do want that," she whispered, "very much."

"Then there's only one solution." Travis sat down in a chair and pulled her onto his lap. "We'll just have to co-own the ranch."

"You won't mind doing that?"

He shook his head. "I no longer need the Bar W." He anchored both arms around her and held her close. "And I don't want anything that keeps me away from you. I love you, Rachel." He touched a hand to the side of her face. "And that's all that counts." Hands at her nape, he brought her head down to his.

When at last they drew apart, she sighed in contentment, the glow of his love for her and hers for him filling her with renewed warmth. "Well, what do you think?" she teased softly. "Shall we find someplace nice and quiet?"

"I have a condo close by."

The prospect of making love with him again filled her with heat and longing. "So what are we waiting for, cowboy?"

He grinned, his eyes twinkling merrily. "Not a damn thing."